William Hepworth Dixon

History of William Penn, Founder of Pennsylvania

William Hepworth Dixon

History of William Penn, Founder of Pennsylvania

ISBN/EAN: 9783337061678

Printed in Europe, USA, Canada, Australia, Japan

Cover: Foto ©Raphael Reischuk / pixelio.de

More available books at **www.hansebooks.com**

HISTORY

OF

WILLIAM PENN

FOUNDER OF PENNSYLVANIA.

BY

WILLIAM HEPWORTH DIXON.

𝔄 𝔑𝔢𝔴 𝔈𝔡𝔦𝔱𝔦𝔬𝔫.

LONDON:
HURST AND BLACKETT, PUBLISHERS,
13 GREAT MARLBOROUGH STREET.
1872.

To

THE RIGHT HON. JOHN BRIGHT, M.P.

THIS HISTORY IS INSCRIBED.

PREFACE.

TWENTY-ONE years have passed since 'William Penn, an Historical Biography,' came out. The book obtained some favour, not in England only, but in Germany and America. Yet it has long been out of print; awaiting that revision which an author who respects his public likes to give his final work. In one-and-twenty years, much light has come to us from public offices, both home and foreign; and in dealing with a mass of new materials I have been led to write my book afresh. The change of title hardly corresponds to the material change. It would be no misuse of words to say that 'William Penn: Founder of Pennsylvania,' is substantially a new book.

6 *St. James's Terrace, Regent's Park,*
May-day, 1872.

NOTE.

In the first edition of 'William Penn' appeared an Extra Chapter on the charges brought by Macaulay against Penn. The five specific censures were confronted with the actual names and dates, and every fact alleged as ground for censure was shown to be no fact at all. With a consent most rare in matters of this kind, the press accepted this defence, and almost every one expected that the calumnies would be withdrawn.

On some points he gave way; especially as to William Kiffin and the Prince of Orange.

In his first edition he had represented Penn as being 'employed by the heartless and venal sycophants of Whitehall' to seduce Kiffin into the acceptance of an alderman's gown, and failing to induce that sturdy Baptist to comply. I met this statement with the words of Kiffin; words which proved that Penn was *not* employed 'in the work of seduction;' and that Kiffin *did* accept 'an alderman's gown.' Macaulay fenced with the first citation, but the second smote him, and he added to his text that Kiffin took the alderman's gown.

In his first edition he had said in reference to the Prince of Orange : 'All men were anxious to know what he thought of the declaration. . . . . Penn sent copious disquisitions to the Hague, and even went thither in the hope that his eloquence, of which he had a high opinion, would prove irre-

sistible.'   It was shown that not a word in this paragraph
was true.   Penn sent *no* copious disquisitions to the Hague
in 1687.   He did *not* go over in the hope that his eloquence
would prove irresistible.   He did not go at all.   Macaulay
drew his pen across this passage; replacing what was proved
to be a falsehood by a sneer.

My hope was that Macaulay would in time withdraw his
charges as disproved.   I had some reason for this hope.
His mind was racked by doubts, and he was often busy
with this portion of his book.   It is within my knowledge
that his latest thoughts on earth were given to Penn and
that which he had said of Penn.   Some part of what he
might have done, the world can guess from what he did.
He ceased the work of calumny.   In what he wrote after
1857, there is not a single sneer at Penn.   His indexes
were greatly changed.   He struck out much that was false,
and more that was abusive. Penn's Jacobitism was no longer
'scandalous,' his word was no longer a 'falsehood.'   Penn
was no longer charged with 'treasonable conduct,' with
'flight to France,' and with 'renewing his plots.'   What
else Macaulay might have done can only be surmised; but
it is fair to think that changes in his index would have been
followed by amendments in his text.   I know that he was
far from satisfied with his 'Notes' of 1857, and that he was
engaged in reconsidering the defence of Penn when he leaned
back in his chair and died.

Unhappily he passed away, and made no other sign.
The accusations in his text remain: and it is only just that
the defence of Penn, extended and adapted to the present
time, should reappear.

CONTENTS.

LIFE OF WILLIAM PENN.

CHAPTER I.

OLD AND NEW FORTUNES (1644).

THE Penns of Penn were an old family, living in Bucks during the wars of the Red and White Roses, three or four miles from the town of Beaconsfield, in the parish from which they seem to have got their name. These Penns of Penn have long since passed away.

In very old times a branch of this family removed to the north of Wiltshire, where they held a small estate in land, a hundred pounds a-year, on the skirts of Bradon forest, on the borders of the shire. Their seat was called Penn's Lodge, a 'genteel, ancient house,' and in the town of Minety, across the border, they had a second house. The last of these old Penns of Bradon forest was William Penn of Penn's Lodge and Minety, who survived his only son, also a William Penn, and dying in 1591 at a great age, was buried in Minety Church, near the altar. On the old man's death the property was sold to pay his

B

debts, and this connexion of the Penn family with Penn's Lodge and Minety ceased.

This patriarch of failing fortune left two grand-sons, William and Giles, to begin the world afresh. Giles went to Bristol, took to the sea, and entered into trade. He sailed into the North Sea; he crossed the Bay of Biscay; he visited the Spanish ports; he caught some glimpses of the pirate holds. The skipper had his ups and downs; for some of his ventures turned out ill; the rovers seized his goods, the factors cheated him; yet on the whole he made his way. In Bristol he found a lady to his mind; a Gilbert of Yorkshire, who had recently come into the west country; and marrying her, he took a house in that city for her home, and there his sons, George and William (the future admiral), were in due time born, though at an in-terval of twenty years.

George, the elder born of these two Bristol boys, was early put to work under his father's eye. He learned the business of a merchant, and spent his youth in passing from Cadiz to Antwerp and Rotter-dam, until he fell in love with a lady of Antwerp, a Catholic in creed and a subject of the Crown of Spain. This love was happy, and on being united to the woman of his heart George Penn set up his home at San Lucar, the port of Seville, then a busy, thriving town. George, having no offspring, brought his wife's sisters from Antwerp to live with her, and made for them a pleasant home in that Morisco port, near the English hospice of St. George.

William, the younger born of these two Bristol boys, was put to sea. Captain Giles Penn, his father, roved about the Spanish, Portuguese, and Flemish ports; and William worked his way, under that father's eye, from the lowest work on board his vessel to the highest office on the quarter-deck.

After George's settlement in San Lucar, Captain Giles Penn, the father, turned his keel towards the Moorish ports, then opening up a new and tempting branch of trade. The Moors of Fez and Susa were in want of many things that Bristol could supply —tin, lead, and iron most of all,—and Giles, having paid a visit to the ports, from Tetuan to Sallee, observing the course of trade and picking up the native speech, began to fetch from Bristol such commodities as he found would sell. But this new trade was only to be carried on at daily risk of life. The Spanish court had closed the Barbary ports by paper blockade,—much as they had closed the American ports. Such ports were lawless in a certain sense, the natives having built and manned a swarm of boats in which they roved about the seas and preyed on vessels under every flag. In fact, these Barbary ports were pirate-ports. From Tunis to Sallee the African harbours sent out every spring a fleet of rovers; some of which swept the coasts of Spain on her eastern side, some on her western side; those pushing out as far as the Genoese waters, these coming up into the German and Irish seas. They chased all colours, and they seized all ships. They not only took the goods on board, but sold the officers and crews as slaves. Muley Mohammed,

Emperor of Morocco, tried his best to limit this warfare of the sea to Spain ; but his seat of government was far away from the coast, and his unruly subjects of the sea-ports would not stay their hands to please a young and feeble prince. Sallee, the busiest of these pirate nests, was in revolt against his rule.

A quick and able man, this Captain Penn not only knew that court favour would be useful to him in his perilous trade, but saw how favour could be won at court by simple means. King Charles was fond of falconry, and Giles brought home with him a cast of Tetuan hawks. Charles quickly let him know that he would like more hawks, on which the Bristol skipper told him he could get these birds if the King would give him letters of protection to the Moorish governor of the town. Lord Conway drew up letters in his favour, and Giles went back to Tetuan with the King's command to buy him Barbary horses, as well as hawks. On his return to England he came to town, when he made the acquaintance of Sir Robert Mansel, Edward Nicholas, Endymion Porter, and other gentlemen of the court. Mansel had a great opinion of the skipper, and wrote to Lord Dorchester, then Secretary of State, in his behalf. For Giles was in some trouble about a sale of cargoes in Tetuan ; the proceeds had been seized, and Captain Penn was much afraid of being clapped in jail. His great friends helped him, for the King, in love with his new hawks, was eager for his agent to go out again.

In passing from Bristol to Barbary for several

years, Giles Penn became acquainted with the Moors, their ports, their customs, and their speech. At Sallee he was pained to hear that hundreds of English captives were said to be enslaved in that pirate stronghold; some of them were women; but the port of Sallee being in revolt against the empire nothing could be done for them in the native court. On coming home Penn laid his news before the King, with full reports of what he had seen and done, and hints of measures by which the captives might be released. His plans were laid before the Council and approved. A fleet was manned and victualled for the voyage. Admiral Rainsborough was appointed to the chief command; and there was a talk of sending out Captain Penn as Rainsborough's Vice-admiral. The skipper came to London, lodged at the Black Boy, in Ave Maria Lane, and saw Lord Cottington and Lord Portland, who consulted him on every detail of the expedition, the ships to be sent out, the stores to be laid in, the crews to be impressed, the mode of approaching the pirate-town, and the general policy of the voyage. But after being detained in London more than half a year, he was dismissed with money and thanks; the money not much, the thanks still less. The voyage was a great success. Sallee was taken, the prisoners were released, and Muley Mohammed, on receiving back his revolted port, repaid the citizens, who had bought these English captives from Algerines, the value of their liberated slaves.

To prevent this traffic in English flesh and blood,

the London merchants prayed the King to appoint a consul in Sallee, offering to pay all charges from the profits of their trade ; and when the Council wrote to ask them who should be sent out, they answered Captain Penn. A warrant was accordingly drawn up, and on the 30th of December, 1637, Giles Penn of Bristol was appointed His Majesty's Consul at Sallee.

When Captain Penn went to reside in Sallee, his son William kept his ship, until ship and man were taken together into the service of King Charles. At Rotterdam, the Bristol boy had fallen in with Margaret, a daughter of Hans Jasper—of that town, —a girl with rosy flesh and nimble wit,—and being taken by her comely face, had offered her his heart, and taken up her own in pledge. But William was a prudent lover. Bent on rising in the world, —perhaps rising to be Penn of Penn's Lodge,—he had left the lady in her father's house on the canal, till he could lodge her in a better home than a poor skipper's cabin in a merchant-ship.

In those days every vessel going out of Thames or Severn on a distant voyage was armed ; with five guns, ten guns, twenty guns, as the case might need. She armed according to the seas she had to cross, the pirates to resist ; and every officer on board was trained in all the details of war at sea. The trading navy was a fighting navy. When the country wanted fleets, and men to officer these fleets, she had only to send for the port-reeves and masters of companies, hire the vessels, and engage the officers and crews. The commercial navy was not the reserve ; it was the actual fleet ; but only called and paid in time of war.

In 1639, when the future Admiral was eighteen years and six months old, the Dutch acquired, by two great victories over Spain, a perfect command of the Narrow Seas. Tromp rode within sight of Dover cliffs, and Charles was suddenly smitten with the want of money, ships, and men. The money was refused him ; but he found no difficulty in procuring ships and men. The craft in which William Penn was serving as a skipper seems to have been hired by the crown ; and thus a lad of twenty passed into the public service with lieutenant's rank. Even now he would not marry ; and his rosy Margaret could wait. Knowing his duty as few men know it, he was soon employed, and soon rewarded for success. At twenty-one he was a captain. A few months later, fortune still going with him, he received a regular commission in the King's service, with the promise of the first ship worthy of his fame ; and having got his commission in his pocket, he ran over to Rotterdam and claimed his bride.

From that day forward Penn was always rising. When on shore he lived with his young wife in the naval quarter, near the Tower. His frank and jovial ways were highly relished. He had seen the world ; he sang a stave ; he loved a prank and jest ; and drank his wine with any salt alive. 'Dutch Peg,' with 'more wit than Penn himself,' says Pepys, was jeered at first, until her friends discovered that both she and Captain Penn were folks to rise.

A first step for the young captain of the royal

navy was to find employment for his talent.   The great dispute of King and Commons as to which should command the marine had just been settled (1643) by the appointment of Warwick, in opposition to the will of Charles, to the office of Lord High Admiral.   A part of the fleet, stationed in the Irish seas, adhered to the royal cause under the command of Sir John Pennington, whom the King had vainly tried to make Lord Admiral; but the number of his vessels was not formidable even at first, and capture and desertion soon reduced them to such a state of weakness as to prevent their being troublesome to the Parliamentary chiefs.

One of Pennington's captured ships was the *Fellowship*, Captain Burley, cut out in Milford Haven; a vessel of twenty-eight guns; the third in size and weight then serving in the Irish seas.   This ship was given to Captain Penn, who received his orders to sail in the service of his country; and though his wife Margaret was then in a critical state, expecting to be confined, he went on board. At six o'clock in the morning, all being ready, he shipped his anchor and dropped down the Thames. But he was suddenly recalled to his house on Tower Hill.   The *Fellowship* was detained in the river three weeks, and during these three weeks the Founder of Pennsylvania was born into the world.

The day of his birth was Monday, October the fourteenth, 1644.

CHAPTER II.

AFTER Penn of Penn, and Penn of Penn's Lodge, the boy was christened William. Round in face, with soft blue eyes and curling hair, the boy was 'a love,' not only in his mother's eyes, but in his father's heart. Captain Penn had now a son to fight for; and as soon as Peg was fit to be left, her husband joined his ship, and after visiting his admiral in the Downs, pushed on to Portsmouth, where he took Lord Broghill and his company on board. With Broghill Captain Penn formed a friendship which was never broken till his death, and which descended to his son. On landing Broghill at Kinsale, Penn put to sea, and cruised about the opening of St. George's Channel, from Milford Haven to the Cove of Cork.

In this service he remained some years; the ablest, if not the boldest, cruiser in that section of the Commonwealth fleet. The prizes which he seized were sometimes rich; and he was able to remove his wife and child from the close atmosphere of Tower Hill to the lawns and gardens of a country house. For some brief time he hired a place at Wanstead, in Essex, to which he ran on leave. A daughter Margaret, and a son Richard, were in season added to the nursery in which William broke his toys ; heirs not only to their father's gains, but the fortune made in foreign lands by ' Uncle George.'

The first great grief which fell upon the Wanstead circle came as news from San Lucar in Spain. An English factor living in a Spanish port, George Penn was watched with jealous eyes by native priests and monks, who had, unluckily, access to his house as the confessors of his wife, and of the sisters of his wife. These women were not only Catholics in faith, but subjects of Philip the Fourth. Now George was a prudent man ; a factor who kept his shop, and held his tongue ; so that malice could find no flaw in him, even though it had three or four female confessions every week to work upon. But as he grew in wealth, these priests grew angry at his blameless life. How could a heretic be a blameless man ? Was he ever seen at mass ? Was he known to confess his sins ? Did he honour the Spanish saints ? Spies were set upon him ; his wife was questioned ; his wife's sisters were examined ; and when nothing could be found against him that would justify the civil power in dealing with his case, they got from the Holy Office in Seville a secret warrant for his arrest.

Officers came down from Seville to San Lucar, broke into his house, anathematized him, seized his papers and books, impounded his goods, his plate, his jewels, his furniture, his horses, and his slaves.

They seized the things in his house and magazines, as well as those on board his ships in the port. Having got his person and his goods, they separated him from his wife, and then with holy incantations, cast him out, body and soul, from the Church of Christ, and the society of men.

Nothing escaped the rapacity of these brigands; from the wine in his cellar, to the nail in his wall. The property they seized was worth twelve thousand pounds. His wife was carried off he knew not whither; he himself was dragged to Seville, where he was cast into a dungeon, only eight feet square, and dark as the grave. In this living tomb he was left with a loaf of bread and a jug of water. For seven days no one came near him; and then the jailor brought him another loaf, another jug of water, and disappeared. No one was allowed to visit him in his cell, no letter or message was suffered to be sent out. He vanished from the world as completely as if the earth had opened in the night and sucked him in.

At the end of the first month of his confinement there was a break in the monotony of his life. The masked familiars of the Holy Office came into his cell, took him by the arms, stript him naked, tied him fast to the iron bars of his dungeon door, and one of them, armed with a whip of knotted cords, dealt out fifty lashes on his back. Each month this flogging was repeated, the new stripes crossing and tearing up the former wounds until his body was one festering sore. And all this time he was unable to learn the name of his accuser and the nature of his offence. He could not see his wife. He could not learn whether she was alive or dead.

At every blow they asked him to confess his crimes. What crimes? They could not say: he must confess of his own will and virtue. What was he to say? He would have told them anything, true or false, to stay their hands; for George was not a martyr; and he only wished to live and trade in peace.

Three years elapsed without producing the confessions wanted by the Holy Office. George was then brought into the trial-chamber, and in the presence of seven judges was accused of various crimes :—of being a heretic; of denying some of the seven sacraments; of presuming to marry a Catholic lady; of persuading his wife to change her creed; of meaning to carry his wife into England; of not hearing mass in San Lucar; of not confessing to a priest; of eating flesh on fast-days; and of doubting the miracles wrought by Spanish saints. He pleaded not guilty. But instead of producing witnesses to prove his alleged crimes, the judges ordered him to be tortured in their presence, until he confessed the truth of what was charged against him. For a while his strength and resolution bore him up; but his tormentors persevered, and at the end of four hours of excruciating and accumulating torments, he offered to confess anything they would suggest. Not satisfied with a confession which by the usages of Spain gave up his whole property to the Holy Office, the judges put him to the rack again, and by still more refined and delicate torture forced from him a terrible oath that he would live and die a Catholic, and would defend that form of faith at the risk of his life against every enemy, on pain of being burned to death. He was then cut down from the rack, placed on a hurdle, and conveyed to his former dungeon, where the surgeon had to set his broken limbs, and swathe his lacerated flesh. A little light was now let into his cell; but ten weeks elapsed before he could be lifted from his bed of pain.

Neither George himself nor those who were nursing him back to life, expected that he would quit his cell for any other purpose than to make a holiday for the Sevillian mob. Near to his dungeon lay the public square in which heretics, Jews, and Moors, were burnt in honour of Holy Church. To that infamous square, every man condemned by the Inquisition, and whether he confessed his sins or not, was always led; and George supposed that when his limbs were strong enough to bear his weight, he would be marched like others to the place of death.

He could not know as yet how strong of arm, how quick to save, his country was becoming, since the Stuart dynasty was put away.

Captain Penn, while cruising off the coast of Munster, ran down a prize called the *St. Patrick*, bound for Bilboa in Spain, on board of which he found among his prisoners, Don Juan de Urbina, secretary to the Spanish Viceroy of the Low Countries. Penn seized this great official, and stripping him naked, thrust him into the hold. Don Juan talked big, as men like him are apt to do; and Señor Bernardo, Philip's envoy in London, made complaints to the Council of the insult offered to a man of such high birth and such official rank. Of course, apologies were made; the Don was put into softer hands; and Admiral Swanley was instructed to inquire into the conduct of Captain Penn. Then came out the facts. If such acts of wild justice could not be openly maintained, the tale of George's suffering went to the nation's heart. Don Juan was sent home in another ship, but the prisoner of the Holy Office, in whose cause he had been seized, was snatched from the burning pile.

So soon as 'Uncle George' could walk, he was fetched from his cell in the Inquisition by the seven judges and their households; robed in the San Benito, and carried in the midst of a great procession of monks and priests through the streets of Seville, to the cathedral church. In this church a scaffold was raised, up which they made him mount, so that every eye could see him, as his sentence was slowly read by the secretary of the Inquisition. That sentence opened in the usual way. The prisoner was a heretic; his goods were confiscated; his wife was taken from him; but for certain reasons his life was to be spared. He was pardoned by holy Church; but he was driven out from Spain for ever; his wife was given to a good Catholic for the salvation of her soul; and he was threatened with fire and fagot should he fall away from his newly-adopted faith.

While the three children of Captain Penn were

growing up at Wanstead, Penn was getting rich and rising to higher rank. His prizes yielded him a great deal more than he got in pay ; and some of this money he laid out in land. At twenty-three he was Rear-admiral in the Irish Sea ; at twenty-five he was Vice-admiral ; and at twenty-nine, under the Commonwealth, he was sent as Vice-admiral into the Straits of Gibraltar, the ports and cities of which he had known from his earliest years.

Great changes were taking place on land, of which he took but distant note. Charles Stuart, for whom his father had bought hawks and horses, had lost his crown and life. The hero of Dunbar and Worcester was lord of all. But the change from parliament to protector wrought no change in Vice-admiral Penn, who stuck to his duties and avoided politics. When Cromwell announced to the fleet that he had taken the reins of power into his own hands, Penn was one of the first to send in his adhesion, with that of all the officers under his command.

For the next few years the hand of genius was felt in every department of the administration. While the great powers of the State were in conflict, Spain had treated us with haughty disdain,—France had insulted us at every turn,—even Holland fancied we were no longer worthy of her ire. But Cromwell's arms soon taught them better. Ireland punished and Scotland pacified, he turned his resolute face towards Holland, France, and Spain. The Dutchman lay the nearest and had most provoked his wrath ; but Holland was pre-eminently a naval power, and in dealing with her his invincible infantry was of little use.

Genius finds its own resources. Resolved to infuse into the navy, as he had already done into the army his own heroic spirit, he employed in his fleet two captains of his camp, Blake and Monk; but these officers, though filled with an energy of spirit like his own, were in a great measure ignorant of the sea. All that courage, activity, and resolution could do he expected them to accomplish; but he saw the necessity of placing by the side of these soldiers a worthy sea-captain, and for this important post he selected the young Admiral of the Straits. The Lord Protector knew that Penn was not attached to his person and government; but he needed his services; and seeing that Penn was a worldly man, and of the earth most earthy, he supposed that pensions and honours could secure his sword, if not his heart. What Cromwell wanted was his sword. Vice-admiral Penn had no objection to fight the countrymen of his wife. He was a sailor, as he used to say, and must be faithful to his flag.

When peace was made with Holland, Cromwell turned to Spain, the old and strenuous enemy of his country. England had a thousand scores to settle with the Spanish court; and two great expeditions were prepared in silence in the spring of 1655; one expedition, under Sea-general Blake, to act in Europe, sweep the Spanish coasts, and fight the Spanish fleets wherever he could find them; while a second expedition was to cross the ocean, search the Spanish main, alarm the coasts and islands, take possesion of San Domingo and St. John's—if possible,—and seize some portion of the continent, such as Cartagena.

Cromwell meant to break the power of Spain at sea and in the west.

Penn had served as Vice-admiral under Blake, who was a Somersetshire man, and it was perhaps on Blake's suggestion that the second fleet was placed under Penn's command. Before he went on board the young Vice-admiral made his terms with Cromwell. Penn wanted money and he wanted rank. Both were heaped upon him by the Lord Protector. Under the pretence that an estate which Penn had bought near Cork had suffered by the civil war, Cromwell wrote a letter with his own hand to the Irish commissioners, requesting that, in consideration of good and faithful service to the Commonwealth, lands of the full yearly value of three hundred pounds should be surveyed and set apart for Admiral Penn in a convenient place, near a castle or other fortified place for their better security, and with a good house for him to live in. Cromwell made a special, even a personal, request that his Irish agents would obey this order in such a way as to leave no cause of trouble to either the Admiral or his family; so that they might enjoy the full benefit of this reward in peace while the gallant sailor was engaged in fighting his country's battles in a distant sea. This matter settled, there was nothing but the question of professional rank. Cromwell gave the young Admiral his heart's desire by raising him to the same high rank as Blake. Penn was the only regular sailor who was made a General of the Fleet.

A few days after Penn set sail from Spithead,

with these rewards and honours fresh about him, he despatched a secret offer to Prince Charles, then living at Cologne, to place the whole of his great fleet and army at the prince's disposal, if his highness would indicate a port in which they would be received.

Ever watching for a chance to rise, Sea-general Penn observed when Cromwell's fame was highest, that he stood upon his personal merit, while the nation was rather Royalist than Oliverian. The Lord Protector could not live for ever; after him would come a feeble youth; and then the Commonwealth might fall. In falling it would crush the men who served it; but, for his part, he would not be crushed. Penn cared no more, in truth, for Charles than Oliver. The man for whom he toiled was Admiral Penn; and with a view to the security of Admiral Penn he sent that secret message to Cologne.

Charles thanked the sailor for his message, and he kept his eye on Penn in after days, but for the moment he declined to act. Charles had no ports in which he could receive his ships, no funds to pay the seamen, nothing for a fleet to do, unless, like Rupert, he was minded to embark in a piratical cruise. He told the young Sea-general to complete his voyage, and keep his loyalty for a better time. The exiled court were glad to see the Commonwealth at war with Spain, for they were eager to make friends in Seville and Madrid. Penn's message, though they had to pass it by, was welcome as a sign of disaffection in the service, and supposing that the offer would be made again, they moved the King of Spain, as the most powerful enemy of their country, to allow them one of his ports in which to gather up their fleet.

Though Cromwell knew about the offer, and the answer to it, he was silent in the Council, and allowed the fleet from Portsmouth to proceed upon her voyage.

The expedition failed. Venables, who commanded the army (and was also offering to desert his flag), was beaten under the walls of San Domingo, and but for the rapid march and onset- of a body of sailors, sent by Penn to his assistance, would have been completely mauled. On falling back from Hispaniola the men were so incensed by the failure, that Penn resolved to attack the island of Jamaica, which he conquered and annexed to England at a very slight sacrifice of life.

Sea-general Penn was struck with the resources and the beauties of this island, which in after years he made a subject of his constant talk. A keen examination of the soil and climate, gave him an idea of parting with his Irish lands and laying out his money in the new plantation.

But on Penn's return the Lord Protector was in angry mood, affecting to regard the failure of his great design as due to the incompetency of his chiefs. Land-general Venables threw the blame on Sea-general Penn ; Sea-general Penn threw the blame on Land-general Venables. For reasons which he kept a secret, Cromwell bade his pliant council strip them of their several offices and dignities, and send them under escort to the Tower.

CHAPTER III.

SCHOOL AND COLLEGE (1655-1661).

ADMIRAL PENN's arrest (September 20, 1655) threw his family affairs into confusion. Margaret was at Wanstead with the younger children, Peg and Richard. William was at school in Chigwell. Uncle George had just arrived with proofs of his great losses by the Inquisition : twelve thousand pounds, besides his house, his business, and his wife. He was expecting Admiral Penn to aid him with the Lord Protector, but instead of finding his famous brother powerful at Whitehall, he found him fretting in a dungeon of the Tower.

Margaret fetched her son William to Wanstead, where he fell into a low and feverish state of mind. One day a sort of vision came to him. Sitting in his room he was surprised by a strange feeling in his heart, and by as strange a radiance in his chamber. What it was that filled his veins and flashed into his eyes he could not tell. He was not yet eleven years old. But as he sat alone, in wretched mood, and in a darkish room, he felt a joyous rush of blood along his veins, and saw his chamber fill with what he called a soft and holy light. It was a vision and a visitation. What it meant he could not say; but that he felt the sudden joy and saw the sacred light, he knew and held so long as he could know and hold by any incident of his early life.

The Admiral made every effort to procure his freedom. He was soon aware that he must pay a heavy price for his enlargement. He must crave a pardon from the Lord Protector; he must formally confess his faults; he must surrender his commission as General of the Fleet; he must quit the service of his country. Nor were these conditions all. He was to live in future at his Irish house, near Cork, and was to have no share in the great distribution of Jamaica lands. Unable to do better, he was forced to sign these terms; the Tower was killing him; but on resigning his commission to the Lord Protector he was set at large. Five weeks in the Tower had all but fretted him to death.

Impoverished and dismissed—no longer paid as General of the Fleet—no longer ranked as claimant to a share of the Jamaica lands—no longer suffered to remain near London, Penn broke up his house at Wanstead, gathered in his little folk, and sailed, a poor and discontented man, for county Cork. Macroom, his future home, a town on the river Sullane, twenty miles west of Cork, had been the property of Lord Muskerry, one of the most vigorous partizans of Charles in Ireland. When the royal cause was lost, Macroom was seized by the victorious Roundheads, and the castle and estate were given by

Cromwell's order to his 'faithful' servant, Admiral Penn. The Lord Protector's policy in Ireland was to plant in every shire an English colony, and when he gave a patch of land to any favourite, he was careful that it should be near a castle or a fort. Macroom was strong enough to shield an English colony. A troop of horse and company of foot were stationed in the town, and Penn had been authorised and expected to send out a body of skilful husbandmen. His term of power had been too short for much to have been done; but some few English had arrived whose industry had much increased the worth of Cromwell's gift.

For more than three years Admiral Penn resided with his wife and little ones at Macroom, engaged in planting his estate. His eldest son, to whom this planting was a lesson of immense importance, was a bright and forward lad from twelve to fifteen years of age. Though tall and slim the boy was firmly knit. He liked to run and ride, to scull and sail, and had a passionate delight in country sports. In things of business he was almost like a man.

Besides the castle, town, and manor of Macroom, Penn held the neighbouring castle, town, and manor of Killcrea, the whole containing many thousand acres of good land, with much convenient wood. He bought more land from Roger Boyle, his friend and neighbour, whom he joined in drinking secret healths to Charles. He also prayed Lord Henry Cromwell, son of Oliver, for leases of some districts near his property, alleging that he wished to tenant them with English hands. With sure and patient toil, assisted by his active son, who seemed to have a natural bent that way, the Admiral improved his lands ; here mending roads, there forming nurseries, in a third place planting gardens, in a fourth place building farms. In three years the estate had risen in rental from something like three hundred pounds a-year to eight hundred and fifty-eight pounds a-year.

Good tutors were in plenty at Macroom and Cork, and Penn the Younger made such rapid progress in his learning that at fifteen he was ripe for Oxford, and the Admiral, on talking with his friends, Ormonde and Boyle, resolved that he should go to Christ Church.

This matter was arranged in 1659 ; a year of many changes in the Admiral's prospects. Cromwell died. So soon as sure intelligence of his death arrived in county Cork the Admiral put himself into correspondence with his royalist friends, Boyle and Ormonde ; but on seeing how affairs went on in London they concluded that it would be well to wait events and not commit themselves by any overt act. They had not long to wait. Six months sufficed to wear out Richard Cromwell's force, and when the news of his deposition reached Macroom, Penn threw away his mask, declared for Charles the Second, and immediately set out for the Low Countries to kiss his master's hand.

Charles was so glad to see the Admiral that he knighted him on the spot, and promised him his lasting favour. Penn returned to England, where he found himself, on Monk's suggestion, called to serve in parliament, with his old comrade, Sea-general Montagu, for the town of Weymouth. When the resolution for recalling Charles the Second was adopted by the two houses, Montagu was named commander of the royal fleet, and Penn took ship with him, in order to be one among the first to throw himself at his future sovereign's feet.

The King was kind to him; but Charles had friends much closer to his heart than Admiral Penn. Among these closer friends was Lord Muskerry, his father's partizan, whom he had recently created Earl of Clancarty. Lord Clancarty's house was that Macroom which Penn had been improving with his capital and skill. The King was fixed on giving Lord Clancarty all that he had lost; the Penns must therefore quit Macroom. His Majesty was pleased to say that they should have some other lands; but they must leave at once, in order that Clancarty might go home in peace. To soften this hard blow, the King appointed Penn a Commissioner of the Navy, with a salary of five hundred pounds a-year, and lodgings in Navy Gardens, and he promised to make the Lords Justices of Ireland find among the forfeited estates of Roundheads something that would more than pay him for his losses in Macroom.

Lady Penn being housed in her fine lodgings at the Navy Gardens, Admiral Penn was happy, though he had to keep a wistful eye on the Irish lands. He gave good dinners, kept high company, resorted, as the fashion led him, to the playhouse and the cockpit. Lady Penn set up her coach. The Admiral, who had been a Puritan among the Puritans, became a roystering blade with the returning Cavaliers. He supped at the Dolphin and the Three Crowns, took the comedians into his favour, lived on easy terms with the play-writers, and paid his compliments to every pretty hussy on the stage. Dick Broome, the profligate author of 'The Jovial Crew,' became a guest in his house. Pepys calls this libeller 'Sir William's poet;' and the Navy Gardens were a scene for romps and jinks that faintly echoed the festivities of Whitehall.

Sir William followed in the wake of greater men, for he was bent on rising in the world. His Irish friends were gaining great rewards from Charles. Boyle was created Earl of Orrery, and named Lord President of Munster. Ormonde, with the higher grade of marquis, was become Lord Steward of the Household and Lord Lieutenant of Ireland. Penn was made Governor of the town and Captain of the fort of Kinsale ; a post which gave him the title of Admiral of Ireland, with fees amounting to four hundred pounds a-year. Penn had therefore gained in these two offices of Naval Commissioner and Governor of Kinsale nine hundred pounds a-year from the grateful King. But Charles, who wished to bind him closer to his person, wrote with his own hand to the Lords Justices in Dublin that a good estate, of equal value to the one restored to Lord Clancarty, must be set aside for Penn in county Cork, as near as might be to his port and castle of Kinsale.

When Admiral Penn had put his house in order,

he was anxious that his son,—whose talents seemed to him of the finest order, and whose love of business and open-air exercises promised to make him a man of active habits and worldly ambition,—should proceed to the University. In October Penn the Younger went to Oxford, where he matriculated as a gentleman commoner at Christ Church. Oxford was then the seat of wit as well as of scholarship. In the chair of the Dean sat the famous controversialist, Doctor John Owen, soon to become an object of royalist persecution. South, too long repressed, had now obtained a hearing, and, as Orator to the University, he was preparing those sermons which are still regarded by lovers of old literature as models of grace. Jack Wilmot too was there, scattering about him those gleams of wit and devilry which in after-life endeared the Earl of Rochester to his graceless King. Most notable of all the ornaments of Oxford was John Locke—an unknown student of Christ Church, devoting in a sequestered cloister his serene and noble intellect to the study of medicine. Being twelve years older than Penn, it is not probable that these two men contracted more than a casual acquaintance at Christ Church; but in later life they met again—rivals in legislation, and mediators for each other in the hour of need.

Penn, entering on his academical career under the auspices of the King and Duke of York, obtained a good position in the circle of his college. As a student, he gave satisfaction to his superiors; as a boater and rider, he became a favourite with his

set. His reading at this time was solid and ex
tensive, and his acquisition of knowledge was assisted by an excellent memory. For a boy, he left
Oxford well acquainted with history and theology.
Of languages he had more than ordinary share.
Either then or afterwards, he read the chief writers
of Greece and Italy in their native tongues; and
gained a thorough knowledge of French, German,
Dutch, and Italian. Later in life he added to
this stock of languages two or three dialects of
the Red men. But his pleasure and recreation
while at Christ Church was in reading the doctrinal
discussions to which the Puritans gave rise. The
court of Charles had infected the higher classes of
society before the Restoration actually took place;
and that mixture of vice and wit, politeness and
irreligion, which was soon to characterise the youth
of England, was already turning the University
into a den of rakes and dupes. There were not
wanting protests. Many of the young men there
collected had in early youth some better notion of
religion and morality,—and they resisted every attempt to introduce a more lax and courtly ceremonial
into the services of the Church.

Dr. Owen, made Dean of Christ Church by order
of Parliament in 1653, was ejected from his office to
make room for Dr. Reynolds; a change intended,
among other things, to prepare for the introduction
of a more picturesque ritual than had latterly been in
use. This measure was unpopular with the Puritan
students, and Owen kept up a constant correspondence with the members of his college, in which

he incited them to remain firm in their rejection of papistical rites. Under his high sanction, many of them opposed the innovations of the court. William Penn stood foremost. From the trials of his Uncle George he had learnt to loathe the practices of a persecuting Church. Yet it was not without pain that Penn found his conscience at war with the princes whom his father delighted to serve. From the frequent references to these times made by him in after-life, it is evident that his sufferings were acute. As the light of truth dawned on his mind he was surprised and terrified to find how dark all was outside. Everywhere, to use his own expression, he saw that a reign of darkness and debauchery was commencing; and his hope for the future came to lie in a vague, romantic fancy, that a virtuous and holy empire, free from bigotry and from the formalism of a State religion—might be founded in that far-off Western World which had so often formed a topic at his father's hearth. In this fancy his mind discovered a real 'opening of joy.'

While the quarrel of Cavalier and Puritan was raging at Oxford, an obscure person, named Thomas Loe—a layman of that city—took to preaching a new doctrine which was taught by one George Fox. The neglect of forms and ceremonies in the ritual of the Friends, as the New People called themselves, attracted Penn and others, who like him were in revolt against the restoration of popish usages; and going to hear the preaching of this strange word, the young men got excited, and returned to hear. Their absence from chapel was noticed; their superiors became alarmed ; the young defaulters were arraigned and fined. This indignity drove them wild ; and as the fines were laid at the moment when a new rule about college gowns came out, the youngsters banded themselves together to oppose the orders of the court by force. They marched through the streets. They not only refused to wear the new gown, but declared war against all who put it on. In the gardens of Christ Church, in the quadrangles of colleges, they set upon the courtly youths and tore the vestments from their backs. In these affairs young Penn was always in the front ; and on the facts being proved against him he was censured and expelled.

CHAPTER IV.

THE WORLD (1661–1666).

ON hearing of his son's offence of Non-conformity, the Admiral was deeply grieved. The world was going well with him. He was a Naval Commissioner, a Member of Parliament, Governor of Kinsale, Admiral of Ireland, a Member of the Council of Munster, and a favourite of the Duke of York. The King was kind to him and something more. The Lords Justices had found him an estate in Shangarry Castle, county Cork. An English peerage lay within his reach, and in his choice of title he had fixed his mind on Weymouth, the port for which he sat in parliament. That such a lad as his son William, with his love of sport and business, should become a ranter and a mystic, was so droll a fancy, that the Admiral could only laugh it off. Yet he was troubled with reports from Oxford, and his rivals at the Navy Gardens noted with a secret joy his clouded brow, his wistful manner, and his silent tongue.

The boy was brought to London, to the Navy Gardens, in the hope that a course of hard dining and late dancing might do him good. His mother, Lady Penn, was of a merry mood, and Peg, his sister, was a perfect romp. Sir William kept a pleasant table; entertained the best of company; enjoyed a supper at the Bear, and was a frequent visitor in the pit of Drury Lane. Broome's comedy of the 'Jovial Crew,' a satire on the Puritans, was then being acted at the old Cock-pit, and Sir William took his son to see it. 'To the theatre,' writes Pepys under date of November 1, 1661, 'to see the Jovial Crew. At my house Sir William sent for his son, William Penn, lately come from Oxford.' William Penn was not corrected in his notions by the Jovial Crew.

Sir William tried all courses with his son. He shut him up; he took him to the play; he had him whipt; he joked and laughed at him; he treated him with silent rage. But nothing he could do prevailed. The boy continued in a low and serious frame of mind; he shunned society; he sang no ballads; nay, he even gave up dog and gun. He wrote to Dr. Owen, who replied to him, as to a favourite pupil; and the young man could not be induced, by dice and cards, by plays and suppers, to admit that he was wrong in resisting the King's commands about wearing the college gown.

Yet every one who came near Penn observed that he was strong in wit and purpose, even as he was soft of face. Every one liked him, and spoke well of him; and of those who knew him well, the Admiral loved him most. To quarrel with this favourite, more than was needful for his good, was what the scheming Admiral had neither will nor power to do; and after giving much thought to what he ought to try he changed his method of proceeding with his son. It occurred to him that the best way to withdraw a young man from sombre thought and inferior company would be to send him to the gay capital of France. His son had not yet seen the world :—he proposed to him to set out immediately for Paris. Some of his college friends were going into France to study, and it was soon arranged that he should join them. Some of these young men were of the highest rank, and every door in France would open to their knock. At Paris, where they stayed a few weeks only, Penn was presented to Louis Quatorze, and became a welcome guest at court. There he made the acquaintance of Robert Spencer, son of the first Earl of Sunderland, and Lady Dorothy Sydney—sister of the famous Algernon Sydney. France was very gay, and in a few weeks William Penn forgot the gravity of his life. Returning late one night from a party, he was accosted in the dark street by a man who shouted to him in angry tones to draw and defend himself. At the same moment a sword gleamed past his eyes. The fellow would not listen to reason. Penn, he said, had treated him with contempt. He had bowed his head and taken off his hat in salutation :—his courtesy had been slighted, and he would have satisfaction made to his wounded pride. In vain the young Englishman protested he had not seen him,—that he could have no motive for offering such an insult to a stranger. The more he showed the absurdity of the quarrel, the more enraged his assailant grew; he would say no more — the only answer which he deigned was a pass with his rapier. Penn's blood was now stirred; and whipping his sword from its scabbard, he stood to the attack. There was but little light; yet several persons were attracted by the clash of steel; and a number of roysterers gathered round to see fair play. A few passes proved that Penn was the more expert swordsman; and a dexterous movement threw the French gallant's blade into the air. He might have run the man through, and those who gathered round the combatants expected him to do so. Penn picked up the fallen sword, and gave it back with his politest bow.

On hearing how his son was living at Paris, Admiral Penn felt glad that he was far away from Puritans like John Owen and Quakers like Thomas Loe. He thought of a career in life for him, and spoke to Ormonde on the subject. Ormonde said the lad would make a soldier, and the Admiral fixed his mind on the career of arms. But William was too young for life in camp, and he had much as yet to learn from books. He must be sent to school. His father, therefore, made arrangements with Professor Amyrault of Saumur, on the river Loire, to board and teach him, and in sunny Anjou Penn the Younger spent the two years which he should have passed in Oxford, reading the classics and the fathers, pondering over theological mysteries, and mastering the poetry, the language, and the history of France.

At nineteen years of age he left Saumur and passed through Switzerland into Italy. Spencer was a companion of his travels, and in some part of his journey he fell in with Spencer's uncle, Algernon Sydney, then in exile, and became at once his pupil and his friend.

In the summer days of 1664, while William Penn was not yet twenty years of age, he was recalled to London by his father, who was no less eager to see him back on private than on public grounds.

Uncle George, who had been teasing Charles for justice several years, died before his case was heard in council, leaving to his younger brother all his claims on Spain. Poor George had trudged from park to lodge, waylaying Charles and James, and forcing them to hear his plaints, until the King, who knew that he had suffered grievous wrongs, proposed to send him to Madrid as envoy to the court of Philip the Fourth. If George were in Madrid, as envoy from his sovereign, justice might be done to him; but the appointment was hardly made before the sufferer died; when all his claims against the Spanish Crown devolved on Admiral Penn—a vast addition to his cares and a perpetual drain upon his purse. The sum originally seized at San Lucar was twelve thousand pounds in English money. Twenty-one years had passed, and as the price of money in the south of Spain was ten or twelve per cent, the claim had grown from twelve to forty thousand pounds. If Penn demanded less he would be moderate. This affair required attention which the Admiral could not give. Sir William was in fact at sea.

So soon as Charles the Second was restored the Dutch revived their ancient dream of naval supremacy, and their pretensions had at length outwearied the patience of Whitehall. War was declared. James, Duke of York, Lord Admiral of England, divided his fleet into three squadrons, one of which he gave to Prince Rupert, a second to Lord Sandwich, and the third he kept in hand. Not one of these commanders had ever directed a great naval fight; not one was qualified, by experience and ability, to contend against veterans like De Ruyter and De Witt. Sandwich was a soldier, Rupert a freebooter, and James, though he had distinguished himself under Turenne, was yet a stranger to the quarterdeck. It was not safe to trifle with such seamen as the Dutch. James wanted the best captains, the best sailors in the kingdom, and in spite of Sandwich's jealousy and Rupert's rage, the royal Duke consulted Admiral Penn. Sir William Penn advised him to employ in his service the old and dauntless captains of the Commonwealth. 'Take no notice of their religion, and I will answer for their courage,' said Penn. The Duke of York had strength enough to resist the royalist clamour when this advice was known; and many of Blake's old captains were appointed to commands by James. That all the benefit of Penn's skill and courage might be given to his country Penn was named Great Captain Commander, and ordered to take his station on the Duke's flagship, to direct the most important movements of the fleet.

While he was thus employed at sea, Sir William thought it well to have his son at home ; in part to watch the family affairs in Cork, in part to save him from arrest in France. The French were leaning towards alliance with the Dutch, and if the treaty, then in secret preparation, should be·signed, a hostage like the Admiral's eldest son was very likely to be seized.   As fast as post could carry him Penn returned from Italy through Savoy, and arrived about the middle of August, 1664, at the Navy Gardens, to the great delight of Peg and Lady Penn.

The boy was nearly twenty years of age ; but what a change from the moody, silent lad who went from home two years ago ! He had a fine outside ; a little over-fine, some critics said. ' A most modish person,' little Mr. Pepys exclaimed ; ' grown a fine gentleman.' He wore French pantaloons ; he carried his rapier in the French mode ; he doffed his hat on going into a room. His French was perfect, and he spoke like one who had seen the Alps and the Italian cities. 'Something of learning he has got,' wrote Pepys, ' but a great deal, if not too much of the vanity of the French garb, and affected manner of gait and speech.' In person he had grown into a graceful, strong, and handsome man. His face was mild and almost womanly in its beauty ; his eye was soft and full ; his brow was open and ample ; his features, well defined, approached the ideal ; and the lines about his mouth were sweet, yet firm. Like Milton, he wore his hair long and parted in the centre of the forehead, from which it fell over his neck and shoulders in massive ringlets. In mien and manner he was formed by nature, stamped by art—a gentleman.

The Admiral took care to drop all reference to the past. To lessen what was still the risk of a return to old companions, he kept the young man constantly engaged. He carried him to the gallery at Whitehall,—presented him to great persons,—made him pay court visits. The Navy Gardens rang with feast and jollity, for Peg was now growing up, and Lady Penn was more inclined for merriment than ever. Sir William placed his son as a student at Lincoln's Inn, that he might acquire some scraps of law. Allowing him no leisure to indulge in idle fancies, he employed him on the King's business and in his own private affairs. There seemed no fear that he would now go wrong.

Then came the crisis of the war. On the 24th of March, 1665, the Duke of York, accompanied by Penn as Great Captain Commander, and many great persons, went on board the *Royal Charles*. The younger Penn was on his father's staff, and saw during the few days he remained at sea some service between the Dutch and English fleets. Meanwhile his mother and the ladies left behind in the Navy Gardens kept high jinks. 'Going to my Lady Batten,' says Pepys, 'there found a great many women with her, in her chamber, merry; my Lady Penn and her daughter among others, when my Lady Penn flung me down on the bed, and herself and others, one after another, upon me, and very merry we were.' Admiral Batten was on board the fleet with Admiral Penn. The little Clerk of the Acts was the only man left in the Navy Gardens to make pastime for these merry wives. Dick Broome himself could hardly have imagined a more 'jovial crew.'

On Sunday, twenty-third day of April, 1665, Penn the Younger landed at Harwich with despatches from the Duke of York to Charles, and from Sir William Coventry to Lord Arlington, Secretary of State. He pressed for horses, as the Duke of York's instructions to him were—that he should get on shore, should ride as hard as horse could carry him, should go at once to the King's apartments, and should make a full report of what was being done at sea. By tearing on all night Penn reached Whitehall before the sun was up, and finding that the King was still in bed, he sent a message to Lord Arlington, who rose at once and passed into his master's bedroom. Charles leaped up on hearing that despatches from the Duke were come, and running into the anteroom, met William Penn. 'Oh, it's you! How is Sir William?' Having read the Duke's letter, chatted with the messenger, and asked about Sir William several times, Charles bade the youth go home and get to bed.

In June the fight came off; a striking victory for the English flag; a glory reaped by James, as first in rank, but which his royal highness was too frank in spirit not to share with Admiral Penn. In the same month the plague broke out in London, and the havoc wrought by this disease was chiefly in the districts lying round the Tower. It was a thing to make the merriest romp in the Navy Gardens pause.

When Admiral Penn came home, he was annoyed to see how great a change this plague had wrought in his eldest son. The youth was grave and silent; he had left off speaking French; had ceased to carry his hat in hand; and all but ceased to show himself at court. His days were spent in reading, and the friends who came to him were men of sober life. Again the Admiral's hopes, now nearer fruit than ever, were in check. What could he do with such a moody youth? Suppose the lad turned ranter? He had tried the 'Jovial Crew' before. A good idea struck him. William might be sent to Ireland; first to Dublin, where the Duke of Ormonde would be glad to see him; afterwards to Shangarry Castle, where there was much for him to do, not only on his family estate, but in his office at Kinsale.

To Ireland he was sent. In order to provide him with abundant work, he was appointed Clerk of the Cheque at Kinsale harbour, and encouraged to believe that if he felt inclined to enter His Majesty's service he might get his father's company of foot.

CHAPTER V.

FATHER AND SON (1666–1667).

THE Penns were fond of county Cork, in which they had already spent some years, and as their new estate—when it was free to them—would be larger than any one they could hope to buy in either Somerset or Essex, Admiral Penn was scheming for a settlement of his family in that picturesque and fertile shire. His kinsmen wished him to recover Penn's Lodge near Minety; but the place was small, and he had grown too great for the ambition of a country squire. His house at Chigwell was too paltry for the dignity of a peer. Shangarry Castle, with the lands which had been set apart for him at Rostillon and Inchy, gave him what he could not find in England,—an address, a residence, and a rental of a thousand pounds a-year. His eyes were therefore turned towards county Cork, as likely to become his future home.

Penn sailed for Dublin; where he waited on the Duke of Ormonde. Before going down to Cork, he was to see Sir George Lane, the Irish secretary, and make as many friends as he could win at court.

Lord Ossory, the Duke's eldest son, was absent from Dublin, but Lord Arran was at home, and he and William Penn became fast friends. . The Duke was pleased with Penn, and in a week or two accounts were sent to the Admiral assuring him that in separating his son from his London associates he had turned the current of his thoughts. Instead of moping in his room, the youth was always in the circle, gay and bright, with pretty foreign manners, and a spirit to attempt the boldest things. The Butlers were a family of soldiers, and the pomp and circumstance of war were topmost in the thoughts of Arran and his comrades. Penn was not behind these youngsters. While he was in Dublin, waiting on the court, a mutiny took place at Carrickfergus (May, 1666), where the insurgents seized the castle and alarmed the country-side from Antrim to Belfast. To Arran was assigned the duty of suppressing this revolt, and Penn took service with his friend. The mutineers fought well, but bit by bit were driven into the fort, and then the fort itself was stormed. Young Penn was talked of as the coolest of the cool, the bravest of the brave. Lord Arran was delighted with him; for the young swordsman of Paris had become the proud soldier of Carrickfergus; and the Duke at once wrote off to tell the Admiral he was ready to confer on his son William that command of the company at Kinsale, which they had talked about for him before the lad returned from France.

Though Penn could not be made into a boon companion, a friend of comedians, and a partner in

the romps and jinks of the Navy Gardens, there was
still a chance of seeing him grow up into a soldier of
his country and a bearer of his cross,—a hero of the
stamp of Thomas Grey.   The glory won at Carrickfergus made him long to get his company.   The
fit was on him, and he wanted to appear at Kinsale
as Captain Penn instead of Clerk of the Cheque.
His zeal amused and gratified his parents; but the
Admiral had begun to change his plans.   Affairs
were looking ill at court ; Sir William saw no chance
of going to sea again ; and he was talking of retiring
to Shangarry Castle and his government of Kinsale.
If they should go to Cork, it would be well to keep
the offices they had got; but if his son received
his company of foot he must lose his highly profitable
Clerkship of the Cheque.

'Well, Sir,' said the Duke of Ormonde to his
guest before his courtiers, 'has Sir William given
you his company at Kinsale?'

'He has promised it, your grace,' replied young
Penn; 'and your lordship has promised to favour his
request when made.'

'But has he written nothing?'

'He is far from London, and is busy fitting out
the fleet.'

The Admiral affected to regard his son as being
too young for such a post as Captain at Kinsale.
When Penn was eager, he requested him to live a
'sober life,' and told him in the plainest terms he
was too 'young' and 'rash.'   Heroes of forty-five
are apt to rail at heroes of twenty-two.   The
veteran, when he told his son not to let his 'desires'

outrun his 'discretion,' forgot that he was himself a captain at twenty-one. Before the vision of a life in camp and field was gone for ever, Penn had himself painted with his harness on his back. It was the only portrait for which he ever sat ; and thus the single record which the world possesses of a man whose name is Peace displays him in a coat of shining steel.

When he had warned his son to live a 'sober' life at Kinsale, the Admiral gave him hints about doing his duty to the crown, yet making money in his office of the Cheque.

The post was one of some account. A Clerk of the Cheque had to deal with captains of ships ; to keep the poll-books ; and to certify the accuracy of all accounts. He had the charge of government stores and property, civil and warlike. He had to give out rations and supplies, and to see that the musters on board each ship agreed with the entries on the books. As Clerk of the Cheque Penn would live in county Cork, within easy reach of the family estate, which also needed his constant care.

Sir William's old friend, Roger, Earl of Orrery (known among the literary and scientific Boyles as poet and dramatist), was living at Cork as President of Munster, and in this able and brilliant nobleman Penn soon found a steadfast friend.

Penn resided chiefly at Kinsale, attending to the duties of his office ; giving out rope and tar, paying seamen's wages, counting tallies, and living, as the Admiral wished him to live, a 'sober' life. His superiors in the King's service were well pleased with him; Lord Orrery gave him the rank of Ensign in a company of horse; and during the darker days of the Dutch war we hear of Ensign Penn running to and fro; fitting out ships, throwing chains across the harbour, rallying soldiers in the fort. It was still on the cards that William Penn might come to be Captain Penn.

While Ensign Penn was running to and fro about the business of his post, he kept an eye on his own affairs at Shangarry Castle. As in every other grant of forfeited lands, a multitude of suits sprang up; the royal warrant was disputed; and the tenant, Colonel Wallis, was a man who would not yield to either duke or king. In vain the Lords Justices showed him the King's own words. 'The King has no right to give away these lands; the law alone can say if they were forfeit to the crown.' Much prudence was required in dealing with Colonel Wallis, but the young and soft negotiator brought the fiery old soldier to a calmer frame of mind.

In London things were jogging on as usual. Margaret Penn had found 'a servant' in Antony Lowther, of Maske, in Yorkshire; a man of good family, wealthy, and devoted to her. Sir William was either at the court, the Navy Office, or the playhouse daily, with Sir William Coventry, Admiral Batten, or some other comrade, pushing his fortunes and deserving all he got. The Admiral was liked by all his equals; and enjoyed the highest favour of the King and Duke of York. Though growing old (and Pepys adds, ' ugly '), Lady Penn kept up her spirits. ' Supped at home, and very merry,' says their garrulous neighbour, ' and about nine to Mrs. Mercer's gate . . . . and there mighty merry; my Lady Penn and Peg going thither with us, and Nan Wright, till about twelve at night; flinging our fireworks, and burning one another, and the people over the way; and at last, our business being most spent, we went into Mrs. Mercer's, and there mighty merry, smutting one another with candle-grease and soot, till most of us were like devils.' Even these high jinks were nothing to what came in the early hours. Pepys carried the whole party to his lodgings in the Navy Office, where they drank still more, and then began to reel and dance. Pepys and two other men put on women's clothes. They dressed the maid-servant like a boy, and got her to dance a jig. ' Nan Wright, my wife, and Peg Penn,' says the Navy Clerk, ' put on periwigs; thus we spent till three or four in the morning; mighty merry, and then parted, and to bed.' A very jovial crew!

It was in London, not at Kinsale or Dublin, that the question of the Irish lands was to be settled. The Land Commissioners, appointed by the Crown to hear the multitude of cases which had risen during twenty years of grants, confiscations, for-feitures, and restorations, were then sitting; but the Admiral had begun to feel a greater confidence in his son's tact and judgment than his own. He wrote to his son, desiring him to get the family affairs into an orderly state and then come over and see the Commissioners; at the same time giving him some worldly hints as to the conduct of the victualling department of Kinsale Castle, and begging him to make the passage in calm weather, so as to run no risk. Penn joyfully obeyed his father's summons, as he had not seen his mother and sister for a long time, and he arrived in London in the month of November. The business was arranged. After hearing evidence on both sides, the Land Commissioners confirmed the grant of Shangarry Castle to Sir William Penn.

Assured of this addition to his fortune, the Admiral was less intent about his brother George's claims. He set up several coaches; he arranged his daughter's marriage with Lowther; and in the face of his expected barony of Weymouth, talked of buying Wanstead House.

Antony and Peg were married, rather quietly, on the 15th of February, 1667. Sir William gave his daughter a large fortune; some said fifteen thousand pounds! His cousin, John Gorges, member for Cirencester, begged him to purchase the old place in Wiltshire; but Penn's Lodge, the 'genteel ancient house,' was not a big one, and his thoughts were steadily directed towards the county Cork, his future home. Peg's dress and jewels were like those of a duchess; and neither the King nor the King's ministers had a coach so fine as hers.

When Peg was happily married, Penn returned to Cork, where he was wanted much. His father saw him go with pleasure; for the romps and feasts of the Navy Gardens drove him into moody ways;

and in despatching him to Ireland he was thinking only of the active life awaiting him in county Cork, the duties of his office, and the care of his estate.

Soon after Penn arrived, he heard that Thomas Loe the Quaker was about to preach in Cork. He went to hear him, wondering how his riper judgment would receive the eloquence that had stirred him when at Christ Church. Loe gave out his text, 'There is a faith that overcomes the world, and there is a faith that is overcome by the world,' a topic but too well adapted to his state of mind. That evening Penn became a Friend.

Attending Loe's services, he soon began to taste the cup for which he had exchanged the world. In no corner of these islands were the Quakers treated fairly, and least of anywhere in county Cork. Ignorant magistrates supposed they were the Cromwellites come back without their swords ; and only to be ruled with whips and jails. On Tuesday, September 3, 1667, a meeting of these people was called in Cork ; a body of police and soldiers broke upon them, took the congregation prisoners, and carried them before the mayor. On seeing in this crowd, young Ensign Penn, lord of Shangarry Castle, the mayor proposed to set him free on giving his word to keep the peace ; but Penn denied that in meeting for worship, either he or any of his fellow-prisoners had been guilty of a breach of law. He would not give his word. 'Unless you give bonds for your good behaviour,' said the mayor, 'I must commit you with the rest.'

'On what authority do you act ?'

'A proclamation of the year 1660,' replied the mayor. Penn knew that proclamation well. It was an act against the Fifth monarchy-men; fiery souls, with whom king-killing was not murder; and he told the mayor of Cork that these poor Quakers met to worship God, and not to pull down thrones and states. The mayor was zealous for the King, and as the heir of Shangarry Castle would not yield, he too was lodged in jail.

From his prison Penn wrote to Orrery, as President of Munster. Lord Orrery sent an order to the mayor of Cork for Penn's discharge; but the incident made known to all the gossips of Cork and Dublin that Ensign Penn, the volunteer of Carrickfergus, had taken up with a lot of ranters and canters. His reply to these scorners was an open appearance among the Friends, as one of that persecuted sect.

The Admiral's friends in Dublin wrote to warn Sir William of his son's relapse. The Admiral was beside himself with rage. Was this the end of all his arts? Recalling his son to London, where he arrived a few days before Christmas, 1667, Sir William met him with a frown, which passed away as he observed his manner and attire. The young man's bearing was polite and easy, and his dress, adorned with lace and ruffles, sword and plume, was that of gentlemen at court. But in a few days he was undeceived. Observing that his son omitted to unbonnet, as the newest fashion was at court, the Admiral asked him what he meant.

'I am a Friend,' the young man said, 'and Friends take off the hat to none but God.'

Then how would he behave at court? Would he, a king's officer, Ensign Penn, Clerk of the Cheque, the son of a Navy Commissioner, wear his hat in presence of his prince? Penn asked for time to think this question over.

' Why?' exclaimed the angry Admiral; 'in order to consult the Ranters?'

' No, sir,' said the young man softly; 'I will not see them; let me go into my room.'

Penn slipped aside, and after some time, spent in prayer, he came back to his father with his final word—he could not lift his hat to mortal man.

' Not even to the King and to the Duke of York?'

' No, sir; not even to the King and to the Duke of York?'

The indignant Admiral turned him out of doors.

CHAPTER VI.

HAT-HOMAGE (1667–1668).

To live an easy life and wear the coronet of an English peer? To pass through shadows and to dwell with the despised of men? Such was the choice now offered to the young swordsman of Paris, the modish gentleman of the Navy Gardens, and the volunteer of Carrickfergus. Was it craze of mind which led him to offend a generous father, to renounce a pleasant home, and sacrifice his prospects in the court, about some scruple as to taking off his hat? A man of sense might think so, if this lifting of the hat were all. But lifting, and not lifting, of the hat was very far from being all. It was a sign, and one of many signs.

With us to raise the hat is easy; we are used to it. Our hats are made for lifting, and we raise the hat in cases where our fathers would have bent the knee. Hat-homage is our social creed. But in the reign of Charles the Second it was new and strange. A hat is made to wear, not carry in your hand. Men wore their hats in house and church, as well as in the street and park. Men sate at meals in felt, and listened at a play in felt. 'I got a strange cold in my head,' wrote Pepys, 'by flinging my hat off at dinner.' Every one ate covered. Clarendon tells us that in his younger days he always stood uncovered in the presence of his elders, save at meals, when he and other lads put on their hats. A shopman stood behind the counter in his hat; a preacher mounted to the pulpit in his hat. The audience wore their hats, and only doffed them at the name of God. But with the coming in of Charles a hundred foreign follies had come in. French words, French habits, and French fashions, were the rage. Such wits as Rochester and Sedley brought in French, and fools of fashion cried at every pause of conversation, 'You have reason, sir,' 'In fine, sir,' and the like. Sir Martin Marrall in Dryden's comedy is a type of this new race of courtiers, just as Moody is a type of the Elizabethan men.

Hat-lifting, therefore, was the sign of a depraved and foreign fashion, recently brought into England from abroad. All sober men put on their hats, while wits and foplings carried them in their hands. The homely citizen wore his beaver, and the lord-in-waiting wore a periwig. To wear the hat was English, and to take it off was French.

Even Cromwell had been puzzled how to act towards those who wedded such a doctrine as non-resistance to that of the inner light. What was he to do with men who would not meet him foot to foot, yet claimed to be a law unto themselves? How could he manage men who told him they would not accept his rule, yet offered him their cheeks and necks to smite? A sword that cut a path through Naseby field was useless in the presence of this unresisting force. He tempted them with smiles, with gifts, with places, but these simple souls would have no part in him and in his rule. 'Now,' said he, 'I see there is a people risen whom I cannot win.' These Friends were men of peace. If what they did was wrong, they took upon their backs the burden of that sin. Such sects as Levellers and Anabaptists he could meet as sword encounters sword; but with the Quakers there was nothing he could strike. They courted stripes and chains. They bowed their heads to fine and sentence; taking his decrees as so much penance laid on them in love. They would not fly before his troops, and if he wished to kill them they were ready for the cross. However fixed his purpose, they were not less fixed in theirs—to weary out and overcome his strength.

The system of these Friends was one of State affairs as well as Church affairs; announcing that all men are equal before the laws; that all men have a right to express opinions; that all men have a right to worship God according to their conscience; not because such and such things were done by ancient tribes; not because it is well to have certain balances and checks; but on account of the inward, independent, indestructible light in every human soul. Each man is a separate power, and therefore has a separate right. This system met with bold denial every claim of prince and pope to curb the individual will, and every claim of prelate and inquisitor to search the individual mind. It held that every man's own light—his conscience or his reason—is the safest guide. To doff the hat, to bend the knee, to call a man by such vain names as lord and prince, was sin against the Lord and Prince of heaven. For God, the Friends declared, had made men peers, and setting up these marks of separation was dividing men without a cause, and trifling with the noblest work of God.

To a young man holding such a gospel what was a baron's coronet—what a seat in the House of Lords?

Shut out from his home in the Navy Gardens at the age of twenty-three, Ensign Penn was not left to starve in the streets. Lady Penn sent him money from her private purse. His new friends made him welcome in their homes ; for this young soldier came amongst these pious people as a brand plucked out of a burning fire. This time of exile from the Navy Gardens was a trial to his faith. He loved his mother and his sister Peg, the merry matron and the romping girl ; and for the Admiral he entertained a high, though not unreasoning, respect. On every side he had to count some loss. With his opinions he could not hold his Ensign's rank, he could not keep his Clerkship of the Cheque. These small things had to go the way of greater things.

The set-off to his loss was not so obvious to a worldly eye, and Admiral Penn could not be made to see that he had any set-off at all to count. In giving up his rank, his office, and his home, as well as sacrificing the hope of greater things to come, the young man felt he was obeying the summons to forsake his father and mother for a higher good. He found no comfort in the romps and revels, in the tavern dinners and the evening plays. The creed of Fox was to him a saving creed. Such men as Fox and Loe were notable for the purity of their lives. What they professed to be they were; not so the titled people whom he met in his father's haunts. At the theatre in Drury Lane, to which his mother and sister went so often, he had seen virtue mocked, and truth abused, and female modesty put to shame. The park, where his father loved to be seen, was thronged with harlots and bravoes; with women who sold their smiles and men who were ready to sell their swords. He knew that the royal palace was a nest for every crawling thing. Look where he would upon that society from which he was shut out, he saw little beyond vanity, rottenness, and death. In the highest place of all— that chamber in which, not long ago, Cromwell had poured out his soul in prayer, and Milton had pealed his organ-note—a herd of gamesters, courtesans, and duellists, diced and drank the live-long night.

A young man, pure in heart, might well turn anchoret in such a world.

The politics of Fox had also their attraction for this idealist of twenty-three. For four or five years he had been poring over Sydney's dreams. One Commonwealth had failed. He wished to see a new experiment in freedom; an experiment conducted, not by orators and soldiers acting in a worldly spirit, and with personal ends in view; but a religious and fraternal commonwealth, where every member would devote himself to God and man. Penn loved that great republican like a son, but he could never give his heart up wholly to the idea of a country governed in the pride of intellect and virtue. Fox supplied what Sydney wanted—faith in things unseen and passionate belief in individual men. Penn found that he could feel and act with both these leaders; looking up with Sydney to the free government of Pericles and Scipio, yet denying with Fox that past example is of higher use to man than inner light.

After a few months of absence from the Navy Gardens, Penn was suffered to return, but still the Admiral held aloof from his rebellious son. He would not speak to him; he would not sit at table with him. Penn hung up his sword and coat of mail, and put into a trunk his lace and plume. He dressed in homely garments, and resigned his lucrative Clerkship of the Cheque.

CHAPTER VII.

SWORD AND PEN (1668).

ALONE in his rooms at the Navy Gardens, he who had just laid down his sword, took up his pen. While the Admiral was fighting through a court intrigue of Lord Arlington and Sir Robert Howard, as the minions of Prince Rupert, Penn was engaged in struggling with the sins and sufferings of a host of men whom he regarded as agents of the Prince of Darkness. But his only weapon was, as yet, the pen.

A startling call was made to princes, priests, and people, to examine for themselves the Quaker doctrine of the inner light, in a tract called 'Truth Exalted; in a short but sure testimony against all those religious faiths and worships that have been formed and followed in the darkness of apostacy,— and for that glorious Light which is risen and shines forth in the life and doctrine of the despised Quakers, is the alone good old way of life and salvation'— a boyish piece, signed, 'William Penn, whom divine love constrains in holy contempt to trample upon Egypt's glory, not fearing the King's wrath,

having beheld the majesty of Him who is invisible.'
This kind of protest was not relished by such
courtiers and buffoons as Arlington; the less so
when they found how prompt the young man was
to practise what he taught. In face of shrug and
sneer, Penn walked among the scoffers of the Mall, his
sword and feather laid aside, in simple garb, salut-
ing those he met as thee and thou, and keeping on
his hat in presence of the greatest lords. Such men
of wit and rank as Rochester observed him with a
pleasant smile, and bucks and bloods of lower standing were restrained from offering insult to the man
of peace by what they knew of his dexterity in
fence. In company with George Whitehead and
Thomas Loe, he waited on the Duke of Buckingham,
as one who had both power and wit to help him in
his cause, and standing covered in. his Grace's
chamber, urged upon that flighty nobleman the
policy of tolerating all opinion in the Church. The
Duke sat still, while Penn denounced the stocks
and pillories, to which good men were daily sentenced
for their conscience sakes, while he recited Saxon laws
and Norman charters, and appealed to jurists of a
later time. His Grace not only thanked his guests
for coming to his house, but told them he was of
their mind in such things, and would help them
when he could. Not much was to be got from the
mercurial Duke. They went to Arlington, Secretary
of State, but Arlington, who was angry with the
Admiral, put these Quakers to the door.

A few weeks after 'Truth Exalted' saw the
light of day, the writer gave his second essay in

polemics to the world. One Jonathan Clapham, Rector of Wramplingham, in Norfolk, had abused the Quakers in 'A Guide to True Religion,' with grotesque severity. Penn answered Clapham in 'The Guide Mistaken,' an extremely fierce and personal piece of writing, such as the religious public loved to read. All writing was in that day highly spiced; the plays with an indecent wit, the sermons with ridiculous compliments, the controversies with personal spite. In following up the fashion of his time, Penn always called a fool a fool. His nights and days were therefore full of strife, and in these early times, before his spirit had been tempered by the Tower and Newgate to a softer wisdom, he was rather Ensign Penn than Quaker Penn.

At this time—summer time of 1668—there lived in Spital Fields a minister of good repute named Thomas Vincent, once a student of Christ Church, Oxford, afterwards a chaplain to Robert Sydney, Earl of Leicester, and pastor of St. Mary Magdalen, Milk Street. He had been ejected from his living at the Restoration, and had afterwards obtained a pulpit in Spital Yard. This Vincent was a sound scholar and an eloquent, though a coarse divine. Now two of Vincent's hearers, happening to stray from Spital Yard chapel to a Quaker meeting-house in the city, out of simple eagerness to know what people like the Children of Light could say for themselves, were caught, as Penn himself had been caught by Thomas Loe. These followers of Vincent left his chapel in Spital Yard, on which he turned in wrath on the seducers of his people, calling them blasphemers, hypocrites, and schismatics, and denouncing them to his flock as worthy of the fiery pit. For Vincent, though a good and worthy man, employed the controversial language of his time.

These violent words inflamed the Friends, and two of their recognised chiefs, the aged George White-head and the youthful William Penn, repaired to Spital Yard to ask from Thomas Vincent, as their right, a time and place where in the presence of his congregation they might answer his attacks. At first the minister of Spital Yard refused, but on their suit being pressed more warmly he consented on condition that they left the choice of time and place to him. To this condition Whitehead and Penn agreed, when Vincent named a certain evening as the time, and his own pulpit as the place. Such controversies were a fashion of the age; as popular as plays and bull-baits, even when they turned on abstract articles of faith.

When Penn and Whitehead came to Spital Yard, attended by a body of their friends, they found the chapel densely packed by Vincent's people. Not a man could enter save the speakers, and these speakers saw too plainly that their chance of a fair hearing was but small. Yet they passed in.

George Whitehead, as the elder, rose to state his views, but Vincent took exception to this course. The better way, he said, would be for him to put questions, and for the Quakers to reply, as then the Quakers would stand condemned out of their own mouths. Penn could not see the justice of this line, but Vincent's people cried, 'Yea, yea, let it be so!' Alone in that vast crowd of men, the Quakers were obliged to yield, and let the wrangle take such form as Vincent pleased. Then Vincent rose and asked the two 'blasphemers' whether they owned one Godhead, consisting in three distinct and separate forms? Whitehead and Penn asserted that the dogma so delivered by Vincent was not found in Holy Writ. Vincent answered by a syllogism. Quoting St. John, he said :—'There are three that bear record in heaven, the Father, the Word, and the Holy Spirit, and these three are one.' These three, he argued, 'are either three manifestations, three operations, three substances, or three some-things else besides subsistences; but they are not three manifestations, three operations, three sub-stances, nor anything else besides three subsistences; hence, there are three separate substances, yet only one deity.' Whitehead rejected the term 'subsis-tences' as not of scriptural authority, and wished to hear from Vincent what he meant by it—in vain. Penn laid this point before the public in a pam-phlet called 'The Sandy Foundation Shaken;' an attempt in author-craft which brought him into con-flict with men as swift to strike as Vincent, and with greater power to hurt than the excited folks in Spital Yard.

'I found it so well writ,' says Pepys, in speaking of this pamphlet, 'as I think it too good for him ever to have writ it; and it is a serious sort of book, not fit for everybody to read.' Much wiser men than Pepys thought with him; for in some good people's view, to hold that God is One, is to deny that Christ is also God. While Vincent railed against 'The Sandy Foundation' as a book denying Christ, he also called upon the civil power to put it down by force. This cry exactly suited Arlington, then hot in quarrel with his colleague at the Navy Office, Sir William Penn. As he had not been able to hurt the father, he seized too eagerly on any chance of injuring him through his son.

Like nearly all the pamphlets of that time, 'The Sandy Foundation Shaken' was printed without a license from the Bishop of London; and the fact, however common, laid both printer and author open to proceedings by the crown. A recent act (14 Car. II. c. 33), had made it unlawful for any private person to print a book without a license; and Lord Arlington at once arrested John Derby, printer of 'The Sandy Foundation Shaken,' and committed him prisoner to the Gatehouse till he should disclose the author's name, submit himself to mercy, and confess his fault.

The full title of Penn's pamphlet was 'The Sandy Foundations shaken; or those so generally believed and applauded doctrines of One God subsisting in three distinct and separate persons,—the impossibility of God's pardoning sinners without a plenary satisfaction—and the justification of impure persons by an imputative righteousness— refuted from the authority of Scripture testimonies and right reason by W. P. j., a builder on that foundation which cannot be removed.' W. P. j. was known to stand for William Penn, junior, son of

the Navy Commissioner Sir William Penn; but
Arlington refrained from troubling the young writer
till that gentleman put on his Quaker hat, walked
down to Piccadilly, asked to see his lordship,
and declared himself to be the author of that tract.
He meant, he said, no harm.   In printing his 'Sandy
Foundation Shaken' without a license he was only
following where much older persons led.   No writers
of such pamphlets ever thought of troubling his grace
of London, Bishop Henchman, for a formal leave to
print their works.   Of course a technical offence
had been committed.   If his Majesty was pleased
to press the law against him, he would answer it
as best he could.   But Derby was an innocent
partner in his fault, and therefore Penn desired to
take his printer's place.

Lord Arlington was but too prompt to take him
at his word.   Not having power to commit under
the Licensing Act, the proper course for Arlington
was to have caused Penn to be carried before a
justice of the peace.   A magistrate could hear the
charge, compare the evidence, and on confession
send him to trial for a misdemeanour.   Such a
magistrate would have taken bail for his appearance
at the sessions, and in case the bail was not sufficient might have lodged him in the Fleet.   But
Arlington, in his haste to wound the Admiral, called
his officers, arrested Penn, and sent him off—un-
heard, uncharged, and uncommitted—to the Tower.

CHAPTER VIII.

IN THE TOWER (1668).

YOUNG Penn was carried through the City to the Tower on Wednesday afternoon the sixteenth day of December, 1668; through streets piled up with snow and in a frost the like of which few Londoners had felt before that year. The Thames was full of ice. Old men were frozen in the public squares. The Pool was almost blocked with drift, and all the rigours of an Arctic winter raged and howled about the swampy precincts of the Tower.

Sir John Robinson, Lieutenant of the Tower, was much surprised and more alarmed to see this prisoner at the By-ward Gate. The officer who brought him in had no authority for his detention there, nor any statement of the charge against him. Robinson was asked to take him in, and hold him safe, without a lawful warrant; asked, in fact, to keep him prisoner at his personal risk. It was an unsafe game for Robinson to play. Such acts of power as Penn's arrest were not unfrequent, and Sir John, a bold and ready fellow, had been placed in the Lieutenant's Lodgings so that points of law and right should not be raised. But Robinson had been some years in office; he was growing rich and timid; and when counting up his spoils, he trembled lest the fate of Blount and Helwys might become his own. He felt that he had kept the keys too long; he knew that villains bolder than himself were bidding for his post. A pack of hounds were hanging on his steps, and if they caught him at a slip would fasten on his heel. The great men at St. James's would not heed his cries. No promise had been kept to Helwys; none was likely to be kept with him. He must protect himself. One step beyond the line, and he might find himself, like Blount, a prisoner in the dungeon he had ruled so harshly and so long.

The nicer points of law were not within his province. He was not aware of Penn's offence; and, therefore, not aware that his offence was matter of statute-law; that the mode of proceeding was defined by a recent act; that every form prescribed in this recent act was being violated by the Secretary of State. But if Sir John was blind to his prisoner's case, he was quick enough to see his own. As a King's officer he was bound to answer in the courts of law for every exercise of an illegal power. A judge would only hear from him one plea in bar —a lawful warrant from the King in council to restrain his prisoner. If the Admiral should seek relief in the court of King's Bench, Sir John, being called upon to produce his son, would not be suffered to reply that he was acting on a verbal message from the Secretary of State.

The fierce old sailor at the Navy Gardens was a

man to dread.   Sir William was a favourite with
the fleet, a comrade of the Duke of York.   If war
should come again, he might be one of the most
powerful men in England; if the King should die,
he might have greater power to make and mar than
twenty such comedians in high place as Arlington.
A man like Admiral Penn would never pardon those
who helped to heap this shame upon him in the
person of his son and heir ; and if the furious sailor
caught such persons in his grip, he could be trusted—
as Sir John supposed—to show them no more mercy
than he had showed to Don Juan de Urbina, when he
seized that royal secretary, stript him of his clothes,
and flung him, naked and astonished, down into the
hold.   Sir John sent off a messenger to beg that
Arlington would give him at once a legal order to
receive his prisoner.

Arlington had no more right to sign such order
than Sir John himself.   All warrants of commitment
to the Tower were signed by the King's Council ;
understood as being the King in council ; and unless
a prisoner were concerned in some offence against
his Majesty's crown and life, it was unusual to commit him to the Tower.   Again, the fault of Penn was
misdemeanour, not high treason, and the mode of
dealing with that form of misdemeanour was prescribed by law.   On looking at his hasty work, the
Secretary saw that he had gone too far, unless he could
convert the charge confessed by Penn into some graver
matter than the publication of a pious and unlicensed
book.   He therefore called his coach, and braving the
frosty air, drove down in person to the Tower.

F

Neither Lord Arlington nor Sir John Robinson was yet aware how much officials had to gain from the Quaker doctrine of non-resistance. Other sects had learned to say by rote, 'Whosoever shall smite thee on the right cheek, turn to him the left also.' Many persons said, 'Bless them that curse you, do good to them that hate you.' But the young Quaker took these gracious rules to heart, and strove to wear down malice by his patient and forgiving mood. No gleam of the white passion that consumed the Admiral was likely to be seen in his converted son.

Arlington sent for Penn to the Lieutenant's house, and putting on a big black look, demanded what the paper was about which Penn had dropped that morning in Lord Arlington's room. A paper! Penn replied that he had dropped no paper in the Secretary's room.

'Come, come,' urged the great man, looking bigger and blacker; 'a paper had been picked up; it lay on the floor where he had stood; a paper full of rant and treason against his Majesty. The culprit would do well to own his crime and say who his confederates were. King Charles, their gracious sovereign, could be mild with young and penitent offenders; but with old and hardened sinners he was justly stern.'

Penn answered that he had no paper, no confederates, no designs. He had not dropped a paper in Lord Arlington's room, and he had nothing that concerned his Majesty to confess. The book which he had written was directed against Vincent's argument, not against his Majesty's throne and life. He avowed the writing of that book, and told the Secretary he was ready to answer for it in the courts of law.

Though baffled in his aim Lord Arlington affected to be pleased with Penn's disclaimer of the paper; and on leaving Penn at the Lieutenant's lodgings, he assured him he would go and see the King at once, when he would make the best of his case with Charles, and held out hopes that in a few hours Penn would be free to join his family at the Navy Gardens.

Driving back to Whitehall Palace, Arlington sought an interview with Charles. Harry Bennet, first and only Baron Arlington, was a man after the King's own heart—a mimic and buffoon, who heightened the effect of every wink and parody in private, by the affectation of a grave and sombre carriage in the park and street. The man had lived in Spain and caught the manner of a grandee of that formal and punctilious country; but in Charles's cabinet, among the odalisques and spaniels, he could throw his mask aside, and strut and bray, and whine and cackle, till the painted women and their royal patron shouted with delight. Young Penn — so grave of face, so plain of speech—was just the subject for a low comedian to display in such a place,—a boy who told the truth, who thee-ed and thou-ed, who wore his hat, who quoted Saxon laws, and wanted to be put in jail.

King Charles, at all times ready to protect the favourites who amused his idle moments, took upon himself the charge of Penn's arrest as well as Derby's. But on what pretence could Penn's commitment to the Tower be justified? When all was said, the offence of printing an unlicensed pamphlet was a misdemeanour only, and the manner of proceeding with offenders was prescribed by law. The copies must be seized as evidence against the printer and his employer. The printer and his employer must be taken to a justice of the peace, who, having heard the charge, and seen the proofs, could send the case for trial in the public courts. Not one of these legal forms had been observed with Penn. Charles, lolling in his cabinet, was puzzled how to act, until a lucky thought occurred to him. Vincent was known to have called 'The Sandy Foundation Shaken' a blasphemous pamphlet; meaning that Penn's denial of the 'three subsistences' was blasphemy against the Son and Holy Spirit. Charles and Arlington caught the word. By virtue of his royal office, Charles was a defender of the faith, and if a book were blasphemous, the writer of it might be held his prisoner, not as chief of the State, but as head of the Church. Yes; here was light for them—so far. A young man, who was talked about as having 'turned ranter,' or some such 'dreadful thing,' might be restrained for blasphemy without exciting grave remark. But there was still for Arlington the slip in point of form. No Secretary of State had power to send a prisoner to the Tower; the lawful right was in the Council; in the King, supported and advised by men appointed to their office and responsible to the law. Unless His Majesty would help him here, poor Arlington was but too well aware how much he lay exposed to future suits and fines. His Majesty would help him. Sending for the Council Register, Charles held a mock meeting of the Council —he and Arlington—and put the following entry on the book, as though the act had been done in regular course :—

At the Court at Whitehall, the 16th of December, 1668.

Present : the King's Most Excellent Majesty, &c.

The Right Hon. the Lord Arlington, His Majesty's principal Secretary of State, having this day represented to His Majesty in Council that William Penn, author of the blasphemous book lately printed, intituled, 'The Sandy Foundation Shaken,' etc., had rendered himself unto His Lordship, and that thereupon, in order to His Majesty's service, he caused him to be committed to the Tower of London, and likewise that he had caused John Derby, who printed the said book, to be sent prisoner to the Gate House; which His Majesty, well approving of, did order that the said Lord Arlington be and he is hereby authorized and desired to give directions for the continuing the said William Penn and John Derby close prisoners in the respective places aforesaid until further order.

This fraudulent entry in the Council book is to be noted for two singular facts, besides the fraud. The 'Sandy Foundation Shaken' is described in it as a 'blasphemous book ;' not as a book alleged to be blasphemous by an opponent ; but as a book which the King and lords are satisfied is blasphemous. It is not likely that either Charles or Arlington had read the book ; for it was hardly out of press, and was a grave and pious work. Lord Arlington had not been bound to read it in his office, for the seizure had been caused by want of license on the title, not by matter of offence supposed to lie in the book itself. But proof was nothing to a man like Charles, who made himself accuser where he ought to have been the final judge. His next point was to make the imprisonment close. A close prisoner in the Tower was in a harder case than ordinary prisoners. He was locked up in his cell with a keeper. If a servant waited on him, that servant was kept a prisoner too. He was but scantily supplied with fire. At fixed and early hours, his lights were all put out. He could not see a friend except by special license from the Council. He was not allowed to send for either doctor, parson, or attorney. He was not permitted to write a letter, to receive a present, to discharge a debt. He was obliged to eat the prison fare. All these restraints, by which the blackest traitors were not always bound, were to be put on Penn in order to induce unthinking people to believe that he was guilty of some serious crime.

But this mock council and this fraudulent entry, though they covered Arlington, would not cover Robinson. An act of commitment, to be legal, must be signed by several members of the Council on his Majesty's behalf. At any moment Robinson might be ordered by a judge to produce his prisoner, and he begged Lord Arlington to let him have a regular warrant, duly signed, which he could plead in bar of any action brought against him. Then, a meeting of the Council — of some pliant members of the

Council—was convened in haste, on Friday, when seven members met the King, and put their signatures to the following warrant :—

At the Court at Whitehall, the 18th of December, 1668.

Present: the King's Most Excellent Majesty, &c.

Whereas William Penn hath by His Majesty's particular command, signified by the Lord Arlington, principal Secretary of State, been committed prisoner to your custody for composing and causing to be printed a blasphemous treatise, intituled, 'The Sandy Foundation Shaken,' etc., and the said Lord Arlington having this day in Council acquainted His Majesty therewith, His Majesty was pleased to approve well of what by the diligence of the said Lord Arlington had been done therein, and accordingly to order that the said William Penn should remain and continue prisoner in your custody. These are therefore in His Majesty's name to charge and require you to keep and detain close prisoner within that His Majesty's Tower of London the person of the said William Penn, until His Majesty's pleasure shall be further signified. Dated the 18th day of December, 1668.

A warrant signed by Ormonde, Carbery, and Sandwich, was enough for Robinson, who felt when he received their names that he could turn the key upon his prisoner and retire to sleep in peace.

CHAPTER IX.

BLASPHEMY AND HERESY (1669).

THOUGH Arlington was backed by Charles, he knew that he had gone too far, unless he could complete his task. He had induced his Majesty to let the thing go on by putting Penn's proceedings in a comic light, and making Charles believe that ten or twelve days in a dark and wintry vault would bring that youngster to his knees. Charles knew how Admiral Penn himself had winced and fainted in the Tower. If Penn's young spirit could be broken, Arlington was safe; for if the writer of 'The Sandy Foundation Shaken' were brought to own his fault, admit the charge of blasphemy, and beg Lord Arlington to intercede for him, the Admiral could not afterwards resent the injury of his commitment to the Tower.

Arlington's first care was to make the world believe that Penn was not a prisoner of the State; that Bishop Henchman, whose authority was touched, had been the mover; and that Penn would have to answer for his crime before the Consistorial court. Some persons were deceived by Arlington's reports;

among these persons Penn himself. One day a servant from the Navy Gardens, who was suffered to attend him in his chamber, said the rumour in the city was that my Lord of London was exceedingly angry with him, and had answered some who spoke about the charge of blasphemy, 'Penn shall either recant or die a prisoner.' Penn was staggered for a moment; he was only twenty-four years old; and Arlington had led him to expect release from day to day. Then turning to his servant, he replied, 'Now all is well.' He knew the worst, and rose to meet it like a man. 'I wish,' he added, ' they had told me so before, since the expecting of release put a stop to some business.' Penn was much deceived about the prelate. Henchman was not present when the Council signed his order of commitment, nor was any other officer of the Church, save Charles, as born Defender of the Faith. This born Defender of the Faith was not much versed in sacred lore; but if he had one serious purpose in his brain, it was that men should not be troubled in his kingdom for affairs of faith. He stood in need of much indulgence, and he tried to keep his creed a secret from the world. To rouse religious passion was alike against his humour and his interest. Not a single case of blasphemy had been tried since he began to reign. But Arlington was in a strait, and Charles imagined that the easiest way to pull him through it was to frighten the young gentleman in the Tower ; to pardon his offence without the scandal of a public trial ; and, on due submission, to restore him, cured of his ridiculous whimsies, to his father's house. But Charles, like Arlington, was apt to count his victories before his adversary's sword was down.

'Thou mayst tell my father,' said the prisoner to his servant, 'my prison shall be my grave before I will budge one jot. I owe my conscience to no mortal man. I have no fear. God will make amends for all.' The Admiral was lying in a sick bed, unable to attend the meetings of his board, and only strong enough at intervals to crawl across the bridge and see his son. Court feuds were running high; the Admiral's friends were losing ground; and Coventry, his closest comrade, was unlikely to retain his seat. The state of parties vexed him. At the Navy Board his rivals were intriguing to get rid of him. He dared not hope for new commands at sea. His health was breaking fast. On every side he saw the twilight closing round his house.

To lend some show of fairness to his seizure of Penn's 'Sandy Foundation Shaken,' Arlington, who heard that Vincent was engaged in printing a reply to that pamphlet, called 'The Foundation of God Standeth Sure,' despatched an officer to the house of Thomas Johnson, printer, with instructions to seize the copies of Vincent's book; Vincent had no more thought of asking for a license than Penn had done, and the Secretary had a legal right to seize his papers, carry him to a justice of the peace, and have him tried for breach of law. Tom Widdower, the King's messenger, who went to search Johnson's premises, found the types and papers gone;

they had been carried off the previous night; but Widdower got a clue to their hiding-place in the cellars of William Burden, one of Johnson's friends. A fortnight after Charles had been pleased to order Penn to be kept a prisoner in the Tower, and Derby in the Gatehouse, Widdower was authorized to take the bodies of Johnson and Burden into his custody, to seize all copies he could find of Vincent's book, and bring the two prisoners, with their types, before one of his Majesty's principal Secretaries of State. No search was made for Vincent. After nine days had been spent by Burden and Johnson in the messenger's house, the men were liberated on petition to the King, and not a second word was said about this printing of unlicensed books. The book itself was out. When Vincent heard of Johnson's types being seized, he found a second printer, got his work set up, and in a week 'The Foundation of God' was scattered far and wide in the religious world. This pamphlet bore no license from the Bishop of London, and it had no printer's name affixed. It was a product of the secret press; yet no proceedings were commenced by Arlington, and Vincent paid no visit to his Majesty's Secretary of State.

Days, weeks, passed by. The winter wore away, and Penn sat waiting in his dungeon for the royal mood to change. From time to time the King sent down some person skilled in fence to search his mind. These persons found him very gentle in his ways, but not inclined to yield in what was now the central point. They told the King that Penn had given them 'reasonable, good satisfaction;' but his

Majesty wanted more than Penn could give. The weeks of his imprisonment grew months. In March, his friend, Sir William Coventry, was brought into the Tower a prisoner, on a charge of challenging the Duke of Buckingham to fight. Coventry, a Privy Councillor, was lodged in Raleigh's old prison, the Brick tower, on the northern wall, where he re-. mained for sixteen days, and then, completely broken in his spirit, made a full submission, and retired a ruined man. From time to time adroit and learned persons came to visit Penn; but these divines could say no more than that they found him in a 'reasonable' state of mind. The Admiral, who heard of these reports, resolved to make an effort for his son's relief. For ten weeks he had been unable to attend the Navy Board; but on the thirtieth day of March, he went in person to White-hall, where he presented a petition to the King, and took the seat which he had held so long. In his petition he expressed his sorrow for those failings of his son which had incurred his Majesty's dis-pleasure; but while he admitted that the youth had fallen away from his Church, and so provoked the King to anger, he expressed a confident hope that God would bring him back to true religion, and a full conviction that he would do nothing to the prejudice of his Majesty's crown and govern-ment. He referred to the 'reasonable satisfaction' which his son had given and begged his Majesty to set him free.

The Admiral's appearance at the Navy Board stirred up the faction of his enemies, and when the

Council met next day to read his petition, a majority of the councillors were dead against his prayer. Instead of setting Penn at liberty, the King in Council gave an order for Humphrey Henchman, Bishop of London, to proceed against him in the Consistorial Court, for an offence not hitherto asserted—namely, 'blasphemous heresies'—not alleged 'blasphemy' and alleged 'heresies,' but for these heinous crimes, now ascertained by Charles himself. 'His Majesty,' so ran the royal order, 'having taken into consideration that the book printed and published by the said William Penn, entitled, The Sandy Foundation Shaken, containeth in it several dangerous and blasphemous heresies to the scandal of the Christian religion, did this day order and require the Right Reverend Father in God, the Lord Bishop of London, to take cognizance, and to proceed to the examination and judging of the said heretical opinions, according to such rules and forms as belong to the Ecclesiastical Courts by the laws of this kingdom, and in such a manner as hath been formerly accustomed in like cases.' Henchman's officers were to have free access to the Tower; and Penn, accompanied by his keeper and a guard, was to be brought in person to defend himself in that prelate's court.

But nothing came of these commands. No doubt the Bishop sent his chaplains to the Tower, and had reports of Penn's condition laid before him; but he took no step to bring the young offender to a public trial. Not a friend of Penn, and looking on him as a deserter, still the Bishop could not bring upon his church the odium of a persecution which she had not raised.   For what was this offence of blasphemy, alike according to the Common Law and constant ruling of the Consistorial Courts? Denial of God and of His providence; contempt of Jesus Christ; scurrility and mockery of the words of Holy Writ. Could any one of these three forms of blasphemy be found in 'The Sandy Foundation Shaken?' No; not one; and Bishop Henchman knew it. Penn contended for the Unity of God. A few extreme divines might hold that such an article of faith excludes the equal rank of Christ, and therefore is a practical denial of the Trinity. But Penn denied that such an inference was true. If he denounced, as unscriptural, the dogma of a separate existence of Father, Son, and Holy Ghost, he had not said they were not equally divine. A sober ruler of his see, the Bishop shrank from a discussion of such topics in a public court with such a man as Penn. Our creeds and articles use the words substance, essence, union, and personality, in reference to the Trinity in a way to stir up subtle and vexatious doubts; and in a court like that of Charles the Second, with men like Rochester and Buckingham for critics, with women like Barbara Palmer and Nell Gwyn for auditors, the scandal and excitement of a public trial would disturb his church. The young man would appear in sober garb; he would refuse to swear an oath; he would decline to doff his hat; he would address the judge as 'thee' and 'thou,' instead of as 'my lord.' There would be laughter, jokes, and sneers. The young man might be trusted to defend his pamphlet with the highest spirit. He was so young in years, so pure in life, so quick in wit and eloquence, so comely in his face and person, that the sympathies of serious people would be with him. Henchman could not see his way. The King's command was not obeyed; and Penn was left a prisoner in the Tower, till Arlington could find some other means of finishing the work he had begun in too much haste and hate.

Arrested for one alleged offence, detained for another alleged offence, without a legal warrant, without a formal accusation, denied a trial, and confined in prison for the mere convenience of a Secretary of State, Penn asked himself in what respect the proceeding of a Protestant Privy Council differed from those of a Catholic Holy Office? Charles was but another name for Philip; Arlington for Torquemada. If the balance leaned to either side, it leaned to that of Spain. The Catholic persecutors of his Uncle George were moved by nobler forces than the Protestant persecutors who had lodged him in the Tower. At San Lucar, the members of the Holy Office who arrested George believed that what they did was right. But Charles and Arlington were but too well aware that what they did was wrong.

Allowed the use of pen and ink, Penn took to writing, as the prisoner's solace, and compiled the first strong outline of a book which still enjoys pre-eminent favour in the serious world. 'No Cross, no Crown,' this prison book, was written in defence of Quaker habits, such as wearing the hat, dressing in sober tints, refusing titles of respect ; but thirteen years elapsed before the work assumed that larger shape in which it was to find acceptance from the whole body of professing Christian men.   The title of his book was quaint.   It stood, in the original draft, 'No Cross, no Crown ; or several sober reasons against hat-honour, titular respects, You to a single person, with the apparel and recreations of the time ; being inconsistent with scripture, reason, and the practice, as well of the best heathens as the holy men and women of all generations, and consequently fantastic, impertinent, and sinful; with sixty-eight testimonies of the most famous persons of both former and latter ages for further confirmation.   In defence of the poor despised Quakers against the practice and objection of their adversaries.   By W. Penn, junior, an humble disciple and patient bearer of the cross of Jesus.'   Four good texts were added to the page, of which the first expressed the prisoner's mood,—'But Mordecai bowed not.'   And William Penn bowed not, even though they kept him prisoner in the Tower.

CHAPTER X.

STILLINGFLEET (1669–1670).

'No Cross, no Crown is a serious cross to me,' said Admiral Penn on reading this unworldly book. 'No Cross, no Crown' arose out of the writer's own position. He was suffering for opinion : he was suffering at the hands of men who professed to be the servants of God. He wished to present clearly to his own mind and to impress upon others the great Christian doctrine that every man must bear the cross who hopes to wear the crown. To this end he reviewed the character of the age. He showed how corrupt was the laity, how proud and self-willed were the priests. The second part of 'No Cross, no Crown' consists of a collection of the sayings of heroes and sages of all nations in favour of the same doctrine—namely, that to do well and to bear ill, is the only way to lasting happiness.

In prison Penn was free. No gates could close upon his fancy ; no restraints could chain his thoughts. The light of heaven was on his window-panes ; the peace of God was in his soul. The strength with which he bore his trial brought him back his father's heart.   Surprised to see how easily his son could brave privations which had broken his own hard spirit, Admiral Penn began to think there must be something genuine in his son's principles. Of course he hated all this stuff about equality and titles of honour, but he could not help being proud of having such a son.   That son was more troubled about his father and mother, than his father and mother were about himself. Dark clouds were lowering on their roof.   The Admiral never went to the Navy Board after the thirtieth day of March.   He was requested not to come again.   In April he resigned his seat at the Navy Board, and his official residence in the Navy Gardens.   He retired with Lady Penn to Wanstead. Peg was with her husband in Yorkshire; Dick was on his travels in foreign countries.   Admiral Penn was well-nigh sick to death, and in his loneliness he begged the Duke of York to interfere once more for his misguided son.

No length of weary days and nights induced the prisoner to unsay one word that he had said. To Arlington he wrote a manly letter of appeal against the treatment he was suffering at the Secretary's hands. Protesting that in a proper state of civil society men are not to be pursued and punished for opinions, he asserted, with a touch of humour, that the Secretary might be satisfied with denying his opponent any share of heaven, and leaving him his little corner of the earth. That men should not be free to eat, drink, sleep, walk, trade, and think, because they differ as to things which belong to a future life, he said, was dangerous and absurd.   He held that men's opinions must be reached by reason, not by force. In his own case those who persecuted him had discovered their mistake, and dared not bring him to an open trial. He invoked his English right to know the charge preferred against him, and be called to his defence. 'I make no apology,' he added, 'for my letter as a trouble (the usual style of supplicants), because I think the honour that will accrue to thee by being just and releasing the oppressed, exceeds the advantage that can succeed to me.'

All hope of seeing the prisoner yield was passing out of Arlington's mind, as well as out of that of Charles. 'They are mistaken in me,' said the prisoner; 'I can weary out their malice. Neither great things nor good things ever were attained without loss and hardship. He that would reap and not labour, must faint in the wind.'

The King was growing tired of a business which he had commenced in idle mood; and when the Duke of York renewed his suit, Charles called his chaplain, Edward Stillingfleet, into his cabinet, and begged him to go down into the Tower, and bring the young man there a prisoner to his senses, so that he might pardon him and set him free.

Canon Stillingfleet, though he was only thirty-four years old, was thought to be the ablest controversial speaker in the Church. On all sides he was counted as a prodigy of nature. At the age of eighteen years he had been a fellow of his college. At the age of twenty-four he had published his Ireni-cum; and at the age of twenty-seven his Origines

Sacræ. Dons at Cambridge and councillors in London vied with each other in promoting this accomplished scholar. Lord Southampton, at the instance of Archbishop Shelden and Bishop Henchman, gave him the rich living of St. Andrew's, Holborn. He was preacher at the Rolls and lecturer at the Temple; he was canon residentiary of St. Paul's; and was the most popular preacher at Whitehall. 'I carried my wife and her woman,' writes Pepys, 'to Whitehall Chapel and heard the famous young Stillingfleet, who is newly admitted one of the King's chaplains, and was presented, they say, to my Lord Treasurer for St. Andrew's, Holborn, where he is now minister, with these words: "That the Bishops of Canterbury, London, and another, believed he is the ablest young man to preach the Gospel of any since the apostles."' Henchman had employed his pen in controversy with the Jesuits. At the age of thirty-four he was already hailed as Stillingfleet the Great.

This eminent divine, so well prepared for argument with men like Penn, repaired to his apartments in the Tower. Of course the prisoner was no match for him in learning, but his gentleness and fortitude impressed the Canon's heart. With nothing but an open Bible, Penn contested every inch of ground with one who had a perfect library of the Fathers and the Councils in his memory. He wanted Penn to yield so far that Charles could set him free as an act of royal grace. Penn wanted to confront his enemies in a court of justice. 'Tell the King,' he said to Stillingfleet, 'that the Tower is the worst argument in the world.' His visitor would not press that point; he was too kind a man to take the Secretary's view. The Canon spoke of the King's favour to his family, of the Admiral's position in the service, of the prospects of advancements he was casting to the winds. Penn heard him plead in silence, for he held him, as all good and intellectual people held him, in the highest honour; but the words he uttered in the Tower were empty sounds. It was a case of conscience, not of policy, and Penn was only one of many, who had been arrested for opinion's sake. His private ease was nothing, while so great a principle was at stake.

Penn could not own a fault where he was not in fault, and by his weakness put his persecutor in the right. 'Whoever is in the wrong,' urged Penn, 'those who use force in religion can never be in the right.' The Canon carried these words to his royal master.

Not once, but many times, the great divine went down to the Tower, to hold discourse with Penn. On questions of theology, the prisoner heard his visitor with zest. Stillingfleet brought down some of his recent writings, which he left for Penn to read; and Penn, being made aware that other persons than Thomas Vincent were assailing him as one who had denied the divinity of Christ, composed a pamphlet in reply entitled, 'Innocency with her open face, presented by way of apology for the book entitled The Sandy Foundation Shaken,' which he sent into the world at once. 'That which I am credibly informed to be the greatest reason for my imprisonment,' he wrote, 'and that noise of blasphemy which has pierced so many ears of late, is my denying the divinity of Christ.' He utterly repudiates such ' denying :' and proceeds to give some proofs of the divinity of Christ. The tract owed much to Stillingfleet, not only in quotations but suggestions. Every page betrayed the writer's study of his eloquent and learned visitor's recent works, especially of his discourse on Christ.

As nothing further could be got from Penn—no owning of his fault, no prayers to Arlington, no promise for the future—and as Charles had now been teased for seven whole months about the matter, which the Admiral and the Duke of York would not allow him to forget, his Majesty was pleased to declare himself satisfied with Stillingfleet's report and ' Innocency with her open face.' An order, under date of July 28, 1669, was sent to Robinson, instructing the Lieutenant of the Tower to deliver up his prisoner to Sir William Penn.

It was not in human nature that Lord Arlington should be pleased, and it was probably from him that a report was spread of Penn being discharged on hard conditions. ' Young Penn, who wrote the blasphemous book,' said one of the court gossips, ' is delivered to his father to be transported.' Admiral Penn was ill; so ill, that he could rarely stir from Wanstead. Nothing had been done, as yet, about the purchase of a house and lands. Lowther was looking through the Yorkshire wolds for an estate, and hoping to secure a country place near Maske ; but Admiral Penn, who clung to his design of settling in county Cork, desired his son to go at once to Shangarry Castle, where the property required a master's eye. Sir William hoped that in the management of his estate the young man's worldly passions would revive; and six weeks after his son's discharge from the Tower the Admiral sent him down to Bristol, on his way to county Cork.

'If you are ordained to be another cross to me,' said the Admiral, 'God's will be done; and I shall arm myself the best I can against it.' He was very sore at heart.

Arrived in Cork, Penn found the prison of that city full of Quakers; men of English race and faith, whose main offences were, as he conceived, that they were hard workers and cautious traders. Jealousy had much to do with this repression of the Light, 'which was at least as much from envy about trade as zeal for religion.' From an early day the Friends had learned to buy and sell, and prosper in the ways of trade. The hour of Penn's arrival saw him at the jail. Next day he held a meeting in the prison-yard, where he exhorted his brethren to be steadfast in their faith, and firm in their resistance to an unjust exercise of power. Without going on to Shangarry Castle, he set out for Dublin, where he called a meeting of Friends, and having put the case in form, he carried a memorial of their griev- ances to his friend the Duke of Ormonde. Arran, Lane, and others who remembered him at Carrick- fergus in his plume and corslet, helped him to pro- cure a hearing. A commissioner was directed to report on the Quaker prisoners who had been committed by local justices, and in the following summer an order was signed by Ormonde for the free discharge of every one who was in prison for opinion's sake.

Penn stayed at Shangarry Castle nearly ten months; until, in fact, his father's plans began to change. The Lowthers found a good estate, some twenty miles from Maske, which he was now disposed to purchase; and he told his son to try if he could sell the Irish lands. It not being easy to procure a customer for Shangarry Castle, the Admiral bade him ask if any of the tenants were disposed to buy their lots. These tenants were too poor. 'I wish you had well done all your business there,' the Admiral wrote to his son, 'for I find myself to decline.' Penn took the hint, and gathering up his papers started for his father's house, where he was quickly reconciled to his father's heart.

CHAPTER XI.

A FRESH ARREST (1670).

PENN was soon disturbed by new persecutions. Liberty of Conscience—with its consequence, Free Worship—was the question of that day ; a question of much practical difficulty even to those who could admit that it was right in principle. The Duke of York, presumptive heir to the throne, was an avowed Catholic. Charles was suspected of a leaning towards the ritual followed by his wife, his brother, his brother's wife, and his own favourite mistress. Some of the courtiers were apostatising ; others were supposed to be only waiting a more favourable moment to desert their Church. If Popery threatened from above, Puritanism was no less terrible below. The country swarmed with the disbanded hosts of Cromwell—men as hostile to the establishment as to the monarchy. Sects were daily multiplying in number. In the midst of all these causes of dismay, a power which Parliament had given the Church for her defence against the non-conforming bodies was renewed. The Conventicle Act declared it seditious and unlawful for more than five persons, exclusive of the family, to meet together for religious worship according to any other than the national rite ; and every person above the age of sixteen years attending any such meeting, was liable, for the first offence, to be fined five pounds or imprisoned during three months ; for the second offence, to be fined ten pounds, or imprisoned six months ; for the third offence, to be fined a hundred pounds or transported beyond the seas for seven years ; and for every additional offence to a hundred pounds of fine. This Act was renewed in April, 1670.

Penn soon became a victim of this enactment. Taking no notice of attempts to interfere with their modes of worship, some of the Quakers went on Sunday, the 14th of August to their meeting-house in Gracechurch Street. They found the house closed, the doors guarded by soldiers. Penn took off his hat and began to preach. The constables came forward and arrested him. At the same time, but in another part of the crowd, they arrested Captain William Mead, an old soldier of the Commonwealth, now a draper in the city. Penn demanded their authority for his arrest ; the officers produced a warrant, signed by Sir Samuel Starling, Lord Mayor. Penn and Mead were taken from the place of meeting to the City magistrates. When Penn refused to doff his hat, Sir Samuel threatened to send him to Bridewell and have him flogged, though he *was* the son of a Commonwealth admiral ! On being reminded that the law would not allow him, he committed Penn and Mead to the Black Dog, a sponging-house in Newgate Market, to await their trial at the Old Bailey. From this place of durance Penn wrote to his father, glorying in his sufferings for a great principle, but expressing his deep regret at being dragged away from home at such a time.

On Thursday, September 1st, 1670, the prisoners, William Penn the Younger, and Captain William Mead, were placed in the dock. Penn stood before his judges, less as a Quaker pleading for the rights of conscience, than an Englishman contending for the ancient liberties of his race. That he had violated the Conventicle Act he knew; that he meant to violate that Act he also knew. Penn held that the new Act was equally hostile to the Bible and the Great Charter. This was the point at issue—Does an edict possess the virtue and force of law, even when passed by Crown and Parliament, which abolishes any one of our fundamental rights? A most important point; and very dear to England were the issues to be tried. Penn raised the constitutional question, 'If we now plead guilty to the facts alleged against us—as in common cases we should do—this Act will acquire additional force: if we deny our guilt, as we may do, and throw the burden of proof on the court, we shall show to all the world the evil animus of our persecutors; we shall also be able to raise the question whether this new and oppressive law be in harmony with the Great Charter, and other fundamental laws.'

Both Penn and Mead resolved to plead not guilty to the charge, and throw the burden of proof on the other side. They thought it well to hire no counsel, and conduct the case themselves; the rather that they meant the trial to be taken as a civil inquisition, not as a simple form of ascertaining whether they were guilty of the fact or not.

Sir Thomas Howell, Recorder of London, tried the case. Around him sat Sir Samuel Starling, Lord Mayor; Alderman Sir Thomas Bludworth, Alderman Sir William Peake, Alderman Sir Richard Ford, and Alderman Sir Joseph Sheldon; the two sheriffs, John Smith, and James Edwards. Sir John Robinson, Lieutenant of the Tower, was present as Alderman of Dowgate; also Sir Richard Brown, the Lord Mayor of the Restoration year. In all ten justices occupied the bench. When the clerk of the court bade the crier call the jury, twelve citizens of London answered to their names: Thomas Vere, Edward Bushel, John Hammond, Charles Milson, Gregory Walklet, John Brightman, William Plumstead, Henry Henley, Thomas Damask, Henry Michel, William Lever, and John Baily. These good men and true were sworn to try the prisoners at the bar and find according to the evidence adduced. The indictment, charging the two prisoners with holding a tumultuous assembly, ran :—

'That William Penn, gentleman, and William Mead, late of London, linen-draper, with divers other persons to the jury unknown, to the number of three hundred, the 15th day of August, in the twenty-second year of the King, about eleven of the clock in the forenoon of the same day, with force and arms, &c., in the parish of St. Bennet, Gracechurch, in Bridge Ward, London, in the street called Gracechurch Street, unlawfully and tumult-

uously did assemble and congregate themselves together, to the disturbance of the peace of the said
lord the King : And the aforesaid William Penn
and William Mead, together with other persons to
the jury aforesaid unknown, then and there assembled and congregated together ; the aforesaid William Penn, by agreement between him and William
Mead, before made and by abetment of the aforesaid
William Mead, then and there in the open street,
did take upon himself to preach and speak, and
then and there did preach and speak unto the aforesaid William Mead and other persons there in the
street aforesaid, being assembled and congregated
together, by reason whereof a great concourse and
tumult of people in the street aforesaid, then and
there, a long time did remain and continue in contempt of the said lord the King and his law ; to the
great disturbance of his peace, to the great terror
and disturbance of many of his liege people and
subjects, to the ill-example of all others in the like
case offenders, and against the peace of the said lord
the King, his crown and dignity.'

Such was the form and matter of a charge which
was to be a memorable fact in the development of
our civic liberties. No other verdict than acquittal
could have been expected by a man with eyes to
see and sense to understand. The very date assigned
to the offence was wrong, for Penn was taken on
Sunday, August 14, and the indictment charged him
with addressing a tumultuous and disorderly assembly
in Gracechurch Street, on Monday, August 15,
when he was living at the Black Dog. Penn and

Mead were indicted for 'conspiring together by agreement, before made between them.' They had never met, never spoken, never written to each other; they were perfect strangers till they found themselves in custody on a common charge. They were accused of being armed. Both Penn and Mead had long ago laid down their swords; and both were men of peace, in that extreme degree that they would not have raised a weapon even in self-defence.

'What say you, William Penn and William Mead, are you guilty as you stand indicted, in manner and form as aforesaid, or not guilty ?'

Penn: 'It is impossible that we should be able to remember the indictment verbatim, and therefore we desire a copy of it, as is customary on the like occasions.'

Howell: 'You must first plead to the indictment before you can have a copy of it.'

Penn: 'I am unacquainted with the formality of the law, and before I shall answer, I request two things of the court:—first, that no advantage be taken against me, nor I be deprived of any benefit I might otherwise have received ; secondly, that you will promise me a fair hearing and liberty of making my defence.'

Court: 'No advantage shall be taken against you. You shall have liberty ; you shall be heard.'

Penn: 'Then I plead not guilty in manner and form.'

Like questions being put to Captain Mead, and the same assurances being given to him, he also pleaded not guilty in manner and form; on which the court adjourned for dinner until three o'clock.

Assembling after dinner, the court commanded Penn and Mead to be placed at the bar. They took their places; but the judges changed their minds; and Howell, the Recorder, called the ordinary felons on his list. Penn, Mead, and the twelve jurymen were detained till eight o'clock at night, when they were told the court would take their case on Saturday.

CHAPTER XII.

OLD BAILEY (1670).

ON Saturday, September 3, the court assembled for the case of Captain Mead and William Penn.

The prisoners were coming into court with their hats on; a too zealous officer knocked them off; on which Sir Samuel Starling bellowed from the bench, 'Sirrah! Who bade you put off their hats? Put them on again.' As neither Mead nor Penn resisted, the officer picked their hats from the floor and set them on the prisoners' heads. When they had thus been covered by command of the court, Recorder Howell asked them if they knew where they were, to which Penn answered that they knew.

Howell: 'Do you know it is the King's court?'

Penn: 'I know it to be a court, and I suppose it to be the King's court.'

Howell: 'Do you know there is respect due to the court?'

Penn: 'Yes.'

Howell: 'Why do you not pay it then?'

Penn: 'I do so.'

Howell: 'Why do you not pull off your hat then?'

Penn: 'Because I do not believe that to be any . respect.'

Howell: 'Well, the court sets forty marks a-piece on your heads as a fine for your contempt of court.'

Penn: 'I desire it may be observed that we came into court with our hats off—that is, taken off—and if they have been put on since, it was by order of the Bench; and therefore not we, but the Bench should be fined.'

The jury being sworn, Sir John Robinson, suspecting that Edward Bushel, one of the jurors, known to be a religious man, objected to take an oath, pretended not to have seen him kiss the book, and desired him to be sworn again. Bushel was sworn a second time. Lieutenant James Cook was called.

Cook: 'I was sent for from the Exchange to go and disperse a meeting in Gracechurch Street, where I saw Mr. Penn speaking to the people, but I could not hear what was said on account of the noise. I endeavoured to make way to take him, but I could not get near him for the crowd of people; upon which Captain Mead came to me about the kennel of the street and desired me to let him go on, for when he had done he would bring Mr. Penn to me.'

Court: 'What number do you think there might be there?'

Cook: 'About three or four hundred people.'

Richard Read, a constable, was called.

Howell: 'What do you know concerning the prisoners at the bar?'

Read: 'My lord, I went to Gracechurch Street, where I found a great crowd of people, and I heard Mr. Penn preach to them, and I saw Captain Mead speaking to Lieutenant Cook, but what he said I could not tell.'

Mead: 'What did William Penn say?'

Read: 'There was such a great noise I could not tell what he said.'

Mead: 'Observe this evidence; he saith, he heard him preach; and yet saith, he doth not know what he said.—Take notice (to the jury) he means now a clean contrary thing to what he swore before the Mayor when we were committed. I appeal to the Mayor himself if this be not true.'

Sir Samuel Starling would not answer yea or nay.

Court: 'What number do you think there might be there?'

Read: 'About four or five hundred.'

Penn: 'I desire to know of the witness what day it was?'

Read: 'The 14th day of August.'

Penn: 'Did he speak to me, or let me know he was there? For I am very sure I never saw him.'

The court would not allow this question to be put.

Another witness was called: his name not given.

Unknown Witness: 'My lord, I saw a great number of people, and Mr. Penn I suppose was speaking, for I saw him make a motion with his hands and heard some noise, but could not understand what was said. But for Captain Mead, I did not see him there.'

Howell: 'What say you, Mr. Mead,—were you there ?'

Mead: 'It is a maxim in your own law—*Nemo tenetur accusare seipsum*—which, if it be not true Latin, I am sure it is true English—No man is bound to accuse himself. And why dost thou offer to ensnare me with such a question ?'

Howell: 'Hold your tongue, sir.'

Penn: 'I desire we may come more close to the point, and that silence be commanded.'

'Silence in the court !' said the crier.

Penn: 'We confess ourselves so far from recanting or declining to vindicate the assembling of ourselves to preach, to pray, or worship God, that we declare to all the world, we believe it to be our indispensable duty to meet incessantly on so good an account; nor shall all the powers on earth be able to prevent us.'

Brown: 'You are not here for worshipping God, but for breaking the laws.'

Penn: 'I affirm I have broken no law; nor am I guilty of the indictment that is laid to my charge; and to the end that the Bench, the jury, myself, and those who hear us may have a more direct understanding of this procedure, I desire you would let me know by what law it is you prosecute me, and on what law you ground your indictment ?'

Howell: 'Upon the common law.'

Penn: 'Where is that common law ?'

Howell: 'You must not think that I am able to sum up so many years and over so many adjudged cases, which we call common law, to satisfy your curiosity.'

Penn: 'This answer is very short of my question; for if it be common, it should not be so very hard to produce.'

Howell: 'Sir, will you plead to your indictment?'

Penn: 'Shall I plead to an indictment that has no foundation in law? If it contain that law you say I have broken, why should you decline to produce that law, since it will be impossible for the jury to determine, or agree to bring in their verdict, who have not the law produced by which they should measure the truth of the indictment?'

Howell (waxing warm): 'You are a saucy fellow. Speak to the indictment.'

Penn · 'I say it is my place to speak to matter of law. I am arraigned a prisoner. My liberty, which is next to life itself, is now concerned. You are many mouths and ears against me; and it is hard if I must not make the best of my case. I say again, unless you show me and the people the law you ground your indictment upon, I shall take it for granted your proceedings are merely arbitrary.'

Howell: 'The question is whether you are guilty of this indictment.'

Penn: 'The question is not whether I am guilty of this indictment, but whether this indictment be legal. It is too general and imperfect an answer to say it is common law, unless we know both where and what it is: for where there is no law, there is no transgression ; and that law which is not in being, so far from being common law, is no law at all.'

Howell : 'You are an impertinent fellow. Will you teach the court what law is ? It is *lex non scripta.* That which many have studied thirty or forty years to know, would you have me tell you in a moment ?'

Penn : 'Certainly if the common law be so hard to be understood, it is far from being very common : but if the Lord Coke in his Institutes (vol. ii. p. 56) be of any weight, he tells us that—common law is common right, and common right is the Great Charter privileges, confirmed by 9 Henry III. cap. 29 : by 25 Edward I. cap. 1 : and by 2 Edward III. cap. 8.'

Howell : 'Sir, you are a very troublesome fellow, and it is not for the honour of the court to suffer you to go on.'

Penn : 'I have asked but one question, and you have not answered me—though the rights and privileges of every Englishman are concerned in it.'

Howell : 'If I should suffer you to ask questions till to-morrow morning, you would be never the wiser.'

Penn : 'That would depend upon the answers.'

Howell (writhing) : 'Sir, we must not stand to hear you talk all night.'

Penn : 'I design no affront to the court, but to be heard in my just plea. And I must plainly tell you, that if you deny me Oyer of that law, which you suggest I have broken, you do at once deny me an acknowledged right, and evidence to the whole world your resolution to sacrifice the privileges of Englishmen to your sinister and arbitrary designs.'

Howell: 'Take him away! My Lord, if you do not take some course with this pestilent fellow to stop his mouth, we shall not be able to do any thing to-night.'

Starling: 'Take him away, take him away! Put him into the bale-dock.'

Penn: 'These are so many vain exclamations. Is this justice or true judgment? Must I be taken away because I plead for the fundamental laws of England? However (addressing the jury), this I leave upon your consciences, who are my sole judges, that if these ancient fundamental laws, which relate to liberty and property—and are not limited to particular persuasions in matters of religion—must not be indispensably maintained—who can say he has a right to the coat upon his back? If not, our liberties are open to be invaded—our wives ravished—our children enslaved—our families ruined—our estates led away in triumph. The Lord of heaven and earth be judge between us in this matter!

Howell: 'Be silent there!'

Starling commanded the officers of the court to carry the prisoner to the bale-dock—a well-like place at the farthest end of the court, in which he could neither see nor be seen. Thither Penn was forced under a protest against their right to remove him before the jury retired. Mead then addressed himself to his peers.

Mead: 'You men of the jury,—Here I stand to answer an indictment which is a bundle of lies; for therein I am accused that I met *vi et armis, illicitè et tumultuosè.* Time was when I had freedom to use a carnal weapon, and then I thought I feared no man; but now I fear the living God. I am a peaceable man; and therefore ask, like William Penn, an Oyer of the law on which our indictment is founded.'

Howell: 'I have made answer to that already.'

Turning from the bench to the jury, the old soldier told the twelve, that if the Recorder would not tell the court what constituted a riot and an unlawful assembly, he would quote for them the opinions of Lord Coke. A riot, said that great legal writer, was when three or more met together to beat a man, or enter his house by force, or cut his grass, or trespass on his land. Howell took off his hat to the prisoner, and making a low bow, said, in a tone which he meant to be withering, 'I thank you, sir, for teaching *me* what is law.'

Mead: 'Thou mayst put on thy hat: *I* have no fee to give thee.'

Brown: 'He talks at random: one while an Independent—now a Quaker—next a Papist.'

Mead: 'Turpe est doctori cum culpa redarguit ipsum.'

Starling: 'You deserve to have your tongue cut out.'

Mead: 'Thou didst promise me I should have fair liberty to be heard. Am I not to have the privilege of all Englishmen?'

Mead was also removed to the bale-dock; and the court proceeded to charge the jury.

Howell: 'You, gentlemen of the jury, have heard what the indictment is; it is for preaching to the people, and drawing a tumultuous company after them; and Mr. Penn was speaking. If they should should not be disturbed, you see they will go on. Three or four witnesses have proved this — that Mr. Penn did preach there, that Mr. Mead did allow of it. After this, you have heard by substantial witnesses what is said against them. Now we are on matter of fact, which you are to keep and to observe, as what hath been fully sworn, at your peril.'

Penn (from the bale-dock, at the top of his voice): 'I appeal to the jury, who are my judges, and to this great assembly, whether the proceedings of the court are not most arbitrary and void of all law, in offering to give the jury their charge in the absence of the prisoners! I say it is directly opposed and destructive to the right of every English prisoner, as declared by Coke in the 2d Institute, 29 on the chapter of Magna Charta.'

Howell (with playful humour): 'Why you are present; you do hear. Do you not?'

Penn: 'No thanks to the court that commanded me into the bale-dock. And you of the jury, take notice that I have not been heard; neither can you legally depart the court before I have been fully heard, having at least ten or twelve material points to offer in order to invalidate their indictment.'

Howell: 'Pull that fellow down; pull him down. Take them to the Hole.'

So Penn and Mead were taken out of the baledock and carried to the hole in Newgate—the nastiest place in the most loathsome gaol in England, a den which Penn describes as so noisome that the Lord Mayor would think it unfit for pigs to lie in. Howell commanded the jury to agree in their verdict according to the facts. They retired; the court remained sitting; the vast concourse of people keeping an eager eye on the door which led into the jury-room. An hour and a half had passed before the door opened, and eight of the twelve jurors walked into court. They could not agree, they said; the other four stood out against the court. Howell commanded the uncomplying four to be brought into his presence; they came. Bushel was one of them; in fact, the leader of the four.

Robinson: 'I know you. You have thrust yourself upon this jury.'

Bushel: 'No, Sir John. There were threescore before me on the panel, and I would willingly have got off, but could not.'

Robinson: 'I tell you, you deserve to be indicted more than any man that has been indicted this day.'

Starling: 'Sirrah, you are an impertinent fellow! I will put a mark on you.'

Sent back to their room, the twelve jurors were absent longer than before; at length they came into court, when Penn and Mead being sent for, silence was commanded.

Clerk: 'Are you agreed in your verdict?'

Vere the Foreman : 'Yes.'

Clerk : ' How say you ?   Is William Penn guilty of the matter whereof he stands indicted in manner and form, or not guilty ?'

Vere : ' Guilty of speaking in Gracechurch Street.'

Court : ' Is that all ?'

Vere : ' That is all I have in commission.'

Howell : ' You had as good say nothing ?'

Starling : ' Was it not an unlawful assembly ? You mean he was speaking to a tumult of people there ?'

Vere explained that on those points the jurors were not agreed.   The court began to converse with each juryman apart, and some of these jurymen expressed themselves in favour of the views taken by the bench; but Edward Bushel, John Hammond, and two or three others, declared that they could admit no such term into their verdict as 'unlawful assembly.'

Howell : ' The law of England will not allow you to depart till you have given in your verdict.'

Vere : ' We have given in our verdict; we can give in no other.'

Howell : ' Gentlemen, you have *not* given in your verdict; you had as good say nothing as what you have said.   Therefore go and consider it once more.'

The jurors asked for pen, ink, and paper, and the court adjourned for half an hour.   When the jury returned they handed in a written verdict,— again finding William Penn guilty of speaking to an assembly met together in Gracechurch Street,—

and acquitting William Mead. This act was signed by all the twelve. On hearing it read aloud, Sir Samuel Starling shouted at the whole jury, 'What, will you be led by such a silly fellow as Bushel—an impudent, canting knave! I warrant you, you shall not come upon juries again in a hurry.' And then turning on Thomas Vere, the foreman, he exclaimed, 'You are a foreman indeed! I thought you understood your place better.' Howell came directly to the point.

Howell : 'Gentlemen, you shall not be dismissed till you bring in a verdict which the court will accept. You shall be locked up, without meat, drink, fire, and tobacco. You shall not think thus to abuse the court. We will have a verdict by the help of God, or you shall starve for it.'

Penn : 'My jury, who are my judges, ought not to be thus menaced. Their verdict should be free— not forced.'

Howell : 'Stop that fellow's mouth, put him out of court.'

Starling (to the jury): 'You have heard that he preached; that he gathered a company of tumultuous people; and that they not only disobey the martial power, but the civil also.'

Penn : 'That is a mistake. We did not make the tumult, but they that interrupted us. The jury cannot be so ignorant as to think we met there to disturb the peace, because it is well known that we are a peaceable people, never offering violence to any man, and were kept by force of arms out of our own house.'

One of the jury pleaded illness, as a reason why he should not be locked up without fire, food, or water.

Starling: 'You are strong as any of them. Hold your principles and—starve.'

Howell: 'Gentlemen, you must be content with your hard fate; let your patience overcome it. The court is resolved to have a verdict.'

The whole Jury: 'We are agreed; we are agreed; we are agreed.'

'Let the constables be sworn,' said Howell, 'to keep them in a room apart, with neither meat nor drink, with neither fire nor light.' The constables were sworn, and the unhappy jurors dragged away.

CHAPTER XIII.

TRIAL OF THE JURY (1670).

NEXT day was Sunday, but the court assembled at the Old Bailey as on other days. At seven o'clock the jurors' names were called, and each man answering to his name, the clerk inquired,—

Clerk: 'Are you agreed upon your verdict?'

Vere: 'Yes.'

Clerk: 'What say you? Look upon the prisoner at the bar. Is William Penn guilty of the matter whereof he stands indicted, in manner and form as aforesaid, or not guilty?'

Vere: 'William Penn is guilty of speaking in Gracechurch Street.'

Starling: 'To an unlawful assembly?'

Bushel: 'No, my lord. We give no other verdict than we gave last night.'

Starling: 'You are a factious fellow; I'll take a course with you.'

Bludworth: 'I knew Mr. Bushel would not yield.'

Bushel: 'Sir Thomas, I have done according to my conscience.'

Starling : 'That conscience of yours would cut my throat.'

Bushel : 'No, my lord, it never shall.'

Starling : 'But I will cut yours as soon as I can.'

Howell (merry): 'He has inspired the jury ; he has the spirit of divination ; methinks he begins to affect me,—I will have a positive verdict, or else you shall starve.'

Penn : 'I desire to ask the Recorder a question. Do you allow the verdict given of William Mead ?'

Howell : 'It cannot be a verdict, because you are indicted for conspiracy—and one being found Not guilty and not the other, it is no verdict.'

Penn : 'If Not guilty be no verdict, then you make of the jury and of the Great Charter a mere nose of wax.'

Mead : 'How!   Is Not guilty no verdict ?'

Howell : 'No, it is no verdict.'

Penn : 'I affirm that the consent of a jury is a verdict in law ; and if William Mead be not guilty, it follows that I am clear, since you have indicted us for conspiracy, and I could not possibly conspire alone.'

Howell found it convenient not to notice this way of viewing the case. A scene of great confusion followed, with threats on the part of the magistrates, met by unflinching firmness from the jurors. Again the twelve good men were sent to their room ; again they returned with the same verdict of 'Guilty of speaking in Gracechurch Street.' It was clear they could do no more according to the evidence laid before them. When Vere announced

the result of their third examination, the legal con-
ductor of the trial roared :—

Howell : 'What is this to the purpose ?   I say, I
will have a verdict.'   And then scowling fiercely at
Bushel, cried, 'You are a factious fellow.   I will set a
mark on you ; and whilst I have any thing to do with
the city, I will have an eye upon you.'

Starling (to the other jurors) : 'Have you no more
wit than to be led by such a pitiful fellow ?   I will
cut his nose.'

Penn : 'It is intolerable that my jury should be
thus menaced.   Is this according to the fundamental laws ?   Are they not my proper judges by
the Great Charter of England ?   What hope is there
of ever having justice done when juries are threatened and their verdicts rejected ?   Has not the
Lieutenant of the Tower made one of them out
worse than a felon ?'

Howell : 'My lord, you *must* take a course with
that fellow.'

Starling : 'Stop his mouth.   Gaoler, bring fetters,
and stake him to the ground.'

Penn : 'Do your will : I care not for your fetters.'

Howell (suddenly enlightened) : 'Till now I never
understood the reason of the policy and prudence
of the Spaniards in suffering the Inquisition among
them ; and certainly it will never be well with
us till something like the Inquisition be brought
into England.'

Starling told the jury they must retire until
they could agree upon a verdict of guilty.   They
refused.   They had consulted three several times ;

they had agreed to a a verdict and signed it; they could give no other.

Howell: 'Gentlemen, we shall not always be at this pass with you. You will find that next session of Parliament there will be a law made that such as will not conform shall not have the protection of law. Mr. Lee,' addressing a law-officer of the court, 'draw up another verdict that they may bring it in special.'

Lee: 'I cannot tell how to do it.'

Jury: 'We ought not to be returned, having all agreed and set our hands to the verdict.'

Howell: 'Your verdict is nothing. You play upon the court. I say you shall go and bring in another verdict or you shall starve; and I will have you carted about the city as in Edward the Third's time.'

Vere (who had fasted thirty hours): 'We have given in our verdict, in which we are all agreed; if we give in another, it will be by force, to save our lives.'

Starling: 'Take them up to their room.'

Officer: 'My lord, they will not go.'

The Sheriff was told to use force.

They were again locked up for the day and night; left without food, without fire, without water,—to endure the agony of another night of raging fever, brought on by thirst and want of rest. They spent the night in anxious talk. They could not sleep for pain. Their chamber was unutterably foul; for Howell had refused them every article of chamber furniture. Some wandered in their thoughts.

Some said they must give way or die. But those who fought for freedom of conscience—for the rights of jurors—supported from within by a strong sense of martyrdom, held on. They were prepared to die; but never to betray the cause of right.

Next day the court sat again. It was. Monday morning and the proceedings began soon after sunrise. Yet the room was crowded. As the jury came into court, the men were pale and dark, but firm and resolute. The forms were gone through in succession, while the agitated audience tried to read the faces of the jurors.

Crier: 'Silence in the court on pain of imprisonment !'

Clerk: 'Gentlemen, are you agreed in your verdict ?'

Jury: ' Yes.'

Clerk: ' Who shall speak for you ?'

Jury: ' Our Foreman.'

Clerk: ' Look upon the prisoners. What say you, is William Penn guilty of the matter whereof he stands indicted in manner and form, or not guilty ?'

Vere: ' You have our verdict in writing with our hands subscribed.'

Clerk: ' I will read it—'

Howell: ' No. It is no verdict. The court will not accept it.'

Vere: ' If you will not accept of it, I desire to have it back again.'

Court: 'The paper was no verdict, and no advantage shall be taken of you for it.'

Clerk: 'How say you : is William Penn guilty or not guilty?'

Vere: 'Not guilty.' (Movement and emotion in the court.)

Clerk: 'Then hearken to your verdict.' (Reads) 'You say William Penn is not guilty, and you say William Mead is not guilty. Say you all so?'

Jury: 'We do.'

The court was not content ; each man, it said, must answer for himself. The names were called over one by one in the hope that some one more timid than the rest would side with the bench. In vain ; each juror answered to the call, and distinctly and without qualification pronounced—'Not guilty.'

Howell: 'I am sorry, gentlemen, you have followed your own judgments and opinions rather than the good advice which was given you. God keep my life out of your hands ! But for this the court fines you forty marks a man and imprisonment in Newgate till the fines be paid.'

Penn: 'Being freed by the jury, I demand to be set at liberty.'

Starling: 'No. You are in for your fines.'

Penn: 'Fines ! What fines ?'

Starling: 'For contempt of court.'

Penn: 'I ask if it be according to the fundamental laws of England that any Englishman should be fined except by the judgment of his peers ? Since it expressly contradicts the 14th and 29th chapters of the Great Charter of Engand, which says, No free man ought to be amerced except by the oath of good and lawful men of the vicinage.'

Howell (with severe and simple logic): 'Take him away; take him away; take him out of the court.'

Penn: 'I can never urge the fundamental *laws* of *England*, but you cry out, "Take him away; take him away!" But this is no wonder, since the *Spanish Inquisition* sits so near the Recorder's heart. God, who is just, will judge you for all these things.'

The two prisoners and the twelve jurors alike refused to pay the fines—the first as a matter of conscience; the second, because, under the influence of Bushel, they were induced to dispute the power of the court to inflict this fine. The fourteen gentlemen were all removed to Newgate.

From his prison chamber, Penn wrote to his sick father daily; and his letters breathe the most affectionate and devoted spirit. He deplores the Admiral's illness, and his own compulsory absence from his bed-side; but the cause of English freedom is at stake, he is detained contrary to law, and he beseeches his family not to think of paying the fine in order to get him out. However anxious to be near his father at such a time, he would do nothing unworthy; he would trust in God and in the justness of his cause. Even when Bushel and his fellows had been acquitted, Penn and Mead refused to pay their fines, but a few days after their removal, a turnkey came to them with news that some unknown friend had paid their fines—and they were free to go away.

Admiral Penn was lying on his death-bed. The excitement caused by his son's arrest, imprisonment, and trial, had made him worse; and when William hastened home from Newgate to Wanstead he was scared to find that, in the opinion of medical men, his father had only a few days to live.

'Son William,' said the veteran, 'I am weary of the world; I would not live my days over again, if I could command them with a wish; for the snares of life are greater than the fears of death.' The Admiral had ceased to think of his great disappointment; but he retained his patriotic ardour to the last. He bewailed the corruption of the age, the profligacy in high places, the daily traffic in justice, the contempt into which the court was falling, the rottenness at home, the decline of power abroad. He gave his children three maxims as a legacy: 'First—Let nothing in this world tempt you to wrong your conscience; so you will keep peace at home, which will be a feast to you in the day of trouble. Secondly—Whatever you design to do, lay it justly and time it seasonably, for that gives security and despatch. Lastly—Be not troubled at disappointments; for if they may be recovered, do it; if they cannot, trouble is vain: if you could not have helped it, be content; there is often peace and profit in submitting to providence, for afflictions make wise: if you could have helped it, let not your trouble exceed your instruction for another time. These rules,' said the Admiral, 'will carry you with firmness and comfort through this inconstant world.'

The dying man had risen into that region which is above the fear and favour of the world. His frame of mind was calm, confiding, and religious.

He talked a good deal with his son; and in the end not only forgave him, but approved of what he was doing. 'Son William,'—these were almost the last words he uttered,—'if you and your friends keep to your plain way of preaching, and also keep to your plain way of living, you will make an end of priests to the end of the world.' For himself, however, he died, as he had lived, a member of the Church. He added, 'Bury me near my mother; live all in love. Shun all manner of evil. . . . I pray God to bless you all, and He will bless you.'

Eleven days after the trial Admiral Penn was gone. With a life-interest in his estate reserved to Lady Penn,—his daughter Margaret being married,—he left the whole of his property, his plate, his household furniture, the money owing to him by government, his lands in England and in Ireland, his claims in Spain, his claims in Jamaica, his gold chain and medal, and the sole executorship of his last will and testament to his Quaker son. Altogether this property was of very considerable amount. Besides the claims on the State for money lent to it and for arrears of salary—not much under 15,000*l.*—the estates brought their owner, on the average, about fifteen hundred pounds a-year.

Fearing, not without good cause, from what had happened, that, unless his son were held up and supported by powerful friends, his life would be one continual act of martyrdom, Sir William had sent from his death-bed to both the King and the Duke of York to solicit at their hands those kind offices to his son which they had been ever ready to ex-

tend towards himself. The royal brothers had returned a flattering answer. James undertook the
office of guardian and protector to the young man :—
the natural origin of that connexion between the
Quaker gentleman and the Catholic prince which
afterwards created so much talk. As Penn told the
delegates of Magdalen College, in after days, the
questions which made him intimate with the prince
were such as affected his property, not his creed.

CHAPTER XIV.

GULI SPRINGETT (1670–1671).

GULIELMA MARIA, daughter of Sir William Springett, of Darling, in Sussex, one of the leaders of the Parliamentary forces during the first years of the civil war, was living with her mother at the village of Chalfont, in Buckinghamshire, when her future husband first saw her. Guli was the delight of a small circle, including persons no less famous than John Milton, Thomas Ellwood, and Isaac Pennington. To Pennington, who was Guli's step-father, Ellwood owed his introduction to his great master. When the ravages of plague had driven the bard from London, he went down to Chalfont with his pupil, knowing that friends were living there who shared his opinions and revered his genius. Rarely is an unpretending village honoured with such company as Chalfont boasted in those days. Pennington occupied the Grange, which he rebuilt and beautified; Milton lived in a cottage at a distance; Ellwood had a house midway between the residences of his friends. To Guli, Ellwood had been a mate from childhood; one of her little playfellows in the hop-gardens of

Kent, and in his manhood he was one of her most constant and devoted squires. It is not easy to decide which of the attractions of Chalfont — his master or his mistress — was the greater for Ellwood. To Milton he was warmly attached; and though his love for Guli Springett was true and earnest, it was not so fierce as to be beyond control. Sought and flattered by men of all ranks, by peers and commoners, by courtiers and puritans, Guli must have been well aware of her power. She cannot fail to have felt flattered by Ellwood's silent homage. As he never gave offence by obtruding passion on her thought, she graciously received his attentions, and contracted for him a friendship which lasted without a day of coldness on either side until her death.

Guli was fond of music. Music was Milton's passion. In the poet's cottage, in the philosopher's grange, the hours flew past, between psalms of love, converse from the bard, old stories of the war, in which the elder people had played their parts, and favourite passages from that stupendous work which was to crown the aged poet. It was to these friends that Milton first made known that he had written Paradise Lost; it was also in their society that Ellwood suggested to him the theme of Paradise Regained. Immortal Chalfont!

Penn, going down to Chalfont to see his friend Pennington, was struck by Guli's charms. He saw, he loved, he prospered in his love. All other suitors were forgotten, and the heart of Guli Springett passed from her for ever. In the handsome person,

in the social station, in the sober bearing of her
suitor, Guli found the hero of her waking dreams.
The circumstances of the time, and recollections of
the past, were not without their influence on his
love.   To understand these influences, it is requisite
to look on the romantic story of Guli's house.

The father of Sir William Springett died in the
third year of his marriage, leaving a widow and three
infant children—one of them unborn—to inherit a
good name and a moderate fortune.   His widow devoted herself to the education of her children, and
they grew up to be an honour to their native land.
She was herself a character.

'To her son William,' says Lady Springett, in
a memoir which she wrote for Guli Penn's eldest
son, 'she was a most tender and affectionate mother,
and always showed great kindness towards me;
indeed she was very honourable in counselling her
son not to marry for an estate, and put by great
offers of persons with thousands, urging him to consider what would make him happy in a choice.'
Mary Proud, the memoir-writer—a daughter of Sir
John Proud, a colonel in the service of the Dutch
Republic—was then living in the same house with
the Springetts; and being a young girl of great
beauty and spirit, of nearly the same age as Sir
William, and of his own station in society, both
mother and son not unnaturally cast their eyes
on their fair ward.   Lady Springett, writing more
than forty years after these events, in describing
them to her grandson, Penn's eldest son William,
says, 'She proposed my marriage to him, because

we were bred together from children, I being nine, he twelve years old when we first came to live together. She would discourse with him in this wise :—that 'she knew me, and we were known to one another;' she said, 'she should choose me for his wife before any one with a great portion, even if I had no portion, because of these things and of our equality in outward conditions and years. She lived to see thy mother (Guli) three or four year old.'

Colonel Springett, Guli's father, had spent his money as freely as his blood. He had served without pay, and kept a mess-table for his officers at his own expense ; so that when he died at three-and-twenty his affairs were not a little out of order, but the energy and prudence of Lady Springett kept them from falling into ruin. Other cares assailed the widow. Her husband had fought and died for his religious opinions ; and even before then he had inspired her with all his own religious fervour, which she, with her woman's nature and in her lonely condition, soon allowed to overmaster her. The details she has left of the agony of heart suffered during the first two years of her widowhood, are full of that solemn striving after a better life which may be accounted either wisdom or insanity according to the point of view. At length she met with one, who, like herself, was out at sea. This man was Isaac Pennington. In the manuscript history of her life she tells the story :—'My love was drawn to him because I found he saw the deceits of all notions, and lay as one that refused to be comforted, so that he was sick and weary of all that appeared ; and in this my heart clove to him, and a desire was in me to be serviceable to him in his desolate condition, for he was alone and miserable in the world—and I gave up much to be a companion to him in this suffering.' Some time after their marriage they found the comfort they were seeking in the system preached by George Fox, of which William Penn was now the champion.

What wonder that the graceful and intrepid Penn should be a welcome visitor at Chalfont; what wonder that the fair Guli, herself a Quaker, should smile on her new suitor, and consent to be his wife !

CHAPTER XV.

BOND AND FREE (1671–1672).

WHILE Penn was living in the poetic circles of Chalfont, he began to study the Catholic Question seriously, and in his twenty-sixth year he gave the world his thoughts upon it. In his 'Caveat against Popery' he refutes the dogmas of that Church; but he makes a large distinction between Catholic and Catholicism; a distinction never made in that age, and too seldom made even now. While he denounced the creed as contrary to reason and Scripture, to conscience and human liberty, he pleaded for toleration to the men who had been trained to think it true. Toleration to doctrine he was forced in conscience to condemn; but toleration to the disciple he affirmed with all his might. Here was a new and startling theory. Few men were then prepared to understand it; fewer still to act upon it; yet the theory was true, and made its way.

When Admiral Penn was dead, and William Penn his son had dropped from sight at court, the city Dogberries, Starling and Robinson, thought the time for their revenge had come. Their plot was certain to succeed. It was a punishable offence to refuse the oath of allegiance when it was offered by a magistrate; and as a Quaker could not take an oath, it was only necessary to seize his person, put him to the proof, and then commit him for contempt. To mask the evil animus, the arrest must be on other grounds; they chose to consider the Quakers' meeting-house in Wheeler Street, which Penn attended, an illegal meeting; though they would not trust a jury on the point. These City aldermen set spies on Penn, who made reports to them of his comings and goings, his sayings and doings. They learned his daily haunts; and often in the morning they could tell how he intended to bestow his day. Their agents were about his heels; and as he feared no evil and had nothing to conceal, their plot soon took effect. On his return from Bucks, he went to Wheeler Street as usual, when a sergeant and picquet of soldiers entered the room, and as he rose to address the people, pulled him down and dragged him into the street, where a constable and assistants being in readiness, they carried him to the Tower, lodged him in a dungeon, and left a guard at his door. After a lapse of three or four hours he was brought before his enemies. Robinson, Sheldon, and a few other magistrates were present.

Robinson: 'What is this person's name?'
Constable: 'Mr. Penn, sir.'
Robinson: 'Is your name Penn?'
Penn: 'Dost thou not know me?'

Robinson : 'I don't know you. I don't desire to know such as you.'

Penn : 'If not, why didst thou send for me hither?'

Robinson : 'Is that your name, sir?'

Penn : 'Yes, yes, my name is Penn. I am not ashamed of my name.'

Robinson : 'Constable, where did you find him?'

Constable : 'At Wheeler Street, at a meeting; speaking to the people.'

Robinson : 'You mean, he was speaking to an unlawful assembly.'

Constable : 'I don't know indeed, sir; he was there, and he was speaking.'

Robinson : 'Give them their oaths.'

Penn : 'Hold, don't swear the men; there is no need of it. I freely acknowledge I was in Wheeler Street, and that I spoke to an assembly of people there.'

Robinson : 'He confesses it.'

Penn : 'I do so. I am not ashamed of my testimony.'

Robinson : 'No matter; give them their oaths. . . . Mr. Penn, you know the law better than I do, and you know these things are contrary to law.'

Penn : 'If thou believest me to know the law better than thyself, hear me, for I know no law I have transgressed. . . . Now I am probably to be tried by the late act against Conventicles; I conceive it doth not reach me.'

Robinson : 'No, sir. I shall not proceed upon that law.'

Sir John Robinson named the Oxford Act; but in a moment Penn showed him that the law so called could not apply to him. Driven to their kennel, the two Dogberries brought out the oath of allegiance, and Sir John cried out abruptly and angrily, 'Wilt thou take the oath?' 'This is not to the purpose,' replied Penn, in the midst of an ingenious protest against their endeavour to apply to his case fragments of different and dissimilar laws. 'Read him the oath,' roared the lieutenant. Penn refused to swear; alleging as his reason that his conscience forbade him to take up arms at all, much more against his sovereign.

Robinson: 'I am sorry you put me upon this severity. It is no pleasant work to me.'

Penn: 'These are but words. It is manifest that this is a *prepense malice*. Thou hast several times laid the meetings for me, and this day particularly.'

Robinson: 'No. I profess I could not tell you would be there.'

Penn: 'Thine own corporal told me that you had intelligence at the Tower, that I should be at Wheeler Street to-day, almost as soon as I knew it myself. This is disingenuous and partial. I never gave thee occasion for such unkindness.'

Robinson: 'I knew no such thing; but if I had, I confess I should have sent for thee.'

Penn: 'That confession might have been spared. I do heartily believe it.'

Robinson: 'I vow, Mr. Penn, I am sorry for you. You are an ingenious gentleman; all the world must allow that; and you have a plentiful estate.   Why should you render yourself unhappy by associating with such a simple people?'

Penn: 'I confess I have made it my choice to relinquish the company of those that are ingeniously wicked, to converse with those who are more honestly simple.'

Robinson: 'I wish thee wiser.'

Penn: 'I wish thee better.'

Robinson: 'You have been as bad as other folks.'

Penn: 'When and where? I charge thee to tell the company to my face.'

Robinson: 'Abroad—and at home too.'

Sheldon: 'No, no, Sir John.   That's too much.'

Penn: 'I make this bold challenge to all men, justly to accuse me with ever having heard me swear, utter a curse, or speak one obscene word— much less that I make it my practice. . . . Thy words shall be my burden, and I trample thy slander under my feet.'

Robinson: 'Well, Mr. Penn, I have no ill-will towards you.   Your father was my friend, and I have a great deal of kindness for you.'

Penn: 'Thou hast an ill way of expressing it. . . .'

Robinson: 'Well, I must send you to Newgate for six months, and when they are expired you will come out.'

Penn: 'Is that all?   Thou well knowest a longer imprisonment has not daunted me.   Alas, you mistake your interests; this is not the way to compass your ends.'

Robinson: 'You bring yourself into trouble.

You will be heading of parties, and drawing people after you.'

Penn: 'Thou mistakest. There is no such way as this to render men remarkable.'

Robinson: 'I wish your adhering to these things do not convert you to something at last.'

Penn: 'I would have thee and all men know that I scorn that religion which is not worth suffering for, and able to sustain those that are afflicted for its sake. . . . . Thy religion persecutes, mine forgives. I desire God to forgive you all that are concerned in my commitment, and I leave you all in perfect charity.'

Robinson: 'Send a corporal with a file of musqueteers with him.'

Penn: 'No, no; send thy lacquey. I know the way to Newgate.'

During the whole of his long period of six months in jail, Penn was busily employed in writing; and as the results of this labour, not less than four important treatises came from his hand: 1. The Great Case of Liberty of Conscience. 2. Truth rescued from Imposture. 3. A Postscript to Truth exalted. 4. An Apology for the Quakers. Three of these works are of considerable length; and one of them, 'The Great Case of Liberty of Conscience,' is not only in itself a noble piece of work, but, from the nature of its subject, one which ought to be familiar to every one. Besides these larger works, the prisoner wrote many letters on public and private business. The young lady of Chalfont, from whom he had so lately parted, would naturally occupy not a few of his thoughts; but the cause in which they were jointly embarked had the first claim on his services. Besides long letters written to a Catholic who had taken offence at his 'Caveat against Popery,' and to the Sheriffs of London on the state of Newgate, and the abuses practised by the jailers on such as either could not, or from scruples of conscience would not, buy their favours; he wrote a dignified and temperate letter to the High Court of Parliament, then known to be contemplating a more rigorous enforcement of the act against conventicles, explaining the principles of his body as to civil and political affairs, proving that the freedom they claimed was in no way dangerous to the State.

When his term of imprisonment was up, he went abroad for a time; at first into Holland, and afterwards into Germany, neither of which countries he had seen in his earlier travels. He could speak the Low Dutch pretty well, and made some converts to his opinions. Embden was one of the cities in which he made a great impression. The first meeting was held in the house of Dr. Haesbert, who was deeply struck with the new doctrines proposed by the English missionary; and after giving the matter three months' consideration, Haesbert openly embraced them, and was the first Quaker in that part of the continent. About twelve months later Frau Haesbert joined him, and a godly meeting was in course of time formed in Embden, which looked to Penn with the feelings of a converted country to the apostle of its conversion. In the days of persecution which soon came upon them—when the members of the new sect were flogged in public, cast into loathsome dungeons, fed on bread and water, mulcted in heavy fines, and even banished from their native land—his voice was ever raised in their defence, and his influence used for their protection.

There were at this time many other religious communities in Holland in which Penn took a deep interest—various members of the great Puritan party of England, who had crossed over into that country on the return of the Stuarts, with the intention of ultimately migrating to the new world. To all these exiled sects America was the land of promise, the subject of their daily talk and nightly dreams. Many ships filled with emigrants had already gone out. At religious meetings and in domestic circles the accounts sent home by the adventurers of the perils of the sea-voyage, of the beauty and fertility of the new country, were read and re-read; and hardly a year passed by that did not witness the departure of a fresh band of these devout and sturdy founders of the great republic. The stories told by those who for a time were left behind of the trials from which they and their fellows had fled, of their unconquerable desire to found a free state in the depths of the wilderness, where every man should be able to worship God according to his conscience, of the dangers which their predecessors in the good work encountered and overcame, of their own anxiety to follow them to their new home— all this was deeply interesting to Penn, and served to revive the romantic dreams in which he had found comfort while at Oxford. Though his thoughts on this subject assumed as yet no practical shape, his mind became more and more fixed, during this tour, on the land to which he saw the best men of his age going out as settlers. The germ of Pennsylvania was quickening into life.

CHAPTER XVI.

MARRIED LIFE (1672–1673).

PENN was anxious to be near Guli Springett once again. Calling to see his mother at Wanstead on his way to London, he made a short stay in the capital, visiting old friends, reporting the results of his journey, and then posted down to Bucks. Received by the people of the Grange with open arms, by Guli Springett as her lover, and by Ellwood and Pennington as a champion of their faith, he passed in their society a considerable time, dallying with the days of courtship, and making preparations for his marriage. Not wishing to disturb Lady Penn at Wanstead, he took a house at Rickmansworth, six miles from Chalfont; and when everything was ready for Guli's reception, the marriage rites were performed in the early spring of 1672.

Their honeymoon lasted long. The spring and summer came and went, but Penn was still with his young wife at Rickmansworth. No flattery of friends, and no attack of foes, could draw him from that charming house. Since his expulsion from his father's house he had never known so much repose.

Seeing him surrounded by all that makes domestic happiness complete—a charming home, a beautiful and loving wife, a plentiful estate, the prospect of a family, and a troop of attached and admiring friends,—those who knew him only at second hand imagined that the prisoner of Newgate and the Tower would now subside into the country gentleman, more interested in cultivating his paternal acres than in the progress of an unpopular doctrine. Those who reasoned so knew little of William Penn, and still less of the lady who had now become his wife. Some months given up to love, Guli would have scorned the man who could sink down into the sloth of the affections; who by outward showing to the world would have represented her alliance as bringing weakness to his character instead of strength.

The next three years of Penn's life were spent in working, writing, preaching. Guli rode with him from town to town, and as she had no little ones as yet in the nursery, she could give up all her time to missionary work. As she was past her thirtieth year, it seemed as though the name of Penn might only live in what her husband wrote and said. He never laid his pen aside. Beyond his labours as a preacher, he composed in these three years no less than twenty-six books of controversy, some of which were rather long, and two political pamphlets—his treatise on Oaths, and England's Present Interests considered.

A controversy with Thomas Hicks, a Baptist minister, on the Inner Light, first drew him out of his retreat ; and led him to indite his 'Christian Quaker,' his 'Reason against Railing,' and his 'Counterfeit Christian detected.'   Men's minds were much unsettled. Two converts, fancying they felt a call, set off for Rome in order to convert the Pope. They had not been long in the Eternal City ere they were arrested as dangerous heretics and placed in confinement :—one of them, John Love, was sent to the Inquisition, where he died in a short time with such aids as the Holy Office used for the suppression of heresy ; the other, John Perrot, was sent to a hospital for the insane. England could not quite abandon them, and after a good deal of interest had been made in his behalf, John Perrot was set at liberty; on which he returned to his own country, where he soon gave his former friends so much trouble that they wished him back again in the Roman bedlam. It was in the conduct of men like Perrot that the weak side of the new Christian Democracy came out. Soon after his return to England, he began to preach the doctrine that even in prayer the hat should not be removed except at the Divine instance. This was felt by Penn to be a dangerous development of his own idea. Not uncover to God ! It was not only absurd, but destroyed the argument on which his own re- fusal to unbonnet to the King was justified. Firm measures were taken with the innovator ; but, as usual with such men, Perrot refused to conform, and was expelled the society. Thereupon he pub- lished a pamphlet called the 'Spirit of the Hat,' -—which Penn answered in 'The Spirit of Alexander the Coppersmith.' More pamphlets followed —Penn, as usual, having the last and strongest word.

In April, 1673, Penn's brother Richard died at Wanstead, where his mother still resided. Dick was buried at Walthamstow, and as he died a single man, his fortune passed to his elder brother.

The session of 1673 was occupied by a dispute in the House of Commons as to the King's right to issue declarations of Liberty of Conscience without consent of Parliament. A majority of the Commons declared that his Majesty had exceeded his powers. Charles took time to consider his answer; and at last replied that his ancestors had exercised this disputed right. The Commons said it was not so; on which his Majesty, who said he was insulted, threatened to dissolve the House. But his more cautious and politic friend, Louis Quatorze, advised him to submit, in order to gain time till peace was finally concluded with Holland, when the regiments engaged on the Continent could be used against his enemies in England; Louis offering to supply him with money and forces from France sufficient to crush every attempt to resist his royal will. Charles adopted this counsel. The very evening on which it was offered by Colbert on behalf of his august master, the King sent for a copy of his declaration and tore it up in the presence of his ministers. Next day this act of grace was made public; the two Houses of Parliament received the intelligence with shouts of satisfaction; in the evening bonfires burst upon the capital, and every one seemed glad that Liberty of Conscience was withdrawn.

Hardly were these fires extinguished ere the Test Act, hurried through the Commons with indecent haste, was sent up to the Peers, and in less than ten days one of the most disgraceful laws ever passed in England was added to the book of statutes. Its authors professed to strike only at the Papists; and to prove their sincerity they introduced another bill for the relief of Nonconforming Protestants; but delay followed delay; the debates were adjourned from time to time; one clause after another was amended or struck out; and prorogation overtook them before their work was finished, and the whole body of Dissenters was left at the mercy of any one who might be moved to rake the old penal statutes up against them.

Foremost of these sufferers were the Quakers. At this juncture Penn produced his work on 'England's present Interest.' Every line of this production seems written with indignant hand— 'There is no law under heaven, which has its rise from nature or grace, that forbids men to deal honestly and plainly with the greatest'—thus he begins; and addressing himself to those in authority, he proceeds to show how the old charters of liberty have been violated, adducing specific instances of each. He goes at great length into the origin of English liberties; with a view to show that they are older in date than our religious feuds. 'We were a free people,' he says, 'by the creation of God and by the careful provision of our never-to-be-forgotten ancestors; so that our claim to these English privileges, rising higher than Protestantism, can never justly be invalidated on account of nonconformity to any tenet or fashion it may prescribe. This would be to lose by the Reformation.'—His concluding advice tō the ruling power is—1. To conserve all the ancient rights and liberties of the people; 2. To grant entire freedom to opinion in matters of faith; and, 3. To endeavour to promote the growth of true and practical piety.

Though the composition of this work kept Penn at home a good part of the year, his attention was continually diverted to special cases of oppression; and the letters written by him to magistrates, sheriffs, lieutenants of counties and others in behalf of individual sufferers, would fill a volume.

Justice Fleming had been an old friend of the Springetts, and years before this date had been very kind to Guli when she paid a visit at his house in Westmoreland. Penn's letter of remonstrance to Fleming, written on receipt of some complaints of his harshness towards the Quakers in his magisterial capacity, is concluded in language of much courtliness and beauty. One can fancy Guli looking over Penn's shoulder as he wrote these words— 'However differing I am from other men *circa sacra*, and that world which, respecting men, may be said to begin when this ends, I know no religion that destroys courtesy, civility, and kindness.'

Penn had been five years absent from court; but the arrest of George Fox, his spiritual chief, by the Worcester justices, and his imprisonment in

Worcester Castle on a charge of refusing to take the oaths—George 'would not swear at all'—induced him to appear once more in that familiar scene. Penn went with Captain Mead to Sackville, who advised that they should see the Duke of York, as being the only man with power enough to help them. If the Duke would back their cause, then he, Charles Sackville, would assist them also; but he could not move in such a work alone. They went to the Duke's palace, and by means of the Duchess's secretary, tried to gain admission; but they found the house so full of people and the Duke so busy, that the secretary could not obtain admission for himself. They were going away very sadly, when Colonel Aston, of the Duke's bed-chamber, seeing his old friend Penn, whom he had lost for a long time, asked him into the drawing-room. Aston went into the Duke's closet; and James, on hearing who was there, at once came out, saying how glad he was to see his ward again. James listened to the request about Fox with much courtesy, and said he was against all persecution for religion's sake. In his youth, he confessed, he had been warm against sectaries, because he thought they used their conscience only as a pretext to disturb the government; but he now thought better of them, and was willing to do to others as he hoped to be done by. He wished all men were of that opinion; for he was sure no man was willing to be persecuted for his own belief. He would use his influence with the King. But where had Penn been all these years, and why had he not called before? He had promised the

Admiral to look after his son ; but that son had never shown himself at court. James told his ward to come whenever he had any business ; he should always be pleased to see him ; and would do his best to fulfil towards him the duties of a guardian.

CHAPTER XVII.

HOLY EXPERIMENT (1673–1676).

LOVE of country was one of the most powerful sentiments of a Puritan. But he had other inspirations.
Love of personal freedom—claim to the free utterance of his thoughts—determination to bend his
knee only at the shrine which his conscience owned
—these things were stronger than the love of country,
even than the love of life. Not lightly, not hastily,
did the founders of the New World turn their backs
on the land which had given them birth. Years of
wrong and insult were required to loosen their tena-
cious hold of the soil which had been ploughed and
reaped by their Saxon fathers. When endurance
was at length exhausted, they departed more in
sorrow than in anger; quitting the ports they were
never more to behold again with blessings on their
lips, and with their faces like their hearts still
turned towards dear old England. In the days of
peace and concord, now and then recurring in the
most unsettled times, the tide of emigration ebbed;
but when the act of indulgence had been cancelled
by the King, and the fury of persecution began to

fill the jails with victims, plans for founding a New Home beyond the seas, away from the old political and religious rivalries of Europe, for the persecuted of all creeds and nations, were revived.

To Penn this dream had been more or less familiar from his youth. At twelve years old the victories of his father in Jamaica turned his fancies towards the West. By usage Admiral Penn should have received his share of the conquered lands, and but for his arrest by Cromwell, an estate—a very large one—in that island, would have come to Penn. It might come any day. The Admiral's claims against the crown were still unsettled, and the King might choose to pay his debts by giving up the lands which Cromwell had withheld. In the retirement of his family in Ireland Penn had been employed in planting an English colony on foreign soil ; at Wanstead and in the Navy Gardens the subject of buying an estate in the New World had been often raised ; in his hour of excitement and disobedience at Oxford, he had turned to these earlier projects and laid out a new Oceana or Utopia in his fancy ; at the yearly meetings of his own religious society the settlement of Quakers in Jamaica, in New England, and on the Delaware, had been frequently discussed. The journey he had recently made into Holland and Germany had roused the gathering zeal of years. At Amsterdam, at Leyden, in the cities of the Middle Rhine, his imagination was excited by the stories he had heard from relatives and friends of those who had crossed the Atlantic in their barks. At length his mind began to fix itself on what he called the Holy Experiment of planting a religious democracy in the western world.

His first connexion with the continent on which he was to build himself a monument was in the affairs of New Jersey. No reader need be told that in the reign of Charles the Second many of the colonies in America were either given or sold away to private persons. In accordance with his principle of misrule, the King made over to his brother James the province of New Netherland, then stretching from the shores of the Delaware river to the Connecticut river, even before a single rood of land had yet been wrested from the Dutch. Two months before the conquest of that country, James in turn had ganted to Lord Berkeley and Sir George Carteret, in equal shares, the region lying between the Hudson river and the Delaware river. When the English forces took possession of the country, these old names and boundaries were removed, and in honour of Sir George Carteret (a Jersey man) the province became New Jersey. As the object of nearly all noble owners of such estates was to make money, they offered such concessions—or constitutions—as would attract a crowd of able, energetic, and wealthy men. Without being advocates of civil and religious liberty, the speculators not unfrequently established in their colonial possessions enlarged and liberal laws. The owners of New Jersey offered some concessions in this spirit. A number of Puritans set sail from the port of New Haven, with a view to establish themselves in the new territory; and having reached the Passaic, they held a council there with Indian tribes, changed the name of the settlement to New Ark, and laid the foundations of a democratic state. Under their free and vigorous rule the province rapidly increased; the Quakers took an interest in it, and a few of them went out. But Berkeley in a short time grew dissatisfied; disputes arose about quit-rents and privileges; and the Earl found his ease disturbed by murmur and remonstrance from men into whose hands he had passed away the reins. These troubles made him anxious to sell his share; and as Fox had just returned from a visit to the English settlements in America, the Quakers opened a communication with Berkeley, who agreed to sell his share in the province for a thousand pounds. The buyers, John Fenwick and Edward Billing, quarrelled, and the matter was referred to Penn. The letters still extant show that Fenwick was disposed to resist the award; but a rebuke from Penn, in which he spoke in noble and affecting language of the meanness of such quarrels, brought him round. 'Thy grandchildren,' said the expostulator to his client, 'may be in the other world before the land thou hast allotted will be employed.'

Fenwick, with his family and a number of emigrants, set sail in the ship *Griffith* for New Jersey, and ascending the Delaware a considerable distance, found a fertile and pleasant spot, where they landed their goods and chattels, formed a settlement, and called the town Salem—place of peace and rest. Meantime the affairs of Billing got involved. Unable to meet his creditors, Billing gave up his property into the hands of trustees. Penn was one of these trustees. Full of his old dreams of a model state, and fresh from the study of Harrington and More, Penn was not content to carry on the government of the province as he found it, simply as a commercial venture, and without regard to the working out of great ideas. Sydney's lessons had made a deep impression on his mind; and Locke's constitution for Carolina was ever present to his thoughts. The first attempt to lay the foundations of a free colony was obstructed by the joint ownership of the soil, as even within the limits prescribed by law, the trustees of Billing could only exercise a semi-sovereignty, while Sir George Carteret remained co-partner. The object, then, which lay in front of every effort for the good of the settlers, was such a division of the province as should separate Carteret's share from the rest; and this result was obtained by Penn after a troublesome negotiation, on giving up the best half of the estate to the agents of the old proprietor, which was henceforth known as the province of East New Jersey,—that retained by the Quakers being called from its geographical position West New Jersey. By these two names the provinces were known for many years.

Left free to act, the trustees began their operations by dividing the land into a hundred lots, ten of which were made over to John Fenwick in satisfaction of his claims. The other ninety lots were put up for sale, and the creditors being satisfied, Penn got power to carry out his own ideas in the work of

L

settling a fundamental pact. As yet the mind of the legislator was itself in ferment. Harrington and the classic republicans still exercised a powerful influence over him; and it was not till some years later that his genius—aided by Algernon Sydney— found its highest expression in the laws and charters of the state which bears his name.

An outline of the new constitution for West New Jersey may be given in a few words :—the rights of free worship were secured—the legislative power was given in a great measure to the people— representatives were to be elected, not in the old way of acclamation, but by the ballot-box—every man of mature age and free from crime was an elector and was eligible for election—the executive power was vested in ten commissioners, to be appointed by the general assembly—the office of interpreting the law and pronouncing verdicts was confided to the juries, as Penn contended was the case in England by the ancient charters—and the judges, elected for two years, sat in the courts simply to assist the juries in arriving at a correct decision— the state was made to charge itself with the education of all orphan children—no man was to be shut up in prison for debt. By these provisions and the laws which were to follow, Penn believed he was laying a foundation for those who came after him to understand their liberties as Christians and as men.

While he was toiling at the grounds of his Holy Experiment, Penn had the happiness to become a father. Guli bore him a son, whom Penn called Springett, after her heroic sire. As he was now a family man, he thought it right to have a house of his own, besides Shangarry Castle in county Cork; and after looking through the lovely southern shires, he fixed on Worminghurst, in Sussex; as a high and healthy spot, seven miles from Shoreham, with noble timber in the park, and air kept fresh by breezes from the sea. For this estate he paid four thousand five hundred pounds; and got a bargain in it, since the surplus wood was worth, as he supposed, two thousand pounds. Sydney had a place in the neighbourhood. On this noble Sussex down Penn nursed his first-born son, and perfected his frame of government for a Free State.

When this document was finished, the trustees met and resolved on its publication in the shape of a letter, which they signed. A brief description of the soil, air, climate, natural productions, and other features of West New Jersey followed; and it is characteristic of Penn that he added a cautionary postscript to his countrymen against indulging, without sufficient cause, in the thought of seeking for a new home—of leaving their native land either out of curiosity, from a love of change, or in the spirit of gain. Yet Worminghurst was soon besieged with applications for plots of land in the Free State. Two companies were formed to establish trade and promote emigration, one in Yorkshire, and one in Middlesex. The members of the Yorkshire company were chiefly creditors of Billing; as a set-off to their claims, they received from the trustees ten of the original hundred parts of land. By cancelling these debts the property was freed.

The purchasers of land at once made preparations for the voyage. Before there was as yet a people in West New Jersey, Penn found it desirable to have an authority, legally constituted, to conduct the enterprise; and with this view he proposed to institute a provisional government—himself selecting some of its members, Fenwick's party and the two companies nominating the other members. Thomas Olive and Daniel Wills were appointed to act as commissioners by the London company; Joseph Helmsly and Robert Stacey by the Yorkshire proprietors; Richard Guy was named on behalf of the former emigrants; and to these were added Benjamin Scott, John Kinsey, and three others. These ten persons were to exercise the powers of the ten commissioners mentioned in the fundamental laws until such time as a popular government, chosen in a legal and orderly way, could be organised, on which their functions were to cease.

Penn organised the emigration, and engaged the good ship *Kent*, Gregory Marlow, master, to carry out the commissioners, their families and tenants, to the number of two hundred and thirty persons. The vessel was moored high up in the Thames; at the hour fixed for her departure the emigrants went on board accompanied by their friends; and the master was just on the point of weighing anchor, amid the tears and embraces of relatives about to part for ever, when a light and gilded barge was seen to be gliding over the smooth waters towards them. Something in the appearance of the *Kent* had caught the attention of its occupants, for the boatmen, now seen to be attired in the royal livery, used their oars as if they had been ordered to come alongside. It was the King. He asked the name of the ship and whither it was bound. Being answered, he inquired if the emigrants were all Quakers, to which they answered Yes; on which he gave them his blessing, and pulled away.

Two other vessels followed the *Kent*; one of them sailed from Hull with a body of emigrants from Yorkshire, the other from London freighted with a hundred and fourteen persons from the southern counties. When the new-comers arrived at their destination, Andros, governor of New York, claimed jurisdiction over them and their territory, justifying his claim by reference to the feudal law and the colonial charter; but both parties fortunately were moderate in their tone, and while the question of rights was referred to the mother country, the Quakers entered into treaties with the natives for the purchase of land, and under a sail-cloth, set up in the forest of Burlington, began to assemble for public worship. The native tribes came from their hunting-grounds to confer with these peaceful strangers, who carried purses in their hands to pay for what they required, instead of muskets to seize on it by force. 'You are our brothers,' said the Sachem chiefs, after hearing their proposals, 'and we will live like brothers with you. We will have a broad path for you and us to walk in. If an Englishman falls asleep in this path, the Indian shall pass him by and say—He is an Englishman; he is asleep; let him alone. The path shall be plain.

There shall not be in it a stump to hurt the feet.' Commenced under such auspices, West New Jersey prospered. Land was sold and cleared. The Sachems kept the peace. The population multiplied. Some letters written by the leaders of their party in England to these happy colonists are still extant; from these it would be inferred that in a very few years West New Jersey had become a new Arcadia —that the Holy Experiment was a safe success— that Penn had realised the State which Sydney had conceived and Harrington had dreamed.

CHAPTER XVIII.

WORK AND TRAVEL (1677).

HAVING got his Holy Experiment under shape, Penn turned his thoughts to those Dutch and Rhenish towns in which he had planted Quaker congregations. Not a few of these societies had fallen into bad ways; some were suffering persecution; some were rent by quarrels; all were anxious for his presence. Those who suffered from their feudal lords were eager to be told about that Free State which he was helping to found in the great deserts beyond the sea. For each he had a message full of hope. The Princess Elizabeth, who held her court at Herwerden, begged her 'affectionate friend' to pay her a second visit now that his affairs allowed him time.

Leaving Guli and her child at Worminghurst, he rode to Harwich, where he found George Fox, Robert Barclay, and other Quakers waiting for him. Armed with books and tracts, explanatory of Quaker doctrines, printed in various languages, English, French, Dutch, and German, they took their passage in a ship commanded by one of Admiral Penn's old officers, who out of affection for his former patron let them convert his quarter-deck into a conventicle. When they came in sight of Brill, Penn and Barclay, anxious to land ere nightfall, stept into a boat. Before they got ashore, the sun went down; the gates were closed; and as no houses stood outside the walls, they had to make their beds in a fisherman's boat. At dawn the passengers landed and started immediately for Rotterdam, where they held meetings of their friends. Penn spoke in Dutch, while the eloquence of George Fox had to be interpreted word for word. Meetings had been prepared for them in all the towns along their route, and three Dutch converts, Claus, Arents, and Bocliffs, came to them from Amsterdam to conduct them on their way. At Leyden and at Haarlem, where they held meetings and spread abroad a knowledge of their tenets, other deputies from Alchmaer and Embden met them. Their journey through the country was a triumph. At Amsterdam they organised the scattered Quakers and settled some of the nicer points of doctrine—such as the non-necessity for priest or magistrate as a witness to the ceremony of marriage. Another matter which came before them was the suffering of their disciples in various countries, especially the case of certain inhabitants of Dantzic, which city then formed a part of the Polish republic. Sobieski, King of Poland, was at the time on a visit to Dantzic ; and Penn advised that a petition should be presented to him in the name of the suffering citizens, briefly detailing their wrongs and asking at his hands the right to worship God according to their faith. This petition

Penn was desired to draw up, which he did in suitable and noble terms, quoting most happily a saying of Stephen, one of Sobieski's most illustrious predecessors—'I am a king of men, but not of consciences; king of bodies, not of souls.'

Leaving Fox at Amsterdam, Penn and Barclay went to Herwerden, where the Electress gave them a friendly welcome. This pious woman, daughter of Frederick, Prince Palatine of the Rhine and King of Bohemia, was a granddaughter of James the First, a cousin to the reigning King of England, and a sister of Prince Rupert—the old rival and enemy of Admiral Penn. The Princess treated Penn with courtesy and affection; his gratitude survived her; and in one of the subsequent editions of 'No Cross, no Crown' he added her name to his list of benefactors and examples to mankind.

Penn and Barclay stayed at an inn of the town, but visited the court daily, holding meetings and discoursing before her Highness on the principles of their creed. They dined at the common table of their hotel, where they met with many strangers, to whom they distributed books and tracts. One of these, a student at the college of Duysburg, told them of a 'sober and seeking man of great note in the city of Duysburg,' which determined Penn to pay a visit to that town. As the last service drew to a close, Elizabeth walked up to Penn, took him by the hand, and leading him aside, began to speak of the sense she had of God's power and presence; but emotion choked her utterance, and she sobbed out, 'I cannot speak to you; my heart is full!' Penn whispered some few words of comfort. When she gained her voice, she pressed the missionaries to visit her again on their return from the Upper Rhine. Penn promised to do so if they could. She asked them to sup with her that evening, which they at first refused; but the lady would not be denied, and they yielded so far as to take some bread and wine. 'We left them,' says Penn, 'in the love and peace of God, praying that they might be kept from the evil of this world.'

Next morning Barclay set out to join Fox at Amsterdam, while Penn and Keith took places in an open cart for Frankfort. Pushing on through Paderborn, 'a dark Popish city,' and Cassel, where they were 'tenderly received,' obstructed by the heavy rains, bad roads, and primitive vehicle, they arrived in Frankfort just a week after leaving Herwerden. About three miles from Frankfort they were met by two merchants who came forth to welcome them, and report that many of their fellow-citizens were prepared to receive the faith. Doctors, lawyers, ministers of the Gospel, noble ladies, peasants, and handworkers, came to hear them preach. One girl cried out, 'It will never be well with us till persecution comes, and some of us be lodged in the stadthouse.' Penn did not neglect the temporal liberties and worldly interests of his Church. America was a theme of conversation; and among those who took an interest in the colony were Franz Pastorious, Von Dewalle, Dr. Schütz, and Daniel Behagel, all of whom emigrated in a few years. From Frankfort Penn addressed a letter to 'the

Churches of Jesus throughout the world,' in which he exhorted the faithful to take up the cross, to curb the pride of life, and to redeem the time.

Going up the Rhine, the travellers passed through Worms on the fifth day, and in the evening arrived at Kirchheim, six miles from Worms. In this small place the missionary made a deep impression, and the fruits of that day's preaching are still visible in Pennsylvania. The home of which he told them beyond the seas was hardly less welcome to the Protestants of Kirchheim than that better home which he promised them beyond the skies.

Penn was anxious to do something for this handful of true believers, and he went to Mannheim to consult with the Prince Palatine, and ascertain what encouragement that Prince would offer to a colony of virtuous and industrious families, in the event of a considerable number being willing to remove into his territory; also to learn how they would stand in respect to their refusal to take oaths, bear arms, and pay ecclesiastical taxes. On his arrival at Mannheim, finding the Prince had gone to Heidelberg, he contented himself with writing a letter to his Highness, and returned to Worms that evening by the boat.

From Worms they dropped down the stream to Cologne, and met their disciples at the house of a merchant, who at their departure furnished them with a letter of introduction to Dr. Mästricht of Duysburg, which city they were now anxious to visit, not only on account of what the student had told them of 'the sober and seeking man of note,' but because they had been informed by the Princess Elizabeth that the young and beautiful Countess von Falkenstein, whose father lived in that neighbourhood, was seriously inclined.

Duysburg, a Calvinistic city, lay in the territory of the Elector of Brandenburg. On their arrival they sought out Dr. Mästricht and delivered their letter. He told them they were very fortunate in the time of their visit, as, it being Sunday, the young Countess would have left her father's castle and crossed the river to Mulheim, where she would, as usual, spend the day at a clergyman's house. He cautioned them, however, not to make themselves public, as much for the young lady's sake as for their own,—her father, a coarse and rigorous person, being already much displeased with her. Thus warned, they set out for Mulheim. On their way they met with Heinrich Schmidt, a schoolmaster, who told them the Countess had returned. To him they gave the letter from Dr. Mästricht. In an hour he came to say the Countess would be glad to see them, but knew not where, as her father kept so strict a hand over her. She thought it would be best for them to cross the water and go to the house of her friend the clergyman. While they were talking, the Graf with his attendants came from the castle, and seeing persons in a foreign dress standing near his gate, sent one of his retinue to inquire who they were, what they wanted, and whither they were going. Before the Graf received his answers, he walked up and questioned them in person. Penn replied, that they were Englishmen from Holland, and were going no farther than to his own town of Mulheim; on hearing which answer, one of the Graf's gentlemen walked up to the strangers with a frown on his face, and asked them if they knew before whom they stood; and if they had not yet learned how to deport themselves before noblemen and in the presence of princes? Penn answered, he was not aware of any disrespect. 'Then why don't you take off your hats?' said one. 'Is it respectful to stand covered in the presence of the sovereign of the country?' The Quakers took no notice of his gesture, but replied that they uncovered to none but God. 'Well, then,' said the Graf, 'get out of my dominions; you shall not go to my town.' Penn tried to reason with the offended Graf von Falkenstein, who called his men, and bade them lead these Englishmen out of his estates.

It was dusk; they were alone in a strange land; for after conducting them to a thick forest, the soldiers returned to the castle and left them to find their own way back. This forest was three miles in length, and the roads being unknown to them, and the night dark, they wandered in and out. At length they came into an open country, and were soon below a city wall. What city? It was ten o'clock; the gates were shut. In vain they hailed; no sentinel replied. The town had no suburbs; not a single house or building stood beyond the ditch. They lay down in an open field, in search of such repose as they might find on the marshy ground of the Lower Rhine. At three in the morning they got up, stiff with cold, and walked about till five, comforting each other with the assurance that a great day for Germany was at hand, 'several places in that country being almost ripe for the harvest.' After the cathedral clock struck five the gates were opened, and the outcasts gained the shelter of their inn.

Mästricht was 'surprised with fear, the common disease of this country,' says Penn, when he heard of the affair with Graf von Falkenstein. He asked minutely what had passed, and was relieved to find they had not named the Countess. For themselves he thought they had escaped pretty well, as the Graf usually amused himself by setting his dogs to worry persons who were found loitering near his castle gates.

Failing to see the young Countess, Penn had the satisfaction to receive from her a message by the hand of her page. In return he wrote to her a long letter of consolation; and so he went his way.

Dropping down the Rhine — proclaiming their mission in all towns and preparing men for emigration — the travellers at length arrived at Amsterdam. There they found that Fox had gone to Harlingen, whither Penn followed him; and so they stayed in Holland and in the countries about the Elbe and the Lower Rhine until the winter set in, when they again returned to England, by way of Rotterdam and Harwich. On the passage home they met a violent storm. They were at sea three days and nights; the rain fell in torrents; the wind set dead against them; the vessel sprang a leak; and labour at the pumps, both night and day, could hardly keep the hold from filling. Fear fell on the seamen; but no sooner had the danger passed away, than they resumed their wanton mood.

On landing at Harwich, Fox proposed to hold a meeting in that town, and then going on by Colchester and other places make their way towards London. Penn was anxious to be at Worminghurst; and while his friends were willing to travel luxuriously in a cart bedded with straw, he mounted the best horse he could find and rode away.

CHAPTER XIX.

THE WORLD (1673).

FOR two years after his return from Germany, Penn was much in the world and much about the court. His position was a strange one. Standing aloof from all intrigues in that intriguing court; taking no direct and personal part in politics; a candidate for no office; seeking no honour, no emolument that courts can give; accustomed from his youth to mix on equal terms with peers; acquainted with the leading spirits of the day, yet free from their ambition and their lust of pleasure; no man's rival in either love, business, or gallantry; his neutrality in personal and party strife secured to him a larger share of intercourse with leading men than any other individual of the time enjoyed. While graced so highly by the Duke of York, it was easy for him to maintain a high standing with the wits, ministers, and favourites, who daily thronged the galleries of Whitehall; and far beyond that circle he enjoyed the confidence of men whom no such blandishments could win. Not only was he intimate with the Catholic Duke of Ormonde, and his sons, the Earl of Ossory and Lord Arran, but also with that champion of Protestant doctrine, the pious Tillotson. His virtues were appreciated by the Whig Lord Russell, the Tory Lord Hyde, and the Republican Algernon Sydney. Of other men with whom he lived at this time on terms of intimacy, there were the Duke of Buckingham, the Earl of Shaftsbury, the Marquis of Halifax, the Earl of Sunderland, the Earl of Essex, and Lord Churchill. Some of these friends adopted his views on the great subject of Liberty of Faith. Buckingham was supporting a more liberal policy in parliament; and Penn tried very hard to induce him to devote his splendid talents to this national reform. By Penn's advice the Duke made more than one attempt; but the Church party was too wary to be surprised, too powerful to be overthrown; and then a new face, a fresh whim, a fit of the spleen, would distract his grace. In the Duke of York—and in him alone—Penn found a steadfast friend to Liberty of Conscience. Penn availed himself of the royal favour to obtain a pardon for his brethren when they fell under persecution, and to urge on the great work of securing an Act of Toleration from the House of Commons.

But the family with which he held the most intimate relations was that of Sydney. With the several members of this gifted race he lived on friendly terms. Estranged from each other, they put confidence in Penn—appealed to his wisdom in their difficulties, and sometimes placed their interests in his charge. Towards Henry Sydney, a man younger than himself, Penn retained an affection which had commenced in early life; but to his great brother Algernon he was at once a friend and pupil. Henry was nearly twenty years younger than his illustrious brother. He had seen but little of the best period of the Revolution, and had never known the purer and more moderate of its chiefs. Gifted by nature with a handsome face and a voluptuous imagination, he had easily taken up the courtly habits which he found in fashion when he entered life. Between the brothers there was little sympathy, and not much love. In his infancy Algernon had been remarkable for his fine wit and natural sweetness. In the civil war he had made a name for wisdom in the council and for valour in the field. A sincere republican, he had opposed the designs of Cromwell with as much zeal as he had shown in fighting against the King. Abroad at the Restoration, he had lived in exile rather than unsay a single word of his political faith. For seventeen years had he lived abroad; his friends had made great efforts to obtain for him a pardon; but as he would concede nothing, the negotiations had always failed. The utmost that could be drawn from him —though wasting away with sickness—was a declaration to the effect that he was willing to submit to the King, since Parliament had done so. He could on no account regret what he had done, renounce his old opinions, or even ask a pardon. To those who bade him distrust the instincts which made him a wanderer and a beggar in a foreign land, he said, 'I walk in the light which God hath given me. If it be dim or uncertain, I must bear the penalty of my errors. I hope to do it with patience, and that no burden should be very grievous to me except sin and shame. God keep me from these evils, and in all things else dispose of me according to His pleasure.'

After an absence of seventeen years Sydney was allowed to return to his father's death-bed. Penn saw him; they discussed his schemes. A man of Sydney's strength could not remain inactive. Old Commonwealth men looked up to him. A vanquished body, they had great traditions; and were very powerful in the towns. If Sydney never hid his preference of a republic to a monarchy he was willing to help in bringing about reforms in the government,—and one great object of the men with whom he acted was to procure an act of Parliament giving Freedom to Conscience. Buckingham's vanity was flattered with the thought of being at the head of this body of reformers, but the French agent, M. Barillon, saw and said that he was swayed by Sydney.

An impression was produced on the two houses, and in the early part of 1678 there had arisen a more friendly feeling towards Non-conformers. The House of Commons no longer refused to hear of grievances; and Penn presented a petition to that body on behalf of suffering Quakers who had been confounded with the followers of Rome in order to involve them in a common fault and fine. A committee was named to see if it were possible to relieve the great body of Protestants from penalties which had been legally imposed on Catholics. Penn was heard by this committee. 'If,' he said, 'we ought to believe that it is our duty, according to the doctrine of the Apostle, to be always ready to give an account of the hope that is in us to every sober and private inquirer, certainly much more ought we to hold ourselves obliged to declare with all readiness, when called to it by so great an authority, what is *not* our hope; especially when our very safety is eminently concerned in so doing, and when we cannot decline this discrimination of ourselves from Papists without being conscious to ourselves of the guilt of our own sufferings, for so must every man needs be who suffers mutely under another character than that which truly belongeth to him and his belief. That which gives me more than an ordinary right to speak at this time, and in this place, is the great abuse which I have received above any other of my profession; for of a long time I have not only been supposed a Papist, but a Seminary, a Jesuit, an emissary of Rome, and in pay from the Pope; a man dedicating my endeavours to the interest and advancements of that party. Nor hath this been the report of the rabble, but the jealousy and insinuation of persons otherwise sober and discreet. Nay, some zealous for the Protestant religion have been so far gone in this mistake, as not only to think ill of us, and to decline our conversation, but to take courage to themselves to prosecute us for a sort of concealed Papists; and the truth is, we have been as the wool-sacks and common whipping-stock of the kingdom : all laws have been let loose upon us, as if the design were not to reform, but destroy us ; and this not for what we are, but for what we are not. It is hard that we must thus bear the stripes of another interest and be their proxy in punishment. I would not be mistaken. I am far from thinking it fit that Papists should be whipped for their consciences, because I exclaim against the injustice of whipping Quakers for Papists. No ; for though the hand, pretended to be lifted up against them, hath lighted heavily on us, yet we do not mean that any should take a fresh aim at them, or that they should come in our room ; for we must give the liberty we ask ; and cannot be false to our principles, though it were to relieve ourselves. We have good-will to all men, and would have none suffer for a truly sober and conscientious dissent on any hand. And I humbly take leave to add, that those methods against persons so qualified do not seem to me to be convincing, or indeed adequate to the reason of mankind.'

To doubt the policy of whipping Papists, was in that age fatal. Penn, however, spoke the truth ; and spoke it years before John Locke had given it form and breadth. The Church was still a persecuting Church ; the Catholics were intolerant in their practice ; Puritans, Independents, Presbyterians, each appealed in turn to stocks and whipping-posts.

The committee resolved to insert in a bill then before Parliament a clause providing relief ; and in this amended form the bill, having passed a third reading in the lower House, went up under promising auspices to the Peers. The friends of

Toleration were already congratulating each other on a first victory, when, from an obscure and unexpected quarter, burst a storm.

Titus Oates was a minister of the Church of England till his dissolute life had caused him to be expelled. He joined the Roman Catholics; he entered the Jesuits' College at Valladolid; he afterwards removed to that of St. Omer; from both of which he was removed in shame. In these colleges he had heard conversations on the prospects of Catholicism in England, and suggestions for carrying on the good work of its recovery to the ancient faith. A quick imagination framed from these materials the Popish Plot. Oates said he had been trusted by the Jesuits in Spain and France with the conveyance of certain letters and papers; that he had opened these documents out of curiosity; that he had become possessed of dark and terrible secrets. England, he asserted, was to be the scene of a bloody drama. Charles was to be killed. William of Orange was to be also killed. Even James, the Catholic Duke of York, would not be spared. The price of these great crimes had been already paid. Every true Protestant would be murdered. A French army was to land in Ireland. When the reformed faith was put down, the whole country would be given up to the Jesuits. What the real facts—if any—underlying all these fables were, has never been discovered. Men of sober sense believed there were some facts. Sydney, than whom no man in that age had a more thorough knowledge of the Catholic courts, believed in a plot, as Penn believed in a plot. Sir William Temple thought there was a plot.

England was in a temper to receive with eagerness a story of intrigue. The fears of every good Protestant were fed with rumours of the royal apostasy ; and the only cordial friend of the reigning house, the King of France, was known to be a bigoted servant of his church. Some vague idea got abroad that Louis had supplied the court with money. Charles was suspected of a secret leaning towards the religion of his wife and his mistresses, and the Duke of York was an avowed and obstinate Catholic. Contrary to the wishes of Parliament, James had married an Italian ; should there be issue of this alliance, there was a fear that a line of Catholic princes might succeed him. Thus, the feeling of the country was alarmed ; and wild as were the stories told by Oates, they found a willing audience in the streets.

On seeing how much was made of Oates by men of rank and fashion, Bedloe, Dangerfield, and other scoundrels, brought out newer, more astounding tales. The wiser people only laughed at these impostors ; but the affair of Coleman and the murder of Godfrey gave such colour to the charge as made it dangerous to express in public any doubt as to the plot.

CHAPTER XX.

ALGERNON SYDNEY (1678–1679).

SYDNEY and Penn were anxious to have the alleged plot sifted to the quick ; Sydney to uncover Royalist intrigues, and Penn to satisfy his mind about the Jesuits. Sydney looked for a convenient seat. Penn could not go into the House of Commons, but he used his pen to help in what he felt to be his country's need. He issued one address to Quakers. Fearing, in the general consternation, lest some might be led astray, he exhorted them not to be drawn out of their sober course by rumours of plots and conspiracies, but to stand aloof, discharging their duties, in the perilous times which were at hand. He wrote a second address to Protestants of every denomination. These duties done, he wrote a tract entitled 'England's great Interest in the Choice of a new Parliament,' composed with a view to promote the choice of wise and liberal members at the approaching poll.

In the address to Protestants of every party, Penn reviewed the moral question. He began by showing the fallacy of vicarious virtue. If the people would be honestly governed, they must be honest themselves. Vice is the disease of which nations die. No just government ever perished— no unjust government ever long maintained its power. Virtue is the life of society. All history proves it; but if immorality is the chief destroyer of nations, unwise policy is only a little less injurious than active vice. Foremost among errors of policy is the attempt to interfere with thought. Act, not thought, is the proper subject of law. A man's conception of such abstractions as fate, free-will, election, and the like, is not a thing to punish. No less mischievous is the fallacy of measuring conduct by belief. The test of faith is practice. He who acts well believes well. Morality is debased when tested from above. Virtue may be necessary to the state of grace, but grace is not indispensable to virtue. It is a grand mistake to disparage morality under pretence of looking to higher things.

'England's great Interest in the choice of a new Parliament' was political. Sydney and he were much together at this time; and Sydney's hand is traceable in the pamphlet. Sydney was a frequent and cherished guest at Worminghurst. 'All is at stake!' says Penn. 'The times demand the utmost wisdom. The new Parliament will have the gravest duties:—to investigate the plot and punish its authors; to impeach corrupt and arbitrary ministers of state; to detect and punish representatives who have sold their votes to shorten the duration of parliaments; and, finally, to ease Dissenters from the galling cruelties of the Conventicle Act and other similar acts. Such work required bold and able men.' In sketching his man for the day, he had Sydney chiefly in his mind. 'The man for England should,' he urged, 'be able, learned, well affected to liberty; one who will neither buy his seat nor sell his services; he must be free from suspicion of being a pensioner on the court; he should be a person of energy and industry, free from the vices and weaknesses of town gallants; a respecter of principles, but not of persons; fearful of evil, but he should be courageous in good; a true Protestant; above all, a man unconnected by office and favour with the court.'

The writs were issued. Sydney was proposed for Guildford. Penn was at his side.

Hitherto Penn had taken no part in politics. His moral sense was hurt by scenes of low corruption—by the eating and drinking, by the revelries and disorders, by the insolence of officials, by the envy, malice, and uncharitableness to which elections then gave rise. But in the interests of his friend these scruples went for nothing. For Sydney and his cause Penn would have done much more than give a few weeks to canvassing electors, making liberal speeches, and quoting the great charters of our liberty. But government was little pleased to see him acting as the friend of Sydney, and the government had power to make him feel the King's displeasure. His account was still unsettled. Neither principal nor interest of the debts owing to his father had been paid; and it was evident that any settlement of his claim would rest on the good will of Charles and James. It was his interest therefore to be well at court. But he was acting with Sydney; a man who had borne arms against the Stuarts in his ardent youth, and in his riper manhood still avowed himself a partisan of the Commonwealth. To lie under suspicion of republicanism was enough to ruin any public man. When Sydney's hope of sitting for Guildford became known, the Court prepared to oppose his candidature with all its power; but Penn paid no respect to this hostility, and boldly put in peril the chief part of his worldly fortune rather than stand apart.

The day of election drawing nigh, the Court party became very active. Colonel Dalmahoy was sent to stand as 'a King's friend;' the mayor and recorder of the town were bought; bribery, treating, intimidation, all the baser practices, were brought to bear on Guildford. Soldiers were discharged from service on promising to vote for Dalmahoy. Non-residents were sought. Paupers were made to tender votes. To make the Commonwealth-men odious, Penn was accused of being a Jesuit, Sydney was branded as a regicide. For upwards of three weeks the town was a scene of disorder. Both parties feasted their supporters; for the sternest virtue of that age was held to be compatible with cakes and ale.

At length the day of election came. In spite of everything the Court could do, Sydney had promises of a majority of votes. Penn went with his friend to the hustings and made a powerful speech. 'Don't listen to him; he's a Jesuit,' shouted the Recorder; but the people laughed at their Recorder, not at Penn. That officer called for a New Testament and tendered Penn the oaths—well knowing that he would not take them. Penn, the better lawyer of the two, said quietly, the offer of an oath in such a place was contrary to law. At this rebuke the Recorder lost all patience, called his men, and pushed the speaker from his seat.

This use of violence was made too late. Sydney had a majority of votes. But having gone such lengths as he had done to serve his sovereign, the Recorder refused to sanction Sydney's poll, on the plea that he was not a freeman of the town.

Penn and Sydney held a conference of their friends, at which it was resolved to petition against the return of Dalmahoy, and persons were appointed to watch the movements of the enemy and make reports. It was late in the evening when Penn parted from Sydney; he had been from home some time; and he was getting anxious about Guli and the little folks. As he rode along, his mind was deeply troubled at the scenes he had just witnessed —the profligacy and unfairness of the Court party, —the indifference of so many electors,—the contumely heaped on his noble friend, because he and his party 'had a conscientious regard for England.' When he got home he found his family in health; but instead of giving himself up, as usual with him, to domestic intercourse, he went to his room and wrote to Sydney.

'Dear Friend,—I hope you got all well home, as I, by God's goodness, have done. I reflected upon the way of things past at Guildford, and that which occurs to me as reasonable is this, that so soon as the articles or exceptions are digested, we should show them to Sergeant Maynard, and get his opinion of the matter. Sir Francis Winnington and Wallope have been used on these occasions too. Thou must have counsel before the Committee; and to advise first upon the reason of an address or petition with them, in my opinion, is not imprudent, but very fitting. If they say that (the conjecture considered, thy qualifications and alliance, and his ungratefulness to the House) they believe all may amount to an unfair election, then I offer to wait presently upon the Duke of Buckingham, Earl of Shaftsbury, Lord Essex, Lord Halifax, Lord Hollis, Lord Gray, and others, to use their utmost interest in reversing this business. This may be done in five days. I was not willing to stay till I come, which will be with the first. Remember the non-residents on their side, as Legg and others. I left order with all our interest to bestir themselves, and watch, and transmit an account to thee daily. I bless God, I found all well at home. I hope a disappointment so strange (a hundred and forty poll-men as we thought last night considered) does not move thee. Thou, as thy friends, hast a conscientious regard for England; and to be put aside by such base ways is really a suffering for righteousness. Thou hast embarked thyself with them that seek, and love, and choose the best things; and number is not weight with thee. 'Tis late, I am weary, and hope to see thee quickly. Farewell.'

A petition on behalf of Sydney was sent to the House of Commons. Terror of the Popish plot had spread, and seldom before had England returned so implacable and intolerant a parliament. Another crisis soon came on. Monmouth had been sent into banishment, and his mother branded as a wanton. These acts of the Catholic party added fuel to the flame :—and the Houses met in a most threatening mood. Their rage was prompt. Danby was committed to the Tower. The Duke of York was banished the realm. The Whigs —the party led by Shaftsbury and Russell—were on the eve of a decisive victory—when Charles again dissolved.

Sydney prepared to stand again, but not for Guildford. Penn, after riding much about the southern counties, testing the feeling of constituencies, urged him to try the rape of Bramber, where the name of Sydney bore with it assurance of success. The rape of Bramber lay within five miles of Worminghurst, where the Penns had strong connexions ; Springetts, Ellwoods, Faggs, Temples ; and on all of whom they felt that they might count. Penn fell to work with zeal, and in a few days all these families were in Sydney's camp. He tried to enlist the Pelhams in the same cause, though in a recent county election he had opposed that family in favour of Sir John Fagg. As soon as the writs were out, Penn rode to Bramber.

Quick and ardent, he communicated his own zeal to others, and with Sir John Fagg and Sir John Temple as his helpers, he commenced an active canvass. When he spoke of Sydney's virtues, things looked well; but when his partners in the canvass treated the men to beer in Sydney's name, they looked much better. As the rape of Bramber had scarcely a hundred inhabitants, it was not difficult to treat them all. Captain Goring, the court candidate, broached his ale and tossed his cakes. Parsons, the second liberal candidate, treated for himself and Sydney also; meaning, if he saw no chance of carrying both the seats, to yield in Sydney's favour at the poll. Both Fagg and Temple thought their friend's election sure.

In this emergency, the Court resorted to the vilest arts. Knowing the influence which the name of Sydney exercised, Lord Sunderland, whose genius now directed every movement at the palace, formed the plan of opposing brother to brother—arraying one Sydney against another Sydney. Sunderland, being Sydney's nephew, was aware of the divisions in his family. He knew that Henry Sydney, weak by nature, would do anything to please the King. Henry had received some proofs of royal favour, and had reason given him to hope for more. He had been graciously allowed to buy Godolphin's place of Master of the Robes for six thousand pounds. He had been sent to Holland as envoy extraordinary to the Prince of Orange. He could not quarrel with Whitehall; and so he let his name be put up by his brother's foes.

When this design was whispered in the rape of Bramber, Penn would not believe it. But he knew the danger, should report prove true; for the first effect of it would be to carry the Pelham interest to the other side. Penn felt that no time should be lost, and urged on Sydney the importance of his coming down at once:

'DEAR FRIEND,—I am now at Sir John Fagg's, where I and my relations dined. I have pressed the point with what diligence and force I could; and, to say true, Sir John Fagg has been a most zealous, and, he believes, a successful friend to thee. But, upon a serious consideration of the matter, it is agreed that thou comest down with all speed, but that thou takest Hall-Land in thy way, and bringest Sir John Pelham with thee,— which he ought less to scruple, because his having no interest can be no objection to his appearing with thee; the commonest civility that can be is all desired. The borough has kindled at thy name, and takes it well. If Sir John Temple may be credited, he assures me it is very likely. He is at work daily. Another, one Parsons, treats to-day, but for thee as well as himself, and mostly makes his men for thee, and perhaps will be persuaded, if you two carry it not, to bequeath his interest to thee, and then Captain Goring is thy colleague; and this I wish, both to make the thing easier and to prevent offence. Sir John Pelham sent me word, he heard that thy brother Henry Sydney would be proposed to that borough, or already was, and till he was sure of the contrary, it would not be decent for him to appear. Of that thou canst best inform him. That day you come to Bramber, Sir John Fagg will meet you both; and that night you may lie at Wiston, and then, when thou pleasest, with us at Worminghurst.'

Penn wrote a second letter to Pelham to protest against the scandal of Henry's name being used in his absence to the prejudice of Algernon; expressing his fears that this ungenerous act would lead to greater feuds in the Sydney family. Sunderland moved the wires at will; and what with feasting and drinking—the Pelhams contributing half a fat buck—the men of Bramber were divided at the poll. Henry obtained as many votes as his brother. Algernon got the casting voice, and was declared duly returned. Penn now considered his friend about to take his seat, where his counsels and his example might be of service to his country. But as soon as the Houses met, his return was cancelled by a court intrigue.

This second disappointment made a deep impression on the mind of Penn. It drove the rage of Guildford from his thoughts. That Dalmahoy should be willing to take advantage of an honest adversary, that a petty official, whom the court could make or mar at pleasure, should be ready to stain his fame, were things conceivable to him. But that a nephew and a brother—members of an illustrious house, and men whom he had known for years—

should serve the purpose of a base cabal, to the dishonour of their blood, these things were inconceivable to him.   If the nearest relatives of Sydney would not pause at such an act of baseness, what was left for virtue but to flee away from a corrupt society and court?

CHAPTER XXI.

A NEW COUNTRY (1680).

TURNING from the rape of Bramber and the gallery of Whitehall, Penn looked in mind across the ocean. He had made another effort; he had failed; but though he never sank in hope, he felt that there was hardly room in England for a new experiment in freedom to be made. The people were too much divided; some too rich and some too poor; some too learned, some too ignorant; for a frame of government in which every man ought to be the equal of every other man. On finding that a trial could not well be made in England, Penn adopted the romantic scheme of giving up his fortune and his future life to trying this experiment in lands beyond the sea.

In place of the great sums of money due to his deceased father—not a penny of which had yet been paid—he offered to accept a stretch of desert, lying backwards towards the unknown west, beyond the Delaware. This tract was then a wilderness, with here and there a house of wood and thatch, in which some Dutch or Swedish farmer lived. To this wild country he proposed to lead out a colony of citizens, to seek those fortunes and enjoy those liberties in the New World which the evil passions of the older world denied them.   There was poetry and chivalry in such a thought.   The soldier of Kinsale, with the adventurous genius of his race, would be in modern times a hero of romance.   To be a leader of adventurers was not his highest aim.   He wished to found in that wilderness a Free Colony for all nations—an original and august conception; one to keep his name for ever in the memories of mankind. His experiment was to bear witness to the world that there is in human nature virtue for self-government.   In the colony of his brain there should be equal laws.   The sovereignty—judicial, representative, administrative—should be with the people. Every office should be filled by men elected to their functions, and paid out of the public revenue for their services.   The state should employ the best of servants, and admit no masters.   There should be no privileged order.   In Utopia there should be no power, not even his own, above the law.   Justice should be equally administered.   To the natives of the soil he would offer protection, the useful arts, European comforts, above all the gospel.   Love should brood over all his projects.   Freedom of the conscience—equality of political and civil rights—respect for personal liberty—and full regard for the rights of property : these were the points of his scheme.

The block of country lay to the north of that Catholic province of Maryland, which was owned by

Baltimore. For eastern boundary it had the state of New Jersey, with the affairs of which Penn was now familiar. It had only one outlet to the sea ; by means of the river Delaware ; but it stretched inland over an undefined country, across the Alleghannies to the banks of the Ohio on the west, and to Lake Erie on the north. The length of this province was nearly three hundred miles ; its width about one hundred and sixty miles ; and it contained no less than forty-seven thousand square miles of surface ; little less than the entire area of England. Much of the land was hilly, and the hills were green with wood. The Indians hunted elk and deer over its plains, danced the war-dance, and smoked the pipe of peace beneath the shade of its majestic oaks. Nature, it is true, had not been prodigal in this region ; mountain chains covered a large portion of its area ; and while the adjoining states of Virginia, Maryland, and New York, were alive with industry, hardly an English settler had as yet thought of sitting down in this bleaker clime. The winters were severe on the eastern slopes, and men supposed they must be colder in the valleys on the west. Yet the land was rich in many of the best elements of wealth. Between Cape Henlopen and Cape May, the Delaware offered a basin in which the commerce of a great continent would have room. The Susquehannah, the Delaware, the Ohio, the Alleghanny, and a host of rivers either watered the interior of the country or washed its boundaries. It was rich in mineral treasures. Iron was found in a thousand mines; to the west of the Alle-

ghannies lay inexhaustible fields of coal; and an-
thracite beds of the same fossil were found in
almost every part of the province.   Near the banks
of the Ohio lay concealed a treasury of salt-springs.
Limestone was abundant; in the south-east there
was a quarry of marble not unworthy of Italy and
Greece.   Nor was the whole of the province like
the slopes of the mountain districts.   Though the
rock lay near the surface, it was covered with
loam.   Sand and alluvial deposit existed in the
same locality.   Brooks and streams ran down its
valleys, glens, and gorges, fertilising the soil and
breeding myriads of ducks, curlews, geese, and other
water-fowl.   Remarkable for fertility were the lower
flats about the Skuykill and the Delaware.   Between
the head-waters of the Alleghanny and Lake Erie,
and on both banks of the Susquehannah, the soil
was rich and capable of culture.   When the forest
should be felled and the surface cleared, wheat,
barley, rye, Indian corn, hemp, oats, and flax,
would take their place.   The climate had the
softness of the south of France; and the purity of
the atmosphere reminded Penn of Languedoc.   The
forests supplied woods of almost every kind,—
cypress, cedar, chestnut, oak, and walnut.   Poplars
were common.   Oaks of several kinds were found.
The pine, the cedar, and the wild myrtle filled the
air with fragrance; and a slight breeze brought
from the heart of boundless woods a stimulating
scent.   Beasts of prey were absent; but the woods
abounded in wild game, and the venison was superior to anything of the kind out of England.

Fowls grew to an uncommon size ; turkeys to forty or fifty pounds weight a-piece. Partridges and pigeons made the fields vocal with their cries. The rivers yielded fish, especially perch and trout, shad and rock, roach, smelt, and eels. Oysters, crabs, cockles, conch and other shell-fish, were abundant. Fruits grew wild about the country—grapes, peaches, strawberries, plums, chestnuts, and mulberries; while the eye was charmed with the virgin flowers of spring and with the forest radiance of the fall.

But these advantages were not all known. Penn never suspected he was asking for a kingdom in return for a debt of sixteen thousand pounds. He had no hope of making money by his province ; and to his death he never dreamt that it would pay him back the money he had spent. For years it was a waste. In that age people looked on a settlement among the Alleghannies as their descendants look on a removal into the gorges of the Rocky Mountains. Men went thither who could settle nowhere else. When Gustavus Adolphus came to the throne of Sweden he found nearly the whole of the American continent in the possession of one or other power ; but anxious, as he said, 'to convert the heathen and to extend his dominions ; to enrich the treasury and lessen the public taxes,' he sent out colonists from Sweden to take possession of the unoccupied country on the Delaware. This colony was the beginning of a state. They found a few Dutch settlers there, who had at first no friendly feeling towards the new comers. But they found that these industrious neighbours would be useful to them; for the Swedes turned their attention to farming, while the Hollanders preferred to fetch and carry, and to buy and sell. They suited each other. With the Swedes went out a number of Finns; and a village was formed by them at Wicocoa, now within the suburbs of Philadelphia. The Swedes bestowed the name of New Suabia on the whole country, and scattered themselves far and wide over its surface. They had, however, advanced but a little way towards the formation of a state when Penn became a petitioner to the King. Not a single house had been built at Philadelphia—a spot marked out by nature as the site of a great city; for such of the Hollanders as fixed their residence at the confluence of the two rivers were content to harbour in the holes and caves.

The red men were a branch of the Lenni Lenapé. This name, signifying 'the original people,' was a common term, under which were included all the Indian tribes speaking dialects of the widely-spread Algonquin language. An obscure tradition among them pointed to a great migration from the west, in ages long ago. They may have been the remnants of a conquering race which had subdued and swept away the civilised people whose monuments still arrest attention in the great valley of the Mississippi. The northern regions were held by Iroquois—a race of red men famous in the history of New York under the name of the Six Nations. As compared with whites, the tribes presented the same general characteristics — they were hardy, cunning, cruel, brave. They claimed the lordship of the soil as theirs by immemorial right.   But as they hunted only, the grounds were of no use to them except so long as the rivers yielded fish and the forests yielded game.   Men who have no fixed place of residence—no altars and no homes—have yet to acquire the means whereby a sense of property in the soil grows up.   The Iroquois and the Lenapé built no cities—permanently kept no fields.   Wherever the woods afforded sport the lodge was pitched. The men tightened their bows and sharpened their hatchets ; the women planted a rood or two of maize ; and when the forest spoils and field produce were got in, they marched to more attractive spots. Their sachem was an hereditary ruler ; but the order of succession was by the female line.   The children of the reigning sachem could not succeed him in his regal office, but the next son of his mother, after whom came in the sister's eldest son.

Such was the country which Penn petitioned the King to grant him in lieu of his claim.

A year was wasted in debates.   The Royalists lost all patience when they heard that Penn was asking for a grant of land, to put in practice certain theories held to be Utopian by wise and moderate politicians, and denounced by courtier and cavalier as dangerous to the Crown and State. Events had slackened his hold on James.   Penn had publicly expressed his belief in the Popish plot ; he had influenced his friends openly to support Sydney ; he had himself become a leader among the Republicans.   He had committed a still greater offence in the eyes of James—he had stood between that prince and his prey. As lord-proprietor of the whole province of New Netherlands, James had claimed the right to levy an import and export tax upon all articles entering or leaving its ports. So long as James retained the land as well as the seignorial right, this claim was not disputed; consequently traders carrying goods to or from New Jersey paid to his agents a duty of ten per cent. When Billing got the land, this tax was felt to be a wrong; the colonists invited Penn to act for them; and, having considered the justice of their case, Penn proceeded against his royal guardian in the law courts. Sir William Jones decided the case in favour of Penn and the colonists; the Duke at once submitted; but it is impossible to believe that he would not feel sore at his defeat. To the coldness of the prince was added the active hostility of Lord Baltimore, whose ill-defined possessions were supposed to be invaded by the new boundary-line. Baltimore was one of those who stood in Oates's black list; he was not in the country; but he had friends at court, who watched his interests; and Penn's petition was no sooner laid before the council, than a copy of it was sent to his agent, Burke, who took such measures as he thought most likely to defeat it. All the dilatory forms of the Royal Council were used; the Lord Commissioners of Trade and Plantation wrote long letters about trifles to the Attorney-general, and the Attorney-general wrote with similar tact to the Lords Commissioners. Penn's time and hopes were wasting. Sunderland was an active friend; and Hyde, Chief Justice

North, and the Earl of Halifax, were also on his side. These prudent friends advised him to be silent as to his Free Colony until his patent had been signed. The name of Freedom was offensive at Whitehall.

CHAPTER XXII.

PENNSYLVANIA (1680–81).

At first, the Duke of York was not in favour of the grant; and the Attorney-general, Sir Joseph Warden, was instructed to oppose it in his name. James thought the boundary line too loose, the rights of seigniory too large. But Sunderland kept the King's attention fixed on the alternative mode of paying off the score. A peerage and a sum of sixteen thousand pounds were due. If Penn were willing to accept a lordship on the Deleware in lieu of a barony on the Wey, a patch of waste woodland in lieu of sixteen thousand pounds in money, Sunderland thought the King would make a very good bargain for the crown. Sir Thomas Thynne was hankering after Weymouth; the royal treasury was empty; and the King could hardly make another man Viscount Weymouth while the Admiral's dues were still unpaid.

This argument in favour of the grant decided Charles. Had there been money in the coffers, Penn would not have gained his prayer, and Pennsylvania would have been reclaimed and planted by another race of men. Five months after Penn's petition was sent in, Sir Joseph wrote to inform Secretary Blathwayte that the Duke of York consented to Penn's request. What now remained, was the arrangement of details. But this task occupied a second five months. The chief questions which came up for discussion had reference to boundaries and constitutions. Agents of the Duke of York were heard by the Privy Council; Burke appeared for Lord Baltimore; and both parties laid down objections to the boundary-line as drawn by Penn. Penn's counsel made the best of their position; their client being anxious to obtain a well-marked line; but the parties could not come to terms. At length, the grant was made by the Council with no proper understanding of the question, in a vain hope that the proprietors would be able to arrange their differences among themselves. This omission led to much dispute in after-times. The terms of the charter then came on. Penn had forgotten some of our less liberal laws and usages; but the Attorney-general and the Lord Chief Justice remedied his defects by adding clauses to the charter. They reserved all royal privileges. They provided for the authority of Parliament in questions of trade and commerce. Acts of the colonial legislature were to be submitted to the King. Above all, they reserved to the mother country the right to levy rates. The Bishop of London got a clause inserted claiming security for the English Church.

All these preliminaries being arranged, the Lords

of Trade and Plantations submitted the draft of a charter constituting Penn proprietor of his great estates. On Thursday, February 24, 1681, Charles set his signature to the document, too happy to cancel a very large and troublesome debt.

A council was called for Saturday, the 5th of March, at Whitehall, which Penn was summoned to attend. The name which Penn had fixed on for his province was New Wales; but Secretary Blathwayte, a Welshman, objected to have the Quaker country called after his native land. Penn proposed Sylvania, on account of the magnificent forests. Penn means great and high; and Charles, who loved a word of double meaning, added Penn to Sylvania; partly as a compliment to his old admiral, and partly as descriptive of the country. Penn, being fearful lest it would appear in him a piece of vanity to allow a principality to be called by his name, appealed to the King, and offered twenty guineas to the Secretary, to have it changed. Had he appealed to Blathwayte, and bribed the King, he might have had his wish. But Charles took upon himself the name; and the patent was then issued in the usual form.

The document itself is in the office of the Secretary of Pennsylvania; it is written on rolls of strong parchment, in the old English handwriting, each line underscored with red ink; the borders are emblazoned with devices, and the top of the first sheet exhibits a portrait of King Charles. It briefly sets forth the nature and reasons of the grant, and loosely describes the boundaries of the province. This document, not yet two centuries old, is regarded in America with veneration.

Four weeks after Charles had signed his patent, Penn sent out his cousin, Colonel William Markham, with his orders to take possession of the country, to inform the natives of his coming over, and assure them of his friendly feeling; to select a piece of land near Trenton Falls on which to build a house, and settle with Lord Baltimore the question of their frontier lines.

The grant of his petition was a great event for Penn. Penn knew the grandeur and the purity of his design. If Sydney felt that the cause of freedom was at issue, Penn believed that the experiment involved no less than the cause of human nature and of God. While waiting the turns of his negotiations he saw how one false step, one rash word, one imprudent concession, might put the whole of his great scheme in peril. When the charter was issued he exclaimed, 'God hath given it to me in the face of the world. . . . He will bless and make it the seed of a nation.'

In this spirit he commenced his labours as a legislator. Warned by the failure of the constitution drawn up by Locke and Shaftsbury for Carolina, which their friends had declared would last for ever, —Penn resolved, at Sydney's instance, to secure a democratic basis for his scheme, and then allow the details to fall in with time. He therefore drew a frame of government, the preamble of which — like the declaration of rights and principle prefixed to modern constitutions — contained his leading

ideas on the nature, origin, and object of government. His sentiments, as exhibited in this document, are liberal, wise, and noble. He begins by
expressing his conviction that government is of
divine origin: and bears the same sort of relation
to the outer that religion does to the inner man.
An outward law, he says, is needed in the world
because men will not obey the inward light; in the
words of an Apostle, 'The law was added on account
of sin.' They err, he says, who fancy that government has only to coerce the evil-doers; it has also
to encourage the well-disposed, to shield virtue,
to reward merit, to foster art, to promote learning.
As to models of government, he says little. Vice
will vitiate every form; and while men side with
their passions against their reason, neither monarchy
nor democracy can preserve them from corruption.
Governments depend more on men than men on
governments. If men are wise and virtuous, the
governments under which they must live also become wise and virtuous; it is therefore essential to
the stability of a state that the people be educated in
noble thoughts and virtuous deeds. A people
making their own laws and obeying them faithfully,
will be a free people, while those laws exist, whatever be the *name* of the constitution under which
they live.

The counsels of Halifax and Sunderland were not
lost. Without using terms which would have roused
the jealousy of Whitehall, Penn contrived to express
the chief of his ideas in a clear and practical shape.
He concludes his preface by saying that 'in reverence

to God and good conscience towards men,' he has formed his scheme of government so as 'to support power in reverence with the people, and to secure the people from the abuse of power, that they may be free by their just obedience, and the magistrates honourable for their just administration.'

The constitution, a rough draft only, followed. It had been drawn up with care by Penn and Sydney. Sydney went down to Worminghurst for the purpose; and there the two lawgivers drew up the first outlines. Every phrase employed was tested by the most advanced theories of democracy and by the practice of ancient and modern nations. Penn changed his terms whenever Sydney expressed a doubt. When the first rudiments were moulded into shape, Sydney carried the papers home with him to Penshurst, to consider and re-consider the various clauses; when his mind was fully satisfied as to their form and substance, he brought them back. So intricate, so continuous, was this mutual aid, that it is now impossible to separate the work of one legislator from that of the other—Penn's share from Sydney's—Sydney's share from Penn's.

The constitution begins by declaring that the sovereign power resides in the governor and freemen of the province. For purposes of legislation, two bodies are to be elected by the people—a Council and an Assembly. The proprietor, or his deputy, is to preside at the council, and to have three votes. These votes are the only power which he reserves to himself or to his agents. The functions of the council are, to prepare and propose bills—to see the laws duly executed—to watch over the peace and safety of the province—to determine the sites of new towns and cities—to build ports, harbours, and markets—to make and repair roads—to inspect the public treasury—to erect courts of justice, institute primary schools, and reward the authors of useful inventions and discoveries. This body, consisting of seventy-two persons, is to be chosen by universal suffrage for three years; twenty-four of them retiring every year, whose places are to be supplied by new elections. The members of the assembly are to be elected annually. The votes are to be taken by ballot; the members are to be paid; and the suffrage is to be universal. There are no property qualifications, and the whole country is to be divided into sections. The assembly has no deliberative power. All acts of the council are to be laid before it for approval or rejection. It has the privilege of making out a list of persons to be named as justices and sheriffs, of which list the governor is bound to select one half.

To this outline of a .constitution are added forty provisional laws, relating to liberty of conscience, to choice of civil officers, to provision for the poor, to processes at law, to fines, arrests, and other matters of a civil nature. These provisional laws are to be in force until the council has been properly elected, when they are to be either accepted, amended, or rejected, as the popular representatives think proper; Penn agreeing with Sydney, that no men can know what laws are needful so well as those whose lives, properties, and liberties are concerned. On this point the constitutions of Pennsylvania and Delaware, and after them the constitution of the United States, owe an eternal obligation to Sydney. Penn, like More, like Harrington, and the writers on Utopian schemes, desired to have a fixed system of public law. He would have drawn his constitutions and offered them to the world as the conditions of settlement in his new colony. Shaftsbury and Baltimore had adopted such a mode. With ruling instinct, Sydney saw that a democracy is incompatible with a foreign body of constitutional law. He proposed, therefore, to leave this question open. Having fixed the great boundary-lines of the system—secured freedom of thought (always Penn's first care), sacredness of person and property, popular control over all the powers of the state, financial, civil, proprietorial, and judicial—the lawgivers left the new democracy to develope itself in accordance with its natural wants. America owes much to Sydney.

An outline of the new political system being drawn up, Penn began to organise. The elements were prepared. So soon as it was whispered that the champion of trial by jury had become the owner and governor of a province in the New World, and that he proposed to settle it on the broadest principles of popular right, from nearly every large town in the three kingdoms, and from many cities of the Rhine and Holland, agents were despatched to treat with the new lord for lands. Societies were formed for emigration. A German company started up at Frankfort. Franz Pastorius came to London, where he bought fifteen thousand acres lying in one tract on a navigable river, and three thousand acres within the liberties of the new city. Liverpool furnished many purchasers and settlers, London more. At Bristol a company was organised under the name of Free Society of Traders in Pennsylvania; and in the autumn Penn rode down to that city to confer with Moore, Ford, Claypole, and other adventurers on their plans. Penn was anxious to encourage skilful manufacturers of wool to migrate from the neighbourhood of Bristol and the valley of Stroud; for in the early stage of his experiment these were the staples on which he based his expectations of success. Desiring freedom for trade as well as freedom for the person, he resisted every temptation to reserve to himself profitable monopolies, just as in his constitutions he had refused to retain official patronage. A few weeks after the charter was issued, Thurston and Maryland sent an agent to offer him a fee of 6000*l*. and 2½ per cent as rental, if he would allow a company to be formed with an exclusive right to trade in beaver-skins between the Delaware and Susquehannah rivers. Other proprietors granted such monopolies; Penn's right to grant them was unquestionable; but he felt that such monopolies were unjust, and he refused the money and the yearly rent. A Free Society of Traders realised one of his own ideas, and he afforded the Bristol company great facilities. Nicolas Moore, a lawyer, was appointed chairman of this company. Having bought twenty thousand acres of land, they published articles of trade, and commenced preparations for the voyage. Some persons from the principality joined the Bristol colonists, and zeal being backed by money, things were soon so far advanced that a vessel filled with emigrants, and taking out the chairman, Nicolas Moore, was ready to set sail.

CHAPTER XXIII.

CLEARING GROUND (1681–82).

PHILIP FORD, a Bristol Quaker and a leading member
of the Free Society of Traders, gained the confidence
of Penn, and was appointed as his agent in the
western port. This Ford was one of those sedate
and sallow rogues who made a business of religion,
and was lashed by every writer for the comic stage.
He had the face of Cantwell and the hand of Over-
reach. Penn saw that he was quick and cere-
monious, and fancied he was honest and sincere.
For many years he was the agent through whose
hands receipts and payments on the largest scale
were made, but many years elapsed before the family
of Penn became aware how much of what was properly their own stuck fast to Ford.

When Markham landed on the Delaware he
made known a letter from Penn to the people of
Pennsylvania, under date of April 8, 1681, announcing the issue of his patent, and explaining the
spirit in which he should proceed to plant a free
state in that country. Then he called the Indian
sachems into council, and surprised the redskins by

inquiring whether they would sell a piece of land near the Trenton Falls to the new lord; and if so, what would be their price? The new lord, whom the great King had set to rule and own the country, was, he said, a just man, who would neither do them wrong himself nor suffer any of his sons to do them wrong. He meant to live with them in love; to buy their lands if he should want it; and to trade with them in open market, as a white man bought and sold with white men. In July the terms of sale were fixed; in August they were signed by Markham on behalf of Penn, and by the various sachems who had claims on the estate; and Colonel Markham set about to clear the woods and stake the buildings of the homestead afterwards known as Pennsbury Manor. Markham had less success with Baltimore than with the Indians; but his opening moves in that game of chance and skill—the boundary question—left a deep impression of his tact. He was in truth too able and too worldly in such things to be a fitting deputy for an idealist like Penn.

While Markham was buying Pennsbury Manor from the sachems, Penn was putting out in London articles of concession for intending colonists. In these concessions he described the country and the constitution, and he dwelt with vigour on the line of conduct he intended to pursue towards natives of the soil. From Cortez and Pizarro downwards, Europeans in America had treated the aborigines as property. Not content with robbing them of their lands, their lakes, their hunting-grounds, their ornaments of pearl and gold, the pale-faces from Seville and Cartagena had seized their persons and compelled them, under terror of the rod, to toil and die. When some of the bolder spirits among these natives fled from the faces of their tyrants, they were hunted down like wolves, and either worried by blood-hounds or sent to painful death in the mines. Even Puritan settlers, flying from an unjust rule at home, had been at war with natives of the soil, and more than one scene of treachery stains the page of New England history. Penn, strong in his belief in human goodness, would not arm his followers even for their own defence. In his province the sword should cease to be the symbol of authority; no soldier and no cannon should be seen; he would rely on justice and on courtesy to win the confidence of those whom it had hitherto been the vice of his countrymen to treat as foes.

In the autumn two vessels, called the *Amity* and the *John Sarah*, sailed from the Thames, and a third vessel, called the *Bristol Factor* from the Avon. Penn had now completed his scheme with regard to the Indians, and by the *John Sarah* he sent out three commissioners, William Crispin, John Bezar, and Nathaniel Allen, with written instructions to buy land from them in his name, to arrange a regular course of trade, and enter into treaties of peace and friendship. At sea the two vessels from the Thames parted company. The *Amity* was driven by storms among the West Indian islands, and did not reach the Delaware till the following spring. The *John Sarah* was the first to make land;

but the *Bristol Factor* soon afterwards appeared in the river. As they slowly cut the stream, the passengers observed some cottages on the right bank, forming the Swedish village of Upland, and it being nearly dark, with a long winter night before them in an unknown river, they thought it best to pull up. While the adventurers were enjoying themselves in their own fashion on shore, a sudden frost set in, and next morning they found to their alarm that the vessel was locked in ice. The hospitable Swedes offered them such protection as their scanty homesteads yielded; such as could not obtain the shelter of a roof dug holes in the ground or piled up earthen huts; and here at last they determined to wait patiently for the coming spring. Many of these accidential settlers in Upland were still there when Penn arrived next year.

Meanwhile the friends of the Holy Experiment were busy in England and on the Continent. The Lords of Plantation had left several sources of uncertainty in the grant. The quarrel with Baltimore seemed to threaten angry and expensive litigation; for between the Catholic lord and the Quaker lord irreconcilable views as to the nature and aims of government came in to embitter the dispute. Colonel Markham held conference after conference with Baltimore, but without result. Each appealed to his political friends in England, where the King himself took part with Penn, and felt sufficient interest in the matter to write more than one letter to Lord Baltimore about the boundary lines. Some claims advanced on behalf of the Duke of York were hardly less important to the settlers. James had not consented to forego his seignorial rights over the province. Penn considered it essential to his plans that no hostile power should ever be able to shut his people out from commerce with the world—an event clearly possible if the mouth of the Delaware was to be held by an enemy. To prevent an evil of so much magnitude to the future state, Penn obtained from His Royal Highness a grant of the strip of land fronting the Delaware from Coaquannoc to Cape Henlopen, then called the Territories, now forming the State of Delaware. Some months elapsed before these great affairs could be arranged with the Duke's agents; but on Wednesday, the 24th of August, two drafts of conveyance were sent by his Royal Highness to the Board of Trade, in which he formally made over all his rights and titles in these estates to Penn and his heirs for ever. These important concessions relieved the new proprietor from every immediate fear; and Penn was now become the lord paramount of territories almost as large as England. James behaved to him in all these matters like an honest guardian and a faithful friend.

Excited by his happy fortunes, Penn pushed on his preparations for the voyage with zeal. William Bradford, a printer of Leicester, agreed to go out with his presses. Wallis, the famous mathematician, suggested how much Penn might do to extend the domain of science. Statesmen were at fault as to the geography of America; its natural history was hardly better known to scholars.

Penn agreed to make and transmit to England observations on points of scientific interest; and the Royal Society, then recently founded, elected him a member.

Lady Penn, the merry romp and loving mother, died while he was hurrying on these preparations for his voyage. She was affectionate to her son, without understanding his principles or altogether approving his conduct. Her removal was a blow to him; his sister, Margaret Lowther, being the only one now left to him of his father's blood. For many days he was unable to bear the light; and weeks elapsed before the usual calm returned to his heart—the habitual activity to his brain.

The *Welcome*, which was to take him out to America, was already in the Downs. Compared with many other ships then navigating the Atlantic, the *Welcome*, carrying three hundred tons burden, was a stately bark. On deck a hundred pale and anxious faces gathered; it was getting deep into the autumn, and a winter voyage was then regarded with alarm. The men were well-to-do, and many of them had been used from their birth to all the comforts of life. As yet the Governor was on shore; but his servants, his furniture, his wine, his guns, his horses, his provisions, his wardrobe, his carved doors and window-frames, and the whole interior decoration of the house at Pennsbury Manor, were on board.

The voyage might last from six to fourteen weeks according to the wind and weather, and every man had to be provisioned for the longer term. It is not to be supposed that Friends going out to found a free state denied themselves the consolations of meat and drink. A list of comforts put on board one vessel leaving the Delaware for London on behalf of a Quaker preacher, gives us—32 fowls, 7 turkeys, 11 ducks, 2 hams, a barrel of china oranges, a large keg of sweetmeats, a keg of rum, a pot of tamarinds, a box of spices, ditto of dried herbs, 18 cocoa-nuts, a box of eggs, six balls of chocolate, six dried codfish and five shaddock, six bottles of citron-water, four bottles of madeira, five dozen of good ale, one large keg of wine and nine pints of brandy. There was also much solid food in the shape of flour, sheep, and hogs. Imagine a hundred emigrants so furnished; the grunting of hogs, the screaming of fowls, the bah-ing of sheep, the gabbling of ducks, the litter of bags and boxes, the breaking of bottles, the rolling of barrels, the shouts of the sailors, the anxious faces of men and women about to try a new world—imagine this, and the reader has a picture of the *Welcome* as she lay off Deal on the first day of September, 1682, waiting the arrival of Governor Penn.

Everything being arranged as to the public duties of his mission, the Coloniser gave up his last thoughts in England to Guli and his family. To Springett had been given a brother William, and a sister Lettie. In an age of ' ferries' .it is not easy to conceive the feelings of a man who was about to make the voyage to America. Half a century later a Yorkshire squire conceived it necessary to make his will before starting on a trip

to London; still more needful were such preparations thought when a man proposed to cross the
Atlantic. Penn had wished to take his family out
with him; for it was his wish to settle in the
country now become his own; but information as
to perils and privations to be encountered by the
first settlers, consideration for Guli's health, then
delicate, and for the education of his children,
caused him to abandon this idea. Yet he was not
happy.   Death had snatched away two of those
experienced persons in whose care he could have
left them : Isaac Pennington and Lady Penn. The
grandmother of his little children was at hand.
On Lady Springett, Thomas Ellwood, and other
attached and faithful friends, he felt he could rely;
and yet, with all these solaces, it was a bitter thing
to part from his family for months—for years—and
it might easily be for ever; to encounter danger in
unaccustomed shapes, storms at sea, tropical fevers,
hardships in the wilderness; nay, more—as, in the
faith of an expounder of new doctrines—he was
about to place himself, unarmed, in the power of
savages, too much accustomed to the tomahawk
and scalping-knife—and though a strong believer
in the native virtues of the Redskins, when these
savages were treated well,—he could not help feeling
that before he might have time to impress their
minds with confidence in his integrity of purpose,
some mischance might lead him into peril of his
life.

He made his arrangements as if he were never
to return. His hope was to prepare a home for

those whom he was now about to leave behind; but being doubtful whether Providence had not designed this leave to be his final one, he wrote at length his parting admonitions to his wife and children. This testament is full of wise and noble counsels, earnestly conceived, and tenderly conveyed. Foreseeing that his Holy Experiment might be a drain on his private means, he wishes Guli to be economical, though not parsimonious, in her household. She is to make one great exception, however; in the education of his children she is not to spare. He means the education to be useful and practical. Springett and William are to acquire a sound knowledge of building, ship-carpentry, measuring, levelling, surveying, and navigation; but he desires that their chief attention shall be given to agriculture. Lettie is to pay attention to the affairs of a household as well as to the accomplishments of her sex: 'Let my children be husbandmen and housewifes.' In his parting moments he did not forget that his little children might become the rulers of his province,— and his wishes on this subject were recorded for their guidance. 'As for you,' he writes, 'who are likely to be concerned in the government of Pennsylvania, I do charge you before the Lord God and His holy angels, that you be lowly, diligent, and tender, fearing God, loving the people and hating covetousness. Let justice have its impartial course, and the law free passage. Though to your loss, protect no man against it; for you are not above the law, but the law above you. Live therefore the lives yourselves you would have the people live, and then you will have right and boldness to punish the transgressor. Keep upon the square, for God sees you: therefore do your duty, and be sure you see with your own eyes, and hear with your own ears. Entertain no lurchers, cherish no informers for gain or revenge; use no tricks; fly to no devices to support or cover injustice; but let your hearts be upright before the Lord, trusting in Him above the contrivances of men, and none shall be able to hurt or supplant you.'

On the first of September the *Welcome* weighed anchor at Deal, passed the Foreland with a light breeze. At Deal they shipped a case of small-pox. At first the disease was mild, and they went on; but before they reached the middle of the Atlantic nearly every man, woman, and child, was sick. During two weeks some one died almost every day Of the hundred passengers on board, more than thirty fell. Care, attention, and the Governor's stores, were given without stint. By day and night Penn sat in the cabins of the infected persons, speaking words of comfort to all, giving medicines to such as needed them, and affording the consolations of religion to the dying. In his labours he was much assisted by his friend Pearson, an emigrant from Chester. Want of room and want of fresh provisions were the two chief evils which he could not meet. One boy was born at sea; but many boys and girls, as well as grown-up people, died. The voyage was rather long, and it was deep in October when the low and wooded banks of the Delaware broke on the straining sights of men still struggling with the mortal fear of death.

October 27, 1682, just nine weeks after quitting Deal, the *Welcome* moored off the port of Newcastle, in Delaware, the country lately given up to him by the Duke of York.

CHAPTER XXIV.

IN THE WILDERNESS (1682).

PENN'S landing made a general holiday in the town ; for young and old, Dutch, English, Swedes, and Germans, crowded to the landing-place, each eager to catch a glimpse of the man who was said to come amongst them, less as their lord and governor than as their friend.

Next day he called the people together in the Dutch court-house, when he went through the legal forms of taking possession. Deeds were produced and charters read. The agents of the Duke of York surrendered the territory in their master's name by the usual form of giving earth and water. Penn's great powers being legally established, he addressed the people in profoundest silence. He spoke of the reasons for his coming—the great idea which he had nursed from his youth upwards —his desire to found a free and virtuous state, in which the people should rule themselves. He then explained the nature of his powers ; assuring those who heard him that he wished to exercise them only provisionally and for the general good. He

P

spoke of the constitution he had published for Pennsylvania as containing his theory of government; and promised the settlers on the lower reaches of the Delaware, that the same principles should be adopted in their territory. Every man in his provinces, he said, should enjoy liberty of conscience and his share of political power. As earnest of his intention to proceed on fixed and just principles in the colony, he ended by renewing in his own name the commissions of all existing magistrates.

The people listened to this speech with wonder and delight. They were but simple husbandmen —soft words were not among the things on which they set much store; but that old northern instinct which had led them from the Rhine, the Elbe, and Zuyder Zee, in search of freedom on the shores of the Delaware, told them that the landing of this English Governor was an era in their lives. They had but one request to make in answer; that he would stay amongst them and reign over them in person. They besought him to annex their territory to Pennsylvania, in order that the white settlers might have one country, one parliament, and one ruler. He promised, at their desire, to take the question of a union of the two provinces into consideration, and submit it to an assembly then about to meet at Upland. So he took his leave.

Ascending the Delaware, enjoying the beauty of nature as every bend in the river brought some charm to sight, and breathing the mild air of that southern climate, the adventurers soon arrived at the Swedish town of Upland, then the place of chief importance in the province. Penn was received and lodged in the house of Wade. The spot where he stepped on shore is still shown to strangers with a patriotic pride. Wishing to mark the fact by some striking circumstance, he turned round to his companion Pearson, a man equally eminent for his free spirit and his humane virtues, and observed, 'Providence has brought us safely here; thou hast been the companion of my toils; what wilt thou that I should call this place?' After a moment's thought, Pearson, whose modesty would not allow him to propose his own name, answered, 'Chester; in remembrance of the city whence I came.' So Penn changed the name from Upland to Chester, and as Chester it is known.

Markham and the three commissioners had done their work so well that in a short time after Penn's arrival, the first General Assembly, elected by universal suffrage, was ready to meet. The Friends' Meeting-house, a plain brick edifice, fronting the creek, and opposite to Wade's house, where Penn remained a guest, was selected for the purpose. Nicolas Moore, an English lawyer, and already chairman to the Free Society of Traders, was elected speaker; and as soon as Penn had given them assurances similar to those which he had made in Newcastle, they proceeded to discuss, amend, and accept the Frame of Government and the Provisional Laws. The settlers on the Delaware sent representatives to this Assembly, and one of their first acts was to declare the two provinces united. The constitution was adopted without important alteration; and to the forty laws were added twenty-one others, and the infant code was passed in form.

The new laws only regulated the practical working of ideas and principles embodied in the frame of government; the chief of them providing—that every man should be free to believe in any doctrine whatever not destructive of the peace and honour of civil society; that every Christian man of twenty-one years, unstained by crime, should be eligible to elect and be elected a member of the Colonial Parliament; that every child of twelve, whether rich or poor, should be instructed in some useful trade or skill, all work being honourable in a democratic state, all idleness a shame; that fees of law should be fixed at a low rate, and hung up in every court of justice; that persons wrongly imprisoned should have double damages from the prosecutor; that prisons should be changed from nurseries of vice, idleness, and misery, into houses of industry, honesty, and education. These legislators adopted the humane views of their Governor even where they seemed to be least supported by tradition and experience. The English penal laws were much at variance with Penn's ideas; and at one bold stroke he blotted out the whole catalogue of crimes punished with death excepting only two,—the crimes of murder and treason. The Assembly passed a law embodying this humane and enlightened policy, and also a general act of naturalisation for aliens. There was little talk, much work in this first parliament. On the third day the session was completed, and Penn prorogued the members. They had left their ploughs for half a week; they had met together and made a State.

No reader needs to be reminded how the moral sentiment and state policy of Europe and America have followed in the wake of these ideas. Toleration was in Penn's day but the creed of those who doubted everything; religious men of almost every shade denied it as a suggestion of the evil spirit. Locke could ask for charity towards error, as he found no certitude in truth; but earnest Christians, holding God's Word to be infallible, could show no mercy to the unbeliever. Governor Bradford, one of the noblest of the Pilgrim Fathers, had denounced the folly of toleration as tending to misrule. Endicott had on one occasion said to his prisoner—Renounce your religion or die. President Oakes had looked on toleration as the first-born of all abominations. These were statesmen, but the clergy had been no less hot against opinion. It is doing the religious martyrs of the New World no wrong to say that the cruelties exercised by them on men who differed in opinion were worthy of the best days of the Star Chamber and the Court of Inquisition. Penn was equally before his sect and country. It remained for Howard, Eden, and Romilly, more than a century after that Colonial Assembly met in Chester, to introduce Penn's principles into the administration of our prisons and the reformation of our penal code.

Penn paid some visits to the neighbouring seats of government in New York, Maryland, and the

Jerseys. At West River, Lord Baltimore came forth to meet him with a retinue of the chief persons in the province. Colonel Tailler offered the hospitalities of his mansion in the Ridge, Anne Arundel county, to these visitors, and they held a long and spirited conference. It was impossible to adjust the boundary, and the two proprietors separated with the resolution to maintain their several rights. Penn had sent out a surveyor, Thomas Holme, some months before he himself left England; and this able servant, assisted by Markham and the commissioners, had already held interviews with the Indian sachems, made extensive purchases of land, and acquired so much knowledge of the interior as to enable him to divide the whole province into counties. The lands already bought from the Redmen were now put up for sale at four-pence an acre, with a reserve of one shilling for every hundred acres as quit-rent; the latter sum intended to form a state revenue for the Governor's support. In marking out the various districts Penn set apart equal lots for each of his three children. Two manors of ten thousand acres each he reserved as a present for the Duke of York. Amidst these sales and settlements he recollected George Fox, for whose use and profit he set aside a thousand acres of the best land in the province, free of all claims for quit-rent, costs of transfer, and even of title-deeds.

Penn was no less careful for the Redskins. Laying on one side all ceremonial manners, he won their hearts by his easy confidence and familiar speech. He walked with them alone into the forests. He sat with them on the ground to watch the young men dance. He joined in their feasts, and ate their roasted hominy and acorns. When they expressed delight at seeing the great Onas (native name for Penn) imitate their national customs, not to be outdone in any of those feats of prowess which the Red men value, Penn, in whom the swordsman of Paris and the volunteer of·Carrick-fergus were not lost, leapt up from his seat, entered the lists, and beat them all; on seeing which the younger warriors could hardly control the extravagance of their joy.

Markham had already made his purchase of land, and entered with the natives into a treaty of peace and amity. When he had explained to them the beneficent intentions of the great man who was coming to live and trade with them; when he had told them that, although the King had granted him the whole country, from the Cape of Henlopen to those distant regions stretching away beyond the great mountains to the northern lakes, of which their people had remote traditions, yet he would not take from them by force a single rood of their hunting-grounds, but would buy it from them with their full consent; when he had told them that the great Onas would never allow his children to wrong the Indians, to cheat them of their fish, their wild game, or their beaver-skins; that in his just mind he had ordained that if a quarrel should ever arise in that country between a white man and a red one, twelve men, six Indian and six English, should meet together and judge them; when he laid before them the presents which he had brought as a sign of amity and good-will from his master, the sachems gave the wampum belt to the young colonel, and replied, with all the emphasis of sincerity, 'We will live in peace with Onas and his children as long as the sun and moon endure.'

Beyond this purchase Penn felt that, for the moment, it would be unwise to go. Their hunting-grounds were dear to them. Had he shown desire to possess their lands before he had secured their friendship, suspicions would have been engendered in their minds. The experiment he had to conduct was so novel that care was needful at every step. It would have been madness to offend the Iroquois, while the settlers in his villages refused to carry arms. Not till he had spent seven months in the country would he make proposals for the purchase of unoccupied lands. Having now become intimate with Taminent and other of the native kings, who had approved these treaties, seeing great advantages in them for their people, he proposed to hold a conference with the chiefs and warriors, to confirm the former treaties and form a lasting league of peace.

On the banks of the Delaware, in the suburbs of the rising city of Philadelphia, lay a natural amphitheatre, used from time immemorial as a place of meeting for the native tribes. The name of Sakimaxing—now corrupted by the white men into Shackamaxon—means the place of kings. At this spot stood an aged elm-tree, one of those glorious elms which mark the forests of the New World. It was a hundred and fifty-five years old; under its spreading branches friendly nations had been wont to meet; and here the Redskins smoked the calumet of peace long before the pale-faces landed on those shores. Markham had appointed this locality for his first conference, and the land commissioners wisely followed his example. Old traditions had made the place sacred to one of the contracting parties,—and when Penn proposed his solemn conference, he named Sakimaxing as a place of meeting with the Indian kings.

Artists have painted, poets sung, philosophers praised this meeting of the white men and the red. The great outlines of nature are easily regained. There the dense masses of cedar, pine, and chestnut, spread away into the interior of the land; here the noble river rolled its majestic waters down to the Atlantic. Along its surface rose the purple smoke of the settler's homestead; on the opposite shores lay the fertile and settled country of West New Jersey. Here stood the gigantic elm which was to become immortal from that day; there lay the verdant council-chamber formed by nature on the surface of the soil. In the centre of this group stood William Penn; in costume undistinguished from the English settlers, save by the blue silk sash of office. His dress was not ungainly. An outer coat, reaching to the knees, with rows of buttons; a vest of other materials; trousers extremely full, slashed at the sides, and tied with strings; a profusion of shirt-sleeve and ruffles; and a hat of the cavalier shape (wanting only the feather), from beneath the brim of which escaped the curls of auburn hair,—were its chief and not ungraceful ingredients. At his right hand, in the uniform of an English soldier, was Colonel Markham; on his left Pearson, the brave companion of his voyage; and near his person, but a little backward, stood a picturesque and various band of followers; old Swedes encased in the uniforms worn by them in the camp of Gustavus Adolphus; Dutch and German settlers in the province; Quakers in the sober suits of the first Puritans; sailors in their rough and ready habits; members of his council and his government; and though last, not least in importance, old Captain Cockle, interpreter in general to the Red men. When the Indians approached in their old forest costume, their feathers sparkling in the sun, their bodies painted yellow, red, and blue, the Governor received them with the easy dignity of European courts. The reception over, the sachems retired to a short distance, and after a brief consultation among themselves, Taminent, chief sachem, a man whose virtues are still remembered by the sons of the forest, advanced a few steps, and putting on his head a chaplet, into which was twisted a small horn, sat down. This chaplet was his symbol of power; and in the customs of the Lenni Lenapé, whenever the chief placed it on his brows the spot became sacred, and the person of every one present inviolable. The older sachems sat on his right and left; the middle-aged warriors ranged themselves in the form of a crescent round them; and the younger men formed a third and outer semicircle. All being seated, the old king announced to the Governor that the natives were prepared to hear and consider his words. Penn then rose to address them. Thirty-eight years old; light and graceful in form; he was 'the hand-somest, best-looking, lively gentleman,' a lady who was near him had 'ever seen.' The Great Spirit, he said, who ruled in the heaven to which good men go after death, who had made them and him out of nothing, and who knew every secret thought that was in the heart of white man or red man, knew that he and his children had a strong desire to live in peace, to be their friends, to do no wrong, but to serve them in every way. As the Great Spirit was the common Father of all, he wished them to live together not merely as brothers, and the children of a common parent, but as if they were joined with one head, one heart, one body together; that if ill was done to one, all would suffer; if good was done to any, all would gain. He and his children, he went on to say, never fired the rifle, never trusted to the sword; they met the red men on the broad path of good faith and good will. They meant no harm, and had no fear. He read the treaty of friendship, and explained its clauses. It recited that from that day the children of Onas and the nations of the Lenni Lenapé should be brothers to each other,—that all paths should be free and open—that the doors of the white men should be open to the red men, and the lodges of the red men

should be open to the white men,—that the children
of Onas should not believe any false reports of the
Lenni Lenapé, nor the Lenni Lenapé of the children
of Onas, but should come and see for themselves,
and bury such false reports in a pit,—that if
the Christians should hear of anything likely to
hurt the Indians, or the Indians hear of anything
likely to harm the Christians, they should run, like
friends, and let the other know,—that if any son
of Onas were to do any harm to any Redskin, or
any Redskin were to do harm to a son of Onas,
the sufferer should not offer to right himself, but
should complain to the chiefs and to Onas, that
justice might be declared by twelve honest men,
and the wrong buried in a pit with no bottom,—
that the Lenni Lenapé should assist the white men,
and the white men should assist the Lenni Lenapé,
against all such as would disturb them or do them
hurt ;—and, lastly, that both Christians and Indians
should tell their children of this league and chain
of friendship, that it might grow stronger and
stronger, and be kept bright and clean, without
rust or spot, while the waters ran down the creeks
and rivers, and while the sun and moon and stars
endured. He laid the scroll on the ground. The
sachems received his proposal for themselves and
for their children. No oaths, no seals, no mummeries,
were used ; the treaty was ratified on both sides
with yea,—and, unlike treaties which are sworn and
sealed, was kept.

CHAPTER XXV.

PHILADELPHIA (1682–4).

WHEN Penn had sailed, he held a note in his mind of six things to be done on landing : (1) to organize his government; (2) to visit Friends in Delaware, Pennsylvania, and New Jersey; (3) to conciliate the Indians; (4) to see the Governor of New York, who had previously governed his province; (5) to fix the site for his capital city; (6) to arrange his differences with Lord Baltimore. The subject of his chief city occupied his anxious thought, and Markham had collected information for his use. Some people wished to see Chester made his capital; but the surveyor, Thomas Holme, agreed with Penn that the best locality in almost every respect was the neck of land lying at the junction of the Delaware and the Skuylkill rivers. Both these rivers were navigable, at least for small vessels; the Delaware being a noble stream, and the Skuylkill broader than the Thames at Lambeth Reach. The point was known as Wicocoa. In all respects the site agreed with Penn's requirements. Facing the river the bank was bold and high, the air pure and wholesome; the neighbouring lands were free from swamp; clay for making bricks was found on the spot; immense quarries of good stone— not a little of it the whitest marble—lay within a few miles. These advantages not being found elsewhere, Penn soon decided in its favour, and taking an open boat at Chester Creek, sailed up the river to this chosen spot. The land was owned by three Swedes, from whom Penn purchased it on their own terms; and then, with the assistance of Holme, he drew his plan. In everything relating to his Holy Experiment, he thought on a grand scale. Not content to begin humbly, and allow house to be added to house, and street to street, as people wanted them, he formed the whole scheme of his city—its name, its form, its streets, its docks, and open spaces—fair and perfect in his mind, before a single stone was laid.

According to his original design, Philadelphia was to cover with its houses, squares, and gardens, twelve square miles. Two noble streets, one of them facing a row of old red pines, were to front the two rivers; a great public thoroughfare lying between the houses and the river banks. These streets were to be connected by the High Street, an avenue perfectly straight, a hundred feet in width, to be adorned with lines of trees and gardens surrounding each clump of dwelling-houses. At a right angle with the High Street, Broad Street, of equal width, was to cut the town in halves from north to south. The whole city, therefore, was divided into four sections. In the exact centre

a public square of ten acres was reserved ; and in
the middle of each quarter a similar square of
eight acres was set apart for the comfort and
recreation of posterity.   Eight streets, each fifty
feet wide, were to be built parallel to Broad Street,
and twenty of the same width parallel to the rivers.
Penn encouraged the building of detached houses,
with rustic porches and trailing plants about them ;
his desire being to see Philadelphia ' a green country
town.'

A house was hardly built, a cave was hardly
dug, in which to shelter comers from the cold
of winter, ere the colonists poured in. As soon as
it was known that Penn had sailed for his province,
hundreds of persons in the old country followed
him ; and since the spring not less than twenty-
three vessels had entered the Delaware filled with
emigrants, most of them anxious to remain at the
' green country town.' Along the high bank of
the Delaware nature had formed a number of caves,
and these were seized by some of the colonists,
and made as habitable as time and circumstances
would permit. Some settlers lodged under the
branches of huge pines ; he blessed his stars who
was fortunate enough to secure the shelter of
a tree in the vicinity of his house. Women, who
had been used to all the luxuries of the earth, went
out to help their fathers and husbands ; brought
in wood and water ; cooked the victuals ; tended
sheep and pigs ; some of them acted as labourers
while the house was building, anxious to carry
mortar or lend a hand at sawing a block of wood.

If a murmur ever once arose, the thought of that 'woful Europe' which they had left behind soon checked the sigh. A wilderness was better than a jail. Before enthusiasm every obstacle must give way; and in a short time every family had found some sort of shelter from the winter frost.

The first frame completed was a tavern, ferry-house, and general place of trade. For many years the Blue Anchor maintained a high reputation in the province; being a beer-house, an exchange, a corn-market, a post-office, and a landing-place combined. This house became the key of the infant city, and was connected with the leading incidents of its early days. The Blue Anchor was formed of large rafters of wood, the interstices being filled with bricks brought from England, in the manner of Cheshire houses of the Tudor and Stuart reigns. It had twelve feet of frontage towards the river, and it stood full twenty-two feet backwards, into what was afterwards Dock Street. Modern magnates of Philadelphia may smile at the dimensions of a house of so much interest to their fathers, but posterity will feel for ever grateful to the founder of their city, that in an age of means so limited and results so small, he clung to his own conceptions, laying down the outlines of his city with as much order as if sure that he was rearing the capital of a mighty state. Other houses, such as they were, were soon completed. Within a few months of the foundation, Penn could announce to the Society of Traders that eighty houses and cottages were ready; that the merchants and craftsmen had fallen into their callings; that the farmers had partly cleared their lands; that ships were continually coming with goods and passengers; and that plentiful crops had been obtained from the soil. Enterprise then took bolder flights. One settler named Carpenter built a quay three hundred feet long, by the side of which a vessel of five hundred tons could be moored. The first mayor of the town made a rope-walk; and stone houses, with pointed roofs, balconies, and porches, ceased to excite remark. One year from the date of Penn's landing in the New World, a hundred houses had been built; two years later there were six hundred houses. Penn's correspondence with his friends in England is full of honest exultation. To Lord Halifax he writes, 'I must without vanity say, I have led the greatest colony into America that ever any man did on private credit.' To Lord Sunderland he says, 'With the help of God and such noble friends, I will show a province in seven years equal to her neighbour's of forty years' planting.'

But the material growth of his city occupied only a part of Penn's attention. He took early and regular steps for the protection of morals and the promotion of art and scholarship. Before the pines had been cleared from his ground he began to build schools and set up a printing-press. These were not the least marvellous of the many novelties introduced into Philadelphia. In other American settlements such luxuries had slowly followed in the wake of prosperity. In December 1683, Enoch

Flower opened his school in a hut, formed of pine and cedar planks, and divided into two apartments by a wooden frame. A Philadelphian of the present age may smile at the simplicity of Enoch's charges and curriculum, though his ancestors thought such matters worthy of a place in their minutes of council : 'To learn to read, four shillings a quarter : to write, six shillings : boarding a scholar—to wit, diet, lodging, washing, and schooling—ten pounds the whole year.'

Six years afterwards a public school was founded, in which the famous George Keith was the first master. The office of teacher was held in high estimation. Keith was allowed fifty pounds a-year, a house for his family, and a set of school-rooms, over and above all the profits made by the payments of his scholars ; in addition to which he received a guarantee that his total income should never fall below a hundred and twenty pounds in any year—a very considerable sum in those days in a society so small and primitive. William Bradford, the printer who went out with Penn, set up his craft. In Massachussetts, no book or paper had been printed until eighteen years after the first settlement ; in New York seventy-three years had elapsed before a press was got to work ; in every other colony founded by England the interval had been greater still ; and in the two provinces of Virginia and Maryland the governors had set their faces against the press. The first book printed in Philadelphia was an Almanac for 1687, which must have been printed in the preceding year. Another institution which Penn established deserves to be classed with his intellectual legislation. The post-office had been at work in England but a few years; yet so convinced was Penn of its utility that he at once issued orders to Henry Waldy to run a post and supply travellers with horses. From the Falls of Trenton to Philadelphia the carriage of a letter was charged three-pence—to Chester five-pence — to Newcastle seven-pence — to Maryland nine-pence. From Philadelphia to Chester the charge was two-pence—to Newcastle four-pence—to Maryland six-pence. The post travelled once a-week!

When the members of Penn's first free parliament met, he saw how hard it is to frame laws and constitutions for a political society at a distance; for instead of the full number of members, each county sent up only twelve, three for the Council, nine for the Assembly, making seventy-two persons —no more in all than the number he had originally fixed for the Council. They bore with them a written statement of the reasons which had led the electors to disregard the letter of his writs; a statement concluding with a prayer that this act of self-judgment might not cause the proprietor to think of altering their charter. Penn was no formalist; and as they came with full powers, he told them they were at liberty to change, amend, or add to, the existing laws; he was not wedded to his own conceits, but would consent to any changes they might wish to make.

The Assembly appointed Thomas Wynne as

speaker. Some parts of the Frame of Government acted as a restraint on the freedom of the Assembly, especially that clause which reserved to the Governor and his Council the sole right to propose new laws. From the first day of meeting the Assembly set this restriction at nought, but in return they wished to invest the Governor with a veto on all the doings of parliament. This last was necessary; the King's sanction being required to make every act of the colonial legislature binding, it was obvious that no law would be received in England which came unsupported by the Governor's vote. These and other points in which changes seemed desirable were discussed. Amendments were suggested and new frames drawn up. The House was anxious to obtain the privilege of conference with the Governor. An opinion was expressed that it might be well to make a new charter on the principles laid down in the Frame of Government, but in other respects to be the growth of the New World and to bear date from the new capital.

This design amounted to a transfer of the legislative power from the Council to the Assembly; and Penn saw with no little uneasiness the grasping spirit of his parliament. He called his Council together and laid before them the prayer of the Assembly. Had the Council been complete they might have fought; but fearing controversy with the larger house of representatives, they advised that an open conference should be held to ascertain the general opinion. The Assembly was then summoned, and the Governor asked them distinctly yea or nay, whether they desired to have a new charter. They replied—yea, unanimously. He then addressed them in a few words :— He expressed his willingness to meet their wishes, and gave his consent to a revision of the charter; at the same time telling them they should consider their own duty as well as his desire to oblige them, and he hoped they would not find it difficult to reconcile the two.

A general committee being appointed to draw up a new charter, in ten days it was prepared, and on the 30th of March, 1683, it was read, approved, and signed by the proprietor—subject, of course, to the revision of the crown lawyers in England. The Council was reduced to eighteen—the Assembly to thirty-six members. Governor and Council still retained the initiative; but the Assembly obtained some privileges and left the way open for the acquisition of more as circumstances might favour their designs. The constitution remained the same. All power was vested in the people. They elected members of Council and members of Assembly. Judges were elected to their seats; and Penn gave his power to suspend them. In the neighbouring state of Maryland, Lord Baltimore appointed magistrates, officers of government, members of council, every class of functionaries. Penn could not name either a street-sweeper or a parish-constable. ' I purpose,' he explained to a friend, ' to leave myself and my successors no power of doing mischief, that the will of one man may not hinder the good of a whole country.'

The Assembly established courts of justice for each county with the proper officers to each; they voted an impost on certain goods exported or imported for the Governor's support, which he declined. He would not hear of imposts; and a tax-gatherer was for many years an unknown figure. To prevent law-suits, three Peace-Makers were chosen by every county-court to hear and settle disputes between man and man according to the right. Law was only to be invoked as a last resource. Twice a-year an Orphans' court was to meet in each county to inquire into and regulate the affairs of widows and orphans. All this early legislation reads like pages out of Harrington and More.

The little parliament having finished its labours and adjourned, Penn made a journey up the river to a spot where Markham was engaged in building Pennsbury. The time was near when he had agreed to meet Lord Baltimore at Newcastle and settle, if they could, their boundary lines. They met, but with no more success than in the previous year. There is but little doubt that, in accordance with the terms of their several grants, both proprietors could legally claim some parts of the territory; and neither of them felt inclined to surrender what he deemed his right. Lord Baltimore wrote off to Blaythwaite and Halifax an account of the interview, giving it in such a way as to serve his own interest at the distant court. Penn learned that his rival had written to London without his privity; he suspected Baltimore of not conveying a fair report of what had taken place between them; and he instantly sat down and wrote to the Board of Trade. He expressed his surprise that Baltimore should have given a report of their conference without his knowledge and consent, protested against its being received as a true report, and proceeded to give his own version of the meeting at full length. In order that he might be represented on the spot by one in whose truth, judgment, and fidelity, he had perfect confidence, he sent his cousin Markham as his agent to the court in London, provided with letters to the King himself, to the Earl of Sunderland, to Henry Sydney, and to the officers of the colonial department. In the early spring of 1684, Baltimore quitted Maryland for London; a movement which suggested to Penn the need of being likewise on the spot; even if causes of deeper and more painful interest than the loss of a few hundred miles of territory had not begun to crowd on him.

About the time that Lord Baltimore departed from the colony, letters arrived for Penn bringing with them a long list of calamities. His wife Guli was seriously ill; his friend Sydney had perished on the block; Shaftsbury and Essex were both in prison; persecution of nonconformers had begun to rage; Oxford had put forth the doctrine of passive obedience; and his enemies were heaping calumnies on his name.

Penn felt that he must go at once. Summoning the chiefs of all the Indian tribes in his vicinity to Pennsbury, he concluded with each a separate treaty of peace. He told them he was going beyond the seas for a little while, but would return to them again if the Great Spirit permitted him to live. He begged of them to drink no more fire-water, and forbade his own people to sell them brandy and rum; he put them in the ways of honest trade and husbandry; he obtained from them a promise that they would live at peace and amity with each other and with the Christians. The new city engaged his daily thoughts; he felt some comfort in seeing it steadily rising from the ground; and as the news from Europe darkened, he was more and more anxious that Philadelphia might become a haven of safety in the coming storm.

The brig *Endeavour* being now ready to leave the Delaware, he named a mixed commission to conduct the affairs of government in his absence. Thomas Loyd was named president; Colonel Markham (who was to return immediately) secretary; assisted by Thomas Holme, James Claypole, Robert Turner and two or three others. Going on board, Penn addressed to Thomas Loyd and the rest a parting letter, in which he thus apostrophised the city of his heart :—

'And thou, Philadelphia, the virgin settlement of this province, named before thou wert born, what love, what care, what service, and what travail, has there been to bring thee forth and preserve thee from such as would abuse and defile thee ! My soul prays to God for thee, that thou mayest stand in the day of trial, that thy children may be blessed of the Lord, and thy people saved by His power !'

CHAPTER XXVI.

AT HOME (1684–85).

WHEN Guli Penn fell sick, she wrote to ask her old friend Ellwood to ride over and direct her husband's business. Ellwood lived not far from Worminghurst, and would have come to her at once, but for a trouble of his own. A book of his, which had been circulating in the neighbourhood by the means of William Ayrs, a barber and apothecary, had got into the hands of Sir Benjamin Tichborne, a stupid justice of the peace, who thought it dangerous to the King. Sir Benjamin summoned Ayrs before the county bench; on which the barber ran to Ellwood's house to let him know. Ellwood was seeing Ayrs and giving him his word that on the day of hearing he would go before the magistrates and own his book, when Guli's messenger arrived. What could he do in this new stress? He could not leave the barber to his fate; yet if he stayed to answer at the petty session, Guli Penn might die before he reached her house. There was a middle course. He might go round to Tichborne park, and take the blame upon himself.

Leaping to horse, he rode to Tichborne, where he found Sir Benjamin and a brother-justice, Thomas Fotherly, and told them who he was and why he had come to own his book. They heard him in a sullen mood, and were about to have him seized, when it occurred to them to ask him why he had come before the day appointed for his case. Ellwood showed them Guli's note. 'While I thus delivered myself,' he writes, 'I observed a sensible alteration in the justice, and when I had done speaking, he said he was very sorry for Madame Penn's illness (of whose virtues and worth he spoke very highly, but not more highly than was her due). Then he told me that *for her sake* he would do what he could to further my suit; but he added, "I can assure you the matter which will be laid to your charge is of greater importance than you think."' On Ellwood pledging his word to appear when called upon, he was allowed to leave; he got to Worminghurst that day; and 'Madame Penn' improved so fast, that when her husband landed at Shorcham from his ship, she was able to go down and meet him at that Sussex port.

After passing three or four days with his family, Penn went to Newmarket, where he saw the King and Duke of York, who both received him kindly, and assured him that justice should be done about his boundary lines. Baltimore was on the spot, but the King's health was now failing, and the affair was suffered to languish,—both parties hoping from either the justice or the friendship of his brother. Feeling that possession was nine parts of the law, and knowing that his neighbour would not oppose force to force Lord Baltimore ordered his relative Colonel Talbot to seize the territory in dispute and hold it in his name. With three musqueteers Talbot invaded some farm-houses, proclaimed Lord Baltimore proprietor, and threatened to expel any one who should refuse to admit his claim. Talbot threatened a descent on Newcastle; but the Government of Pennsylvania having issued a declaration of their proprietor's right over the disputed tract, and announced an intention to prosecute the authors of the recent outrage in the English courts, Talbot waited for fresh orders to come out. The feint of war had answered its purpose, that of raising suspicions in England as to Penn's pacific ideas. The moment this disturbance was heard of, foes began to whisper that the preacher of peace was mounting guns and fortifying towns. But Penn explained that when he went to America a few old guns were lying on the green by the Session-house at Newcastle, some on the ground, others on broken carriages, but that there had been no ball, no powder, no soldier there from the day he landed; and he could no more be charged with warlike propensities on this account, than a man might be who happened to buy a house with an old musket in it.

On the 6th of February, 1685, Charles the Second breathed his last; and James the Second quietly succeeded to his throne. The reign of Charles had been the most shameful in our annals; vice had reared its head in the highest places, and the first rank of the peerage had been filled with wantons; the honour of the country had been sold to the enemy of its freedom and its faith; persecution had ravened through the land. Penn counted up the families ruined for opinions in that reign to more than fifteen thousand. Of those who were cast into jails, not less than four thousand had died. As Duke of York, James had often lifted up his voice against these atrocities; and when he came to the throne, a statement of the wrongs, in mind, in body, and estate, endured by unoffending men was placed in his hands. Penn waited on him at Whitehall to remind him of the good-will he had formerly professed towards all conscientious persons, and to beg his interference in behalf of the many religious men and women then in jail. The King was affable. He talked to Penn with his old frankness, and when the Quaker spoke of the penal laws then in operation, and expressed a hope that the poor Quakers languishing in Marshalsea, Newgate, and the Gatehouse, would find relief, James took him into his private closet, where they long remained in talk. Penn has preserved the substance of what passed. His Majesty said he should deal openly with his subjects. He was himself a Catholic, and he desired no person to be disturbed on account of his opinions; but he would defer making any distinct promise until the day fixed for his coronation, and even then he could only exercise his prerogative to pardon such as were already suffering unjustly. With a new parliament would rest the power to establish liberty of conscience.

James was better than his word. He charged his judges to discourage persecution on the score of religious differences; he opened his prison-gates to every person who was confined for refusing to take oaths of allegiance and supremacy. Twelve hundred Quakers obtained their freedom by this act of justice. Opinions varied at that time—and vary still —as to James's motives. Simple men saw in these orders the acts of a prince who had tasted the bitterness of persecution. Penn believed that this liberty of worship granted by James was neither a delusion nor a snare.

As friend, as patron, and as guardian, the new King seemed well disposed to Penn. He directed the Board of Trade to collect the papers having reference to his controversy with Baltimore, especially the authorised and sworn versions of what had taken place between Markham, Penn, and Baltimore, in their private conferences; and when this was done, Penn went through the form of praying that his Majesty would command the Board of Trade to decide the question without delay. It is not necessary to enter into the details of this settlement. Ignorance of the geography of America had led the original granters of the charters to include some parts of the Peninsula in both the patents. But as Baltimore's right had priority of date, and had never been cancelled, his supporters argued, with fair show of reason, that the latter grant was invalid, the King not being able to give away lands which were not his own. On the other hand, as the Maryland charter expressly stated that only lands which were wild and waste were assigned to Lord Baltimore, it was urged with equal cogency that the tract on the Delaware, then settled and cultivated by the Dutch and Swedes, could not have been included in the patent. While the Duke of York remained master of these territories, the Maryland proprietor had been silent about his claims, and it was only when he found the new Governor about to plant a democracy in his immediate neighbourhood, that he became anxious about the unproductive strip of ground lying between the Chesapeake and the Delaware. James settled the question—for a time —by dividing the territory in dispute into two equal parts, the eastern half of which he transferred to Lord Baltimore as his by right, and the western half of which he added to the crown, so as to place it beyond the reach of future litigation, with a view to granting it to Penn on new conditions, with a perfect title.

Penn now saw that he had work to do—and work which no one else could do—at home. The laws against opinion under which Penn had suffered, still existed ; hundreds of poor Quakers were still confined for tithes and jailor's fees ; and the Church party, instead of showing a friendly disposition towards Dissenters, proposed that the House of Commons should petition James to put the penal laws against them into execution. At such a time he felt that Providence had placed him near the throne ; that on him had fallen, in a violent time, the work of daily mercy and mediation. He accepted his position with a full sense of its perils ;

but he trusted to the sanctity of his office, 'the general mediator for charity,' for a liberal construction of his acts. To him and his, the ordinary laws afforded no protection; a fine or fee was a sentence of imprisonment to a man who in his conscience could not pay fines and fees. A judge might order a poor wretch to be set at liberty, but then the jailor showed his list of charges, and unless the judge were willing to pay them out of his own purse, the wretch was sent back again to jail. Conscience was at war with law, and the only hope of obtaining justice, not to speak of mercy, for the sufferers lay in the royal right to pardon and relieve.

To be near the court, Penn hired apartments in Holland House at Kensington, and brought Guli and his family to town. The house was large, and he had many visitors. His influence with the King was known, and every man with a grievance found in him a counsellor and a friend. Envoys were sent from the American colonies to solicit his influence in their behalf; members of his sect and of many other sects crowded to his levees; sometimes not less than two hundred persons were in attendance at his door.

One of the earliest favours which Penn is known to have begged from the new King will be remembered to his honour as long as a taste for letters shall endure. In the preceding reign, when Shaftsbury had fled to the Continent, John Locke, as one of his friends, had fallen under court suspicion; but so serene and blameless was the life he had led at Oxford that the Council feared to try him.

Charles had employed his creatures at Christ Church to entrap Locke into some unwary expression—some word of sympathy for the alleged conspirators—any, even the least remark which malice might construe into a crime. But Locke had given them no assistance in their work. At length, on treachery failing, force had been employed. Sunderland conveyed to the authorities of the college his Majesty's commands to strip the unmoved philosopher of his honours and dignities, and expel him from the University. These authorities had put their doctrine of absolute obedience into practice; and a week later the Secretary of State could thank the college in his Majesty's name for their ready compliance with his orders. Locke, then on the Continent, had been cast out from the University of which he was the chiefest ornament, and going to reside at the Hague, had busied himself in finishing his great work on the Human Understanding, and in furnishing the friends of liberty with new arguments in favour of toleration. Touched with a situation in some respects so like his own in earlier life, Penn put his influence to the test by asking permission for his old acquaintance to return to England. James had been a party to his banishment; and it was felt to be a signal instance of his favour that he promised what the intercessor asked for, without a scruple and without conditions. Penn at once wrote off these tidings to the Hague; but the illustrious exile, conscious of no crime, while noting his deep sense of obligation to the mediator, refused to accept the proffered pardon. And in this view of his duty Locke continued steadfast. When Pembroke offered his services to obtain a similar concession from the King, he returned the same answer. That he thankfully remembered the un-solicited kindness of his 'friend Penn' was seen in the good offices he was able to render in return after the Revolution. Locke's friend, Popple, was less scrupulous. Being involved in troublesome affairs in France, Popple applied to the 'general mediator.' Penn, convinced of Popple's honour and innocence, went to M. Barillon, and procured from that ambassador such a representation of Popple's affair at the court of Versailles as soon put an end to his troubles. The future Secretary of State re-tained a warm sense of gratitude to his benefactor, and events afterwards placed it in Popple's power in some measure to repay his debt. Nor did Locke himself scruple to ask that for others which his pride rejected for himself.

CHAPTER XXVII.

AT COURT (1685–86).

THE reign of James brought back the troubles of an earlier time. The names of Cavalier and Roundhead were revived. Monmouth and Argyle were secretly preparing for invasion. Public passion was aflame. When Titus Oates was placed in the pillory after his trial, people were excited to a serious breach of the peace. The zeal of fanatic Churchmen was inflamed to frenzy on seeing James go publicly to mass. Sermons and speeches against Popery were delivered in all churches, chapels, coffee-houses, and places of general resort. Even in the royal chapel at Whitehall the rites and ceremonies practised by the sovereign were denounced as contrary to the Word of God and to the laws of England. In the midst of these distractions, James held on his course. He clung to his own notions of religion with a tenacity worthy of an Englishman; and refused to purchase the support of his ancient friends, the Cavaliers, by any sacrifice of his bigotry to their intolerance, even when Argyle had landed in the north, and the signal of revolt was daily expected in the west.

A committee of the House of Commons, under the influence of the Church party, proposed to petition the King for the instant execution of all the penal statutes against Dissent. Though some of the King's personal friends were present they were silent. James, informed of what had taken place, sent for his friends and laid before them so clearly his determination to err on the side of mercy (if he must err at all), that they went away convinced of his sincerity, and took their measures with such success that the motion was condemned as an insult to the sovereign and rejected without a division. Penn began to feel some hope that Parliament would find itself in a temper to discuss a general act.

Literature came to the aid of freedom, from an unexpected quarter. Penn's acquaintance with the Duke of Buckingham was of old standing; and the public fancied it was at Penn's instigation, or through his influence, that the Duke brought out his Essay on Religion. Buckingham argues for universal charity towards opinion. He says he had long been convinced that nothing can be more anti-Christian nor more contrary to sense and reason, than to molest our fellow-Christians because they cannot be exactly of our minds in all that relates to the worship of God. The effusion breathes this spirit; and it is not a little to the author's credit that during a life of more than ordinary fickleness and change he never wavered from this view. He concludes his discourse with the paraphrase of a thought often expressed by Penn, to the effect that if Parliament refused to adopt a more liberal policy towards opinion, the result would be 'a general discontent, the dispeopling of our poor country, and the exposing us to the conquest of a foreign nation.' A pamphlet on such a subject by the author of the Rehearsal naturally excited much attention. The wit of the court was answered by wits of the coffee-house. Some of these answers were rather smart. One writer alludes to the great rake taking up with Whiggism in her old age, when she is a poor cast-off mistress, that porters and footmen turn away from in scorn; and wonders how his grace can think of making himself the champion of any thing so out of all countenance as religion and toleration. The graver argument adduced by these writers against any concession to the sectaries, was the alleged peril of the nation. Liberty, they said, was fraught with danger. There had been liberties in the time of Charles the First, —and Charles the First lost his head: there was toleration under the Commonwealth, — and the Commonwealth fell!

One of the disputants charged the Duke with having been misled by Penn; and being thus dragged into the lists, a duty to maintain the right urged Penn to add his testimony to the principle of enlightened policy advocated by the Duke. A vein of satire runs through his discourse. He expresses his great pleasure in seeing a work in defence of religion from such a pen, and sincerely hopes that the witty writer may soon begin to enjoy those felicities of a good life which he has proved himself able to describe. When that day arrives, he says in conclusion, he will be happy to press the gentlemen of England to imitate so illustrious an example. At first, the King affected to take no notice of this literary combat; but when he found the Church party in alarm, and heard from those about him that nothing else was talked of in the coffee-houses, he began to read the book. Barillon saw its importance from the first; and as soon as Buckingham's pamphlet appeared, he caused it to be translated, and sent over to his master as a key to the new and serious questions which were now dividing England into hostile camps.

The expeditions under Monmouth and Argyle failed. These events and the trials and executions to which they led belong to the domain of general history. Penn's connexion with them was but slight. He was himself an object of suspicion to the court. Though it is not imagined that he gave the followers of Monmouth any reason to believe he approved their projects, it is known that they regarded him as a friend to their cause, and that in their plans they set him down as one of the half-dozen persons who might help to bring over the American colonies to accept a Protestant revolution. The ministry were conscious that his sympathies were not with them, and they professed to regard him as a partisan of the Prince of Orange. Against these suspicions and misgivings he had no protection save the private favour of the King. Penn strove to mitigate the sufferings of men who had been drawn into rebellion. God had given him an asylum for the oppressed; and when the prisoners were sentenced to transportation beyond sea, he offered them a home in Pennsylvania, where the climate would agree with them, and their offences would be looked upon with lenient eyes.

When the trials in the country were over and those in London began, Penn was still more anxiously employed in the work of mediation. One of the first victims of royal rigour was an old acquaintance of his own. Five years before this time, when the court was moving heaven and earth to defeat the Sydney party in elections, two liberals, Henry Cornish and Slingsby Bethel, had the courage to stand for the office of sheriffs in the city of London; and in spite of bribery and threats, they carried the election. The mob gave vent to their triumph by party cries; and James took this defeat to heart as if it had been a personal insult. From that day Cornish was a marked man; and when the Rye-House plot exploded, he was believed to be involved in it past recovery. The evidence, however, was not complete, and he had now been two years at large after the execution of Sydney, and was congratulating himself on his escape, when James obtained the evidence required. He was arrested, tried, found guilty, and gibbeted in front of his own house in Cheapside. That Cornish was accused and sentenced as the accomplice of Sydney was not without its weight with Penn; but the mediator took a higher view; he declared his belief that

the condemned man was innocent of the crimes
alleged against him, and he begged the King to
pause ere signing warrants for his death.   His
arguments failed to touch the King.   Another case,
pending at the same moment, interested his feelings, not less strongly.   Elizabeth Gaunt, a lady
of religious temperament and of spotless life, whose
time and fortune had been spent in visiting prisons
and relieving the wretched, had in a moment of
compassion given the shelter of her house to one
of the fugitive rebels; but as the government
declared its determination to punish those who har-
boured traitors with as much severity as the traitors
themselves, the scoundrel whom she had tried to
save informed against his humane protectress, and
she was thereupon arrested, found guilty, and condemned to be burnt at Tyburn.   For her Penn also
interceded—but in vain.

Penn stood near Cornish to the last,—and vin-
dicated his memory after death.   The creatures of
the court, annoyed at the indignant bearing of
the city merchant on the scaffold, gave out that
he was drunk.   Penn repelled the charge : he said
he could see nothing in his conduct but the natural
indignation of an Englishman about to be murdered
by form of law.   From Cheapside Penn went to
Tyburn.   The poor lady met her fate with calmness
and resignation.   She had obeyed the merciful
promptings of her heart in sheltering a fellow-
creature from the blood-hounds of the law; and
when grave judges pronounced this act worthy
of fire and faggot, she submitted to the King's

pleasure in silence. As she arranged the straw about her feet, that the flame might do its work more quickly, the whole concourse of spectators burst into tears. To the last she asserted her innocence, her loyalty, her respect for the laws. But she did not repent of what she had done. The cause in which she suffered was, she said, the cause of humanity—the cause of God.

Penn was able, when he afterwards pleaded with his sovereign for mercy, to quote these instances of persons who had gone down to the grave protesting their innocence. But some of James's ministers disliked his interference; and to punish his presumption they contrived not only to postpone his legal investiture with the Delaware province, though, as he enjoyed it in fact, there could be no reason for withholding it in form, but under pretence of a general measure of reform for the colonies, they also gave orders to the crown lawyers to issue a *quo warranto* against his province of Pennsylvania, and proceed against him with such vigour as to compel him to vacate his charter.

James was then at Windsor Castle; Penn went to see him; and in less than a week Sunderland wrote to the Attorney-general to suspend proceedings until further orders. Further orders were not issued. James listened to his counsels with interest, even where his own temper forbade him to follow them,—for his manner was soft and winning, and he had not only clear ideas but wit and scholarship to recommend his views. His opportunities were nobly used. If any fault can be found with his conduct, it is that his charity was a little too in-discriminate. A Whig applied to Penn, rather, as he confesses, with a view to ascertain his ideas of political mercy than with any hope of obtaining what he asked, to solicit from the King a pardon for Aaron Smith. Had Penn known Aaron Smith a little better, he might have paused. But Aaron Smith had done one bold and manly thing; he had refused to give evidence against Sydney. Smith had been a prisoner in the Tower, and government had offered him a full discharge, if he would com-promise the patriot's life. 'I cannot tell you any-thing,' he had said, 'that would touch a hair of Sydney's head.' When Penn was asked to speak for Aaron Smith, he therefore undertook the task. A few days afterwards, when alone with James, he made his request. The King started at the name, —flew into a violent passion,—replied in his angriest tone that he would do no such thing,— that six fellows like Smith would put the three kingdoms in a flame,—and threatened in his wrath to turn the petitioner out of doors. Yet Penn would not desist. He got, with trouble—for Smith was obstinate—a letter from the delinquent; and taking an opportunity, when James was in a good humour, and the scene in the closet had faded from his recollection, he again pressed the suit of mercy, and obtained a pardon for the exile.

Bonds of friendship grew between the Quaker and the Catholic, who had suffered proscription, pillories, and exile together, in the common name of religion. Even when he was suffering under laws directed against Papists, Penn had never proposed to escape by joining in the hue and cry after Romanists. While he condemned their creed, he contended for their liberty of thought. All that he asked for himself he gave to them. Yet not without drawing suspicion upon himself. Hearing none of the usual cant about Popery from his lips, some ignorant folk began to fancy he must be a Papist in disguise. He was often seen at court; he was known to have much favour with the King; and courtiers, waiting in the ante-chamber while he was closeted with their master, could think of no other explanation. Once, when Penn was travelling in the country in a stage-coach, the passengers beguiled the time by talking on the usual topics of the day. One man asked Penn how he, Barclay, and Keith, had come to have so much learning and such love of letters, seeing that Quakers professed to despise these things? 'I suppose,' said Penn, 'it comes of my having been educated at Saumur.' Mistaking the name, his questioner reported that Penn had been educated at St. Omer. At St. Omer the Jesuits had a seminary. How easy the conclusion then! He must be, not a Papist merely, but a Jesuit. Soon afterwards it was reported in every coffee-house in London that Penn had matriculated in the Jesuits' College,—had taken holy orders in Rome,—and now regularly officiated at the service of mass in the private chapel at Whitehall. All this was said in spite of his lay habits,—his wife and children,—his public preaching,—his Caveat against Popery! Nor did these simple lies content the curious; more mysterious and romantic incidents came out. A tale got abroad of a monk who had abjured his faith and fled away to America for safety. Attracted to Pennsylvania, the poor fellow had placed himself unwittingly in the power of his superior,—who had got him secretly kidnapped by his own familiars and sent to Europe, to be there delivered over to the awful retributions of his Church. Some men of sober judgment lent unwilling ear to these reports. Tillotson was one of this class. Tillotson had once told him it was reported that he kept up a secret corresspondence with Rome, and particularly with some of the Jesuits there; at which his visitor seemed much surprised and more amused. Nothing more was said that day—nor was it for a long time after, as Penn had gone out to his province, and on his return he had either forgotten the circumstance or was too busy to attend to such mattters. When Tillotson heard of Penn being a Jesuit, he could not deny it on certain knowledge; and as they were known to have been on intimate terms, the gossips found support for the rumour even in Tillotson's silence. Then it was noised abroad that Tillotson affirmed of his own knowledge that Penn was a Jesuit.

Few men despised clamour and false representation more than Penn; and yet he thought it time to speak when those who should have known him better were said to countenance such reports. He wrote to his old friend:—he was grieved, he said, to hear the reports in question, whether it was the public which abused Tillotson, or Tillotson who had misunderstood him. He would only say, for he could not join in a cry to ruin those he differed from, that he abhorred two principles in religion, and pitied those who held them—obedience on mere authority without conviction, and persecution of man on pretence of serving God. When truth was clear, he thought union was best; where not, he thought charity best. He agreed with Hooker, that a few words spoken with meekness, humility, and love, are worth whole volumes of controversy — which commonly destroys charity, the best part of religion.

Tillotson replied without reserve. He had, he admitted, been troubled with doubts, and had sometimes spoken of them. He was sorry for it. He admired his old friend's wit and zeal; and so soon as he distinctly stated that he was *not* a Papist, he would do all in his power to correct the rumours that were about. Penn answered at once that he had no correspondence with the Jesuits, nor with any other body at Rome—that he wrote no letters to any priest of the Popish faith—that he was not even acquainted with any priest belonging to that communion. Yet, he added, though not a Romanist, he was a Catholic; he could not deny to others what he claimed for himself—thinking faith, piety, and providence, a better security than force; and that if truth could not succeed with her own weapons, all others would fail her. On the receipt of this letter Tillotson called on Penn; their intimacy was renewed. Tillotson did what he could to put an end to false report; but they whose purposes it served were unwilling to be set right, and the rumour not only spread more and more, but Tillotson's name was still coupled with it. Tillotson thereupon placed in his friend's hands a written disavowal, to be shown to such as should repeat the slander. It was years, however, before Penn heard the last of his Jesuitism.

Penn would gladly have returned to his colony, but the King pressed him to remain until an Act of Parliament had legally and firmly established freedom for thought. Penn's heart was yearning for the other world. The repose of the Delaware, the rising greatness of Philadelphia, haunted his dreams, and mingled with the scenes of his daily life. The favour of the King had powerful drawbacks, and he longed to escape from the atmosphere of a court into the forests of Pennsylvania. But a sense of duty kept him in England. By speech and writing, by his influence with the great, and by his power with Dissenters, he was working day and night at his great task. The chief obstacle was the mutual ignorance and bigotry of court and parliament,—and he strove to enlighten them on the policy of toleration. His 'Persuasive to Moderation' is an able and learned history of opinion and experiment on the subject. He called history to witness—he quoted the wisdom of the wise, and the experiences of time, in support of his argument. The paper was addressed to the King and Council; and contributed to procure that general pardon which emptied the jails of many thousands of prisoners,—

including twelve or thirteen hundred Quakers. Still this act of grace was due to the King; the penal laws remained in force; the sufferers were liable to be seized again. The bigots murmured at every fresh pardon, and the maintenance of the Test Act became the avowed policy of all parties in opposition. The hopes of Churchmen were already turning to the Hague; and the Prince of Orange, while professing liberal sentiments, took care to confirm them in their opposition to the King. Penn went over to the Hague—not in the formal character of an envoy, but so accredited as to satisfy the Prince that he spoke by authority—to ascertain his opinions. William had taken a fancy to the Tests, and though he allowed Penn two audiences, he adhered to his own plans. Penn was instructed to make the most liberal proposals, if William would aid the King to obtain a repeal of the Tests. James promised to consult him in everything, and to put his friends in the highest places. The Prince remained inflexible. He would consent to an Act of Toleration, but he would not consent to a repeal of the Tests—those bulwarks of the Church! While at the court of Holland, Penn mixed with the exiles who thronged the streets—the old comrades of Sydney and Argyle; he studied their views, and made acquaintance with their miseries. With Burnet he had long and frequent discussions; but the Protestant zeal of the doctor was only inflamed by his firm adherence to his old opinions. They met with suspicion—Burnet accusing Penn of leaning to Popery—Penn accusing Burnet of bigotry and intolerance; and they parted with coldness, and on the Churchman's side with hate.

Penn's hopes turned more and more towards Pennsylvania. There he had secured a home for the oppressed. Time, he knew, would make it a nation. He would help on the good work as fast as he might be able. So, having finished his business at the Hague, he went to Amsterdam, where he engaged Wilhelm Sewell—an old friend and correspondent—to translate his accounts of Pennsylvania into Flemish, and circulate them among the able and industrious farmers of the Low Countries. He travelled through Holland and into the Rhineland, bearing everywhere the tidings that a land of freedom was springing up in the New World, where every man enjoyed his full share of political power, and every class of opinions was respected. To the citizens of the Upper Rhine he could report the success of the German colony. At a short distance from Philadelphia their countrymen had built a town, which, in affectionate remembrance of the fatherland, they called Germanopolis. It rose in a beautiful and fertile district; on the spot were a number of fresh springs; in the vicinity were oak, walnut, and chestnut-trees in abundance; and the surrounding country was in many places favourable to the vine.

CHAPTER XXVIII.

MEDIATION (1686–89).

ON Penn's return to London he appealed to the King and Council in behalf of the English exiles. There were two classes of English in Holland. The most numerous was that of political offenders. At first Penn tried to obtain a general pardon; but the King would not give way so far. To individual cases he was open, and several pardons were obtained from him in his more gracious moods. But there were many who had merely fled from religious fear; and Penn reminded James that it would be in strict accordance with the gracious intentions he had formed, to offer these men indemnity and recall. Thus pressed, the King issued an order to that effect, and a great number of persons, who had not been engaged in treasonable acts against the government, returned to their homes. The indemnity was traced entirely to the influence of Penn; and the posterity of some of the men whom it restored to their country cherished for many years a grateful memory of his aid.

The failure of Penn's mission to the Prince of

Orange hurried matters to a crisis. James, resolved
to effect his purpose, not unnaturally, though most
unwisely, began to lean more and more towards
his great Catholic neighbour. Penn saw the danger
of such an alliance more clearly than the King, and
he counselled James against even raising the suspicion of a desire to rely on France. But James
was mad. It may be true that he had changed his
views ; instead of asking toleration for the faith
which he believed to be right, he meant to aim at
a complete subversion of the Established Church.
There is a change of tone in the correspondence
with Versailles. From the probabilities of gaining
a Bill of Toleration, the discussion assumes the
King's aim to be the reintroduction of Popery as
a state religion. James's son-in-law being with his
enemies, and Parliament being determined to thwart
his plans, James tried his right to suspend the
whole body of the penal laws. With one exception,
that of Street, his judges were of opinion that the
King had power to suspend these enactments. James
was not long in making use of his prerogative. On
the 18th of March, 1687, he called his privy council
together :—he told them he ·intended to use his
royal right. Experience had shown the uselessness
of penal laws. They did not prevent new sects
from springing up. They were a perpetual cause
of soreness and discontent. It was time to put an
end to these civil troubles. Conscience was a thing
not to be forced ; he was resolved to give all classes
of his people that right of opinion which he claimed
himself. On the fourth day of April, 1687, came

out his Majesty's gracious Declaration to all his loving subjects for Liberty of Conscience. By this famous act the King suspended all the penal laws against free thought in matters of religion, and forbade the offer of either test or oath to persons taking office under the crown.

It was a wise and noble measure, most unwisely introduced. Locke might have written some of its sentences, while others might have been inspired by Father Petre. Penn, though gladly snatching at the boon of freedom, was annoyed that he must gain it from prerogative instead of by consent of Parliament.

Apart from flaws of origin, this Declaration of Liberty of Conscience was received with different feelings. Whigs and Tories equally disliked it. They had not been harried by the magistrates. Their brethren were not languishing in jails, and ruined by repeated and increasing fines. The laws were on their side, for they had made these laws themselves. To them the King's declaration of Liberty was but a declaration of 'Indulgence;' and by this papistical and opprobrious nick-name they described it in a hundred pamphlets, sermons, squibs, and songs. Dissenters, on the other hand, were loud in gratitude. Their prison-doors flew open. Many of them got into the army, navy, and civil service. From persecuted wretches, only fit for stocks and jails, they acquired the rights and dignities of Englishmen. Some of the more wealthy and intelligent were made magistrates and sheriffs. Quakers began to take some share in public business ; at the next yearly meeting of their body the question was discussed whether they should accept or refuse magistracies. All Dissenters were elated at the change. The Anabaptists were the first to approach the throne with an expression of their thanks ; the Quakers followed ; then came the Independents, the Presbyterians, and the Catholics. Penn was with the Quakers, who agreed to waive the ceremony of the hat. In Sunderland's apartment the deputation uncovered themselves, and leaving their hats behind, went into the presence bareheaded. Penn made a short speech to the King, and then delivered an address from the general body. James assured this deputation he had always been of opinion that conscience should be free, and he appealed to Penn in confirmation of what he told them. He should remain firm to his Declaration of Liberty ; and he hoped to establish it before he died in so regular and legal a manner that future ages should have no reason to change it. Penn needed this assurance. He feared the King's violent temper not less than the bigotry of Parliament. He had no confidence in a freedom resting on the will of James ; and he inserted in the address a hope that means would be taken to get the sanction of both houses to this act. In private he was plainer still. He told the King the only way to secure confidence and to obtain the sanction of Parliament, was to act on open and moderate principles—to banish from his presence the Jesuits and ultra-Papists, who surrounded him daily at Whitehall. In this way only could freedom be fully given to conscience. If James had followed this counsel, he might have died on the throne of his ancestors, and might have left behind an honourable reputation amongst our native kings. He hesitated—and he fell.

The Jesuits had obtained commanding influence, and the King's true friends began to see that their pernicious counsels would bring disaster on his head. Against these Jesuits Penn was straining every nerve, —often using a boldness of expostulation which James would not have brooked from any other man. Penn told him that neither Churchmen nor Dissenters would bear their pride and ambition. The nation, he hinted broadly, was alarmed, but still more indignant. Penn wished to see the Whigs taken into greater confidence, and he kept up an irregular intercourse between their leaders and the court. He carried Trenchard, Treby, and Lawton, to the royal closet, where he urged them to speak openly to the King, disguising nothing of the state of the nation, but placing before him in its true aspect the general opinion of his course. James was much impressed by these discourses. Trenchard was an accomplished courtier; he had lived in exile; and he owed his restoration to his native land to Penn. Lawton, a young man of parts and spirit, had attracted Penn's notice. In politics he was a state Whig. It was at Lawton's instance that Penn had braved the King by asking a pardon for Aaron Smith. One day over their wine at Popple's house, where Penn had carried Lawton to dine, Penn said to his host: 'I have brought you such a man as you never saw before; for I have just now asked him how I might do something for himself, and he has desired me to get a pardon for another man! I will do that if I can; but,' he added, turning to Lawton, 'I should be glad if thou wilt think of some kindness for thyself.' 'Ah,' said Lawton, after a moment's thought, 'I can tell you how you might indeed prolong my life.' 'How so?' asked Penn; 'I am no physician.' Lawton answered: 'There is Jack Trenchard in exile. If you could get leave for him to come home with safety and honour, the drinking of a bottle now and then with Jack would make me so cheerful that it would prolong my life.' The party laughed, and Penn promised to do what he could. He went to the Lord Chancellor, got him to join in a solicitation, and in a few days the future secretary was pardoned and allowed to return to England.

As Trenchard knew the exiles and the opinions current in Holland, Penn felt how serviceable he might be if James would only listen to his advice. Things were so near a change at one moment, that Penn was actually sent by the King to Somers with an offer of the solicitor-generalship; this was before it was offered to Sir William Williams, and consequently before the trial of the seven prelates.

The next step into which the King was urged by his Jesuit friends was an attempt to obtain a footing for the members of his own Church in the Universities. The right of Catholics, as of all other Englishmen, to share in the advantages offered by our national seats of learning liberal men would now concede—though the right is not yet legally admitted. To James it seemed intolerable that descendants of the men who founded and endowed the colleges with their worldly goods should be excluded from them because they had *not* changed their religion. As the presidency of Magdalen College, one of the richest foundations in Europe, was vacant, James desired to see it filled by one who was not unfriendly to Catholics, and he therefore named Antony Farmer for election. Farmer was not legally qualified, and was besides a man of ill repute. The Fellows of the College drew up a petition praying the King to name some other person; through an error this petition did not reach his Majesty for several days; and in the meantime, not hearing from Whitehall, the Fellows elected John Hough, a man of blameless life and moderate abilities, to the chair. Hough and Farmer both appealed to the King,—and James referred the case to his Ecclesiastical Commissioners, by whom Hough's election was declared void, and Farmer's cause was dropped. Some weeks elapsed, that passion might have time to cool. When James sent a new mandate ordering a fresh election, recommending the bishop of the diocese for election, the Fellows would not hear of it. The King was angry. In his journey down to Bath, he received at Oxford the Heads of Colleges; he upbraided them in unkingly terms for disobedience; and he threatened to proceed against them to extremities unless they instantly obeyed.

There was much need of wise and sober mediation. Penn, who was going through the west country on a preaching tour, arrived at Oxford with the King on Saturday afternoon, September 3, and stayed till Monday afternoon, September 5. He was hardly fifty hours in Oxford; yet his stay was long enough to admit of his being drawn into the Magdalen business, and even to his becoming a principal in the dispute.

On Sunday, Mr. Creech, one of the offending Fellows, dined with Penn, and told him such a tale, that Penn was more than half persuaded to adventure in their cause. Being pressed by Creech, he offered to see the Fellows in a body, and to hear their story. Early on Monday he went over to the College. Hough, the selected president, received him. Hunt, Creech, Bailey, and the rest, were present, and explained their case; citing their college charter, by the terms of which Antony Farmer could not hold the office of president. Penn saw that they were right, and that the court, in forcing them against the law, was wrong. Not satisfied with letting them perceive that he was with them in his mind, he offered, then and there, to write a letter in their behalf to James. They took him at his word, and in their presence he composed a letter which they made good speed to place in James's hands. Their case, Penn told his Majesty, was very hard; they could not yield without an evident violation of their oaths. Such mandates, he continued, were a force on conscience, and were therefore contrary to the King's profession and intention. James could not be moved. Though Penn left Oxford on the

Monday, Hough and his little senate had already come to look upon him as their friend. Bailey wrote to him after he quitted Oxford, as one who had been so kind as to appear in their behalf already, and was reported by all who knew him to employ much of his time in doing good, and in using his credit with the King to undeceive him of any wrong impressions he might entertain. All the contemporary accounts are conceived in the same spirit. Creech says he appeared in their behalf. Sykes is equally emphatic. Indeed the letter to the King would be decisive, were there no other evidence. That letter emboldened the Fellows to draw up a strong petition, which they signed and carried to Lord Sunderland, who promised to lay it before the King.

The King refused to listen. Remonstrance and entreaty were in vain. Though Penn denounced his measures as contrary to his often-avowed sentiments in favour of Liberty of Conscience, and Chief Justice Herbert declared them to be against the law, he would not retreat. He professed to believe it impossible for Oxford men to oppose the royal will. A sincere bigot himself, and scrupulously truthful in his words, he could not imagine, after a declaration of unlimited obedience had been promulgated by the University, that the members of a single college would dare to appeal from their own dogma to the free instincts of nature. 'If you are really Church-of-England men,' he said to the deputation, 'prove it by your obedience.'

Magdalen had still much need of Penn's services; and to secure his mediation in their cause, Hough, Hunt, Cradock, and some other Fellows were deputed to wait on him at Windsor, where he lodged. They found him ready to receive them and to hear their story. He expressed his great concern for the welfare of the college, and said he had made many efforts to reconcile the King to what had passed. He grieved that things had gone so far before he was aware of the dispute; in an earlier stage—before the King's self-love had been wounded—the affair would have been easy to arrange. Still he would do his best; and if he failed, it would not be for want of will to serve their cause. He broached the doubts which had occurred to him; the Fellows answered one by one; and after much talk with them, he said his first impressions gained at Oxford were confirmed. He felt that they were in the right. Before the Oxford Fellows saw him, they were afraid that he would make some offer at accommodation; but though he wished the quarrel ended, he would not insult them by advising them to yield. Once he asked the Fellows, smiling, how they would like to see Hough made Bishop. Cradock replied in the same vein of pleasantry—they would be very glad, as the presidency and bishopric would go well enough together. Hough answered (as he says), ' seriously;' and the allusion dropped. Possessed with the fixed idea that James intended to rob them of their college, the Fellows said the Papists had already wrested from them Christ Church and University; the contest was now for Magdalen. This touched Penn nearly; he had written much against Catholic doctrine; and he answered them with fervour— That they shall never have. The Fellows, he said, might be assured. The Catholics had got two colleges; to them he did not dispute their right; but he could confide in their prudence. Honest men would defend their just claims; but should they go beyond their common rights as Englishmen, and ask from royal favour what was not their due, they would peril all they had acquired. He felt sure they would not be so senseless. At the same time he told his visitors that he thought it unfair and unwise in them to attempt to close the national Universities to any class; others besides Churchmen wished to give their children a learned education. To this free counsel Hough—a very high Churchman — made demur. Penn ceased to urge this point. Though he could not well agree with their politics, he said he was willing to be of use to them. Hough suggested that he could promote their interests by laying a true statement of the case before their sovereign. They produced some papers, which he read; these papers he promised to read again to the King, unless peremptorily forbidden. And so the deputation left him.

James was not to be stirred from his purpose. A commission was sent down to Oxford, and the uncompromising champions of Church prerogative were all ejected from the college. Yet they lost little by their temporary removal. His self-love being gratified, the King soon afterwards restored the Fellows to their honours and emoluments; and after the revolution Hough was rewarded for his resistance with a bishopric.

Affairs were now hastening to a crisis. When Dissenters and Commonwealth-men were the only parties likely to fall under the frowns of authority, Oxford could issue precepts of unconditional obedience; but when its own rights and privileges were placed in peril, it was the first and the most obstinate in resisting. A cynic would have smiled at this conversion; but Penn remembered how that precept had clouded the last days of Sydney, and he longed to break away from a scene so full of corruption to the freedom of his own virgin forests. In the very height of his courtly greatness, he wrote to his friends in Philadelphia. 'The Lord only,' he said, 'knew the sorrow, the expense, the hazard of his absence, from the colony;' but his prayers were poured out fervently and with a prostrate soul to Him for aid to return to that beloved country where he was anxious to live and die. The King entreated him to stay in England. He declared himself resolved to establish toleration and to abolish the Test Act; in which good work, he said, he should have to rely on Penn's help and counsel. Though his own affairs were getting daily more and more confused by his absence from Pennsylvania, Penn could not desert the headstrong reformer in his hour of need.

Not satisfied with private mediation, such as he had exerted in the Oxford affair, he took up his pen and wrote the elaborate pamphlet, 'Good Advice to the Church of England, the Roman Catholic, and

Protestant Dissenters'—in which he showed the wisdom and policy, as well as Christian duty, of repealing the Test Act and all other laws against opinion. He admitted frankly, as he had done to the Magdalen delegates, that if he had to choose a state church, he would prefer the one that was by law established to either a Catholic, a Presbyterian, or any other. But he rejected the idea of a supreme and intolerant church. Opinion ought to be free; though at the same time he thought a proper respect should be paid by small bodies of sectaries to the national feeling. Therefore he urged the Catholics, seeing how few they were, and how powerful the feeling was against them, to be content with toleration. His fear was that the King, under ill advice, would take some dangerous step against the Church, and ruin all. To counteract the rashness of James's temper he procured letters from influential pesrons, which he read to him in private, without telling him from whom they came. He took with him several Churchmen to the royal closet, to undeceive the King, as to that passive obedience on which he counted for impunity in his attacks. But James would not believe; he knew the spirit of the English Church; for had not Oxford pledged the body to observe obedience to the royal will, as though it were the voice of God? Lawton almost laughed in the King's face. 'What,' he said, 'does any man live up to the doctrines he professes? The Churchmen may believe that resistance is a sin; but they believe that swearing and drunkenness are sins also —yet many of them drink very hard and swear very often.' 'Ha!' replied James, smiling disdainfully, 'you don't know the loyalty of the Church as well as I do,'—and the bold expostulator bowed his head.

In April (1688) James renewed the Declaration of Liberty of Conscience; and commanded all his clergy to read this document in their churches. Penn was much alarmed. He thought the King was mad. To force the clergy was to violate that very Liberty of Conscience which the King conferred upon his people. Many of the Churchmen could not in their consciences comply with such an order. Penn entreated James to pause; to let the Declaration make its way in peace; to summon parliament, and get this liberty secured by law. The King soon found that Penn was right; his clergy, though professing blind obedience to his will, would not allow his edict to be read; and James, on the suggestion of Jeffreys, sent the seven Bishops who had signed the paper of remonstrance and refusal to the Tower.

By word and act, Penn strove to save these prelates from arrest, and after their commitment to the Tower, he strained his utmost power with James to get a pardon and release for them. When baby James, the Prince of Wales, was born, Penn waited on the King, and pressed him very warmly to perform an act of royal grace. 'On such a happy day,' said Penn, 'everybody ought to rejoice, and everybody would rejoice, if the Bishops were let out, and it was known that a general pardon would be issued soon.' He therefore urged the King to send his order for Sir Edward Hales, Lieutenant of the Tower, to set his prisoners free; and also to let the public understand that a council would be called, and a general pardon issued as soon as it could pass the Seal.

More intimate advisers swayed the royal mind; and long before the parliament was to meet, the King was housed on foreign soil.

CHAPTER XXIX.

IN THE SHADE (1688–91).

THE King's flight became the signal for a rush. The tools, the favourites, the friends, the ministers of James, thought proper to retire from public notice. Curious were the means of escape and ludicrous the incidents attending it. The redoubtable Jeffreys tried to escape in the dress of a common sailor; the subtle and intriguing Sunderland quitted his country in his wife's cap and petticoat. Of the men who had been near the throne for the last three years and a half, Penn was almost the only one who remained in London. Knowing no offence, he turned a deaf ear to every entreaty of his friends to fly. They urged—that he had been too intimate with the King to escape suspicion, and that if he would not follow James he had a refuge open to him in America, where he might remain in peace until the heat of party vengeance passed away. He would not change his course. He would not change his lodgings; he would not keep in the shade. The Council, who assumed the management of affairs, sent to him as he was taking his usual walk, and being told that they were sitting, he at once obeyed the summons to attend. He told them that he loved his country and the Protestant faith, and had ever done his best to serve them. James, he said, had been his friend and his father's friend, and therefore, though he no longer owed him allegiance as a subject, he retained for him the old respect which he had paid him as a man. He had done nothing, and should do nothing, but what he was willing to answer before God and his country.

The Lords were at a loss. They could not free a friend of James without approval from the Prince of Orange. They got over their difficulty by taking security in 6000l. for Penn's appearance in the following term, to answer any charge which might be brought against him. With a threat of prosecution hanging above his head, he was permitted to remain at large. He went to Worminghurst, and watched the drama from his eyrie in the Sussex downs.

Penn was not long left in peace. Fresh causes of suspicion rose ; spies and informers dogged his footsteps ; he was said to be rich, and there were many about the court who wanted money. At the end of February the Lords in Council issued warrants for his arrest. But Penn was made aware of these new accusations, of the witnesses whose evidence was to be taken, and he declined to surrender himself till Easter term. But not to sanction malicious reports by flight, he wrote to Shrewsbury, to say that he was living at his country-house, attending to his private affairs and the concerns of his colony;

that he did not feel justified in giving himself up an unbailable prisoner; that he was already bound over to appear on the first day of term; that he could affirm, without reserve or equivocation, his entire ignorance of any new plot or conspiracy against the government. William acceded to his request to be allowed to remain in the country till his day of trial. By Easter term (1689) men's minds were calmer; and when Penn appeared in court to defend himself, not one of his accusers dared to confront him. Not a whisper was uttered of his being a Jesuit. No man accused him of any wrong. The magistrate declared that nothing had been proved against him. He was free.

Though free in person, he had reason to be anxious for his province. William had desired the crown in order to provide the means of waging war on France. His hope by day, his dream by night, was war; a coalition of the Protestant powers; a declaration against Louis; a victorious march on Paris. War with France, as Penn well knew, however glorious to the arms of William, might be ruin to his province. War in Flanders and Brabant meant fire and sword in Canada, Pennsylvania, and New York. A march of English infantry towards the Sambre and the Meuse might bring a horde of savages to the Susquehannah and the Delaware. How could the colony of peace, the city of fraternal love, be saved? As yet, this war was in the future, and the wisest men were puzzled as to where it might begin. Some thought it would begin on English soil. King James was ready to return. A vast majority of his Scotch and Irish subjects would have hailed him with delight, and even in the English shires opinions were so nicely balanced that observers who had no desire to see him feared that he had only to appear in order to regain what he had lost.

Amidst these doubts, Penn found some comfort in the fact that William stood by the principles he had published at the Hague.

At the risk of giving ground of offence to the Church party, William pressed for an Act of Toleration for Dissenters, and even declared it necessary to afford protection to the Papists. Though his temper was not merciful, he was a politic prince. He knew what power the position he aimed to acquire, as protector-general of Protestants from the fiords of Norway to the Theiss, would give him in the councils of Europe; and he naturally asked himself with what effect he could interfere in behalf of Finn and Magyar, if he gave the Catholic at home a just cause of complaint? Even before his election to the throne he had entered into treaties with the Emperor and the Pope.

Penn was gratified with the results, though they fell short of his desires. The new Act disarmed the petty tyrant. It opened the prison-doors to crowds of Quakers. He hoped it would gradually lead to a still more liberal and enlightened policy, as the dominant parties became aware how great an accession of strength it would bring to the nation. But he had little time to indulge in these reflections. He had little time to dream his dreams of a coming golden age. The King had hardly left for Ireland, where the war was burning fiercely, ere he found his name denounced in public and a proclamation issued for his arrest. This ban was issued on the twenty-fourth of June. Penn was lying on a sick-bed; ill of a surfeit and relapse; and six weeks passed before he could move a foot or even hold a pen. So soon as he could stir, he wrote a letter to Daniel Finch, Earl of Nottingham, in which he said, 'Since the government does not think fit to trust me, I shall trust it . . . . and therefore I humbly beg to know when and where I shall wait upon thee.' Nottingham, a very honest man, a friend of Toleration, was the King's Secretary of State. Fifteen days later Penn was brought before the Council and discharged; there being no evidence of any serious kind against him. Three weeks afterwards the King returned from Ireland to renew with higher zest the war with France.

When war was once begun, the King perceived how much his power of making front against the French in Canada would be strengthened if the full control of all the Colonies from Charleston to Boston were vested in his crown. Vast deserts had been signed away; these deserts were becoming states; and William saw how much they might assist him in his wars. A little had been done already. When the charters were revised by James, some articles had been amended in a royal sense. The charter of New England had suffered much. A good excuse was offered in the state of public feeling in the Colonies for robbing them of rights they dearly prized. Not one of those Colonies had been warm in William's cause. In Maryland and in Virginia the people were either Catholics or Cavaliers. In Pennsylvania they were either Quakers loving peace, or Swedes and French who felt no passion for the strife. Lord Baltimore delayed his proclamation of the new reign, and there were serious thoughts of stripping him of his Colonial crown; but for the moment William held his hand, not liking to disturb existing order in the midst of actual war.

Penn was anxious to go out. He had been several times arrested; his life, to say nothing of his freedom, was no longer safe. No accusation was too monstrous not to find some people who, from either hatred or self-interest, were willing to give it credit. Affairs were going wrong in his province. New York, exposed to the French, was egging on the people of New England to attack New France. Meetings were being held to organise defence; the Colonists were calling on each other; here for money, there for men. The Puritans of New England buckled to their sides the swords which their fathers had worn at Naseby and Marston Moor; and a warlike ardour which was gladdening the stern and martial soul of William spread from Massachussetts to the Carolinas. The Quakers alone were calm. Amidst this martial preparation they declared they had no quarrel with the French, and would not fight. If French and Indians came against them, they said they would go out to meet them unarmed, and tell them so.

What could William do? The Pennsylvanians

would neither defend their own towns, nor pay a war-tax to the frontier governments of Albany and New York. Penn took a more practical view of the crisis. His colony contained others besides Quakers,—Germans, Dutchmen, Swedes, and English,—who would shoulder a musket and draw a sword in defence of their homes. These men had no thought of giving up their goods to the Canadians, their scalps to the Iroquois; and the pacific disposition of the Quaker majority only added zeal to the obtrusive energy of the young and unconvinced. A war party was gaining ground in the colony. Penn felt how necessary it was that he should be on the spot to appease these scruples, and to regulate this rising heat. England had no further need of him. His residence had cost him six thousand pounds—the greater part of which he had given away in charities, in jailors' fees, and in legal expenses attendant on the liberation of prisoners. Preparations for his departure were hastily made; a vessel was engaged to carry him across the Atlantic; the Secretary of State appointed a convoy to protect him on his outward voyage.

When he was ready to start, he was suddenly called to the death-bed of George Fox,—whose decease took place on the 13th of January, 1691. Over his old friend's grave at Bunhill Fields, Penn delivered a long oration. Three weeks after this ceremony warrants were issued by the Council to arrest him on a charge of treason.

Penn was tiring of these daily warrants of arrest, and this time took no pains to help his enemies in their search. He ceased to run about the streets, to preach in public, and to court the general gaze. His wife was very ill, and Springett, his elder son, not strong. His family remained at Worminghurst, on the Sussex down, where he was often with them when the eyes of neighbouring justices of the peace were shut. But he was neither in disguise nor hiding. Though he stayed in London mostly, he lived in his own house, engaged in writing books. 'I know my enemies,' he wrote, 'their true character and history, and their intrinsic value to either this or any other government. I commit them to time, with my own conduct and afflictions.' He was well aware how much a man must pay for leave to do good, but he was ready to pay out that price.

CHAPTER XXX.

A HOUSE OF DOLE (1692–94).

WHEN Penn was under cloud, and driven away, the Council made quick work of his American affairs. Their object was to bring his province under more direct control, and on the tenth of March, 1692, an Order in Council took away his government, and placed it in commission, with a view to joining Pennsylvania with New York. So far as King William meddled, the question was decided on military grounds. Colonel Fletcher was the governor of New York, and William wished to strengthen Fletcher, who was menaced by the French. No case was urged against the rule of Penn, except that it was one of peace. No lack of faith or loyalty was proved against him. William felt that during war the city of fraternal love must be defended from the French and Iroquois, then hovering on the frontier, by a rougher arm than Penn's, and he desired his Council to prepare the draft of a commission for his signature, uniting in a single hand the governments of Pennsylvania, Delaware, the two Jerseys, New York, and Connecticut.

To Penn this blow was crushing. Nearly all his fortune had been sunk in Pennsylvania; he had paid all costs of governing from his private purse. His means were pinched on every side, nor could he tell which way to turn for help. His timber had been cut and sold; his Irish lands were ruined by the war; and Shangarry Castle was sequestered by the crown. His rents were stopped. Guli was worse; and Springett, his intelligent and handsome boy, was entering on that stage of slow decline which led him to an early grave. His second son, in whom the blood of Admiral Penn was strong, required a father's care: for in his mother's weakness he was apt to run into excess. The Fords, too, were beginning to display their teeth, though with a cat-like smoothness and a cat-like patience.

Penn was much in London, where the council were not eager to molest him, though the warrants were allowed to stand. 'God seeth in secret, and will one day reward openly,' he wrote: 'my privacy is not because men have sworn truly, but falsely, against me; for wicked men have laid in wait for me, and false witnesses have laid to my charge things that I knew not.' With whom he lived in these dark days is nowhere told. Not feeling safe at Worminghurst, he was compelled to move from place to place, and leave his sickly wife and drooping child unseen for weeks, except by stealth at dead of night, and in the houses of their friends, where wife and son could come to him unseen. We know that he was busy with his pen. For not to count such trifles as a 'Preface to Barclay's Works,' and a second 'Preface to Burnyeat's Works,' six pieces of importance came from him in this retirement. 'The New Athenian,' 'Just Measures,' and 'A Key Opening the Way,' are three polemical discourses. 'A Brief account of the People called Quakers,' is a picture of his sect, as he conceived that body in his mind. 'Some Fruits of Solitude: reflections and maxims relating to the conduct of human life,' takes in a larger field; and 'An Essay toward the present Peace' is one of those fine efforts of his pen, which help us to understand how a disciple of George Fox could have been the intellectual friend of John Locke.

Speaking of himself in the preface of 'Some Fruits of Solitude,' he says—he 'has now had some time he could call his own, a property he has ever before been short of, in which he has taken a view of himself and of the world, observed wherein he has gone wrong or wasted good effort, and has come to the conclusion, that if he had to live his life over again, he could serve God, his neighbour, and himself, better than he had done, and have seven precious years of time to spare, though he was not an old man yet, and had certainly not been one of the idlest.' Specimens of his maxims will suffice to show the character of the whole collection.—'We are in pain to make our children scholars—not men; to talk rather than to know. This is true canting.'—'They only have a right to censure who have a heart to help: the rest is cruelty, not justice.'—'Love labour: if thou dost not want it for food, thou wilt for physic.' 'To delay justice is injustice.'—'The truest end of life is, to find the life that never ends.'—'To do evil that good may come of it, is bungling in politics as well as in morals.' Many of his maxims are political, 'Ministers of state should undertake their posts at their peril ; if princes wish to override them, let them show the laws—and resign : if fear, gain, or flattery prevail, let them answer for it to the law.'

His second work is more original in form and substance. In 'An Essay towards the present and future Peace of Europe,' he inquires into the polity of nations,—the causes which lead to war,— the conditions necessary to peace. He finds that the great aim of statesmanship is to secure peace and order ; and he demonstrates that these ends are to be obtained more readily and certainly by justice than by war. But the question then occurs —How can justice be obtained for nations except by force ? He reviews the history of society, and finds that in early times individuals stood in the place of states ; every man assumed the right to be a judge in his own cause—every man claimed to be his own avenger. As society advanced from a ruder to a more civilized form, the individuals bound themselves to submit to general restrictions : to give up the old right of judging and avenging their own quarrels for the public good. Why then should not Europeans do for themselves, that which Celts and Teutons, Franks and Scandinavians, have already done on a smaller scale ? As England has its Parlia- ment, France its States-General, Germany its Diet

—each in its sphere over-ruling private passion,—
he proposes that Europe shall have her Congress.
Before this sovereign council he would have disputes
of nation and nation heard; and its decisions
carried out by the united power of Europe. He
refers to Henri Quatre and his League of Peace,
and proves from the United Provinces that peace
might easily be kept if kings and statesmen would
but try.

These dreams were all connected with his great
Experiment.

Colonel Fletcher, a mere soldier, coarse, abrupt,
unlettered, was a stranger to his ideas and intentions; and there was only too much reason to fear
that he would overturn that peaceful and popular
constitution which had been framed with so much
thought. Penn never doubted that in the end he
should be able to regain his colony, and continue,
under happier auspices, his great Experiment; but
he also saw that mischief done in a day might require years of patient government to retrieve. He
therefore wrote a letter to the newly appointed
officer in which he warned him to tread softly and
with caution—as the soil and the government belonged to him as much as his crown belonged to the
King. His charter, he said, had been neither attacked
nor recalled; in the face of the law he was still
master of his province; and as he was an Englishman, he would maintain his right.

To his friends and to the officers of his government in Philadelphia, he wrote, advising them to
insist with moderation on their charters. He told

them to hear patiently; to obey the crown whenever it spoke in the voice of law; to meet asser-
tions that the French and Indians would attack
them, not by quoting their own notions of war and
the friendly relations of the Iroquois—vain arguments to such a man as Fletcher—but by showing
how well their territory was defended by nature,
being equally unassailable by land and sea.

Fletcher began his reign by an attempt to abro-
gate the whole body of the colonial laws. Himself
an ultra-Royalist, the laws of Pennsylvania violated
all his notions of propriety. When the Assembly
objected to this sweeping measure, he showed them
his commission under the great seal of England.
In reply, they pointed to their charter, also under
the great seal of England; and some of those who
held commissions from the proprietor at once withdrew from the Assembly. Before Fletcher went
to Philadelphia, he had written for supplies: the
Quakers had returned for answer, they had nothing
to send him, except their good wishes. Vexed at
their obstinacy, he repaired to the seat of government, and asked them for a subsidy. The Assembly
answered with a list of grievances. No terms could be
made; they would not give up a single law. Fletcher
felt himself committed; and to save his honour,
he proposed to re-enact the code as it then stood.
The Assembly would not consent. 'We are but
men who represent the people,' said John White,
'we dare not begin to re-enact any one of the
laws, lest we seem to admit that all the rest are
void.' Fletcher was in a mess. His object was to

obtain a vote of money; and the colonists would only give it on their own conditions. At last he submitted. On receiving from him a distinct recognition of their legislative powers, the Assembly granted him a penny in the pound,—stipulating, as a salve to tender consciences, that not a farthing of it should be dipt in blood. A permanent advantage remained with the chamber at the close of this dispute; they had bought the right to originate bills; and this right they ever afterwards maintained. Dissatisfied with his new command, Fletcher wrote a letter to the King, urging, in the strongest terms, the impossibility of gaining a regular war-vote in Pennsylvania, and praying his Majesty to consider the propriety of forming that colony, New York, the Jerseys, and Connecticut, into one state, with a general assembly, as the only means of out-voting the Quakers, and compelling them to lend their aid in the common defence. The King's displeasure fell on Penn; and the Privy Council went so far as to order the Attorney-general to inspect his patent, and see if some legal flaw could not be found in it.

In the latter part of the year 1692, Rochester, Somers, Henry Sydney, and Sir John Trenchard, made an effort to put an end to the shame of seeing Penn deprived of his liberty. Ranelagh, Rochester, and Romney, went to the King and laid the whole case before him. William answered that Penn was his old acquaintance as well as theirs; that he had nothing to say against him; that he was at liberty to go about his affairs just as he pleased. The

Lords pressed his Majesty to send this message to Sir John Trenchard, principal Secretary of State, and Romney was selected as its bearer on account of his intimacy with Penn. Trenchard was glad to convey these tidings to his old benefactor; he spoke with feeling of the unsolicited kindness he had received from Penn in the dark times of Monmouth and Sydney; and was pleased to have it in his power to show that he was not ungrateful. Penn was not content that the matter should end in this private way. The act of grace looked like a pardon:—he wanted an acquittal. He asked his friends to get him a public hearing; and in November a council was called at Westminster, before which he defended his conduct so completely to the King's satisfaction, that he was absolved from every charge.

Guli's health was now completely breaking. She had never been herself again since Penn was forced to quit his home. She followed him into his hiding-places; she and Springett, now a bright and gentle child, too grave and learned for his years, and with a wan and hectic face. Her troubles bore her down. At Hoddesden, where they found a sheltering roof, she drooped and died; the 'one of ten thousand, the wise, chaste, humble, modest, constant and undaunted' daughter of Sir William Springett; died in exile, as it were, away from all the comforts of her home. Her end was very sweet, and she was laid among the grassy mounds at Jordans, near the lovely village where she first set maiden eyes on William Penn.

Nothing could arouse her husband from his sorrows till he heard that Colonel Fletcher was proposing to abolish the separate charter of Pennsylvania, and to form one government out of all the northern colonies. William was inclined to Fletcher's policy; for France, victorious on the continent, was menacing America; the Governor of New York would not answer for his province; and the King was but too glad of any plea for strengthening his military powers. Penn thought that if he were in America, his presence might reconcile parties now at variance, and put an end to dangerous complaints. But where could he obtain the funds? The woods at Worminghurst were sadly thinned; two thousand pounds of timber having been already cut. Owner of twenty million acres of land, he could not raise a few hundred pounds. The Irish property had ceased to yield him rent; and his unfaithful stewards, the Fords, pretended they could hardly make his English income meet his outgo. In the depth of his distress a thought occurred to him:—he had spent a fortune on his colony; on the million acres sold there was a quit-rent, which, for ease of the colonists, he had allowed to stand over; and for ten years he had not received a shilling of his due. Why not apply to these prosperous settlers in the land he had made for them, —recently blessed with abundant seasons,—for a loan of ten thousand pounds—a hundred pounds each from a hundred persons? This amount would set him right; the quit-rents and the lands would be security to the lenders. To an old friend, Robert

Turner, he opened his heart, and made proposals, pledging himself, in the event of its success, to sail immediately with a party of emigrants, who were only waiting for a signal; if they refused him this kindness, he knew not where to turn. Then came the old, sad story once again. The men to whom he looked for help — to whom in confidence he laid bare his wants — sought in his distress an opportunity to encroach on his just rights. They said they loved him much — but still they had no mind to lend.

Unable to get help from America, Penn resolved to fight his battle to the end at home. Calling on the friends who had recently done him service, he prevailed on them to take his case once more in hand; if possible, to procure the restoration of his colonial government, with the rank and dignities attached to it by Charles. King William being abroad, he drew up a petition to the Queen, praying her Majesty to order an inquiry into the whole train of facts alleged by him, and if her Majesty was satisfied, to grant him a re-instatement of his rights.

Mary received this petition with favour. Lady Ranelagh had prepared her mind. Mary referred his petition to the Council, who consulted the Board of Trade and the law officers of the crown; and finding no legal flaw in the charter itself, nor any subsequent act to warrant forfeiture, she admitted his claims to be made out. The Lords of Trade and Plantations asserted, — as they were bound to do in dealing as statesmen with a case so peculiar and exceptional, — that although the soil and the government belonged to Penn, as lord proprietor under the great seal, the King's government, still retaining its imperial right, was laid under the necessity of defending the province from its enemies as part and parcel of the empire; but that so soon as war was finished in Europe, and fear of invasion had subsided in Canada, the government must devolve on Penn as owner of the soil. The Five Nations, long in amity with the English, had been won over to the Canadian interest; numerous farms had been sacked and burnt in Albany; settlers had been either massacred or carried off; and it was feared that the friendly Lenni Lenapé would be compelled to join the great confederacy of their tribes. In this event, the forests of Pennsylvania would afford no protection to the unarmed towns and villages scattered over the country; and devoted as he was to peace, Penn saw the folly of maintaining a passive attitude under a tomahawk and a scalping-knife. He promised the Council that as early as convenient he would repair to the colony in person; and in the meantime he undertook to supply money and men for the general defence. Markham was a soldier; there were men in the province who felt no scruple at bearing arms; and Penn had little fear of raising any contingent that the crown might fix. In case he met with opposition from the Assembly, he stipulated that he would then surrender the direction of affairs entirely to the King.

On the ninth of August, 1694—thirty months after the appointment of Colonel Fletcher—an Order in Council was made, restoring Penn to his government, revoking the military commission, and appointing eighty men and their complete equipment and charges as the contingent of Pennsylvania, to be maintained on either the frontiers or at New York, so long as war should last.

CHAPTER XXXI.

LAND OF PROMISE (1694-99).

WITH Guli dead and Springett dying, Penn was not in case to go in person to Philadelphia, and he therefore sent out a new commission to Colonel Markham as his deputy-governor. King William gave his sanction to this act.

Six years elapsed after the restitution of his charter ere he could set his foot again in the Promised Land. Two years he acted as a nurse to his dying boy; his almost constant companion by day and night. Everything that tender nurture, parental watchfulness, and medical skill, could do for him, was done. In spite of all, the youth grew worse and worse;—and fell asleep in his father's arms on the 2nd of April, 1696, in the twenty-first year of his age. Penn's other children still living—Mary and Hannah having died in infancy—were Letitia and William; the latter now his heir, and, as it seemed, the future lord proprietor of Pennsylvania. Springett had the virtues as well as the names of his joint ancestry; to his father's strong sense of political liberty, his fervour and devotion to a great cause, he added the grace and gentleness of his mother and grandmother.   Of all the young people about her in her old age, he had been the favourite of Lady Springett; and it was for his use and instruction that she committed the memoirs of her early life to writing.   But the younger boy was like his grandfather the Admiral; bold and self-willed; quick in quarrel; full of pride and worldly ambition; sensuous in his tastes, and scornful in his words. Yet he, too, had fine qualities :—he was generous even to a fault; he had a keen sense of honour; he had a turn and capacity for business; and he had in a high degree the courage of his race.   From an early period he had shown dislike of the simple routine of his father's house; and sought in the world illicit pleasures which he could not find at home.   Wild blood came out.   He would have liked the old romps of his grandmother, Lady Penn, at the Navy Gardens, and would have joined with pleasure in the Admiral's suppers at the Three Cranes.   With anxious feeling Penn looked forward to the day when he might have to yield the government of his colony to this rash and jovial youth.

Penn meant to settle in America, among the people he had planted in the Promised Land.   To this end he must have a mother to his children and a keeper to his house. He fixed his eyes on Hannah, daughter of Thomas Callowhill of Bristol, a lady he had known for many years.   Hannah accepted him with the understanding that their future home was to be at Pennsbury on the Delaware; and they were married in the city of Bristol in January, 1696. She was a woman of spirit, and made him an admirable manager and wife. They had issue, four sons — Dennis, Richard, Thomas, and John — and two daughters—Margaret and Hannah, the latter of whom died in infancy. It is from Thomas Penn that the present representatives of Penn descend.

With the peace of Ryswick the war ceased in America. As Markham discharged his function of lieutenant-governor with vigour, wisdom, and success, Penn lived in England with his young wife and her young children, varying the routine of his life by making religious tours and writing various works. His daughter Lettie, now growing up to womanhood, was not inclined to go; nor was Hannah in a hurry to depart. The news which came with every post from the seat of government were not of a nature to overcome their feminine objections. Colonel Quarry, a revenue-officer, sent out to America by the crown, and a party to the policy of turning the proprietorial into imperial colonies, found out and courted every person of influence in the colony who fancied he had grievances; and of the information procured from these sources he made the most adroit and malicious use in his correspondence with the Board of Trade. He kept up intimate relations with the leaders of opposition, and by his rank and office gave importance to the local discontent.

When Sydney had counselled Penn to leave all power under his Charter of Liberties in the people's hands,—even power to resist the Governor and annul the Constitution,—he had himself but just returned from exile, and was suffering from the spite and jealousy of a court. Neither Penn nor Sydney had foreseen that, under the form in which they were about to try their great Experiment, two powers would be in presence,—probably in conflict. Republican as it was, the Charter had a foreign element in its author. Towards the settlers in his province, Penn was a feudal lord :—the soil and government were his. Though he had given up many of his rights, enough remained to create strife and bitterness. It was sufficient that he traced his rights to an alien source, to rouse a settler's discontent. The settlers had acquired too much to be satisfied with less than all. Penn's difficulty existed in the nature of things. He had to govern a free people by hereditary right. The Assembly never could forgot he was their master. Though he stood between them and the iron rule at home, his life was one great struggle with settlers who with-held his dues—who disobeyed his orders—who invaded and annulled his rights. A democratic party rose, which led him into trouble in the colony, and even joined his English enemies in their efforts to procure a forfeiture of his grant. Though Fletcher's government was more galling to them than the proprietor's, yet to him they passed and paid a war-tax. A salary they would not grant; and the crown was compelled to allow its servant half this war-tax for his personal use. No governor, from first to last, could work with the

Assembly :— nor did the constitution of Pennsylvania get into a state of free action till the feudal element was cast away.

During this interval, Penn became acquainted with the young Czar, Peter of Russia, then working in the dockyard at Deptford as a carpenter and shipbuilder. With that passion for converting great people which led their brethren to Rome, to Adrianople, and to Versailles, in search of royal proselytes, Thomas Story and another Friend, hearing that the ruler of Muscovy was at Deptford, went to him for the purpose of delivering the new gospel. Peter knew no Latin ; they were ignorant of German ; it was impossible to converse without an interpreter. The Friends were charmed with their reception, and immediately reported to Penn, who spoke High German, that a field was opening in the imperial mind. Penn went down to York Buildings, where the Czar resided, with Prince Menzikoff, and there he saw the object of his visit. As a man who had lived in courts and seen the world, —as the son also of a famous admiral,—Penn got on much better with Peter than the simple-hearted Story. With the practical turn which distinguished him, Peter passed at once to what appeared to him the heart of the matter. You say you are a new people,—will you fight better than the rest? Story told him they could not bear arms. Then tell me, said Peter, of what use you would be to any kingdom if you will not fight? The fact of their wearing their hats amused him ; but he could not be made to comprehend the reason for it. Eager for knowledge of every kind, he listened with courtesy and interest to the discourses of Penn ; he wished, he said, to learn in a few words what the Quakers taught and practised, that he might be able to distinguish them from other men ; whereupon his visitor wrote : ' They teach that men must be holy, or they cannot be happy ; that they should be few in words, peaceable in life, suffer wrongs, love enemies, deny themselves, without which faith is false, worship formality, and religion hypocrisy.' Peter was not converted, but he went occasionally to the meetings of Friends at Deptford, where he behaved very politely and socially, standing up or sitting down as it suited the convenience and comfort of others. Some preachers thought their listener was a convert to their faith ; they were not aware that in his thirst for knowledge he was in the habit of studying every sect.

The complaints of Colonel Quarry, and the rising discontents in the colony, kept Penn alarmed. One charge against his cousin Markham was not cleared away before another rose ; so that his enemies had almost daily opportunities of poisoning the King's mind on that sorest of all subjects—the revenue. The Governor felt unlimited confidence in the faith and purity of Markham ; at the same time he saw that a necessity was arising for his own presence in Philadelphia, and he began to make preparations for his voyage.

The outcry against Colonel Markham and the magistrates of Pennsylvania swelled louder and louder. Markham was a prompt, proud officer, in whose hands the dignity of the government certainly suffered no diminution. Did he encourage contraband traders? Stript of malice, the State Papers still contain evidence which would satisfy most juries; it is certain that he behaved imprudently to those whom he believed to be engaged in a malicious conspiracy against his cousin and himself. He refused to pass the Jamaica act against pirates or smugglers, though he had received it directly from Whitehall, with a request from the Board of Trade that it should be made law. He sent Randolph, one of the commissioners, to prison; he allowed David Loyd, attorney-general for the colony, to use some expressions in open court which were considered as an insult to the King's person. Quarry made the utmost of his imprudent acts. Penn's agents, he said, entered the King's store-houses by force; they carried away the goods which had been lawfully seized from pirates; they protected smugglers coming into the Delaware from New York; they tried to ruin the Admiralty officers, and even threatened to take away their lives. A pirate vessel, he said, had come into the river; Markham had lent no aid in capturing her. Such pirates as were taken prisoners were lodged in a tavern; Quakers not being willing to send them to a jail. The Council, not unwilling to assert the King's authority, made an order depriving Colonel Markham of his powers.

Popple had prepared Penn to expect this measure; and Penn had signified his intention of starting for Philadelphia in a few weeks. On the same day, therefore, in which Markham was deposed, another Order in Council was made, approving of suggestions from the Board of Trade, and recommending them to Penn's attention. Hoping to remain in America, Penn prepared to take his wife and family—excepting his son William, who would not go—with the domestic and personal conveniences desirable in a new country and a permanent home. He left the care of his public interests to the faithful Lawton; and his private business to the faithless Ford.

Embarking at Cowes, in the *Canterbury*, they sailed on the 9th of September, 1699, on a three months' voyage. About the time he left England the yellow fever broke out in Philadelphia, and carried off great numbers; but when he arrived at Chester, things were looking brighter than they had been. A settler named Beaven dragged an old Swedish cannon from a yard and fired it off in honour of the day. The cannon burst, and Beaven had his arm shot off. Some Quakers said it was a judgment on his sin; but Penn took up the man, and put him under medical care, and charged himself with all the cost of curing him. Poor Beaven lingered for some months and then broke down. Penn's cash-book shows the course of his decay: to B. Beaven, 10*s.* 8*d.*; to a woman watching Beaven, 6*s.*; to F. Jervais (a surgeon), 2*l.* 10*s.*; to a grave-digger, 3*s.* 4*d.* Beavan had fired his piece and shot himself. When the *Canterbury* reached Philadelphia, Penn went first of all to visit his cousin, Colonel Markham, and then repaired to the meeting-house to see the inhabitants. His reception was enthusiastic. The people in general had long mourned over his absence, says Thomas Loyd, one of the deputies; and now believing that he would never leave them again to become the dupes of faction and the prey of designing men, they were filled with joy.

Instructions were sent out by the Council for his guidance on the two vexed questions of piracy and revenue; and his first public act on assuming the reins of government was to send forth proclamations against pirates and contraband traders. Not content with proclaiming, he informed his officers and Council that, as they were anxious to preserve his rights and their own honour, they must use every endeavour to put down this illegal trade. He placed himself in friendly communication with Colonel Quarry—who had received from the Admiralty an order to pay the Governor great respect—and discussed with him the best course of proceeding, with a view to re-establish harmony. The revenue agent, mollified by this courtesy, entered readily into his plans. No more complaints were sent to London; and in less than three months from Penn's landing in the Delaware, Quarry had become his friend. The change was marvellous. In his letters to the Lords of Trade and Plantations, he reported that Penn's arrival had completely changed the state of affairs, that offending officers had been displaced, that the pirates were being pursued with rigour, and that two acts had been passed which would meet all evils in the future.

Anxious to put an end to the dispute, Penn called the members of his Council and the general Assembly together some weeks before the usual time. As yet there was no law in Pennsylvania against piracy ; and when the Quakers had refused to commit pirates to the common jail, they could quote their code of laws in justification of their refusal. Here there was an evil to be met. So soon as they had passed two enactments, one against pirates and one against contraband trade, which they did on the Governor's remonstrance,—though reluctantly —he dismissed them for the winter. Now that he was legally armed, he found the task of putting down the pirates much more easy. By the end of February, 1700, he was able to lay before Secretary Vernon and the Board of Trade a statement of his doings ; and in due time received from Whitehall an assurance that his conduct was satisfactory to the crown.

CHAPTER XXXII.

PENNSBURY (1700).

PENN had leisure to settle his family in the place which he had meant to be their future home. Pennsbury was an ancient Indian royalty. It had been chosen as the abode of chiefs on account of its situation. Arms of the great river, which were bent no less than three times round it, had in ruder ages of warfare made an almost impregnable defence. When the estate was first laid out by Markham, it consisted of 8431 acres; but a portion of the ground was left in forest state as a park; and the proprietor from time to time reduced its size by grants to different men. On this land his agent Markham had begun to build, even before his first arrival in the country, a mansion worthy of the owner of a great province; and during his absence in England it had been completed. The front of the house, sixty feet long, faced the Delaware, and the upper windows commanded views of the river and of the opposite shores of New Jersey. The depth of the manor-house was forty feet, and on either wing outhouses were disposed so as to produce an agreeable and picturesque effect. A brew-house, a large wooden building covered with shingles, stood at the back, some little distance from the mansion, and concealed among the trees. The house itself stood on a gentle eminence; it was two stories high, built of fine brick, and covered with tiles. A large and handsome porch and stone steps led into a spacious hall, extending nearly the whole length of the house; a hall which could be used on public occasions for the entertainment of distinguished guests and the reception of Indian tribes. The rooms, arranged in suites, had ample folding-doors, and wainscots planed from English oak. A simple taste prevailed throughout. The oaken capital at the porch was decorated with the carving of a vine and bunch of grapes. These decorations had been sent from England. The gardens of Pennsbury were the wonder of the colony. A country house, with ample garden, was the proprietor's passion; and by a liberal outlay of care and money he made the grounds of Pennsbury unequalled for extent and beauty. Penn sought for able gardeners with a zeal which bordered on enthusiasm. In one of his letters he speaks of his good fortune in having met with ' a rare artist ' in Scotland, who is to go out to America and have three men under him. Orders were given that if this Scotch artist could not agree with Ralph, the old gardener, they were to divide the grounds between them, Ralph taking the upper gardens and the court-yards, the rare Scotch artist having charge of all the lower grounds. Penn gave instructions as to every detail. Lawns, shrubberies, and flower-beds, surrounded the manor on every side. A broad walk, lined with poplars, led to the river brink, a flight of stone steps forming the descent from the higher terrace to the lower. Near the house the woods were laid out with walks and drives; the old forest trees were carefully preserved; the most beautiful wild flowers found in the country were transplanted to the gardens; trees and shrubs not indigenous to the soil were imported from Maryland; while walnuts, hawthorns, hazels, and various kinds of fruit trees, seeds, and roots, were sent from home.

The furnishing of Pennsbury was to match. Mahogany was a luxury then unknown; but Mrs. Penn's spider tables and high-backed carved chairs were of the finest oak. An inventory of the furniture is still extant. There were a set of Turkey worked chairs, arm-chairs for ease, and couches with plush and satin cushions for luxury and beauty. In the parlour stood the great leather chair of the proprietor; in every room were cushions and curtains of satin, camlet, damask, and striped linen; and there is a carpet mentioned as being in one apartment, though at that period such an article was hardly ever seen except in the palaces of kings. Mrs. Penn's sideboard furniture included a service of silver, consisting of cups and tankards, bowls and dishes, tea-pots, salt-cellars and silver forks; blue and white china, a complete set of Tonbridge ware, and a great quantity of damask table-cloths and fine napkins. Penn's table was well served. Ann Nichols was his cook; and he used to observe in his pleasantry, ' Ah, the book of cookery has outgrown the Bible, and I fear is read oftener— to be sure it is of more use.' But he was no favourer of excess, because, as he said, ' it destroys hospitality and wrongs the poor.' The French cuisine in vogue was a subject of his frequent ridicule. 'The sauce is now prepared before the meat,' says he, in his Maxims, ' twelve pennyworth of flesh with five shillings of cookery may happen to make a fashionable dish. Plain beef or mutton is become dull food; but by the time its natural relish is lost in the crowd of cook's ingredients, and the meat sufficiently disguised from the eaters, it passes under a French name for a rare dish.' Penn's cellars were well stocked; canary, claret, sack, and madeira, being the favourite wines consumed by his family and their guests. Besides these nobler drinks there was a plentiful supply of ale and cider. Penn's own wine seems to have been madeira ; and he certainly had no dislike to the temperate pleasures of the table. In one of his letters to his steward, Sotcher, he writes, ' Pray send us some two or three smoked haunches of venison and pork—get them from the Swedes ; also some smoked shads and beefs.' He adds with unction, ' The old priest at Philadelphia had rare shads !'

For travelling, the family had a coach, but, in consequence of the bad roads, even those between Pennsbury and Philadelphia, it was seldom used ; a light calesh in which they chiefly drove about ; and a sedan-chair in which Hannah and Lettie went a shopping in the town. Penn rode about the country

on horseback, and sailed from one settlement to another in his yacht.   He retained the passion for boat-
ing, which he had acquired at Oxford, to the last ;
and that love of fine horses which the Englishman
shares with the Arab did not forsake him in the New
World.   On his first visit to America he had carried
over three blood-mares, a fine white horse not of full
breed, and other inferior animals, not for breeding
but for labour.   His inquiries about the mares were
as frequent and minute as those about the gardens ;
and when he went out for the second time, in 1699,
he took with him the magnificent colt Tamerlane, by
the celebrated Godolphin Barb, to which the best
horses now in England trace their pedigree.   Yet
Tamerlane could not wean his master's affections
from his yacht : a vessel of six oars, with a regular
crew, who received their wages as such—and well
deserved them while the Governor was at home.   In
giving some directions about his house and effects
after his return to England, he writes of this yacht,
' But above all dead things, I hope nobody uses
her on any account, and that she is kept in a dry
dock, or at least covered from the weather.'

The dress and habits of the Penns at Pennsbury
had as little of the sourness and formality which
have been ascribed to the early followers of George
Fox as the mansion and its furnishings.   There
was nothing to mark them as differing from
families of rank in England and America at the
present day.   Pennsbury was renowned throughout
the country for its hospitalities.   The ladies dressed
like gentlewomen ; wore caps and buckles, silk

gowns and golden ornaments. Penn had no less than four wigs in America, all purchased in the same year, at a cost of nearly twenty pounds. To innocent dances and country fairs he not only made no objection, but countenanced them by his own and his family's presence. His participation in the sports of the aborigines has been referred to. All the gentler charities which distinguished him in England continued to distinguish him in Pennsylvannia; he released the poor debtor from prison, he supported out of his private purse the sick and destitute, he gave pensions of three shillings a-week to many of the aged who were beyond labour, and there were numerous persons about him whom he had rescued from distress in England, and whom he supported wholly or in part until their own industry made them independent. Some of the best pages of his history are written in his private cash-books.

In April, 1700, the Assembly met for ordinary business. There had been already many changes introduced into the constitution; and it was well known that a large part, perhaps a majority, of the new parliament would be favourable to a fresh revision. The Holy Experiment was proceeding with more passion and more restlessness than its author had expected; still he would not admit that he felt discouraged. The representatives assumed the right to bring in bills,—they attempted to re-organise the judicial system,—they refused to vote any taxes,—they claimed a right to inspect the records of government,—they wished to displace the officers of his courts,—and they expelled a member of the House for telling them the truth.   Penn bore with them from motives higher and farther-reaching than most of them could understand ; whatever might result to him, he was resolved to realize his dream,—to lay a foundation for that Holy Empire, the thoughts of which had cheered him in his darkest hours.   When the Assembly met in Philadelphia, he addressed them in conciliatory terms :—he began by reminding them that though they were only nineteen years old, they were already equal in numbers and prosperity to their neighbours of twice and thrice that standing ; they had a good constitution, though it was not perfect ; the growth of the province had been so extraordinary that while some of the laws were already obsolete, others were found to be hurtful ; these must be looked to.   If they wished to have the charter amended, he was willing ; he only asked them to lay aside all party feeling, and to do that which was best for all, confident that in the end it would be best for each. So far as regarded a provision for himself, he would only tell them that for nineteen years he had maintained the whole charge of government from his private purse.   He placed himself in their hands, and hoped he should never be compelled to leave them again.

When Penn landed in America, Negro slaves were on the soil.   Hawkins had the merit of first engaging England in the African slave-trade ; but it is fair to state that his royal mistress, Elizabeth, not only approved his expeditions, but joined him in the traffic. No suspicion that this trade was infamous ever crossed her mind. In all the maritime towns of Europe slavery was an ancient institution. The cities of Portugal, Italy, and Spain, were dotted with the dusky forms of Negro and Moorish slaves. The best and most religious men of the sixteenth and seventeenth centuries accepted the existing facts of society without a protest. Columbus introduced the Negro into America; Cromwell did not hesitate to sell his prisoners; Locke provided a place for slaves in his constitution, and forbade them even to aspire to a free condition. Such was the state of things when Penn began to think of it. A century after that period the idea was still general in England that the sale of Africans was a legitimate branch of trade. By a stipulation in the Treaty of Utrecht, Queen Anne became for a time the largest slave-merchant in the world.

It is no demerit in Penn that he did not see at once the evil, and oppose a system which Locke approved. Yet from the first he had his doubts. While acting under the counsels of Sydney, he had provided that, if the Free Society of Traders should receive Negroes as servants, they must at least set them partially free after fourteen years of service— that is, they must become adscripts of the soil; the Free Society giving to each man a piece of land, with the tools for its cultivation, and receiving in return two-thirds of the crops. If the Negroes should refuse these terms, they were to continue slaves. Many years after this date, Penn spoke of slavery as a thing of course; he constantly hired slaves from their owners; and they formed a regular part of his establishment at Pennsbury. But his mind was not at rest; for his neighbours from the Upper Rhine had started the novel doctrine that it was not Christian-like to buy and keep Negroes. Coming from an inland and agricultural country, where the luxury and license of commercial cities were unknown, these German settlers looked on the fact of good men buying and selling human beings,—owning men with immortal spirits,—men who in a few years, according to their own avowed belief, would become not only their own equals, but the glorious peers of angels and archangels,—as something monstrous. They appealed to the Friends;—but Friends declined to say if slavery were right or not. When Penn arrived a second time, he found that many had begun to doubt the lawfulness of owning slaves; and yet, on looking at the matter, he felt certain that between the two races there existed an intellectual inequality which no act of Assembly could remove, and which must of necessity preclude social equality, until by process of education and lapse of time the Negro had been greatly changed. With this conviction he began to work. He tried to get his own religious body to recognise the fact that a black man has a soul, by taking some care for it; whereupon a separate monthly meeting for Negroes was established. Next he looked at their moral condition,—and found them living in their homes like brutes. As they were liable to be sold and carried away to distant parts of the country, it was not convenient to their owners that they should marry; yet, as every Negro child was an additional chattel, worth so many pounds in the slave-market, intercourse between the sexes was encouraged rather than rebuked. Penn was anxious to check this evil by a formal law; and as the breach of a law necessarily involved punishment, he resolved to introduce two bills into the Assembly; one providing for a better regulation of the morals and marriages of Negroes; the second providing for the mode of their trial and punishment in cases of offence. After a stormy debate, the Assembly rejected the first of these bills: —they would not have the morals of their slaves improved. In the will which he drew up before leaving the country, Penn gave their freedom to all his slaves.

CHAPTER XXXIII.

MAKING EMPIRE (1700–2).

THE session being over, Penn returned to Pennsbury; where, besides his household cares, the Indians occupied no little of his mind. Superior in calibre and character to the African race, he fancied these red men might be descended from the long-lost tribes of Israel. When he made the Treaty with them in 1682,—a treaty which they had faithfully kept through a long war under many temptations,—he had proposed to himself to call a council of the chiefs and warriors twice a-year, to renew the treaty of friendship, to adjust matters of trade, to hear and rectify wrongs, and to smoke the pipe of peace. While he remained in the colony this intention was strictly carried out.

The Delaware and Susquehannah tribes had now enjoyed his mild and equitable rule for nearly twenty years, and were anxious to bring other of their tribes within shelter of the same system of law, but more especially their brethren dwelling on the banks of the Potomac. They appealed to Onas; and early in April 1701, he met by appointment to arrange these matters, Connoodaghtoh, king of the Susquehannah Indians, Wopatha, king of the Shawanese, Weewhinjough, king of the Ganawese, and Ahookassong, brother to the Emperor of the Five Nations, and forty other chiefs. A treaty of peace and trade was established by mutual consent, on the same terms as had formerly been granted to the Lenni Lenapé. The red man and the white man were to be as one head and one heart. The Indians were to be protected from the rapacity of traders; and as they bound themselves not to sell their furs and skins out of Pennsylvania, Penn thought it possible to teach them morals by means of trade; and on these terms the Potomac Indians were allowed to settle on his land. A treaty of peace and friendship was also concluded with Ahookassong as the ambassador of his imperial brother, on the part of the Five Nations; an important point, even in a military sense; for, when a war was raging on the frontiers, this measure added a new bulwark to Pennsylvania. Penn lost no time in transmitting the intelligence of his success in these negotiations to the English court.

In the intervals of his more pressing labours, Penn kept up communications with Richard Coote, an Irish peer, then governor at New York, and with Colonel Blakiston, Colonel Nicholson, and other governors of provinces. Questions of great importance had to be arranged; and a conference was held at New York for the purpose of settling the heads of a general regulation for all the colonies, royal and private. Penn took the lead in this conference.

The first thing to engage attention was the coinage; for the same piece was then passing in Maryland for 4s. 6d., in Virginia for 5s., in Massachussetts for 6s., in New York for 6s. 9d., and in Pennsylvania and the two Jerseys for 7s. 8d. A second point was a project for encouraging the timber-trade. A third question was the law of marriage. Great abuses had arisen; and bigamy was almost as common in the colonies as wedlock. A fourth question was the establishment of a general postal system; a fifth, the necessity for a comprehensive act of naturalisation, by which the multitudes of French, Dutch, and Swedes, who came out every year, might gain the rights and privileges of English subjects. In the settlement of boundaries with the French, Penn drew a line through the great lakes,—on the double ground, that those inland waters formed a natural defence, and were the chief centres of the Indian trade. His advice was afterwards adopted by the government. Coote having agreed to these suggestions, Penn returned to Philadelphia, embodied them in a report, and transmitted them to London, where the Lords of Trade received them with much satisfaction.

But while he was thus engaged, Penn received news from England, which compelled him to return in haste. The war with France had given the friends of an imperial system many opportunities; and in the absence of the great proprietors, these partizans had brought a bill into the House of Lords for seizing the private colonies and vesting them in the Crown.

Of course attack on property and private right

was veiled under pretences of the public good. Penn knew the authors of this bill; he felt that they were wilfully deceiving William; and he thought and felt that after what he had already done, he should be able to convince the King. He had not only renewed his own friendly treaties with the natives in his own vicinity, but by urgent counsels had engaged Lord Bellamont to conclude a treaty of peace for all the settlements of the English in North America. Within his own province he had organised a system of signals and watchers, so that the appearance of any suspicious sail in the waters of the Delaware would be instantly reported to the government at Philadelphia. The question of a war contribution had not come before the Assembly, peace being now restored in Europe; but on the great drama known in history as the war of the Spanish Succession opening in calamitous grandeur, William wrote to Penn that he must have either his contingent, or his money ready. Eighty men were to be raised; if not, a sum of 350*l.* was to be paid. Penn laid his charge before the Assembly; but the members talked of their great poverty—doubted whether the other provinces had done their duty—and resolved to postpone considerations of his Majesty's letter until the war had actually commenced. Affairs were in this awkward way when Penn received from Lawton, who was watching every tide and turn of politics on his behalf, the news of what was passing in the House of Lords. No time was to be lost. The owners of Pennsylvania property then in England prayed the House of Lords to postpone discussion of the Colonies Bill till Penn could be heard in person. Penn the Younger, who, amidst his dissipations, kept an eye on politics, demanded to be heard in counsel, and the Lords consenting to his prayer, the case was argued in committee, and some valuable time was gained. The House had been deceived, and the Board of Trade was found to have kept important papers back. In Pennsylvania the feeling against annexation to the crown was all but universal. Having called the representatives together, Penn laid the intelligence he had just received before them. With a single voice they urged him to return at once, and to defend their interests and his own. He said he could not think of such a voyage without reluctance. His wife, Hannah, had recently given birth to a son, and was still in a delicate state of health. He had promised himself a quiet home amongst them in his old age; and even if he should now go away for a season, no unkindness would be able to change his mind; he should return and settle in the country. He advised them to decide what ought to be done for the general security in his absence,—what changes were needed in the constitution,—what new laws were required by the circumstances which had arisen on every side. He recommended the King's letter touching subsidy to their prompt consideration: that question of the war-tax being the key-note of his answer to all misgivings of the court.

The members thanked him for these gracious words, and named committees to draw up statements and prepare the course of business. But in place of aiding him to meet the evil with such means as lay within their reach,—instead of voting the royal subsidy and amending their general laws,—they drew up a list of claims on him, their friend and founder. One of these claims was a request that the price of unsold land should be permanently fixed at the old rent of a bushel of wheat in a hundred; so that while their own estates were being improved tenfold in value with increase of inhabitants, his estate should have no share in this natural increase. Another was a request that he would·lay out all the unsold bay marshes, a rich and highly productive soil, as common land. There was more to this effect. The settlers saw him entering on a fight in which he might be beaten,—for the King was his antagonist and judge,—and sought to wring from his misfortune some large share of personal gain. His calmness under such an insult was surprising; though his heart was strained, his speech was very mild. The inconsistency of their demands was pointed out,—concessions, where no principle was involved, were made,—and the Assembly, perhaps ashamed, returned to something like a better sense. Yet what they gained from him was much: no less than a new charter of liberties. This new charter was argued at great length; and on the 28th of October, 1701, it was finally settled and accepted in the presence of the Council and Assembly. It contained encroachments on the powers of the Governor and his Council: but the chief innovation was the right which the Assembly now acquired to originate bills. They had framed some bills already in the time of Colonel Fletcher; but the act was contrary to law. Henceforth the right they had usurped was guaranteed by Penn.

Then came the question of money. Penn had plenty of land under cultivation; the fields gave him corn and meat; the rivers yielded fish; and the air brought store of birds. To live at Pennsbury was easy. But to take his family across the Atlantic was expensive; a vessel must be hired, and wages must be paid. Yet the Assembly would do nothing in the way of grants; and he was forced to sell as much land as would cover the expenses of his voyage. He hinted that the colony was now rich enough to pay the cost of government; but his little parliament refused to undertake the charge.

Penn's wife and daughter were delighted with the prospect of going home. They felt no love for the wilderness; and more than once had urged the Governor to take them back.

As soon as news got abroad that Onas was about to quit the Delaware, the Indians came in from all parts of the country to take leave of him. A sentiment of fear that he would never more return across the great salt water haunted their untutored minds, and they clung to his assurances of amity and justice with greater force, because they feared that his children would not be to them what he had been. What pale-face had they ever seen like him? A pale-face was to them a trapper, a soldier, a pirate; a man who cheated them in barter, who abused their squaws, who gave them fire-water to drink, who hustled them off their hunting-ground. But here was one pale-face who would not cheat and lie ; who would not fire into their lodge ; who would not rob them of their beaver-skins ; who would not take a rood of land from them till they had fixed and he had paid a price. Where could they look for such another lord ? To comfort them in their distress, Penn introduced them to his Council, and again repeated his desires. The members of his Council pledged themselves to carry out his wish when he was gone, as if he were still living at Pennsbury to punish the guilty and protect the innocent. They took their parting gifts in sorrow ; and after the lapse of a century the memory of that day was found to be still fresh in their descendants' hearts.

The vessel in which the Penn family were to sail being now ready, Penn appointed James Logan as his agent, and Colonel Hamilton, ex-governor of the Jerseys, as his deputy. These appointments were made with the full consent of the Assembly. Hamilton was to be assisted by a Council of ten ; and, at the urgent request of his representatives, who fancied that affairs would go more smoothly if the heir were in the colony, Penn agreed to send over his son William, so that he might learn betimes the nature and wants of the country he would in a few years have to rule.

CHAPTER XXXIV.

CLOSING SCENES (1702–18).

WHEN Penn arrived he found the state of parties changed. William was dying. Anne had been his friend, and when she succeeded to the throne, he was again a welcome guest at court. The bill of annexation was allowed to drop. Penn sent for his son, William, and told him of the promise he had made. The youth was not disposed to leave the brilliant life of London for the solitude of a new country and the stiff decorum of a Quaker town. From school days he had kept the highest company; under his mother's will he had received a fortune of his own— the Springett property in Kent ; and being suddenly set free by his mother's death, and his father's voyage, he had leapt with only too much ardour into every social vice. He drank ; he roved about ; he kept gay women. When his father came home he found the youth in debt, and almost ruined in constitution. This clever but perverted boy was the only remaining son of his lost Guli, and the heir to his colonial government. He had the grace to be ashamed; and on his father promising to pay his debts in

London, and to give him an estate in Pennsylvania for his separate use, he even offered to go out to America, and study the business of that country under guidance of the newly named Deputy-Governor Evans and his Council. Penn gave him an estate of seven thousand acres, which he called from his son's name Williamstadt. He also wrote most urgent letters to his old friends in Philadelphia about his son. 'He has wit,' he said, 'has kept top company, and must be handled with much wisdom.' Logan undertook to give him good advice; to keep such an eye on him as he would keep on a favourite son.

For a few months the young rake behaved pretty well. Logan retained his influence; and between his dog and gun, his hunter and fishing-tackle, his time was pleasantly and innocently, if not very usefully, spent. But after a while an evil intimacy sprang up between the fashionable youth and Governor Evans, an ill-conditioned person like himself; and between them they not only brought discredit on themselves, but filled the whole community with the scandal of their lives. Young Penn, as heir to the government, not only set an example of riot, but protected those who imitated his excess. The young and idle crowded round him; made him their chief; and filled his busy pate with notions of such glory as the stout old Admiral had won. The war question being under discussion in the Assembly, young Penn joined the war party, and on his own authority organised a body of troops in the Quaker city. Nor was this his worst offence.

He and his companions frequented low taverns; got up rows in the streets, and beat the watch. The riot of London seemed to have rushed at once into the midst of that quiet community. A masquerade was established at a public-house kept by Simes. The roysterers caroused till midnight at the White Hart. Women went about the streets in male attire; and two men were brought into court on a charge of being found at night in women's . clothes, contrary to decency and law. But as the elders frowned, the youngsters only gibed and laughed. At length a crisis came. A scene occurred in the streets; a constable was beaten in the performance of his duty; and the city guard was called to quell the riot. Some escaped, but others were arrested :—among the former was Governor Evans, among the latter was young Penn. Next morning Penn was brought before the mayor, and rated. He replied with taunts; he was a gentleman, he said, and not responsible to his father's petty officers. Evans, who took his part, annulled by proclamation these proceedings of the court. This conduct roused the Quaker spirit :—that body indicted young Penn; and in his anger he renounced their doctrines, discipline, and jurisdiction. These disorders were a source of inappeasable grief to Penn in England, and they furnished Quarry, once more active in his work, with solid grounds of censure. The young man soon returned to England deep in debt, though he had sold the fine estate of Williamstadt; as thoroughly disgusted with America as America was with him. He quitted Pennsylvania with the threat that he would soon persuade his father to sell that colony to the crown.

Penn had a father's weakness for this youth— was he not Guli's son? He thought the Quakers of the colony had dealt too harshly with him; that they had not considered his youth. He thought his friends should have seen the conduct of his son in its best aspect, not its worst. That which his son desired from choice, he was impelled towards by necessity. His steward, Philip Ford, had died in January 1702, leaving his affairs to the management of his widow and his son. The widow ruled her son; who would have been as great a scoundrel as his parents had he possessed their gifts. The elder Ford had so contrived to jumble Penn's accounts, as to keep him ignorant how they stood. When asked to sign papers and accounts, Penn seldom troubled himself to read them over, but in simple faith set his name to them and passed them on. Ford knew how to take advantage of this want of prudence. In an evil hour, when Penn was seeking funds to carry him over to America the second time, Ford got from him —as a form—a deed of sale for the colony; on which security, Ford advanced him 2800*l*. This deed was considered by Penn, and professedly considered by Ford, as a mortgage. Ford received money on account of the province, and made such advances as the Governor needed. It was not till Penn returned to England that a first suspicion of his steward crossed his mind. He tried to think himself deceived. But when the Quaker died, his knavery came to the light of day. From an uncertain remembrance of the sums advanced and paid, Penn thought his mortgage nearly cancelled; but the funeral rites of Ford were hardly over, when the widow sent him in a bill for 14,000*l.*, and threatened to seize and sell his province if it were not paid.

Penn was thunderstruck. He asked for accounts. Henry Goldney, a legal Friend, and Herbert Springett, a near relation of his first wife, assisted him. When the accounts were put in shape, it appeared, by his own showing, that Ford had received on behalf of Penn 17,859*l.*; that he had paid 16,200*l.* Yet he claimed 14,000*l*! That the matter should be settled on just bases, and, both parties being Friends, that no scandal should be brought on the society, Penn proposed to refer it to arbitration; but the Fords rejected his proposal. They wanted law—not equity. The courts, they said, would give them the money, and they would have their rights. It was well for Penn that he was able to find a set of the accounts as they had been sent to him from time to time. These papers told him the iniquitous story page by page.

(1.) The Fords had charged him interest on advances; but allowed him none on their receipts. (2.) They had charged him eight per cent interest, though six per cent was the fixed and legal rate. (3.) They had charged compound interest on the 2800*l.*; posting it every six months, and sometimes oftener, so that the overcharge of interest again bore interest, even while the balance of account was on Penn's side of the ledger. (4.) They had charged him fifty shillings as their commission instead of ten shillings for every 100*l.* received or paid by them to his account — even on the overcharges of interest paid to themselves, adding it to the principal every six months, so as to make him pay a commission of 2*l.* 10*s.* to the hundred six or seven times over on the same money. (5.) While he was in the colony Penn had sold a piece of land for 2000*l.*, of which sum he sent 615*l.* to Ford in liquidation of his debt; but Ford, instead of posting 615*l.* to Penn's credit, charged his account with 1385*l.*, as if he had advanced the money, and from that day forward reckoned his commission and his compound interest on this sum. What wonder that the Fords refused to submit their claims to arbitration! The excess of charges on the second, third, and fourth items came to 9697*l.*, reducing the claim of 14,000*l.* to 4303*l.* Penn offered to refund this sum; the widow shook her deed of sale in his face, and threatened him with a suit in chancery if the whole amount were not paid down. Friends interfered; some came from America for the purpose; but the younger Ford grew insolent, and the widow would not listen to their good advice.

Though well aware that the uncancelled deed of sale could not be disputed, Penn allowed the case to go before the Lord Chancellor. The court affirmed the special case of debt; and being armed with this legal verdict, Ford went down with a constable to Gracechurch Street, and tried to arrest his patron in the meeting, while surrounded by their common friends engaged in the act of worship. Herbert Springett and Henry Goldney gave their word that

Penn would come. To get protection from these harpies, he was forced to go into the Fleet; that is to say, into the Liberties of the Fleet. His lodgings were in the Old Bailey, where he held meetings of his sect for worship, and was visited by friends from Whitehall and the Mall. Penn feared that he might have to sell his colony; his son was anxious to be rid of it; and many of his oldest friends urged him to make a bargain with the Queen. Necessity alone could reconcile him to the thought of giving up the guidance of his Holy Experiment,—nor would he ever have dreamt of such a thing had the settlers treated him with justice. 'I went thither,' he says, in a letter to the Judge Mompesson, 'to lay the foundations of a free colony for all mankind. The charter I granted was intended to shelter them against a violent and arbitrary government imposed on us; but, that they should turn it against *me*, that intended it for their security, is very unworthy and provoking, especially as I alone have been at all the expense. . . . . But as a father does not usually knock his children on the head when they do amiss, so I had much rather they were corrected and better instructed, than treated to the rigour of their deservings.'

Logan described the feeling of the colony: 'There are few,' he said to Penn, 'that think it any sin to haul what they can from thee.' Some, he added, were honest; but honest men let rogues have their own way, saying it was not their business. Logan traced their meanness to excess of freedom; and censured his friend for having given them a better charter than they deserved. Against this inference Penn protested; and when he came to treat with the crown for the surrender of his province, he made so many conditions in favour of the colonists, that the Queen's government was obliged to tell him the remainder was not worth accepting, even as a gift.

Young Ford went over to Pennsylvania, where he found out Quarry, Loyd, and other persons much opposed to Penn. Governor Evans, who had now retrieved his character, defended Penn with dignity; and from that moment Evans was an object of attack. When Ford had gained some persons — such as David Loyd — he sailed for London, where he held out threats of raising a disturbance in the colony if his wishes were not met. As Penn declined to see him, he declared that Pennsylvania was his own; that his father had bought it years ago; that he had let it to Penn on a rental; that the rents not being paid, he was resolved to take the country into his own hands; he therefore cautioned the owners of land not to pay any monies to the agents of Penn, at their peril. Widow Ford petitioned the Queen to issue a new charter, making the colony over to her, and to her son. But Lord Chancellor Cowper, having heard the case argued, not only gave judgment against them, but spoke so severely on the merits of the case and the animus of their proceedings, as to cow their spirits.

Fearing lest he should lose the whole, young Ford began to talk of terms. Another instance of the elder Ford's swindling was discovered. In his accounts there was an item of 1200*l.* which, with compound interest, reckoned every six months, amounted in the long-run to 5569*l.* But on looking at the books, it was found that only 500*l.* had been paid by Ford.

Much of Penn's property was gone during the twenty years of his profitless rule in America. He sold the Worminghurst estate to Squire Butler for 6050*l.*, being 1550*l.* more than he gave for it, after having cut down 2000*l.* of wood. This money satisfied some creditors, but not all; and one of them, a man named Churchill, was so importunate as to try to stop Butler's payment of the purchase-money. Under the advice of Goldney, whose purse was as much at his friend's service as his tongue, Penn and his son William made over to Callowhill, Goldney, Oades, and several others, a deed of sale of Pennsylvania for one year, in consideration of the receipt of ten shillings, with intent that these parties might be in actual possession of the province during his settlement with the Fords. Next day the same parties took a formal mortgage of the colony, and paid into his hands 6800*l.* The Fords were paid, their claim having first been lowered one-half.

Disorders continued in Pennsylvania. Evans behaved with far more zeal than prudence. Where he should have won the old Quaker settlers, he offended their prejudices, and broke with them about the war. Procuring a false report to arrive in the city, that the French were coming up the river, he rushed into the street sword in hand, calling on the people right and left to arm and follow him. The terror was extreme. Some burned their effects; many fled into the woods; still more seized their arms. Fixing his standard on Society Hill, he found three hundred well-armed men, some of them Quakers, rally to the flag. His purpose was attained; he knew how many he could count on in a real attack; but the Quakers, to use the words of Logan, were disgusted at the feint, and never pardoned him the fright which he had caused.

Penn was anxious to return. He seemed determined to go over, as things had always gone on smoothly under his control. But his want of means prevented him. At the end of this year he wrote to his agent, 'I assure thee, if the people would only settle 600*l.* a-year upon me as Governor, I would hasten over. . . . . Cultivate this among the best Friends.' But the best Friends would do nothing. When the Assembly met, the quarrel with Evans was at its height. If they passed a bill, he rejected it; if he proposed a bill, they would not pass it. Nothing could be done, and Penn was forced to recall his deputy.

Lord Baltimore was active. After a lapse of twenty-three years, he revived his claim to the second half of the Delaware peninsula; it is possible that he only then discovered that his rival's title to the territory in question had never been completed; and though three successive sovereigns had allowed Penn's right of possession, Baltimore thought there was an opening for his claim, and he advanced it. He petitioned the Queen to repeal the Order in Council, made by her father, dividing the peninsula, and to restore the whole to him in virtue of his original grant. Somers and Sunderland advised Penn to send in a counter-petition to the Queen. The Lords of Trade allowed the question to be opened; but they were unable to settle it on any satisfactory basis; and finding their geography and law alike at fault, they had recourse to the old plan of asking the litigants to arrange it and report. Uncertainty about the boundary-lines soon lost itself in the prior question of title. Penn contended that his deeds were made out, and were all but signed, when James had fled. High personages about the court were eager to obtain an American province; among others, the Earl of Sutherland set up a claim to the Delaware, and the government chose to consider its own claim to the territories on that river as something more than a pretence. When Colonel Gookin was sent out in 1708, and again when Sir William Keith was appointed governor in 1716, the minister gave his sanction with a special reservation of the supposed rights of the Crown in the Delaware province.

Penn was now sixty-five years old. His health was failing; his imprisonment in the Old Bailey had given him a shock. He tried Brentwood; he took a country seat at Ruscombe. Gleams of light broke in upon his later years,—dreams of an unattainable prosperity, which served at least to rouse his sinking spirits. Soon after he recovered his colony, reports arrived that a great silver-mine had been discovered. A remonstrance which he wrote to America produced a good result, and the general peace gave reason to hope for a settlement of his old account with Spain. The silver-mine, on the report of which he built a pleasant castle in the air, was an illusion, but not a greater illusion than his claim on Spain.

Penn reminded the people of Pennsylvania of the sleepless nights and toilsome days, the expense, the load of care, the personal dangers, the family misfortunes, which he had endured for them. What had they done for him? They had found a noble field for their capital and industry; they had got lands, acquired political rights, enjoyed religious liberties; but, not yet satisfied with the enjoyment of these rights, with the increase of their worldly substance, they must turn upon himself. He spoke to them of their past misdeeds, referred to their present unbecoming and uncivil attitude towards his person and government. He made to them a fatherly appeal. The Queen, he told them, was willing to buy his colony and annex it to her crown. In spite of their ill returns, he had been faithful to his promises. He put it to them, as men and Christians, whether they had used him fairly. While they had grown rich, he had become poor; while they had acquired power, he had lost it; while they enjoyed, through his toil and forethought, wealth, influence, and freedom, he had been reduced, through their neglect and avarice, to seek the shelter of a jail. He wished to have an answer to his question, whether they desired to sunder the old connexion? If it were so, let it be declared on a fair and full election, and his course would then be clear.

The answer was emphatic.   When the Assembly met after the general election, not a single man of the aggressive chamber was returned.   The province had been stung with the reproaches of its founder, now in his old age enduring poverty brought on by his too great liberality; and the session which ensued was the most harmonious and most useful in the history of the Assembly.   Penn was gratified with this national response; and the historian dwells on this brief interval of calm and rational legislation with the greater pleasure, since it was the last in which the founder had a conscious part.   Before another gathering of the members took place, his mind was overthrown.

His latest action on the colonial legislature was in behalf of the poor Negroes.   Ten years before this period he had tried in vain to get a formal recognition of their claims as human beings; but the question of slavery had been making progress, and his own ideas had become less dark.   He no longer doubted the injustice of the trade in man.   Four years after the rejection of his bill for regulating the morals and marriages of Negroes, the Assembly tried to discourage slavery by a duty on the importation of Negro slaves.   In 1711 they passed an act prohibiting such importation for the future.   But as soon as this good law reached England it was cancelled by the Crown.

Some years before this time the two Houses of Parliament had put a declaration on the statute-book of the realm to the effect that the trade in slaves was highly beneficial to the country and the colonies.

In the session then sitting (1711), a committee of the Commons recommended the adoption of means to increase the captures of Negroes, that their value might be reduced in the slave-markets of the plantations. The Privy Council was scandalised at a provincial Assembly for proposing measures hostile to the laws and interests of the parent state.

Penn passed much of his time in London, where he had a host of friends in office. Anne was partial to him. He was intimate with men on both sides of the royal gallery—with Tory earls as well as Whig lords. Sunderland was his friend; Godolphin was his friend also. Lord Godolphin thought so highly of his honesty and talent that he often asked him to arrange political and personal matters which required unusual tact. When Anne appointed Dartmouth Secretary of State in 1710, Godolphin asked Penn to see Lord Dartmouth, and assure him that the Lord Treasurer was glad to have him as a colleague, though he could not decently, considering his relations with Lord Sunderland, say so openly and in person. Dartmouth was contented with the Earl's assurance of support.

Early in 1712 Penn received the first of three shocks of paralysis, which laid his reason low. The first shock was not very bad, but in the fall of that year he had a second shock, from which he only rallied after several weeks. A third shock, far more violent than the first or second, took him in his fainting state. His daughter Lettie, and her husband, William Aubrey, were recalled to what was thought to be his dying bed. The younger children were about him, but his eldest boy, the son of Guli, was not there. Since his return from Pennsylvania, and his public renunciation of his father's sect, William Penn the younger had been less and less under the paternal roof. Marriage, and a home blessed with three children — Guli, Springett, and William — had produced no change. He went into the army, but he quitted it in disgust. He tried to get into Parliament, but his opponent bribed higher, and he was defeated at the poll. He sold the Springett estate in Kent, which he inherited under his mother's will. He quitted his young wife and children, leaving them to the care of strangers, to seek the lowest dregs of pleasure and dissipation in the cities of Continental Europe. He returned no more to England. A few years later his family heard that he was living in an obscure town in France, worn out, morally and physically, ruined alike in purse and health. They never saw him more. The darker side of his story was never known to Penn.

Penn's debility grew upon him. From the date of his third attack he was considered in a dying state; but he lingered on in a gentle and sweet decline. To the devout it seemed a dispensation of Providence, that after so long a period of toil and trouble, his spirit should have found an interval of rest. Later on in his long illness, he felt a few more shocks, but they soon passed away, and his bodily health continued good. His temper was serene. He took an interest in the concerns, the pleasures, and the amusements of his young children;

and the abandoned widow of his son was housed at Ruscombe with her little ones. When the sun was warm, he took them out into the fields to gather flowers, and watch them chase butterflies. He was again a little child. When the weather was bad, he gambolled with them about the great mansion, taking an infantine pleasure in running from room to room, in looking at the fine furniture, and gazing from the great windows on the snow or rain. Never before had he looked so happy. He could not speak very much, but a constant smile was on his face. It was only when he saw his wife looking anxious, or when, on going into a room, he found her writing, that a shade of melancholy came into his eyes. Unable now to write, he yet retained a sense of trouble as connected with that writing-desk. No daisies laughed among those papers, and no linnets perched and sang among those shelves. His memory faded more and more; he forgot the names of his intimate friends; his powers of utterance left him; but the mild benignity of his character still came out.

The two friends who were most frequently at his side during this long illness were Thomas Story and Henry Goldney. Neither was in good health; but they considered it a duty to be near their friend. Towards the end of July 1718, Story was at Ruscombe, assisting Mrs. Penn. On the 27th he left on a trip to Bristol; Hannah Penn drove him in her coach to Reading; where she parted from him, with messages to John, her eldest son. When she returned to the house, Penn was no worse than he had been for days past. At noon next day a change occurred; he was seized with fits. She wrote a letter to recall Story; but he had gone too far; and she had to face the trials of the day unaided by a single friend.

Cold shivers quickly followed raging heats. Her doctor thought an intermittent fever was setting in: On the 29th the patient had grown so much worse they could no longer entertain a hope. Hannah then sent a messenger with orders to ride post haste to Bristol, to summon her son John, now a man of three-and-twenty, to his father's bed.

But death rode faster than her messenger. In the first watches of the summer morning, between two and three o'clock, he fell asleep. His widow watched his lips in agony and suspense. They never moved again.

Penn was buried at the village of Jordans, on the 5th of August, 1718, by the side of Guli, his first wife, and Springett, his first-born son. A crowd of people followed the bier from Ruscombe to the grave-yard, consisting of the most eminent Friends, from all parts of the country, and the most distinguished of every Christian church near Ruscombe. When the coffin was lowered into the grave, a pause of silence followed; after which the old and intimate friends of the dead spoke a few words to the assembly; and the people went to their several homes subdued and chastened with the thought that a good man and a great man, who had done his work and earned his rest, had been laid that day upon the bosom of his mother earth.

SUPPLEMENTARY CHAPTER.

In the first edition of Macaulay's 'History of England,' apart from sneers and 'hesitations,' Penn was charged with five offences touching his character as a public man.

He was represented as becoming such a servile courtier, that his own sect looked coldly on him and requited his services with obloquy.   He was represented as extorting money from the school-girls of Taunton, for a set of heartless Maids of Honour.   He was represented as trying to seduce William Kiffin, a fighting Baptist preacher, into the acceptance of an alderman's gown, which gown Kiffin refused. He was represented as going over to the Hague in 1687, and trying to procure the Prince of Orange's support of the King's Declaration for Liberty of Conscience.   He was represented as guilty of simony of a peculiarly disreputable kind in the affairs of Magdalen College.

The third charge has been modified, the fourth withdrawn.   The other charges stand in the Collected Works, with such excuses as Macaulay had hastily put forth in his notes in 1857.

That Macaulay contemplated making further changes in his text may be inferred from several signs. (1) After the year 1857, he ceased his calumnies of Penn.   In all the third part of his narrative, contained in the fifth volume, there is not a single charge, a single sneer, though Penn was still before the public eye, as busy with his colony and with his ministry as in the earlier time.   (2) His indexes were changed in the direction of a much more favourable view of Penn's character and conduct. In the first index we read : 'Failure of his attempted mediation with the Fellows of Magdalen ;' in the amended index we read : 'Negotiates with the Fellows of Magdalen'—a very different thing. The first index refers to 'his scandalous Jacobitism ;' the amended index drops the 'scandalous' Jacobitism. The first index denounces 'his falsehood ;' the amended index substitutes 'held to bail.' The first index says Penn 'takes part in a Jacobite conspiracy ;' the amended index says he 'joins the Jacobite conspiracy,' replacing the active by the passive, the particular by the general. In the first index, Penn is 'charged by Preston with treasonable conduct ;' in the amended index, he is merely 'informed against by Preston.' In the first index, 'he conceals himself ;' in the amended index, he no longer conceals himself. In the first index, Penn's interview with Sydney is 'singular ;' in the amended index, it has ceased to be 'singular.' In the first index, Penn 'escapes to France ;' in the amended index, there is nothing about an escape to France. In the first index, he 'returns to England and renews his plots ;' in the amended index, there is not a word about returning to England and renewing his plots. That all these changes in the index meant a reconsideration of the text, can hardly be denied by any one who knows the principle on which Macaulay worked. (3) It is now no secret, that he was engaged during the last few days of his life, in a review of the evidence produced against his character of Penn.

Macaulay was removed before this portion of his labour was achieved ; and thus the duty comes to me again of citing dates and facts in proof that every statement made by the historian to the injury of William Penn is founded on mistakes of time, of person, and of place. It is a painful duty, but I must not shrink from it. The highest fealty of a public writer is to truth.

I. Writing of Penn in 1685, Macaulay had said :—

'He was soon surrounded by flatterers and sycophants. . . . . He paid dear, however, for this seeming prosperity. Even his own sect looked coldly on him, and requited his services with obloquy.' —*Hist. of England*, i. 506.

This statement was confronted with the records at Devonshire House, in the City. Penn appears from these records to have been in regular attendance at the Society's Meetings all this year. He was elected to the highest offices in his Society. Strong evidence would be required in face of such facts, that in this year of Penn's court life ' his own sect looked coldly on him, and requited his services with obloquy.' No evidence, either strong or weak, is adduced by Macaulay.

II. Writing in his first edition of the Taunton ransom, Macaulay had said :—

'An order was sent to Taunton that all these little girls should be seized and imprisoned. Sir Francis Warc of Hestercombe, the Tory member for Bridgewater, was requested to undertake the office of exacting the ransom. He was charged to declare in strong language that the Maids of Honour would not endure delay, that they were determined to prosecute to outlawry, unless a reasonable sum were forthcoming, and that by a reasonable sum they meant seven thousand pounds. Warre excused himself from taking any part in a transaction so scandalous. The Maids of Honour then requested William Penn to act for them ; and Penn accepted the commission. Yet it should seem that a little of the pertinacious scrupulosity which he had often shown about taking off his hat would not have been altogether out of place on this occasion. He probably silenced the remonstrance of his conscience by repeating, &c.'—*Hist. of England*, i. 656.

It was proved in answer that Penn was not requested to act; that he never accepted any commission; that he had nothing to do with the business.

Macaulay quoted Locke's ' Western Rebellion,' Toulmin's ' History of Taunton,' Letter of Sunderland to Penn, Feb.

13, 1686.   But this appearance of authority was quite fallacious.

Locke never mentions Penn at all; Toulmin never mentions Penn at all; Somerset never mentions Penn at all. The four authorities dwindle down to one authority — 'Sunderland's Letter to Penn, Feb. 13, 1686,' cited by Macaulay from 'the Mackintosh Papers.'   Luckily we know where Mackintosh found this pretended 'Letter to Penn,' and on referring to the State Papers find it is not a letter to Penn at all, but a letter to 'Mr. Penne' (a Mr. George Penne) who was engaged in selling pardons to those who had been compromised by Monmouth's rising.   Here is a copy from Lord Sunderland's Letter-book in the State Paper Office:—

'*Whitehall, Feb.* 13, 1685–6.

'Mr. PENNE,—Her Majesty's Maids of Honour having acquainted me that they designe to employ you and Mr. Walden in making a composition with the relations of the Maids of Taunton for the high misdemeanour they have guilty of, I do at their request hereby let you know that His Majesty has been pleased to give their fines to the said Maids of Honour, and therefore recommend it to Mr. Walden and you to make the most advantageous composition you can in their behalfe.   I am, Sir, your humble servant, SUNDERLAND.'—*Domestic papers*, various, 629, 424.

That this letter was addressed to Mr. Penne, and not to William Penn, is evident.   It bears his name; it refers to his peculiar trade; it engages him to do for one set of clients the sort of business he was doing for another set of clients.   Mr. George Penne was a hanger-on at court, with no objection to the dirty work by which money could be made.   We find him on the scene; we find him vending royal pardons; and we find him claiming the reward which that peculiar service would deserve.   The man was worthy of the work he had to do, and his reward was worthy of such work when it is done.

In a cash-book of the time, still preserved by the Pinney family at Somerton Erlegh House, I find this entry:—

' Bristol, Sept. 1685.

' Mr. John Pinney is debitor to money pd. George Penne, Esquire, for the ransom of my Bro. Aza.   August, 1685. . . . . £65.'

The Pinneys were a good west-country family.   John Pinney, the father of Azariah, was a clergyman, Rector of Norton-sub-Hamdan, by Yeovil.   Others of the house took part in Monmouth's rising, and were sentenced to death. Abraham Pinney was hung at Taunton.   Azariah was condemned to death; but his life was given to Jerome Nepho, who was to take him out to the island of Nevis, near St. Kits, in the West Indies.   But the Pinneys called in the court trafficker in ransoms, Mr. Penne, through whom they bought his freedom, at a cost of sixty-five pounds.   In the year but one following his work at Taunton, Mr. Penne sent in his claim to the King—a claim to set up gaming-tables in the colonies.   In the Privy Council Register of James the Second I find this entry :—

' Nov. 25, 1687.

' George Penne.—Upon reading the petition of George Penne, gent., setting forth that his family having been great sufferers for their loyalty, he humbly begs that his Majesty would be graciously pleased to grant him a patent for the sole exercising the royal Oake lottery, and licensing all other games, in his Majesty's plantations in America, for twenty-one years.   His Majesty in Council is pleased to refer this matter to the consideration of the Rt. Hon. the Lords Commissioners of the Treasury, and upon what their lordships report of what is fit to be done therein for the petitioner, his Majesty will declare his further pleasure.'—Council Reg. i. 540.

Now, what pretence on earth is there for saying that this letter to ' Mr. Penne' was addressed to William Penn? (1) It does not bear his name.   He never spelt his name Penne.   Lord Sunderland, the writer, had been his friend since they were boys; and Sunderland never spelt his friend's name Penne.   (2) It is evidently written, not to a gentleman and a friend, but to a low-class agent.   The maids ' designe to employ you and Mr. Walden;' they 'recommend it to Mr. Walden and you.' Penn was one of the first men in London; he had declined a peerage; he was the lord proprietor of a colony almost as large as England. (3) Not a word occurs in any letter, paper, memoir, or petition of that period hinting that he was 'employed in the affair.'

What said Macaulay in reply to this array of facts?—

'That the person to whom this letter was addressed was William Penn the Quaker was not doubted by Sir James Mackintosh, who first brought it to light, or, as far as I am aware, by any other person, till after the publication of the first part of this history. It has since been confidently asserted that the letter was addressed to a certain George Penne, who appears from an old account-book lately discovered to have been concerned in a negotiation for the ransom of one of Monmouth's followers, named Azariah Pinney. If I thought that I had committed an error, I should, I hope, have the honesty to acknowledge it. But, after full consideration, I am satisfied that Sunderland's letter was addressed to William Penn. Much has been said about the way in which the name is spelt. The Quaker, we are told, was not Mr. Penne, but Mr. Penn. I feel assured that no person conversant with the books and manuscripts of the seventeenth century will attach any importance to this argument. It is notorious that a proper name was then thought to be well spelt if the sound were preserved. To go no further than the persons who, in Penn's time, held the Great Seal, one of them is sometimes Hyde and sometimes Hide: another is Jeffcries, Jeffries, Jeffereys, and Jeffreys : a third is Somers, Sommers, and Summers: a fourth is Wright and Wrighte ; and a fifth is Cowper and Cooper. The Quaker's name was spelt in three ways. He, and his father the Admiral before him, invariably, as far as I have observed, spelt it Penn : but most people spelt it Pen; and there were some who adhered to the ancient form, Penne. For example, William the father is Penne in a letter from Disbrowe to Thurloe, dated on the 7th of December, 1654; and William the son is Penne in a news-letter of the 22nd of September, 1688, printed in the Ellis Correspondence. In Richard Ward's "Life and Letters of Henry More," printed in 1710, the name of the Quaker will be found spelt in all three ways,—Penn in the index, Pen in page 197, and Penne in page 311. The name is Penne in the Commission which the Admiral carried out with him on his expedition to the West Indies. Burchett, who became Secretary to the Admiralty soon after the Revolution, and remained in office long after the accession of the House of Hanover, always, in his " Naval History," wrote the name Penne. Surely it cannot be thought strange that an old-fashioned spelling, in which the Secretary of the Admiralty persisted so late as 1720, should·have been used at the office of the Secretary of State in 1686. I think myself, therefore, perfectly justified in considering the names, Penn and Penne, as the same.'

Perfectly justified ! How would Macaulay have described such reasoning in another man ? Disbrowe misspelt the name of Penn; Burchett misspelt the name of Penn. What then ? Would Burchett's blunder prove that Sunderland could not spell the name of a man whom he had known for twenty years ? The question of spelling amounts to this, and no more. A letter is found addressed to Mr. Penne. There *is* a Mr. Penne. *He* spells his name Penne. Sunderland' spells his name Penne. The Pinney family spell his name Penne. The Lords of the Privy Council spell his name Penne. Everybody spells his name Penne. In deeds, petitions, Acts of Parliament, it is always Penne. Mr. Penne is a pardon-broker. He is down at Taunton. He is actually engaged in selling pardons. Why, then, since there is a man whose name the letter *does* bear—who is a known pardon-broker, actually engaged at the time in Taunton selling pardons—go in search of a man whose name it does *not* bear, and who is *not* known to have been connected with the sale of pardons, either at Taunton or at any other town ? But having argued that the question is open, Macaulay next assumes that it is so. 'To which then of the two persons who bore that name is it probable that the letter of the Secretary of State was addressed ?' This is petition with a vengeance. Which of the two who bore that name ? Penn never bore that name at all. No proof is given that Sunderland ever thought he bore that name. It is not here a question of Burchett's inaccuracy, but of Sunderland's accuracy. Sunderland, a friend of many years, was not a

likely man to misspell the name of Penn of Pennsylvania.
Macaulay added :—

' But, it is said, Sunderland's letter is dry and distant; and
he never would have written in such a style to William Penn, with
whom he was on friendly terms. Can it be necessary for me to
reply that the official communications which a Minister of State
makes to his dearest friends and nearest relations are as cold and
formal as those which he makes to strangers ? Will it be contended that the General Wellesley, to whom the Marquess
Wellesley, when Governor of India, addressed so many letters
beginning with " Sir," and ending with " I have the honour to be
your obedient servant," cannot possibly have been his lordship's
brother Arthur ? . . . . Nothing can be more clear than that
the authorized agent of the Maids of Honour was the Mr. Penne
to whom the Secretary of State wrote; and I firmly believe that
Mr. Penn to have been William the Quaker.'

I firmly believe ! Not a scrap of evidence beyond Burchett's blunder — nothing but ' I firmly believe ' — in face
of every proof direct and indirect.

III. In writing of William Kiffin, a wealthy Baptist
minister, whom the King desired to conciliate, Macaulay
had said : —

' The heartless and mad sycophants of Whitehall, judging by
themselves, thought that the old man would be easily propitiated
by an alderman's gown and by some compensation in money for
the property which his grandson had forfeited. Penn was employed in the work of seduction, but to no purpose."—*Hist. Eng.*
ii. 230.

To this assertion were opposed the facts, as they are
stated by Kiffin himself. Macaulay says that Penn was
employed by the heartless sycophants of the court to seduce
Kiffin into accepting an alderman's gown, and that he failed;
two facts asserted; neither of them true. As to Fact the
first, we read in Kiffin's autobiography : —

'A great temptation attended me, which was a commission from the king to be one of the aldermen of the city of London, which, as soon as I heard of it, I used all diligence I could to be excused, both by some lords near the King, and also by Sir Nicholas Butler and Mr. Penn.'—*Kiffin's Mem.* p. 85.

Kiffin states exactly the reverse of what Macaulay cites. Penn does not go to Kiffin; Kiffin goes to Penn. Instead of being employed in the task of seduction, he is engaged in the work of mediation. In excuse, Macaulay quoted a portion of a sentence following that just given :—

'But it was all in vain; I was told that they (Nicholas and Penn) knew I had an interest that might serve the king.'

I hardly hope to be credited, except on reference, when I say that the names of Nicholas and Penn are not in Kiffin's text! These names are added by Macaulay to the sentence cited from him. Butler and Penn could never have been named by Kiffin in this scandalous connexion, since they were engaged by him to do him good at court. The men who told Kiffin he had an interest that might serve the King, and that he might hope to be paid in either honour or advantage for employing it, were the courtiers, not his own mediators.

As to Fact the second—'employed to no purpose'—Kiffin's refusal of the aldermanic gown, I quoted Kiffin's words:—'The next court day I came to the court and took upon me the office of alderman.' (*Kif. Mem.* 87.) Such words permit no fencing; so a paragraph was added to Macaulay's text, confessing that after all Kiffin took the gown. (*Coll. Works*, ii. 55.)

IV. Penn's visit to the Hague in 1687 to persuade William of Orange to support the Declaration of Liberty of Conscience (which Macaulay styles throughout a Declaration of Indulgence), has been abandoned. As the passage stands, it is absurd, though not malignant; for the change of date and topic throws a sentence on Penn's conversation with

William of Orange about the Test Act of 1686, into the middle of a long paragraph about the Declaration of Liberty of Conscience in 1687.

V. Writing in his first edition of the Magdalen College business, Macaulay said : —

'The agency of Penn was employed. . . . . Penn exhorted the Fellows not to rely on the goodness of their cause, but to submit, or at least to temporise. . . . . He did not scruple to become a broker in simony of a peculiarly disreputable kind.'— *Hist. Eng.* ii. 298.

No authority was cited for this assertion that 'Penn was employed' by the Court. No authority could be cited, for the statement is untrue, in letter and in spirit. Nay, the very opposite of what was said is true. Instead of Penn being 'employed' by the Court, he was engaged in behalf of the Fellows. This is not a fact of inference and conjecture. Clear, abundant, and decisive proofs exist (1) that Penn was not employed in the work of seduction, and (2) that he *was* engaged in the task of mediation. The first proofs are necessarily negative; the second are necessarily positive.

I have in my possessson transcripts of all the letters written by Arnout Van Citters, the Dutch agent in England, on the Magdalen affair. Van Citters travelled with the King, and sent from day to day minute accounts of what was being done in this affair, especially by the Court. In all this correspondence of Van Citters with the States-General, there is not a trace of any employment of Penn; though Penn is constantly mentioned in other matters, and was certain to be named by Van Citters in connexion with Magdalen, had his agency been 'employed.' (*Letters from Bath, Sept.* 17, *from Windsor, Oct.* 14, *from Westminster, Oct.* 31, *Nov.* 4, 7, 11, 25, 28, *Dec.* 2, 5, 9, 16, 19, 23 ; originals in the Secret Box, marked *England, No.* 193.)

So far the negative evidence; the positive evidence is that of the Fellows themselves. The first mention of Penn in the affair is on the 6th of September (1687), when Mr. Creech writes to Mr. Charlett:—

'On Monday morning Mr. Penn, the Quaker (with whom I dined the day before, and had a long discourse concerning the college), *wrote a letter to the King in their behalf.*'—*Ballard MSS. Bod. Oxf.*

Next day, Mr. Sykes, another Fellow, writes to Charlett:—

'Mr. Penn rode down to Magdalen College just before he left this place, and after some discourse with the Fellows wrote a short letter to the King.'—*Sykes to Charlett, Sept. 7, Ball. MSS.*

Four weeks later, when Bailey writes to Penn:—

'You who have been already so kind as *to appear in our behalf.*'—*Baily, Oct. 3, printed in State Trials*, xii. 22.

In face of all these proofs—names, dates, and facts —that Penn was acting on behalf of the College, at the instance of Creech, and by desire of the whole body of Fellows, *not* on the 'employment' of the King, Macaulay's text remains!

Macaulay's warrant for asserting that Penn 'exhorted the Fellows to submit,' or at least to temporise,' is a letter—an anonymous letter, which was sent by some one to Bailey during the dispute. The writer of that letter recommended the Fellows to temporise; but the writer of that letter was *not* William Penn. Bailey, indeed, when he received the letter, thought, 'from the charitable purpose,' that it *might* have come from such a man as Penn; and so it got into print as a note 'supposed to be writ by Mr. William Penn.' (State Trials, xii. 21.) Yet evidence of many kinds exist to prove that it was not 'writ by Mr. Penn.' Except 'the charitable purpose,' there is not one touch of Penn in either form or style. It opens, 'Sir,' and Bailey is addressed throughout as 'you;' two forms which Penn had ceased to use for twenty years. There is a second proof; for Bailey put the writer to a test which satisfied him that his correspondent was some other man than Penn. He answered the anonymous letter by a letter also anonymous, which he forwarded to Penn, inviting him to answer, saying, if Penn had written the first letter, he would know where to send his reply. No answer came. There is a third and stronger proof behind. Hunt, as one of the offending Fellows, had to see Penn shortly afterwards at Windsor, where he seems to have shown him the anonymous letter. Penn denied all knowledge of it. The contemporary manuscript at Magdalen College has a note in Hunt's hand-writing, 'This letter Mr. Penn disowned.'—*Hunt MS. fo. 45, Magdalen College, MSS.*

What said Macaulay to these facts? He wrote:—

'It has lately been asserted that Penn most certainly did not write this letter. Now the evidence which proves the letter to be his is irresistible. Bailey, to whom the letter was addressed, ascribed it to Penn, and sent an answer to Penn. In a very short time both the letter and the answer appeared in print. Many thousands of copies were circulated. Penn was pointed out to the whole world as the author of the letter ; and it is not pretended that he met this public-accusation with a public contradiction. Everybody therefore believed, and was perfectly warranted in believing, that he was the author. The letter was repeatedly quoted as his during his own lifetime, not merely in fugitive pamphlets, such as " The History of the Ecclesiastical Commission," published in 1711, but in grave and elaborate books which were meant to descend to posterity. Boyer, in his " History of William the Third," printed immediately after that king's death, and reprinted in 1703, pronounced the letter to be Penn's, and added some severe reflections on the writer. Kennet, in the bulky " History of England" published in 1706—a history which had a large sale and produced a great sensation—adopted the very words of Boyer. When these works appeared, Penn was not only alive, but in the full enjoyment of his faculties. He cannot have been ignorant of the charge brought against him by writers of so much note ; and it was not his practice to hold his peace when unjust charges were brought against him even by obscure scribblers. . . . In the year of his death appeared Eachard's huge volume, containing the History of England from the Restoration to the Revolution ;

and Eachard, though often differing with Boyer and Kennet, agreed with them in unhesitatingly ascribing the letter to Penn. Such is the evidence on one side. I am not aware that any evidence deserving a serious answer has been produced on the other. (1857.)'

Such *is* the 'evidence on one side.' One man 'ascribes' the letter to Penn; a second 'prints' it as Penn's; a third 'quotes' it as Penn's. Now the first man, Bailey, 'ascribed' it to Penn for a moment only. The second 'printed' it only as 'supposed to be writ' by Penn. The others 'quoted' it in ignorance. It is the first time such a rule has ever been laid down in either law or letters, that when a falsehood has been quoted three times it becomes a truth.

No evidence on the other side! The letter is not in Penn's hand. Is that evidence nothing? The letter is not signed by Penn. Is that evidence nothing? It is not in Penn's style. Is that evidence nothing? It contains words that Penn never uses. Is that evidence nothing? It is denied by Penn. Is that evidence nothing? This denial is made to the Fellows themselves. Is that evidence nothing? The document containing Hunt's memorandum of the denial is preserved at Magdalen College. Is that evidence nothing?

The authority for Macaulay's assertion that Penn 'did not scruple to become a broker in simony of a peculiarly disreputable kind,' is Hough's letter (printed in *Wilmot's* '*Life of Hough*,' 25), describing a meeting which the Fellows had with Penn.

Macaulay's story of this meeting is a comedy of errors. He is wrong on every point — the *time*, the *place*, the *method*, and the *motive*, of this interview. Macaulay describes the *time* of meeting as immediately after James left Oxford, while the King was 'greatly incensed and mortified by his defeat.' This was early in September. The meeting was not really held till five weeks later; October 9, 1687. (*Life of Hough*, 22.) Macaulay gives the *place* as Oxford. It was really held at Eton, near Windsor, where Penn had then a country house (*Law-ton's Mem. in Penn, Hist. Soc. Mem.* iii. p. 11, 218 ; *Life of Hough*, 23.) Macaulay described the *method* of this interview as a visit made by Penn to Hough and other Fellows. The actual method was a deputation from the College to Penn; a deputation of which Hough was the head; a deputation which had to follow Penn to Eton, and to ask his leave to occupy a morning of his time. (*Life of Hough*, 22–3.) Macaulay describes the *motive* of the inter-view as a design of Penn to make the Fellows compro-mise their course. The actual motive was a strong desire on the part of Hough and other Fellows to procure Penn's powerful mediation and support with James. To this, one end they followed him to Eton; and to this one end they begged him to receive them. As their friend, he saw them; as their friend, he wished he had been con-cerned for them a little sooner; as their friend, he feared he was too late a-field to help them; as their friend, he assured them he had the welfare of their college at heart. Penn detained the Fellows upwards of three hours: read the whole of their papers and petitions : and promised he would try to read the whole of them to James. (*Life of Hough*, 23-5.)

Yet all these errors as to time, place, method, and motive, stand untouched in the Collected Works !

Macaulay, speaking of this interview (which he supposes Penn to have sought in the interest of James, not the Fel-lows to have sought in the interest of their College), says that Penn ' began to hint at a compromise,' and thence proceeds to his charge of ' simony of a peculiarly disreputable kind.' I quoted Hough's own words, which show that Penn was so completely on their side, that, even for the sake of peace, this great apostle of non-resistance would not hint that they should yield the point. ' I thank God,' said Hough, ' he did not so much as offer at any proposal by way of accom-modation, which was the thing I most dreaded.' (*Life of Hough*, 24.)

To this Macaulay answered :—

' Here again I have been accused of calumniating Penn; and some show of a case has been made out by suppression amounting to falsification. It is asserted that Penn did not " begin to hint at a compromise;" and in proof of this assertion a few words, quoted from the letter in which Hough gives an account of the interview, are printed in italics. These words are, " I thank God he did not offer any proposal by way of accommodation." These words, taken by themselves, undoubtedly seem to prove that Penn did not begin to hint at a compromise. But their effect is very different indeed when they are read in connexion with words which immediately follow, without the intervention of a full stop, but which have been carefully suppressed. The whole sentence runs thus :—' I thank God he did not offer any proposal by way of accommodation ; only once, upon the mention of the Bishop of Oxford's indisposition, he said, smiling, " If the Bishop of Oxford die, Dr. Hough may be made bishop. What think you of that, gentlemen ?'" Can anything be clearer than that the latter part of the sentence limits the general assertion contained in the former part ? Everybody knows that *only* is perpetually used as synonymous with *except that*. Instances will readily occur to all who are well acquainted with the English Bible,—a book from the authority of which there is no appeal when the question is about the force of an English word. We read in the book of Genesis, to go no further, that *every* living thing was destroyed ; and Noah *only* remained, and they that were with him in the ark ; and that Joseph bought *all* the land of Egypt for Pharaoh ; *only* the land of the priests bought he not. The defenders of Penn reason exactly like a commentator who should construe these passages to mean that Noah was drowned in the flood, and that Joseph bought the land of the priests for Pharaoh. (1857.)'

And so the passage stands !

These five charges were contained in the first part of Macaulay's History, volumes i. and ii., and were answered at the time. The second portion of his ' History' continued the abuse.

Penn, according to Macaulay, was a scandalous Jacobite. He tried to bring a foreign army into England. He told the King a falsehood, which William probably knew to be a falsehood. He narrowly escaped arrest for conspiracy at the grave of Fox. He told Sydney something very like a lie, and confirmed that lie with something very like an oath. He stole down to the Sussex coast, and thence escaped to France. He exhorted James to make a descent on England with thirty thousand men.

Not one of these seven passages was true; not even colourably true; as I must now proceed to show.

VI. That Penn was 'a' scandalous Jacobite is one of those false charges which have been struck out of the later index, with a view (it is to be supposed) of its being ultimately struck out of the text, in which it now unhappily stands :—

'The conduct of Penn was . . . scandalous. He was a zealous and busy Jacobite.'—*Coll. Works*, iii. 261.

That Penn was not a Jacobite at all—that is to say, a man who either shared in James's politics when he was king or strove to bring him back when he had lost his crown— can easily be shown. Penn was the friend of Sydney, Locke, and Somers; and the followers of Monmouth set him down in their private lists as one of those powerful men who might be counted on by them for sympathy and help. The writing of that time is full of evidence that Penn was a Reformer, not a Jacobite.

Hough writes : —

' He gave an account in short of his acquaintance with the king ; assured us it was not popery, but property, that first began it ; that honest people were pleased to call him Papist, he was a dissenting Protestant ; that he dissented from Papists in almost all those points wherein we differ from them, and many wherein we and they are agreed.'—*Wilmot's Life of Hough*, 22.

Clarendon writes :—

' Penn laboured to thwart the Jesuitical influence that predominated.'—*Diary*, June 23, 1688.

Arnaut Van Citters writes:—

' One of these days the well-known Archquaker Penn had a long interview with the King, and, as he said to one of his friends, has shown to the King that the Parliament would never agree to the revocation of the Test Act, and of the penal laws, and that he never would get a Parliament to his mind as long as he did not go to work with greater moderation, and drive away from his presence, or at least not listen to, those immoderate Jesuits and other Papists who surround him daily, and whose immoderate advice he now follows, since the nation and the very Dissenters themselves are too strongly opposed to them, and entertain great apprehensions of them; moreover that he has advised the King, as long as his affairs at home are so changeable and remain in so great uncertainty, above all to be cautious in his connexion with France.'—*Van Citters to Grand Pensioners, Windsor, July* 19–29, 1687.

Johnstone says expressly that Penn was against the Order in Council, commanding that the clergy should read his Declaration of Liberty of Conscience from their pulpits. —*Johnstone Correspon.* May 23, 1688; *Mack.* 241, n.   Lawton says that Penn advised the King to liberate the seven Bishops, and on the birth of his son, the Prince of Wales, to issue a general pardon for all offences against his crown.— *Mem. Penn, Hist.* iii. p. 11, 220

Gerard Croese writes:—

' Penn told the Council that the reason why, although he felt gratefull to James personally, he did not wish to see him back as king, now that he had never been able to agree with him in public affairs.'—*Hist. Quak.* 379.

VII. It is alleged that Penn tried to bring a foreign army into England:—

' It is melancholy to relate that Penn, while professing to consider even defensive war as sinful, did everything in his power to bring a foreign enemy into the heart of his country.   He wrote to inform James, &c. . . . . . Avaux thought this letter so important that he sent a translation of it to Louis.'—*Hist. of Eng.* iii. 587.

Not a word of this paragraph is true, in either form or substance. The authority cited is a letter from Avaux to Louis, June 5, 1689, accompanied by a note of news. The errors as to form are grave enough. 'Penn wrote to inform James'—Avaux does not say so. 'Avaux thought this letter so important that he sent a translation of it to Louis'—Avaux never says he thinks it of much importance; he says nothing of translating it, and he encloses no copy of it to Louis. But errors of form are nothing when compared against errors of substance. Macaulay is wrong as to the time supposed; wrong as to the place supposed; wrong as to the person supposed. Here is Avaux's letter in full :—

'SIRE,   '*A Dublin, le 5 Juin*, 1689.

    'Je n'ay pu envoyer à vostre Maiesté la lettre que j'ay eu l'honneur de luy escrire le 27 du mois passé, avec le duplicata des précédentes, parceque le Roy d'Angleterre n'a point fait partir de bastimens de ce pays cy. Il nous est venu depuis cela des nouvelles assez considerables d'Angleterre et d'Escosse. Je me donne l'honneur d'en envoyer les mémoires à vostre Maiesté tels que je les ay receus du Roy de la Grande Bretagne.

'Le commencement des nouvelles datées d'Angleterre, est la copie d'une lettre de M. Pen que j'ay veue en original. On peut juger pars tout ces mémoires que si Sa Maiesté Britannique estoit en estat d'entrer en Angleterre, elle recouvreroit bientost cette couronne, mais il ne le peut sans la protection de vostre Maiesté, que verra mieux que moy par ces relations cy, ce qu'il y auroit à faire pour le Roy d'Angleterre, si neantmoins vostre Maiesté me permet de luy dire non sentiment, je trouve qu'un secours d'argent avec un bon corps de troupes Françoises, est le plus court moyen qu'il y ait de remettre le Roy d'Angleterre en estat de se restablir sur le throsne, et cet effort qu'on feroit à cette heure, delivreroit vostre Maiesté dans la suitte d'une plus grands despense qu'elle sera peut-estre obligée de faire.

'Le bon effet, Sire, que ces lettres d'Escosse et d'Angleterre ont produit, est qu'elles ont enfin persuadé le Roy d'Angleterre qu'il recouvrera ses estats que les armes à la main, et ce n'est pas peu que de l'en avoir convaincu, car cela luy fera prendre d'autres mesures qu'il n'a fait jusques à cette heure, qu'il a cru devoir menager les Anglois pour les ravoir par amitié.

A A

'Le Roy d'Angleterre a resolu de faire partir incessament un secours de mille ou douze cens hommes, qu'il a dessein il y a desja quelque temps d'envoyer en Escosse.'

The note enclosed by Avaux as a summary of his news is in the following words :—

'MÉMOIRE DE NOUVELLES D'ANGLETERRE ET D'ESCOSSE.

'Le Prince d'Orange commence d'estre fort degoutté de l'humeur des Anglois, et la face des choses change bien viste selon le naturel des insulaires, et sa santé est fort mauvais. Il y a un nuage qui commence à se former au nord des deux royaumes, où le Roy a beaucoup d'amis, ce qui donne beaucoup d'inquietude aux principaux amis du Prince d'Orange, qui estant riches, commencent à estre persuadez que ce sera l'espéc qui decidera de leur sort, ce qu'ils ont tant taché d'eviter. Ils aprehendent une invasion de France et d'Irlande, et en ce cas le Roy aura plus d'amis que jamais. Le commerce est ruiné, tant par les Turcs, que par l'apprehension d'une guerre avec la France, et encore pas nostre flotte mesme, qui prend tous tes esquipages des vaisseaux marchands, sans en excepter que le maistre et un garçon pour chaque bastiment, ce que rend le trafficq si difficile que les marchands s'en plaignent hautement.

'Les divisions sont considerables parmi les grands, et il y a une grande jalousie parmi les Anglois, qui commencent à descouvrir que toutes choses se font par les conseils des Hollandois. L'Eglise Anglicane voit son sort dans le procede du Prince d'Orange en Escosse, où il a chassé les evesques Protestans. Les bons sujets du Roy souhaittent de le voir au plustost, avec une bonne armée au lieu que toute capitulation. Herbert est venu dans Milfort Haven, sa flotte toute en desordre, ce qui augmente beaucoup les desordres dans le pays. Depuis par des courriers qui arrivent chaque semaine, on est informé. Que le Prince d'Orange se defie non seulement des vieilles troupes que Sa Maiesté laissa en Angleterre, mais de presque tous les Anglois, et l'on croit que si Sa Maiesté arrive bien escortée dans le pays, le Parlement mesme se declareroit pour elle. Les gens se defient tant du succez de ce que le Prince d'Orange a fait, qu'ils ne veulent point prester d'argent sur la foy des Actes de Parlement, et mesme ceux qui en ont presté, donnent dix sur cent pour l'assurer. Le Prince d'Orange a cassé les deux Colonels Coningham et Richard, pour n'avoir pas secouru

Londonderry, et fait des efforts pour y envoyer des autres troupes, mais l'allarme du costé d'Escosse estant plus pressante, il s'est contenté d'envoyer quelques navires de guerre de ce costé, pour empescher la correspondance par mer, et a envoyé la pluspart de ses troupes vers les frontières d'Escosse, dont il craint les remue-mens, et tous ses amis commencent à montrer une consternation bien grande, toutes les fois que les nouvelles viennent que le Roy y est allé, dont on parle icy comme d'une chose certain. Depuis l'arrivée de la flotte d'Herbert, nous avon en peu plus de respect pour la force de France par mer, et cela augmenté nos craintes, et l'on ne doute pas que si le Roy revient devant que le Prince d'Orange ayt eu le temps de faire des changemens considerables, qu'il ne soit receu par tous les gens les plus considerables, et mesme la populace commence à souffrir qu'on parle le luy favorablement, ce qu'on n'osoit pas faire devant eux auparavent. Il y a un fort grand nombre qui ont déja enrollé du monde, infanterie, cavalerie, et dragons, et qui ont mesmes leurs chevaux dans des maisons, affidées, et qui ne manguent que l'occasion de paroistre, estant de gens considerables et par leur famille, et par la grandeur de leur bien. On a juste raison de croire, que deux tiers de la vieille armée seroit pour le Roy, en cas qu'il pust venir devant que ces soldats se soient appliquez à quelque autre mestier.'

With these authorities in view, we see the magnitude of Macaulay's errors as to substance.

The time of which Macaulay is writing is June 1690. James was then holding his Court in Dublin; William was on his way to Carrickfergus; Tourbeville was cruising in the Channel; a French descent upon our coasts was hourly expected. But how could Avaux tell his master anything about the state of public feeling? Avaux was at home in France. He had sailed from Cork in the preceding spring. Avaux's letter shows the proper *date* of his intelligence; he is speaking of the months of May and June 1689; a very different time to June 1690.

The *place* from which Avaux forwards news of import-ance (from May and June 1689) is Scotland—not England, as Macaulay says. In May and June 1689, England was calm, and London busy in preparing for the coronation. Scotland was in arms for her ancient line. Dundee was calling for troops, and Avaux trying to persuade his master to adventure in the strife. We see that Avaux, when he comes to business, puts the Scotch affairs in front. 'The good effect, sire, which these letters from Scotland and England have produced,' &c. Louis, in replying, treats the news from England as of no importance, while he answers very carefully as to the Scotch affair.

I give the French king's answer to Avaux:—

'Versailles, June 29, 1689.

'Quant aux relations qu'on a envoyé d'Escosse, qui font voir que le party qui s'est declaré pour le Roy pourroit faire des progrez considerables s'il estoit puissamment secouru, ou seulement apuyé de la presence du Roy, c'est à ce Prince à voir s'il est en estat de l'assister, et d'envoyer dans ledit pays quelque partie des troupes qu'il a en Irlande; et si le secours de mille ou douze cens hommes que vous mandez par vostre lettre du 5, qu'il avoit resolu de faire passer en Escosse, y est heureusement arrivé, malgré tous les empeschemens que le Prince d'Orange et les rebelles y peuvent former, on pouroit esperer d'un semblable succez d'un second passage. Il ne peut pas faire une diversion plus salutaire à l'Irlande que l'occupation que les troupes et le party qu'il aura en Escosse pourra donner à ses ennemis. Pour ce qui regarde sa personne, comme il pourroit arriver telle révolution en sa faveur dans ledit royaume que contre mon opinion, sa seule presence seroit capable de reduire entièrement la ville d'Edimbourg à son obeissance, faire casser tout ce que la convention des rebelles a fait contre l'autorité dudit Roy, et restablir tellement ses affaires dans tout l'Escosse qu'elle donneroit de nouvelles forces à tous les Anglois qui sont mecontens du Prince d'Orange ; il faut luy laisser prendre dans ces evenemens extraordinaires les résolutions qu'il croira luy estre les plus avantageuses, en sorte qu'il ne puisse pas se plaindre qu'on luy ait fait manquer l'occasion de rentrer dan ses estats; mais la principale application qu'il doit avoir à present est de pourvoir à sa deffense et à la seureté de ce qu'il possede en Irlande, à quoy il faut esperer qu'il pourra reussir, si toutes les troupes qu'il a sur pied font bien leur devoir.'

The person from whom Macaulay says that Avaux got his first news was William Penn; but Avaux nowhere says

so.   He only mentions M. Pen.   Who was Avaux's
'M. Pen?' There is no evidence to show that he was
William Penn, and there is plenty of evidence to suggest
that he was *not.* That there were other 'M. Pens' about
the court we know. There was George Penne, the pardon-
broker. There was Neville Penn, a secret agent of the
exiled court. This Neville Penn (whose name is spelt by
different persons Pen, Penn, Pain, and Payne) was then
in England on a secret mission, and the only fair construction of the words of Avaux is, that the news sent from
England by 'M. Pen' were from the King's paid agent,
Neville Penn. This Neville Penn was a zealous Catholic,
a man of talent, and a Jacobite by feeling, even more than
by his dubious trade. That he was hated in the English
Court we know too well. A few months after Avaux sent
his news to Louis, Neville Penn, on flying from England
into Scotland, fell into the power of the new government,
where he was screwed and torn; a first time by command
of Mary, and a second time by command of William; till
the oldest and least scrupulous politician left the council-
table and the torture-chamber in disgust. (*Leven and
Melville Papers*, p. 582.) But let this 'M. Pen' be whom
he may, it is clear that a letter from him in the early part of
1689 cannot have been written by William Penn in connexion with events in June 1690.

VIII. Penn is accused of falsehood :

'Penn was brought before the Privy Council. He said . . . This
was a falsehood; and William was probably aware that it was so.'
—*Hist. Eng.* iii. 600.

No such interview as Macaulay pictures could have
taken place. The dates forbid us to believe it. Macaulay
fixes his imaginary interview immediately before the King's
departure for Ireland. Now, the King left London on the
4th of June, 1690 (*Evelyn's Diary*, iii. 294). The proclamation for Penn's arrest was not issued until King William

had been gone twenty days (*Privy Council Reg. June* 24, 1690); and Penn was still at large on the 31st of July (*Penn to Nottingham, July* 31). On the 15th of August Penn was discharged from custody (*Privy Council Reg. Aug.* 15, 1690). William arrived at Kensington, September 10 (*Gazette, Sept.* 1690). It is therefore physically impossible that the interview described by Macaulay could have taken place, and therefore physically impossible that Penn could have told the King a falsehood, which William probably knew to be a falsehood.

IX. Penn is described as flying from arrest, stealing down to the Sussex coast, and escaping into France—an enemy's country:

'A warrant was issued against Penn, and he narrowly escaped the messenger. . . . . Penn was conspicuous among those who committed the corpse [of Fox] to the earth. . . . . He instantly took flight. . . . . He lay hid in London during some months, and then stole down to the coast of Sussex, and made his escape to France.' —*Hist. Eng.* iv. 23, 30, 31.

This paragraph is one mass of error, as the dates alone suffice to prove. Fox was buried at Bunhill Fields on the 16th of January, 1691 (*Journal of Fox*, p. 366). The order for Penn's arrest was not given until three weeks later (*Privy Council Reg. Feb.* 5, 1691). Penn neither stole down to Sussex nor escaped into France. He lived in London, and occasionally at Worminghurst. Croese writes:

' Penn withdrew himself more and more from business, and at length he confined himself to his new house in London.' (*Hist. Quak.* ii. 102.)

Luttrel, indeed, heard in a London coffee-house a report that Penn had escaped to France, but the report was false. On turning to Penn's Works, the reader will find abundant fruit of the leisure now enjoyed by Penn in his own house. (*Penn's Collected Works*, i. 818–892; ii. 774–807). This ' escape to France ' has disappeared from Macaulay's revised index (*Hist. Eng.* v. 327).

X. Penn told Sydney something 'very like a lie,' and supported that lie by something 'very like an oath':

'A short time after his disappearance, Sydney received from him a strange communication. Penn begged for an interview, but insisted on a promise that he should be suffered to return unmolested to his hiding-place. Sydney obtained the royal permission to make an appointment on these terms. Penn came to the rendezvous, and spoke at length in his own defence. He declared that he was a faithful subject of King William and Queen Mary, and that if he knew of any design against them he would discover it. Departing from his Yea and Nay, he protested, as in the presence of God, that he knew of no plot, and that he did not believe that there was any plot, unless the ambitious projects of the French government might be called plots. Sydney, amazed probably by hearing a person who had such an abhorrence of lies that he would not use the common forms of civility, and such an abhorrence of oaths that he would not kiss the book in a court of justice, tell something very like a lie, and confirm it by something very like an oath, asked how, if there were really no plot, the letters and minutes which had been found on Ashton were to be explained. This question Penn evaded.'—*Hist. Eng.* iv. 30, 31.

As Macaulay cites Sydney's letter to William for his version of this strange interview, I give Sydney's letter to the King in full :—

'*Feb.* 21, 1691.

'SIR,—About ten days ago Mr. Penn sent his brother-in-law, Mr. Lowther, to me, to let me know that he would be very glad to see me if I would give him leave, and promise him to let him return without being molested. I sent him word I would if the Queen would permit it. He then desired me not to mention it to anyone but the Queen. I said I would not. On Monday he sent me to know what time I would appoint. I named Wednesday, in the evening ; and accordingly I went to the place at the time, where I found him, just as he used to be, not at all disguised, but in the same clothes and the same humour I formerly have seen him in. It would be too long for your Majesty to read a full account of all our discourse ; but, in short, it was this, that he was a true and faithful servant to King William and Queen Mary, and if he knew anything that was prejudicial to them or their government, he would readily discover it. He protested, in the presence of God, that he knew of no plot; nor did he believe there was any one in Europe but what King Lewis hath laid; and he was of opinion that King James knew the bottom of this plot as little as other people. He saith he knows your Majesty hath a great many enemies; and some that came over with you, and some that joined you soon after your arrival, he was sure were more inveterate and more dangerous than the Jacobites; for he saith there is not one man among them that hath common understanding. To the letters that were found with my Lord Preston, and the papers of the conference, he would not give any positive answer, but said if he could have the honour to see the King, and that he would be pleased to believe the sincerity of what he saith, and pardon the ingenuity of what he confessed, he would freely tell everything he knew of himself and other things that would be much for his Majesty's service and interest to know, but if he cannot obtain this favour he must be obliged to quit the kingdom; which he is very unwilling to do. He saith he might have gone away twenty times if he had pleased, but he is so confident of giving your Majesty satisfaction if you would hear him, that he was resolved to expect your return before he took any sort of measures. What he intends to do, is all he can do for your service, for he can't be a witness if he would, it being, as he saith, against his conscience and his principles to take an oath. This is the sum of our conference, and I am sure your Majesty will judge as you ought to do of it, without any of my reflections.'—*Dalrymple's Mem.* iii. 183.

Here is a wholly different tale. Sydney never hints that Penn was in a ' hiding-place.' Sydney says, 'I found him just as he used to be; not at all disguised, but in the same clothes and the same humour I have formerly seen him in.' Sydney nowhere suggests that he thought Penn was telling 'something very like a lie.' Macaulay adds, Penn assured Sydney that 'the most formidable enemies of the government were the discontented Whigs.' Sydney never mentions these ' discontented Whigs.' Sydney never asked ' how the letters and minutes which had been

found on Ashton were to be explained.'   Macaulay makes
Penn say, absurdly, that 'the Jacobites are not dangerous.'
Sydney reports him as saying, what was very true, that
some of those who had come over with William, and some of
those who had been the first to join him, were 'more dangerous
than the Jacobites.'

XI. Penn is accused of trying to persuade James to
invade England at the head of thirty thousand men.

'After about three years of wandering and lurking, he made
his peace with the government and again ventured to resume his
ministrations.   The return which he made for the lenity with
which he had been treated does not much raise his character.
Scarcely had he again begun to harangue in public about the
unlawfulness of war, than he sent a message earnestly exhorting
James to make an immediate descent on England with thirty
thousand men.'—*Hist. Eng.* iv. 31.

The authority for this absurd statement is 'a paper
drawn up at St. Germain's under Melfort's direction, Dec.
1828, 1693.'

This paper, which the reader will find in Macpherson's
'Original Papers,' i. 459–463, never mentions the name of
Penn.   It gives a list of many leading men in England who
are said to be interested for the exiled family; but the name
of Penn is not among these men.   Annexed to the 'paper'
are two reports from spies, in one of which occurs the name
Mr. Penn.   But there is nothing to suggest that this 'Mr.
Penn' is William Penn, the Founder and Lord Proprietor
of Pennsylvania, while there is plenty of evidence to show
that he is Neville Penn.   The spy was one Williamson,
who was in London, earning dirty money by the dirtiest
of all dirty trades.   He sent word over to Versailles that
certain peers and gentlemen,—the Earls of Clarendon, Yar-
mouth, Aylesbury and Arran, Sir James Montgomery, Sir
Theophilus Oglethorpe, and Sir John Friend, Mr. Stroude,
Mr. Louton, Mr. Ferguson, Mr. Penn, and Col. Graham,—

implored the King to make a descent on England.　Here is what this spy reports of 'Mr. Penn':—

'Mr. Penn says that your Majesty has had several occasions, but never any so favourable as the present; and he hopes that your Majesty will be earnest with the most Christian King not to neglect it; that a descent with thirty thousand men will not only re-establish your Majesty, but according to all appearances will break the League; that your Majesty's kingdom will be wretched while the confederates are united, for while there is a fool in England the Prince of Orange will have a pensioned parliament who will give him money.'—*Macpherson's Original Papers*, 1, 488.

With the utmost confidence I say that William Penn never spoke and never wrote this stuff.　Penn never used the phrase 'Your Majesty,' here used four times in as many lines.　Penn never called Louis the Fourteenth the 'most Christian King.'　The first expression shows that 'Mr. Penn' was *not* a Quaker; the second expression shows that 'Mr. Penn' *was* a Catholic.　Williamson puts his 'Mr. Penn' below such men as Mr. Stroude, Mr. Louton, and Mr. Ferguson.　Was there any 'Mr. Penn' in James's pay whose place in such a list would be where Captain Williamson puts him?　Yes; we know there was.　'Mr. Penn' was Neville Penn.　Neville Penn was acquainted with Williamson.　Neville Penn was a paid agent.　Neville Penn was intimate with Ferguson, and was connected with Montgomery.　Neville Penn was a Roman Catholic.　Neville Penn would address James as 'Your Majesty,' and assuredly speak of Louis as the 'most Christian King.'　Neville Penn would be sure to call King William 'the Prince of Orange,' and the two houses 'a pensioned parliament.'

It is a second case of mistaken names.　As 'Mr. Penne' who sold pardons in Somerset proved to be George Penne, so 'Mr. Penn' who recommended James to invade England with thirty thousand men, appears to have been Neville Penn.

Thus vanishes the last of eleven charges against the private honour and public service of the Founder of Pennsylvania. For the sake of Lord Macaulay's credit as a writer, it will never cease to be a matter of regret that the amended versions of his index were not introduced into his text.

LONDON:
PRINTED BY JOHN STRANGEWAYS,
Castle St. Leicester Sq.

1, *Leicester Square, London,*
October, 1882.

฿ICKERS AND ŞON'S

𝕷ist

OF

ILLUSTRATED, STANDARD, AND POPULAR

𝔐odern 𝔅ooks.

All new books or new editions are marked thus *.*

IMPORTANT REMAINDER.

BIDA'S ETCHINGS. The authorized Version of the **FOUR GOSPELS,** with the whole of the magnificent Etchings on Steel (132), after drawings by M. BIDA.

4 vols. folio, appropriately bound in cloth, published at £12 12*s.*, reduced to £4 4*s.* net.

4 vols. in 2, bound in half-morocco, with gilt edges, £15 15*s.*, reduced to £5 15*s.* 6*d.* net.

Or, in best morocco, £18 18*s.*, reduced to £10 10*s.* net.

*** BICKERS AND SON have purchased the entire remaining copies of this superb work, which they offer, for a short time only, on the above exceptional terms. As the stock decreases the prices will be proportionately raised.

"An appropriate School Prize."

A New and Cheaper Edition in One Volume. Imperial 8vo, cloth elegant, gilt edges, 15*s.*

INDIA AND ITS NATIVE PRINCES; Travels in Central India, and in the Presidencies of Bombay and Bengal. By LOUIS ROUSSELET, carefully revised and edited by Lieut.-Colonel C. BUCKLE. Profusely Illustrated.

*** This is not an abridgment, but contains the Complete Text of the superb 4to Edition, with more than half its Illustrations.

Bickers and Son's Illustrated Series of 7s. 6d. Gift Books.

Demy 8vo, cloth elegant, gilt edges, 7s. 6d.; calf extra, 12s. 6d. each.

Two New Volumes.

*NAPOLEON BUONAPARTE, LIFE OF. By J. G. LOCKHART, with 9 Illustrations by Eminent Artists, reproduced in Permanent Photography and numerous Woodcuts.

*WELLINGTON, LIFE OF. By W. H. MAXWELL. A New Edition, revised, condensed, and completed; with 12 Illustrations by Eminent Artists, reproduced in Permanent Photography, numerous Woodcuts, and Plan of the Battle of Waterloo.

ROBINSON CRUSOE, THE LIFE AND ADVENTURES OF. By DANIEL DEFOE. With a Memoir of the Author, and Twelve Illustrations by T. STOTHARD, R.A., in Permanent Photography.

THE PILGRIM'S PROGRESS FROM THIS WORLD TO THAT WHICH IS TO COME. By JOHN BUNYAN. With Twelve Illustrations by THOMAS STOTHARD, R.A., reproduced in Permanent Photography.

ROYAL CHARACTERS FROM THE WORKS OF SIR WALTER SCOTT, HISTORICAL AND ROMANTIC. With Twelve Illustrations in Permanent Photography.

THE VICAR OF WAKEFIELD. By OLIVER GOLDSMITH. With Permanent Photographs from Paintings by Mulready, Maclise, and others.

THE GIRLHOOD OF SHAKESPEARE'S HEROINES. A Series of fifteen tales by MARY COWDEN CLARKE. Rearranged by her sister SABILLA NOVELLO. Illustrated with 9 Photographs from paintings by T. F. DICKSEE and W. S. HERRICK.

COOK'S VOYAGES ROUND THE WORLD. With an Account of his Life by A. KIPPIS, D.D. Illustrated with 12 Plates reproduced in exact Facsimile from Drawings made during the Voyages.

DODD'S BEAUTIES OF SHAKESPEARE. By the Rev. WILLIAM DODD, LL.D. Elegantly printed on fine paper. Illustrated with 12 Plates, reproduced in Permanent Woodburytype.

GOLDSMITH (OLIVER), THE LIFE AND TIMES OF. By JOHN FORSTER. Fifth Edition, with 40 Woodcuts.

LAMB'S TALES FROM SHAKESPEARE. By CHARLES and MARY LAMB. Printed at the Chiswick Press, on superfine paper. Illustrated with 12 Plates from the "Boydell Gallery," reproduced in Permanent Woodburytype.

NELSON, THE LIFE OF. By ROBERT SOUTHEY. Illustrated with 12 Plates by WESTALL and others, reproduced in Permanent Woodburytype. Facsimiles of Nelson's Handwriting and Plan of Battle of the Nile.

OUR SUMMER MIGRANTS. An Account of the Migratory Birds which pass the Summer in the British Islands. By J. E. HARTING, F.L.S., F.Z.S., author of " A Handbook of British Birds," a new edition of White's "Selborne," &c., &c. Illustrated with 30 Illustrations on Wood, from Designs by THOMAS BEWICK.

THE NATURAL HISTORY AND ANTIQUITIES OF SELBORNE.
By the Rev. GILBERT WHITE, M.A. Third Edition, with Ten Letters not included in any previous Edition of the Work. The Standard Edition by BENNETT, thoroughly Revised, with Additional Notes, by JAMES EDMUND HARTING, F.L.S., F.Z.S., author of "A Handbook of British Birds," "The Ornithology of Shakespeare," &c. Illustrated with numerous Engravings by THOMAS BEWICK, HARVEY, and others.

"THE GEM POCKET EDITION."

DODD'S BEAUTIES OF SHAKESPEARE. This exquisite little *bijou* is printed on very fine cream-coloured paper, in the best manner of the Elzevir Press. Cloth extra, 2s.

Or bound in roan, with tuck (like a pocket-book), for travellers, 3s. 6d.

Lacroix's Works on the Middle Ages and the Eighteenth Century.

5 Volumes, Imp. 8vo, elegantly bound in Cloth, full gilt sides and leather back, reduced price, £6.

THE ARTS IN THE MIDDLE AGES AND AT THE PERIOD OF THE RENAISSANCE, *New Edition,* including the Chapter on Music. By PAUL LACROIX. 20 Chromo-lithographs and 420 Wood Engravings.

*** This volume can only be supplied with the set.

MANNERS, CUSTOMS, AND DRESS, DURING THE MIDDLE AGES. By PAUL LACROIX. Illustrated with 15 Chromo-lithographic Prints and upwards of 400 Engravings on Wood. £1, 11s. 6d. ; reduced to 25s.
Or in calf, super extra, gilt sides and edges, 31s. 6d. *net.*

MILITARY AND RELIGIOUS LIFE IN THE MIDDLE AGES, AND AT THE PERIOD OF THE RENAISSANCE. By PAUL LACROIX. 13 Chromo-lithographs and 400 Engravings on Wood. £1, 11s. 6d. ; reduced to 25s.

Or in calf, super extra, gilt sides and edges, 31s. 6d. *net.*

THE EIGHTEENTH CENTURY. Its Institutions, Customs, and Costumes. France, 1700-1789. By PAUL LACROIX. Illustrated by 21 Chromo-lithographs and 351 Wood Engravings.

*** This volume can only be supplied with the set.

SCIENCE AND LITERATURE IN THE MIDDLE AGES AND AT THE PERIOD OF THE RENAISSANCE. With 13 Chromo-lithographs and 400 Engravings on Wood. £1, 11s. 6d.; reduced to 25s.
Or in calf, super extra, gilt sides and edges, 31s. 6d. *net.*
Sets elegantly bound in the best morocco, super extra, gilt edges, £9, 9s. *net.*

MUSIC. A Supplementary Chapter to the Arts of the Middle Ages and paged to follow on that volume. With 21 Illustrations and 1 Chromo-lithograph. Wrapper, 2s. 6d.

SHAKESPEARE'S WORKS.

Various Editions.

A New and Improved Edition, in Ten vols. demy 8vo, cloth extra, price £4, 10s.

DYCE'S SHAKESPEARE. The Complete Works of William Shakespeare. With Notes and Copious Glossary. Edited by the late Rev. Alexander Dyce. With finely engraved Droeshout and Stratford Portraits, and Portrait of the Editor.

" Mr. Dyce's 'Shakespeare' is re-issued in a new and improved form. The importance and value of this work can hardly be overrated. . . . In the edition published by Messrs. Bickers and Son the text is printed as it left Mr. Dyce's hands ; but the notes, which hitherto have been placed at the end of the plays, are to be found at the foot of the pages—decidedly an advantageous change."—*Times.*

SHAKESPEARE'S PLAYS AND POEMS. Edited, with a Scrupulous Revision of the Text, but without Note or Comment, by Charles and Mary Cowden Clarke. With an Introductory Essay and Copious Glossary. Four Library 8vo vols. cloth gilt, £1, 11s. 6d.

Or calf extra, £2, 12s. 6d.

*** This splendid edition of Shakespeare's works is copyright, having been carefully revised and amplified by Mr. and Mrs. Cowden Clarke. The Text is selected with great care, and is printed from a new fount of ancient type on toned paper, forming four handsome volumes, bound in cloth extra, calf extra, or in the best morocco.

12th Thousand.

SHAKESPEARE. The Best One Volume Edition, with Essay and Glossary, by Charles and Mary Cowden Clarke. Large 8vo, beautifully printed and bound, cloth extra, 9s.

Or calf extra, 15s.

"The Leicester Square Edition."

The most charming single volume illustrated edition of Shakespeare ever published.

SHAKESPEARE'S COMPLETE WORKS.—Edited by Charles and Mary Cowden Clarke. With Portrait and 21 choice Illustrations from the " Boydell Gallery."

Cloth elegant, gilt edges, 15s.

Or calf extra, gilt edges, £1, 8s.

Morocco, blocked, gilt edges, £1, 16s.

SHAKESPEARE—THE BOYDELL TABLE EDITION. 2 vols. The above text printed on thick superfine paper, with Sixty-six Illustrations. Cloth elegant, gilt edges, £1, 11s. 6d.

Or, in calf extra, gilt edges, £2, 12s. 6d.

Morocco blocked, gilt edges, £3, 7s. 6d.

An illustrated Library Edition of Shakespeare, 4 vols. demy 8vo, cloth extra.

THE BOYDELL SHAKESPEARE. The Complete Works of William Shakespeare. Edited with a Scrupulous Revision of the Text, by Charles and Mary Cowden Clarke. With Glossary, &c. Illustrated with 66 Illustrations from the " Boydell Gallery," *price 2 guineas.*

Or, in calf extra, gilt edges, £3, 3s. net.

English Gentleman's Library.

Demy 8vo, cloth extra (uniform binding), illustrated :—

GEORGE SELWYN AND HIS CONTEMPORARIES. With Memoirs and Notes by JOHN HENEAGE JESSE. With Portraits finely engraved on steel. 4 volumes, demy 8vo, cloth extra, price £2, 2s.

BOSWELL'S LIFE OF SAMUEL JOHNSON. With the Tours to Wales and the Hebrides. A reprint of the first quarto edition, the text carefully collated and restored ; all variations marked ; and new notes, embodying the latest information. The whole edited by PERCY FITZGERALD, M.A., F.S.A. 3 vols. demy 8vo, cloth, 27s.

D'ARBLAY'S (MADAME) DIARY AND LETTERS. Edited by her Niece, CHARLOTTE BARRET. A New Edition, illustrated by numerous fine Portraits engraved on Steel. 4 vols. 8vo, cloth extra, 36s.

GOLDSMITH'S (OLIVER) LIFE AND TIMES. By JOHN FORSTER. The Illustrated Library Edition. 2 vols. demy 8vo, cloth, 15s.; reduced to 10s. 6d. net.

GRAMMONT (COUNT), MEMOIRS OF. By ANTHONY HAMILTON. A New Edition, with a Biographical Sketch of Count Hamilton, numerous Historical and Illustrative Notes by Sir WALTER SCOTT, and 64 Copper-plate Portraits by EDWARD SCRIVEN. 8vo, cloth extra, 12s.

MAXWELL'S LIFE OF THE DUKE OF WELLINGTON. Three vols. 8vo, with numerous highly finished Line and Wood Engravings by Eminent Artists. Cloth extra, 22s. 6d. ; reduced to 15s. net.

MONTAGU'S (LADY MARY WORTLEY) LETTERS AND WORKS. Edited by LORD WHARNCLIFFE. With important Additions and Corrections, derived from the Original Manuscripts, and a New Memoir. Two vols. 8vo, with fine Steel Portraits, cloth extra, 18s. ; reduced to 12s. net.

ROSCOE'S LIFE OF LORENZO DE MEDICI, called "THE MAGNIFICENT." A New and much improved Edition. Edited by his Son, THOMAS ROSCOE. Demy 8vo, with Portraits and numerous Plates, cloth extra, 7s. 6d.

ROSCOE'S LIFE AND PONTIFICATE OF LEO THE TENTH. Edited by his Son, THOMAS ROSCOE. Two vols. 8vo, with numerous Plates, cloth extra, 15s. ; reduced to 10s. 6d. net.

SAINT-SIMON (MEMOIRS OF THE DUKE OF), during the Reign of Louis the Fourteenth and the Regency. Translated from the French and edited by BAYLE ST. JOHN. A New Edition. Three vols. 8vo, cloth extra, 27s.

WALPOLE'S (HORACE) ANECDOTES OF PAINTING IN ENGLAND. With some Account of the principal English Artists, and incidental Notices of Sculptors, Carvers, Enamellers, Architects, Medallists, Engravers, &c. With Additions by Rev. JAMES DALLAWAY. Edited, with Additional Notes by RALPH N. WORNUM. Three vols. 8vo, with upwards of 150 Portraits and Plates, cloth extra, 27s.

WALPOLE'S (HORACE) ENTIRE CORRESPONDENCE. Chronologically arranged, with the Prefaces and Notes of CROKER, Lord DOVER, and others ; the Notes of all previous Editors, and Additional Notes by PETER CUNNINGHAM. Nine vols. 8vo, with numerous fine Portraits engraved on Steel, cloth extra, £4, 1s.

*** The above offered in complete sets, 37 vols. uniformly bound.*

		£	s.	d.
Cloth	net	13	15	0
Half Calf	,,	18	5	0
Calf extra	,,	21	15	0
Tree marbled calf	,,	23	0	0

Reprints of Standard Authors.

NO HANDSOMER LIBRARY BOOKS HAVE EVER ISSUED FROM THE PRESS.

Each Work is carefully edited, collated with the early copies, and printed in the best style on superior paper.

ARNOLD'S (DR. THOMAS) HISTORY OF ROME, AND THE LATER ROMAN COMMONWEALTH. 5 vols. demy 8vo, cloth, £3.

**** The "History of Rome" cannot be supplied separately.

*—— **HISTORY OF THE LATER ROMAN COMMONWEALTH.** 2 vols. demy 8vo, cloth, 24s.

BUNYAN'S PILGRIM'S PROGRESS FROM THIS WORLD TO THAT WHICH IS TO COME. Edition de luxe, containing the complete set of 16 Designs by T. STOTHARD, R.A., reproduced in Permanent Photography from a fine proof set of the original chalk-stipple engravings. Elegantly bound in half roxburghe style, gilt top, 10s. 6d. ; or in half vellum, with vegetable vellum sides and gilt top, 12s. (For Cheaper Edition see page 3.)

COLUMBUS (CHRISTOPHER) LIFE AND VOYAGES OF. Together with the Voyages of his Companions. By WASHINGTON IRVING. 3 vols. demy 8vo, cloth, 22s. 6d. ; reduced to 10s. 6d. net.

New Edition, uniform with "Pepys' Diary."

DIARY OF JOHN EVELYN, Esq., F.R.S., to which are added a selection from his familiar letters and the private correspondence between King Charles I. and Sir Edward Nicholas, and between Sir Edward Hyde (afterwards Earl of Clarendon) and Sir Richard Browne. Edited from the original MSS. by WILLIAM BRAY, F.S.A. With a Life of the author by HENRY B. WHEATLEY, F.S.A. With numerous portraits. 4 vols. medium 8vo, cloth extra, £2, 8s. 0d.

*—— **EDITION DE LUXE** of the above, containing, in addition to the Original Illustrations, 100 Selected Engravings. A few copies remain. Only Sixty (each numbered) were printed. 4 vols. imperial 8vo, half-roxburghe, price £7 net.

FIELDING'S MISCELLANIES AND POEMS, forming Vol. XI. of his complete Works. Half roxburghe, top edge gilt, 7s. 6d.

These Poems and Miscellanies have never before appeared in a collected edition of his Works, and will range with any library 8vo edition.

HERBERT'S POEMS AND REMAINS. With S. T. COLERIDGE's Notes, and Life by IZAAK WALTON. Revised, with Additional Notes, by Mr. J. YEOWELL. 2 vols. Cloth, 21s.

JONSON'S (BEN) COMPLETE WORKS. With Notes, Critical and Explanatory, and a Biographical Memoir by W. GIFFORD, Esq. An exact reprint of the now scarce edition, with Introduction and Appendices by Lieut.-Colonel CUNNINGHAM. 9 vols. medium 8vo, cloth, £5, 5s. ; reduced to £3, 3s. net.

MILTON'S POETICAL WORKS. Edited by the Rev. J. MITFORD. With Portrait and Twenty-seven Illustrations by R. WESTALL, R.A. 2 vols, 8vo, cloth, 21s.

MILTON (JOHN), THE POETICAL WORKS OF. Complete in one volume. Printed in large type, with Life by A. CHALMERS, M.A., F.S.A. Twelve Illustrations by R. WESTALL, R.A., in Permanent Woodburytype. Demy 8vo, cloth elegant, 9s.

MILTON (JOHN), THE POETICAL WORKS OF. With a Life of the Author by the Rev. JOHN MITFORD. A fine Library Edition, printed on rich ribbed paper. 2 vols. demy 8vo, cloth, 15s. ; reduced to 10s. net.

This is an exact reprint, *on superior paper*, of the 2 vols. of Poems in the 8 vol. edition of Milton's Complete Works.

MILTON (JOHN), THE POETICAL WORKS OF. With a Life of the Author by A. CHALMERS, M.A., F.S.A. 8vo, cloth, 6s.

Or calf extra, 12s. 6d.

N.B.—This is on thinner paper than the 2 vol. edition above, and is printed from the same large and elegant type.

MOTLEY'S RISE OF THE DUTCH REPUBLIC. The Library Edition, uniform with the "History of the Netherlands." 3 vols. demy 8vo, cloth, 31s. 6d. (For One Volume Edition see page 9.)

RELIQUES OF ANCIENT ENGLISH POETRY, consisting of Old Heroic Ballads, Songs, and other Pieces of our Earlier Poets, together with some few of later date, by THOMAS PERCY, D.D., F.S.A. Edited, with a General Introduction, additional Prefaces, Notes, &c., by HENRY B. WHEATLEY, F.S.A. 3 vols. medium 8vo, cloth, 36s. ; reduced to 21s. *net.*

*** 25 *Copies printed on fine large Paper, price, in half roxburghe,* 42s. *per vol.*

SHERIDAN (RICHARD BRINSLEY), THE DRAMATIC WORKS OF. With a Memoir of his Life by J. P. BROWNE, M.D., and Selections from his Life by THOMAS MOORE. 2 vols. demy 8vo, half roxburghe, gilt top, 21s.

—— **"THE POPULAR LARGE TYPE EDITION."** The above text, reprinted on thinner paper, forming one handsome volume, demy 8vo, cloth extra, 7s. 6d.

SMOLLETT (TOBIAS, M.D.), THE WORKS OF. With Memoir of his Life. To which is prefixed a view of the Commencement and Progress of Romance, by JOHN MOORE, M.D. A New edition. Edited by J. P. BROWNE, M.D. 8 vols. demy 8vo, half roxburghe, gilt top, £4, 4s.

SPENSER'S COMPLETE WORKS. With Life, Notes, and Glossary, by JOHN PAYNE COLLIER, Esq., F.S.A. 5 vols. medium 8vo. Published at £3, 15s. ; £2 7s. 6d. *net.*

STERNE (LAURENCE), THE WORKS OF. With a Life of the Author, written by himself. A New Edition, with Appendix, containing several Unpublished Letters, &c. Edited by J. P. BROWNE, M.D. With Portrait of Sterne, Engraved on Steel for this Edition. 4 vols. demy 8vo, half roxburghe, top edge gilt, £2, 2s.

TAYLOR'S (BISHOP JEREMY) RULE AND EXERCISE OF HOLY LIVING AND DYING. 2 vols. medium 8vo, 21s.

The Library Edition of Lane's " Arabian Nights."

THE THOUSAND AND ONE NIGHTS; Commonly called The Arabian Nights' Entertainment. A New Translation from the Arabic, with copious Notes by EDWARD WILLIAM LANE, Author of "The Modern Egyptians." Illustrated with many hundred Engravings on Wood from original designs by WILLIAM HARVEY. A New Edition in 3 vols. demy 8vo, cloth gilt, price £1, 11s. 6d. ; reduced to 22s. 6d. Or calf extra, £1, 15s. *net.*

***WRAXALL'S HISTORICAL AND POSTHUMOUS MEMOIRS,** 1772-1784. By Sir NATHANIEL WILLIAM WRAXALL, Bart. With Corrections and Additions from the Author's own MS., and Illustrative Notes by Mrs. PIOZZI and Dr. DORAN. To which are added Reminiscences of Royal and Noble Personages during the last and present centuries, from the Author's unpublished MS. The whole edited and annotated by HENRY B. WHEATLEY, F.S.A. Finely engraved Portraits. 5 volumes, medium 8vo, cloth extra, £3.

*** The Author left a copy of his "Historical Memoirs of My Own Time" with numerous MS. alterations and corrections, to which were afterwards added Notes by Mrs. Piozzi and Dr. Doran. The present edition is printed from this copy. The Posthumous Memoirs also contain notes by Dr. Doran, and the editor has had the advantage of using a copy of both books, with Notes made by a contemporary of Wraxall, at the time of their original publication. Wraxall left a manuscript containing an additional chapter to his Memoirs, which is now printed for the first time. This edition is completed by the addition of an Index to the two works in one alphabet.

"Bickers and Son's Historical Library."

MOTLEY'S (JOHN LOTHROP) RISE OF THE DUTCH REPUBLIC.
A New Edition, complete in 1 vol. medium 8vo, cloth, 9s. *pp.* 920.

PRESCOTT'S (W. H.) HISTORY OF THE CONQUEST OF MEXICO.
A New and Revised Edition, with the Author's latest Corrections and Additions.
Edited by JOHN FOSTER KIRK. 1 vol. medium 8vo, cloth extra, 9s.

—— **HISTORY OF THE CONQUEST OF PERU.** A New and Revised
Edition, with the Author's latest Corrections and Additions. Edited by JOHN
FOSTER KIRK. 1 vol. medium 8vo, cloth extra, 9s.

—— **HISTORY OF THE REIGN OF FERDINAND AND ISABELLA.**
A New Edition. Edited by JOHN FOSTER KIRK. 1 vol. medium 8vo, cloth, 9s.
Prices of above, half calf gilt, 10s.
    ,,   ,,   calf extra, 12s. 6d.

Books of Reference, etc.

**CHAFFERS' (WM.) MARKS AND MONOGRAMS ON POTTERY
AND PORCELAIN** of the Renaissance and Modern Periods, with Histori-
cal Notices of each Manufactory. Preceded by an Introductory Essay on the
Vasa Fictilia of the Greek, Romano-British, and Mediæval Eras, by WILLIAM
CHAFFERS, Author of "Hall Marks on Gold and Silver Plate," "The Keramic Gal-
lery," &c. Sixth Edition, revised and considerably augmented, with 3,000 Potters'
Marks and Illustrations, and an Appendix containing an Account of Japanese Kera-
mic Manufactures, &c. &c., royal 8vo, cloth, 42s.

8TH THOUSAND.

**CHAFFERS' (WM.) THE COLLECTOR'S HANDBOOK OF MARKS
AND MONOGRAMS ON POTTERY AND PORCELAIN** of the
Renaissance and Modern Periods. With nearly 3,000 Marks and a most valuable
Index, by WILLIAM CHAFFERS. Fcap. 8vo, limp cloth, 6s.

₊ This handbook will be of great service to those Collectors who in their travels have occasion to
refer momentarily to any work treating on the subject. A veritable Multum in Parvo.

* —— **HALL MARKS ON GOLD AND SILVER PLATE.** A New Edition,
considerably augmented and carefully revised by the Author. With Tables of Date
Letters used in all the Assay Offices of the United Kingdom. Royal 8vo, cloth,
16s.

₊ This (6th) edition contains a History of the Goldsmith's Trade in France, with Extracts from the
Decrees relating thereto, and engravings of the Standard and other Marks used in that country
as well as in other Foreign States. The Provincial Tables of England and Scotland contain
many hitherto unpublished marks; all the recent enactments are quoted. The London Tables
(which have never been surpassed for correctness) may now be considered complete. Many
valuable hints to Collectors are given, and cases of fraud alluded to, &c.

**CLARKE'S (MRS. COWDEN) COMPLETE CONCORDANCE TO
SHAKESPEARE,** being a verbal Index to all Passages in the Dramatic Works
of the Poet. New and Revised Edition, super royal 8vo, cloth extra, gilt top, 25s.
Calf extra, or half morocco flexible back, 30s. *net.*

**FAIRBAIRN'S CRESTS OF THE FAMILIES OF GREAT BRITAIN
AND IRELAND.** Compiled from the best authorities, by JAMES FAIRBAIRN,
and revised by LAWRENCE BUTTERS. One Volume of Plates, containing nearly
2,000 Crests and Crowns of all Nations, Coronets, Regalia, Chaplets and Helmets,
Flags of all Nations, Scrolls, Monograms, Reversed Initials, Arms of Cities, &c.
Two vols. royal 8vo, cloth, 42s.

LATHAM (DR. R. G.), A DICTIONARY OF THE ENGLISH LAN-GUAGE, founded on that of Dr. S. Johnson, as edited by the Rev. H. J. Todd, with numerous Emendations and Additions. Second Edition, 4 vols. 4to, half-bound morocco, flexible, £4, 10s. *net.*

LITCHFIELD'S POTTERY AND PORCELAIN, A GUIDE TO COL-LECTORS. By F. LITCHFIELD. Second Edition, with Illustrations and marks. Post 8vo, cloth, 5s.

SHAKESPEARIAN THOUGHT (INDEX TO): being a Collection of Allusions, Reflections, Images, Familiar and Descriptive Passages and Sentiments from the Plays and Poems of Shakespeare, alphabetically arranged and classified under appropriate headings, by CECIL ARNOLD. 1 vol. demy 8vo, cloth extra, 7s. 6d. ; reduced to 4s. 6d. *net.*

THE THEORY AND PRACTICE OF LINEAR PERSPECTIVE, applied to Landscapes, Interiors, and the Figure. For the Use of Artists, Art Students, &c. By V. PELLEGRIN. With a Sheet of 16 Figures. Cloth, 1s.

"The Author, himself a painter and accustomed to the manipulation of geometrical methods, was particularly qualified for writing this treatise ; and he has been able, by dint of research and ability, to condense into a small number of pages the laws of perspective, and to extract from a confused mass, rules which are very simple and easily applicable to every possible case."

*** The work has been adopted by the French Government, and is now in general use in the public libraries and schools of France.

Miscellaneous.

BOOK OF COMMON PRAYER. With the Psalter, and with finely-executed woodcut borders round every page, exactly copied from "QUEEN ELIZABETH'S PRAYER-BOOK," and comprising Holbein's "Dance of Death," Albert Durer's "Life of Christ," &c. Crown 8vo, cloth uncut, 10s. ; reduced to 6s. *net.*
 Ditto, cloth extra, 12s. ; reduced to 7s. *net.*
 Ditto, calf antique, 16s. ; reduced to 12s. *net.*

BULWER'S (DOWAGER LADY) "SHELLS FROM THE SANDS OF TIME." A Series of Essays, handsomely printed in crown 8vo, cloth extra, 5s.

BRERETON'S (REV. J. L.) COUNTY EDUCATION. A Contribution of Experiments, Estimates, and Suggestions, Illustrated with Maps, Plans, &c. 8vo, cloth, 3s. 6d.
 Ditto. Cheaper edition. 8vo, paper wrapper, 2s. 6d.

—— **REPORTS OF THE DEVON AND NORFOLK COUNTY SCHOOL ASSOCIATIONS FOR THE YEAR 1874.** 8vo, wrapper, 1s.

—— **THE HIGHER LIFE.** Attempts at the Apostolic Teaching for English Disciples. Crown 8vo, cloth, 3s. 6d.

CREED OF THE GOSPEL OF S. JOHN (THE). Crown 8vo, cloth, 3s. 6d.

CHRISTIAN YEAR (THE). Thoughts in Verse for the Sundays and Holy days throughout the Year. By JOHN KEBLE. Exquisitely printed on toned paper, with elaborate borders round every page. Printed at the Chiswick Press. Small 4to, cloth extra, with Twenty-four Illustrations by FR. OVERBECK, reproduced in Permanent Photography. 15s. ; reduced to 10s. *net.*
 Ditto, antique calf, £1, 10s.
 Ditto, morocco elegant, £2, 2s.

CHRISTIAN YEAR (THE). Another Edition, in fcap. 8vo, with Twelve Photographic Pictures by FR. OVERBECK, selected from the 4to edition. Cloth gilt, 5s.
 Ditto, calf antique, red edges, 12s.
 Ditto, morocco extra, 18s.

—— Another Edition, 32mo, with 6 Photographic Pictures, elegantly bound in cloth extra, gilt edges, 2s. 6d.
 Ditto, morocco extra, 6s. 6d. *net.*
 Ditto, morocco limp, 4s. 6d. *net.*

CHRISTIAN YEAR (THE.) Thoughts in Verse for the Sundays and Holy days throughout the Year. By JOHN KEBLE. Exquisitely printed on toned paper, with elaborate borders round every page. Small 4to, cloth extra, 10s. 6d. ; reduced to 7s. net.
———— Another Edition in fcap. 8vo, without the borders, cloth extra, 3s.
———— Another Edition in 32mo, cloth extra, 1s. 6d.

DARWIN'S THEORY EXAMINED. Crown 8vo, cloth, 2s. 6d.

ELLIS'S (WM.) ENGLISH EXERCISES. Revised and Improved by the Rev. T. K. ARNOLD, M.A. 12mo. 26th Edition, cloth, 3s. 6d.

FAMILY PRAYER AND BIBLE READINGS. 12mo, cloth, red edges, 5s.

GRAY'S POETICAL WORKS. Illustrated by BIRKET FOSTER, handsomely printed. 18mo, cloth, 3s. 6d.

HARTING'S OUR SUMMER MIGRANTS. An Account of the Migratory Birds which pass the Summer in the British Islands. By J. E. HARTING, F.L.S., F.Z.S., author of "A Handbook of British Birds," a new edition of White's "Selborne," &c., &c. Illustrated with 30 Illustrations on Wood, from Designs by THOMAS BEWICK. Fcap. 8vo, cloth elegant, 3s. 6d. (*See page 3 for 8vo. edition.*)

HERBERT'S (GEORGE) POETICAL WORKS. New Edition, edited by CHARLES COWDEN CLARKE, with Introduction by JOHN NICHOL, B.A. Oxon, numerous head and tail pieces. Fcap. 8vo, cloth extra, gilt edges, 3s. 6d.
   Ditto.   ditto.   calf antique, red edges, 8s.

HEROES OF EUROPE. By H. G. HEWLETT. A Companion Volume to the Heroes of England. 12mo, numerous Illustrations, cloth gilt, 3s. 6d.

HUNTINGFORD. A PRACTICAL INTERPRETATION OF THE REVELATION OF ST. JOHN THE DIVINE. A revised Edition of the "Voice of the Last Prophet." By the Rev. EDWARD HUNTINGFORD, D.C.L. Crown 8vo, cloth, 400 pp., 5s.

———— **ADVICE TO SCHOOL-BOYS.** Sermons on their Duties, Trials, and Temptations. By the Rev. EDWARD HUNTINGFORD, D.C.L. 8vo, cloth, 3s. 6d.

———— **THE DIVINE FORECAST OF THE CORRUPTION OF CHRISTIANITY**: a miraculous evidence of its truth. Crown 8vo, cloth, 2s.

"JAMMED," AND OTHER VERSE. Crown 8vo, cloth, 5s.

LECTURES ON ART, delivered at the Royal Academy, London, by HENRY WEEKES, R.A., Professor of Sculpture. With Portrait, a Short Sketch of the Author's Life, and Eight selected Photographs of his Works. Demy 8vo, cloth elegant, 12s. 6d.

MAJOR'S LATIN GRAMMAR. 11th Edition. 12mo, cloth, 2s. 6d.

———— **LATIN READER OF PROFESSOR JACOBS**; with Grammatical References and Notes. 12mo, cloth, 3s.

———— **INITIA GRÆCA.** 12mo, cloth, 4s.

———— **INITIA HOMERICA.** The First and Second Books of the Iliad of Homer, with parallel passages from Virgil, and a Greek and English Lexicon. 12mo, cloth, 3s. 6d.

———— **MILTON'S PARADISE LOST.** With Notes Critical and Explanatory. New Edition, 12mo, cloth, 5s.

———— **MILTON'S PARADISE LOST.** The Last Six Books. With Notes, &c. 12mo, cloth, 3s. 6d.

MOAB'S PATRIARCHAL STONE, being an Account of the Moabite Stone, its Story and Teaching. By the Rev. JAMES KING. Crown 8vo, cloth, 3*s.* 6*d.*; reduced to 1*s.* 9*d. net.*

PEPYS (SAMUEL) AND THE WORLD HE LIVED IN. By HENRY B. WHEATLEY, F.S.A. Second Edition. Contents :—Pepys before the Diary—Pepys in the Diary—Pepys after the Diary—Tangier—Pepys's Books and Collections—London—Pepys's Relations, Friends, and Acquaintances—The Navy—The Court—Public Characters—Manners—Amusements—Portraits of Pepys—List of Secretaries of the Admiralty, Clerks of the Acts, &c., drawn up by Colonel Pasley, R.E. Crown 8vo, cloth extra, 7*s.* 6*d.*

PYTHOUSE PAPERS : Correspondence concerning the Civil War, The Popish Plot, and A Contested Election in 1680. Transcribed from MSS. in the possession of V. F. BENETT STANFORD, Esq., M.P. Edited, and with an introduction by WILLIAM ANSELL DAY. Demy 8vo, half-bound, 10*s.* 6*d.*

QUITE A GENTLEMAN. A short School-boy Correspondence. Cloth, 1*s.* 6*d.*

*** "The little volume entitled ' Quite a Gentleman ' embodies a correspondence between a boy at a public school and his father and mother, the purpose of which is to determine the difficult question, What is it that constitutes the gentleman ? Whether the correspondence be genuine or not, there is the ring of reality about it ; and the ideas set forth are admirable in themselves and excellently put, with a manliness of tone and an avoidance of the goody-goody element which is truly refreshing."—*Scotsman,* Dec. 27th, 1877.

In two Parts, demy 12mo, cloth, 1s. 6d. each.

ROYAL CHARACTERS FROM THE WORKS OF SIR WALTER SCOTT. A Series of Readings for the Young, Historical and Romantic. Selected and Arranged by WILLIAM T. DOBSON.

Part I., 1033-1437 ; Part II., 1470-1745.

" Every teacher knows and has contrasted the difference with which a botanical, geological, or other scientific lesson is drawled over with the interest shown in stories and historical sketches . . . . and therefore the striking and picturesque scenes in the far-off past which are here selected from the works of the great novelist, may live in the imagination and take root in the memory when prosaic facts and dryer theories fail to leave any permanent impression."—*Preface.*

REMINISCENCES OF THE LEWS ; or, Twenty Years' Wild Sport in the Hebrides. By "SIXTY-ONE." With Portrait and Illustrations. Crown 8vo, cloth, 5*s.*

"A thoroughly genuine account of sport. If any one wants to understand the consuming passion for the sport of Highland life, let him read this book."—*Spectator.*

SELECTED PICTURES FROM THE GALLERIES AND PRIVATE COLLECTIONS OF GREAT BRITAIN. A Series of 150 line Engravings from the best Artists, edited by S. C. HALL, Esq., F.S.A., &c. Proofs on India paper, imperial folio, each Plate printed with the greatest care, and accompanied by a descriptive page of letterpress of corresponding size. Four volumes, in four neat portfolios, pub. at £52, 10*s.* ; reduced to £16, 16*s. net.*

Or, bound in Two volumes, half morocco, elegantly gilt ; reduced to £20 *net.*

Or, in whole morocco, super extra ; reduced to £22, 10*s. net.*

A few copies of ARTIST'S PROOFS, atlas folio, also on India paper, and of which only a few copies were printed, Four volumes as above, in four neat portfolios, pub. at £105 ; reduced to £21 *net.*

Or, bound in Two volumes, half morocco, elegantly gilt, £23, 10*s. net.*

SHORT LESSONS ON THE PARABLES OF OUR LORD. Specially for Bible Classes. 2nd Edition, 18mo, cloth, 2*s.*

THE CHRIST OF THE PSALMS ; or, The Key to the Prophecies of David, concerning the Two Advents of Messiah. By CHRISTIANUS. 2 vols. demy 8vo, cloth, 12*s.*

THE THREE PHASES OF CREATION. An Appendix to "The Christ of the Psalms." By CHRISTIANUS. Demy 8vo, wrapper, 1s. 3d.

TRIP TO NORWAY IN 1873. By "SIXTY-ONE," Author of "Reminiscences of the Lews; or, Twenty Years' Wild Sport in the Hebrides." With Illustrations by FREDERICK MILBANK, Esq., M.P. Crown 8vo, cloth, 6s.

VIRGIL. THE FIRST BOOK OF VIRGIL'S ÆNEID. With Vocabularies. Arranged by W. WELCH, M.A. 12mo, cloth, 1s. 6d.

"Without a Master" Series.

LATIN. A COURSE OF LESSONS IN THE LATIN LANGUAGE. 1s. 6d.

FRENCH. A COURSE OF LESSONS IN THE FRENCH LANGUAGE. 1s. 6d.

ITALIAN. A COURSE OF LESSONS IN THE ITALIAN LANGUAGE. 1s. 6d.

SPANISH. A COURSE OF LESSONS IN THE SPANISH LANGUAGE. 1s. 6d.

GERMAN. A COURSE OF LESSONS IN THE GERMAN LANGUAGE.
Part I.   1s. 6d.
Part II.   1s. 6d.
Part III.   1s. 6d.

BOOK-KEEPING. A COURSE OF LESSONS IN BOOK-KEEPING—Single and double Entry. 1s. 6d.

*** These Treatises, as their titles import, are designed chiefly for Persons who either have not the opportunity or the wish to avail themselves of the services of a Teacher ; they will nevertheless be found exceedingly useful to those disposed to study Languages in the usual way—by pointing out to the intelligent Student in what the language consists, and by giving a general notion of its construction, and the leading principles of its pronunciation: these Treatises may render a vast deal of preliminary explanation unnecessary, and so save time and spare much annoyance to both Pupil and Teacher.

A List of New Remainders.

OFFERED AT GREATLY REDUCED NET PRICES.

CADORE; OR, TITIAN'S COUNTRY. By JOSIAH GILBERT, one of the authors of "The Dolomite Mountains," &c. With Map, Illustrative Drawings, and Wood-cuts, large 8vo, cloth, published at £1, 11s. 6d. ; reduced to 17s. 6d. net.

CATLIN'S PORTFOLIO OF ILLUSTRATIONS OF THE MANNERS, CUSTOMS, AND CONDITION OF THE NORTH AMERICAN INDIANS. 31 spirited Chalk Drawings, lithographed in tints, 23½ in. by 16½ in. Folio, half-bound, published £5, 5s. ; reduced to 21s. net.

DORAN'S LIVES OF THE QUEENS OF ENGLAND OF THE HOUSE OF HANOVER. By Dr. DORAN, F.S.A. 4th edition, carefully revised and much enlarged. 2 vols. demy 8vo, cloth gilt, published at 25s. ; reduced to 10s. 6d. net.

ESTIMATES OF THE ENGLISH KINGS FROM WILLIAM THE CONQUEROR TO GEORGE III. By J. LANGTON SANFORD. Crown, cloth, 12s. ; reduced to 5s. net.

EVANS'S THROUGH BOSNIA AND HERZEGOVINA ON FOOT DURING THE INSURRECTION, with an Historical Review of Bosnia. Second edition, demy 8vo, cloth extra, published at 18*s.*; reduced to 5*s.* 6*d. net.*

FIGUIER.—REPTILES AND BIRDS. Best Library Edition, 307 Illustrations, demy 8vo, cloth, 14*s.*; reduced to 5*s.* 6*d. net.*

FRESHFIELD (DOUGLAS W.), TRAVELS IN THE CENTRAL CAUCASUS AND BASHAN. 2 Maps. Coloured Illustrations, and Woodcuts by EDWARD WHYMPER. 18*s.*; reduced to 7*s. net.*

GELL AND GANDY'S POMPEIANA; or, The Topography, Edifices and Ornaments of Pompeii, with upwards of 100 line Engravings by Goodall, Cooke, Heath, Pye, &c. Demy 8vo, cloth, extra gilt. Pub. at 18*s.*; reduced to 10*s.* 6*d. net.*

HORATII OPERA. Cura M. H. MILMAN. 100 Illustrations. Crown 8vo, cloth. Published at 7*s.* 6*d.*; reduced to 3*s.* 6*d. net.*

LONGFELLOW'S POETICAL WORKS. Rossetti's Library Edition (Moxon). Cloth, 7*s.* 6*d.*; reduced to 4*s.* 6*d. net.*
    Ditto, calf extra; reduced to 9*s. net.*

MILTON'S ODE ON THE MORNING OF CHRIST'S NATIVITY. Cloth gilt, 4*s.* 6*d.*; reduced to 3*s. net.*

MORAL EMBLEMS. With Aphorisms, Adages, and Proverbs of all Ages and Nations, from JACOB CATS and ROBERT FARLIE. With Illustrations freely rendered from Designs found in their Works by JOHN LEIGHTON, F.S.A. The whole translated and edited, with additions, by RICHARD PIGOT. 242 Illustrations, beautifully engraved on wood. 4to, cloth elegant, 25*s.* (published at 31*s.* 6*d.*)

PAST DAYS IN INDIA; or, Sporting Reminiscences of the Valley of the Soane and the Basin of Singrowlee. By a late Customs Officer, N.W. Provinces, India. Post 8vo., cloth, 10*s.* 6*d.*; reduced to 3*s. net.*

PICKERING'S DIAMOND CLASSICS.
    Tasso, 2 vols. cloth, 12*s.*; reduced to 5*s. net.*
    Petrarch   „   6*s.*;   „   2*s.* 3*d. net.*
    Dante, 2 vols. „   12*s.*;   „   5*s.*   „

PORTER'S (MAJOR WHITWORTH) HISTORY OF THE KNIGHTS OF MALTA; OR, THE ORDER OF THE HOSPITAL OF ST. JOHN OF JERUSALEM. 2 vols. 8vo, cloth, £1, 4*s.*; reduced to 21*s. net.*

RECOLLECTIONS OF PAST LIFE. By SIR HENRY HOLLAND, Bart., M.D., F.R.S., D.C.L., &c. &c. 10*s.* 6*d.*; reduced to 6*s.* 6*d. net.*

RIDICULA REDIVIVA. (Nursery Rhymes). By J. E. ROGERS. Printed in Colours. 7*s.* 6*d.*; reduced to 3*s. net.*

SCOTT'S BIBLE. Last Edition, 6 vols. 4to, calf antique, red edges; reduced to £5, 5*s. net.*

SHAKESPEARE SCENES AND CHARACTERS. A Series of Illustrations Engraved on Steel, with Explanatory Text, selected and arranged by PROFESSOR E. DOWDEN, LL.D. Royal 8vo, cloth elegant, published at £2, 12*s.* 6*d.*; reduced to 25*s. net;* or in half-rox., 27*s.* 6*d. net.*

SKERTCHLEY'S (J. A.) DAHOMEY AS IT IS. Numerous Woodcuts. 8vo, cloth, 16*s.*; reduced to 5*s.* 6*d. net.*

SOUTH AMERICA, A JOURNEY ACROSS, FROM THE PACIFIC OCEAN TO THE ATLANTIC OCEAN. By PAUL MARCOY. 600 beautiful Engravings on Wood, drawn by E. RIOU, and Eleven Maps in colours, from drawings by the Author. Large Paper Edition, handsomely printed on wove paper, with very fine impressions of the Illustrations. 4 vols. small folio, elegantly bound in cloth gilt, reduced to £2, 10s. (published at £4, 4s.)

SUMNER, DR. (BISHOP OF WINCHESTER), LIFE OF. During a Forty Years' Episcopate. By the Rev. GEORGE HENRY SUMNER, M.A. With a Portrait. Demy 8vo, cloth extra, 14s. ; reduced to 7s. 6d. *net.*

THORVALDSEN, HIS LIFE AND WORKS. By EUGENE PLON. 39 Engravings on Steel and Wood, large 8vo, cloth, £1, 5s. ; reduced to 8s. *net.*

TYROL AND THE TYROLESE: The People and the Land in their Social, Sporting, and Mountaineering Aspects. By W. A. BAILLIE GROHMAN. With numerous Illustrations. Crown 8vo, cloth extra, published at 6s. ; reduced to 3s. *net.*

WHEELER'S TRAVELS OF HERODOTUS. 2 vols. crown 8vo, cloth, 18s.; reduced to 5s. 6d. *net.*

WHEELER'S GEOGRAPHY OF HERODOTUS. 8vo, plates, cloth, 18s. ; reduced to 6s. *net.*

WHETHAM'S (BODDAM-) WESTERN WANDERINGS: a Record of Travel in the United States. 12 full page illustrations, 8vo, cloth gilt, 15s. ; reduced to 4s. 9d. *net.*

WOLF-HUNTING AND WILD SPORT IN LOWER BRITTANY. By the Author of "Paul Pendril," &c. &c. With illustrations by Colonel H. HOPE CREALOCKE, C.B. 8vo, cloth, 12s.; reduced to 4s. 6d. *net.*

𝔑otice.

*** *All Books in this List may be had Elegantly Bound in every style of leather binding. Many are offered at greatly reduced "net prices," and are not subject to the usual discount.*

THE COMPLETE WORKS OF CHARLES DICKENS.

POCKET VOLUME EDITION.

PUBLISHED IN THIRTY ELEGANT LITTLE VOLUMES.

REDUCED NET PRICES IN CABINET.

	£ s. d.
Bound in cloth elegant, primrose coloured edges, in handsome cloth cabinet	1 15 0
„ French morocco, gilt edges, in superior leather cabinet, with lock and key	5 0 0
„ Best Levant morocco, gilt edges, in elegant leather cabinet, with lock and key	6 6 0

SIZE OF CABINET.

Length	12¾ inches.
Width	12 „
Depth	4½ „

REDUCED NET PRICES IN POLISHED EBONISED CASE.

	£ s. d.
Bound in cloth elegant, primrose coloured edges	2 0 0
„ Half Anglo-russia, primrose coloured edges	2 15 0

SIZE OF CASE.

Length	14 inches.
Width	13 „
Depth	4½ „

The Cabinets and Cases are of the best workmanship, and form elegant drawing-room ornaments. If preferred, they may be placed on ornamental brackets *fixed* to the wall.

*** *This edition may be had in 30 vols. cloth extra, without Case or Cabinet, net price 30s.*

BICKERS AND SON, 1, LEICESTER SQUARE.

CHISWICK PRESS:—C. WHITTINGHAM AND CO., TOOKS COURT, CHANCERY LANE.